HOOK

A Neverland Novel

GINA L. MAXWELL

Cover Design: Jaycee DeLorenzo, Sweet 'N Spicy Designs

Editors: Rebecca Barney and Lea Schafer

Created with Vellum

Foreward

PLEASE DO NOT SKIP THIS PAGE

Dear Reader,

Thank you for picking up *Hook*! I'm so excited to take you into the seedier parts of Neverland for a truly epic love story unlike anything I've ever written. With that said, there are two things I want you to know so you can best determine how—or if—you continue from here.

First, if you chose to read this because John works with the FBI and you love a good police procedural…this is *not* the book for you. Believe me, I had every intention of making everything as accurate as possible (as I do with all my characters/stories), but it wasn't long before I realized I'd written myself into a corner with some of the things I wrote in *Pan* (book 1 in the series) and the timelines required to pull this book off.

After struggling to fit my story to reality, I said *screw it* and decided to make reality fit my story. Because when it comes down to it, this isn't a book on how government agencies work. It's not even a book on how criminal organizations work (hint: I didn't worry about those details, either). This is a book about two souls—one broken and one desperate to heal—coming together and fighting for their happily ever after.

So I'm pulling the "creative license card" with this one, people. Just go with it and take the realistic specifics with a grain of salt, just like you do with Hollywood blockbusters. ;)

Secondly, for those concerned about triggering content: Chapter 31 is the only scene that "shows" a past encounter of sexual assault. Nothing graphic or explicit is mentioned and it's fairly brief, but you *are* aware of what's happening as Hook is narrating his thoughts. If you'd rather play it safe and not read the full chapter, I have an alternative way to read it on my website that gives you a quick summary of the scene set up and then the rest of the chapter (after the trigger sensitive material) is posted in its entirety. When you get to Chapter 31, simply navigate back to this page and click on this link. www.ginalmaxwell.com/hook-chapter-31-alternative

One last note: if you need it, there's a Character Glossary in the back.

As always, a thousand thanks for giving my book a spot on your shelf and a place in your heart. I hope you love Hook and John's love story as much as I do.

Literary love and kitten kisses,

Gina

Gina

Dedication

For Captain James Hook

Never has a hero affected me so profoundly
or been more deserving of a happily ever after.

"Always, Captain. Always."

Prologue

HOOK

Four years earlier…

Age 26
Neverland, North Carolina

I'M GETTING MORE KIDS.

Those were the words I overheard earlier today that froze the blood in my veins. Just like it froze every time I heard that same voice bark my name when I was younger.

I'm getting more kids.

Over my dead body.

Fred Croc might have me on a short fucking leash, but I'll be damned if I allow him to use the School for Lost Boys of Neverland to get a new crop of kids for his personal gain and sadistic pleasures. The school was supposed to be an orphanage—a place for boys without families to live and learn. Not with Croc running the show.

As far as he was concerned, we were free labor for his chop shop and convenient targets when he wanted to blow off steam.

Or worse.

Never again.

As I pull off the main road, I cut the headlights so I don't alert Croc and his wife, Delia, in their house behind the school. The moon is less than half full, but it's enough to see by as I drive toward the old, two-story building where I lived for nine years as a forgotten kid in the system. Nine eternal years that I try like hell to forget ever happened. Here's hoping tonight hammers another damn nail in that coffin.

I park in the grass a couple hundred feet away and pop the trunk to grab the two giant plastic containers. The night is quiet. Nothing but the sounds of cicadas buzzing, liquid sloshing at my sides, and grass rustling as I walk to the front stoop.

Setting the cans down, I stare at the heavy wooden door and clench my fists to stop the tremors before they can start. I told myself I'd never come back here, not for anything. My life was never great—even before I was placed here, living with a junkie mom while caring for my baby brother as best I could was no fucking picnic—but here…this was where my nightmare began.

I take three slow breaths through my nose, willing my heart to stop slamming against my ribs like a medieval battering ram. But the memories this place evokes—ones I've relegated to the darkest recesses of my mind—stir my sleeping demons. They're so real I can practically feel them. Every minute I'm here, they'll grow stronger, scratching and clawing their way to the surface. Every cell in my body wants to leave. I'm tempted. So fucking tempted. But I'm here to do a job, and if that means facing the ghosts of my past while I do it, fine.

They won't win.

I worked too damn hard to put this hell behind me.

And I have. I'm *fine*.

I'm fucking *more* than fine.

"Jesus, this place looks like shit." By the time I moved out, it hadn't looked the greatest, but now… Now, I think I'll be doing it a favor. It used to be a well-maintained brick colonial home, a place of hope run by people who were devoted to caring for children with nowhere to go. I'd gotten a brief taste of that utopia with the Andersons, the nice older couple who originally owned the school. But a few weeks after my brother and I arrived, they died in a car crash, and everything changed.

Tracing the words on the weathered plaque nailed to the door, I remember Mrs. Anderson telling me this was her favorite quote.

"The hunger for love is much more difficult to remove than the hunger for bread." ~ Mother Teresa

Difficult? Maybe. But not impossible. It's been a lifetime since I last hungered for love. I learned early on that love isn't necessary to make it in this world, not where I come from. Strength, respect, and smarts. Those are the things that'll get you somewhere. Those were the things *I* hungered for, and they made me into the man I am today. A man who's not afraid to kick over the hornet's nest.

Or set it on fire.

Bottom line, I'm not about to let Croc use this place as a front for his free child labor. And it sure as hell won't become some new kid's version of hell. Not while there's still breath in my body.

Armed with two gas cans, a Zippo, and a grudge the

size of the Atlantic, I check the door and find it unlocked with the security system disarmed. Guess there's no reason to secure an empty building with nothing of value to speak of. I slip inside and leave one can on the main floor, then carry the other to the kitchen where the enclosed staircase to the second floor is located.

I pause at the bottom and peer into the narrow unlit passage. My mouth goes dry and my pulse kicks higher as the memories rush in. Croc thinks I'm just another one of his abused mutts, like a thing he's beaten so much and for so long that I'm afraid to leave my owner. He couldn't be more wrong.

Tonight, I send Croc a message: *GO. FUCK. YOUR. SELF.*

Climbing the stairs, I ignore the creaks trying to drudge up those demons, until I reach the room that spans the entire second story that served as our living quarters. It's like a mini barracks, a dozen single beds with metal frames lining the walls. Each of us had a bed and one dresser drawer to hold our clothes. There were no toys or books, no televisions or video games. We only had each other, our imaginations, and Peter's stories to entertain us. Not that I ever joined in with the other kids. I couldn't, even if I'd wanted to. Which I didn't. I never subscribed to Pan's dumbass theory that we were all family just because we lived under the same roof. We were orphans lumped together through circumstance. The end.

Even still, this room had been my sanctuary. A small part of me hates to destroy the one place in the world I felt safe, but I don't want this to have to be another kid's sanctuary. So down it goes.

I start on one end of the room and trail the gas along the brittle wood floor, over the beds, past the window we sometimes escaped through, and across the dressers until I get to the bathroom. It's large and tiled with three toilet stalls, a community shower area with six sprayers, and six sinks lining the opposite wall under a long, rust-framed mirror.

The rubber soles of my boots are nearly silent on the tile floor as I move to where I can see a specific corner of the showers. My gaze falls to the wall about a foot and a half from the floor where an inch-wide groove is worn down in the grout. I tuck my thumb into my fist out of pure muscle memory, then force myself to relax my hand. My thumb isn't bleeding. It hasn't in years.

Turning away from the missing grout, I grip the edges of a sink until my knuckles turn as white as the porcelain. There's a permanent sea of rage that lies beneath my surface like boiling lava. It burns with every injustice, every instance in my life someone treated me like trash. I can go from low simmer to volcanic eruption in seconds with the right trigger. And this whole goddamn place has them lurking around every fucking corner.

A growl builds in my chest as the rage funnels into my arm and I explode, my fist smashing into the face of the man roaring back at me. Shards of glass litter the tiled floor where thick drops of blood leak from busted knuckles. Lungs heave and nostrils flare with shallow breaths as I stare through what's left of the shattered mirror. I don't see the twenty-six-year-old man with a muscular build and trim beard looking back at me. I see a fourteen-year-old boy with shaggy black hair and too-thin frame. I see guarded blue eyes—his innocence long gone and his innate hunger to be loved plucked out and crushed under a steel-toed boot. And he's blaming me for his pain.

Why didn't you fight back? Why didn't you stop him?

Why didn't you kill *him?*

There it is. The million-dollar question. Answer? I was too scared. No matter how many times I wished for Croc's death, I knew if I failed, the consequences would be unimaginable.

"All in due time," I tell the boy. "You'll have your revenge. I fucking swear it."

I splash gas on anything that isn't tile, then go back to the staircase and pour the rest of it behind me as I head down. Grabbing the full can, I make quick work of dousing the main floor—kitchen, living room, master bedroom where Croc and his wife stayed before they built their house out back, and the schoolroom…until I get to Croc's old office.

The door is closed, but I know what's on the other side —a metal desk that always felt cold against my bare skin, a rolling office chair that squeaked when he shifted, a dusty file cabinet he never bothered to open with metal handles that dug into my chest and stomach. I was the only one he ever brought in there. He said I was privileged. I said we'd have to agree to disagree. At no point did I ever feel privileged to be singled out by Fred Croc, but I accepted it and made sure his "generosity" never went past me. It was the longest four years of my life, and I have no desire to see the inside of those walls again, even for this.

Reaching back, I yank my T-shirt off and tuck half of it under the door, then pour enough gas to soak through to the other side. Of all fucking places, I'd hate for *this* to miss out on the cleansing baptism of my fire. If sins could leave stains behind like traces of gunpowder, this room would explode in a brilliant display of utter devastation.

A dog barks off in the distance, pulling me back to the present. I don't know if it's a stray or Croc's mongrel, but I can't risk getting caught before I finish. Forcing my feet to move, I stride down the hall. On my way out, I grab a framed article hanging on the wall, smash the glass, and pull out the yellowed newspaper column about Fred and Delia taking charge of the orphanage. Then spill a trail of gas behind me as I cross the lawn to my car.

Tossing the empty container to the side, I light a cigarette with my silver Zippo and take a long drag, sucking the smoke deep into my lungs. Exhaling, I stare at the side of the lighter where the engraved words "Captain Hook" are illuminated by the moonlight. It was a gift from Starkey—the last of us to finally "age out" of the system, one of my loyal Pirates…and my eighteen-year-old baby brother.

Not that anyone knows that.

Not even him.

He still has that big-brother-hero-worship thing for me regardless. If I wasn't sure he'd be okay with Smee and the other Pirates watching out for him, I wouldn't go through with this. Starkey is my first and only priority, always has been. Which is why before I turned eighteen and was forced to leave the school, I made sure I had something big to hold over Croc's head to keep him in line, and it worked. He was still a cruel asshole, but he never laid another hand on the kids after that.

But if Croc is allowed to reopen the school, the shit starts all over with a new group of orphans. And I can't let that happen. My leverage on him might spare them his worst, but even his best isn't fit for a fucking goldfish, much less kids.

Once I do this—once I destroy this last reminder—I can finally put my past behind me. I'm determined to do this, and I have no intentions on running. I *want* him to know it was me, and I'll gladly serve the time. Because every minute spent in prison is one I don't have to look my childhood tormentor in the eyes and do his bidding. I need a goddamn break. Since leaving Neverland isn't an option —not until I find a way to bring him down—prison's my only chance for a temporary escape.

Flipping the Zippo open again, I light the wick and stare at dancing flame. I was a lot like it before Fred Croc came along. I might have been a little fucked up, but my fire was contained. Under the right person's care, it could've stayed that way. Maybe even tamped out completely. Instead, Croc pumped it full of oxygen until it blazed out of control and ravaged everything good inside me.

So, fuck him, and fuck this school.

The split knuckles on my hand throb in time with my galloping heart. I ball up the newspaper article, light it with my Zippo, then drop it on the gas-soaked grass. It catches the fire with a satisfying *whoosh* and races down the invisible track, straight through the open front door, and into the building.

I watch the fire grow and feed as it travels from one room to the next, lighting up each window like glowing orange dominoes. It's not long before smoke is billowing from the windows and open door. A few minutes later, the building is engulfed in flames stretching high above the roof as they lick at the sky.

The intense heat practically bakes my bare skin, but I'm rooted to the spot. Now I get why arsonists watch their fires. It's fucking mesmerizing and perfect in its complexity. The power is obvious in its destruction, but also in its healing. Because as I stare at the raging inferno in front of me, I feel a cathartic peace quelling the rage *inside of me*. Not enough to fix what's broken—nothing exists that can ever do that—but enough to satisfy a small part of that boy I saw in the mirror.

Not much time passes before the distant sirens steadily grow louder until finally I'm engulfed in spinning colored lights and shouted commands. I don't fight them when they grab my arms and roughly cuff my hands. I don't struggle when they read me my rights and shove me into the back of a cruiser. And I don't protest with my reasons and justifications for torching the school to the cop who slides behind the wheel.

A judge doesn't need to know why I did it to find me guilty.

I know why…and so does Croc.

As my cruiser starts to pull away from the scene, I find the devil himself glaring at me with bloodlust in his eyes. I don't dare break eye contact first. I refuse to show him any sign of weakness. But once we're on the highway, I blow out a breath and drop my head back on the seat. All I need is a break, a chance to regroup and maybe learn some things on the inside that can help me bring him down in the future. This move is about strategy as much as it is revenge and prevention.

In the meantime, I won't have to answer to Croc, won't have to take his orders and carry out his dirty work. Won't have to ignore those secret smirks that tell me he's remembering things about our past that make me want to simultaneously vomit and rip out his fucking diseased heart with my bare hands.

There's no one who needs my protection right now. Smee will look out for Starkey; they've always been tight like brothers, too. For the first time in my life, I'll only have myself to worry about. And since I'm not worth the trouble, that officially makes me a worry-free man.

I'll pay the price later, one way or another. Croc won't let this go without finding a way to punish me for it. But there isn't anything he can do to me that he hasn't already done. So, whatever it is, I'll survive it. I'll survive him.

It's what I've always done. It's what I'll continue to do until I take him and his entire operation down. And maybe someday I won't simply be surviving, I'll actually be *living*.

But I doubt it.

Chapter One

HOOK

Present Day

Age 30
London, North Carolina

FUCK, I hate the club scene.

I'd rather choke down a glass of metal shavings than admit it to him, but I'd take the hyper-jovial atmosphere of Pan's Friday festivities over going to a nightclub any day. Both settings are rowdy as hell, but the acres surrounding the house where the Lost Boys live is lit up with bonfires and tiki torches instead of strobe lights and lasers. The DJ's playlist is hard rock and heavy metal, not this synthesized EDM shit. Most importantly, you have room to breathe and walk around without having to squeeze through a sweaty sea of people rubbing and grinding on each other like it's mating season for the desperate. It's fucking suffocating.

But the clubs are where the young twentysomethings go to party, and by party, I mean get high. Especially on MDMA-based drugs. Ecstasy used to be the big thing in the early 2000s. When that went out of style, people started rolling on Molly. Now there's a new drug on the scene, engineered and manufactured by a team working for none other than Neverland's up-and-coming crime boss, Fred Croc.

Fairy Dust.

Looks like body glitter, feels like flying. That's the pitch. It's a more intense version of Molly with the added bonus of making the user sparkle under the club lights. They just swipe the ultra-fine powder onto their skin, and, less than a minute later, they're flying high and getting all touchy-feely with everyone around them. Not my thing—no drugs are, thanks to Mommy dearest—but it's only been on the market for a month, and the club kids can't get enough of it, so business is booming.

Tonight, I've set myself up in the VIP lounge at the Quarry, one of the hottest new dance clubs in London, North Carolina. I have three Pirates with me—Smee, Cecco, and Cookson—who are mingling and moving the product. I prefer to sit back and supervise, which is my right as captain. I might not have a choice about selling this shit, but at least I don't have to do it myself.

"Hey there." A girl sits next to me on the couch where I've been nursing my beer, waiting for this job to be over so I can get the hell out of here and get back to my loft.

"Hey, yourself," I force myself to say. Sounding like a normal person who gives a shit about anything doesn't come naturally to me. My instinct is more growl-and-glare than grin-and-gaze. But the surly shit scares off potential customers, so I'm trying to dial it back. For Starkey's sake.

"I'm Brandy. That hot redhead over there said you

could help me out," she says, pointing to the edge of the VIP area.

I flick my eyes over to where Smee, my right-hand man, is standing. He shrugs and holds the sides of his leather jacket open, signaling he's out. But as soon as she looks back at me, he smiles and gives me a wink, then disappears into the crowd.

Fucking Smee. He's not out of Dust. He's sending her over as an offering. The Irish bastard doesn't think I get laid enough. Not that anyone does, compared to him. The man acts like he needs sex to survive instead of air. He enjoys fucking men just as much as women, and he's not shy about it, either. There's a constant parade of ass coming and going from his cabin. But Smee thinks my all-work-and-no-play rule needs bending, so sometimes, he tries to "help out" his captain by playing the role of pimp.

Sometimes, I even let him think it works.

But lately, every time I tap into my spank bank—my mental version of Viagra for when I fuck women—I don't pull up memories of former hookups like usual. Instead, I'm picturing the dozens of filthy never-gonna-happen fantasies I have on a constant reel in my mind about one man in particular—a fucking *cop*, of all things. And as much as I hate this insane attraction to a man I want nothing to do with for multiple reasons, it refuses to go away, so I've learned to live with it. Eventually, I'll have to do something to scrub him from my mind, but I have more important things to worry about right now.

"I like your ring," Brandy purrs, touching the pewter skull ring on my right thumb.

"Thanks." I found it lying in the dirt the day I took back control of my life, so I kept it and it became the inspiration for the Pirates. It's a reminder of who I am and why.

It's a symbol of my mission to end Croc's reign in Neverland. To end his reign over me, and now my brother.

"So, what do you say?" Brandy prods. "Can you help me?"

I turn my full attention on the girl, getting my first good look at her. Time freezes as an image from the past superimposes over her for the briefest of moments. A young, black-haired beauty with a hint of desperation shining in her green eyes…

Blinking the image away, I take a long pull on my beer. Yeah, no. Normally I can fake my interest in the fairer sex, but this girl reminds me of my mother. My very *dead* mother. Without knowing a thing about Brandy, a mix of resentment and pity for her burns in my chest. There's no way I'm touching this girl, even to keep up appearances.

I itch with the need to get out of here, but I have to stay focused. I have a job to do. My brother's life depends on it. "You lookin' for some wings, angel?"

She glances around the roped-off area, but everyone around us is doing their own thing—drinking, laughing, dancing, taking selfies. The usual self-absorbed bullshit of a barely legal crowd. Brushing her long black hair behind her bare shoulder, she smiles coyly, batting her thick lashes at me. "I am. Wanna fly with me?"

"Not tonight, babe. That'll be fifty."

"Dollars?" she says, her eyes flaring wide. She's young, probably around Starkey's age, and I'm guessing she's not well-versed in drug deals.

"That's the cost of admission. You want it or not?"

She leans in and slides a hand over the zipper of my jeans. "Are there any other forms of payment you'd accept?"

Keeping the bored expression on my face, I look her dead in the eyes. "Sorry, cash only."

She pouts, but I'm sure it's more about having to pay fifty bucks than missing out on a quick fuck with me in some darkened corner just to score her and her friends their high for the night. Once the cash is in my hand, I reach inside my jacket and pull out a small resealable bag filled with pearlescent powder. I tuck it into her palm, thinking she'll go to the bathroom to put it on, but apparently, excitement overrides her previous paranoia. She doesn't waste a second before dipping her fingers and painting her body with it. In a handful of seconds, her pupils will dilate, and she's liable to climb into my lap despite my earlier rejection.

Except I'm not sticking around for the show. I saw enough of it the first nine years of my life to last me until I'm cold and dead. I don't know if it's the girl looking like my mom or all the pent-up sexual frustration riding me, but I need air. Right fucking now. Shoving to my feet, I stalk out of the VIP area and weave through the crowd until I finally get to the front entrance and escape outside to suck in the crisp January night.

Firing off a quick text to Smee, I tell him to take over. I don't give him any explanation as to why I'm bailing. I don't have to. I'm his captain, and he never second-guesses me. It's been that way since we were kids at the school—the one I burned to the ground and did two years of a five-year sentence for arson. I'd still be serving my last year right now if I hadn't gotten out for good behavior. Not that my behavior was even remotely good in that place. No, I'd gotten out early for one reason and one reason only—because Croc wanted me out.

Just like he wanted Starkey *in*.

Now the only way for me to get Croc to let my brother out of prison is to sell this first batch of Fairy Dust. Doesn't sound all that hard, but it takes a while to move a million dollars of powder.

I light up a smoke, the crackling sound as I inhale and the sweet taste of the cloves coating my tongue both working to calm my nerves. I climb behind the wheel of my new blacked-out Challenger and focus on the hot shower and the book waiting for me back at my loft in Neverland. But fate has other plans for my evening. I'm only a couple of miles from the Quarry when a set of cherries lights up in my rearview.

"Shit." I briefly contemplate putting my foot to the floor and outrunning them. I know I could with what I've got under the hood, but by now, they already have my plates and info. If I bring attention down on the club—and by extension, Croc's operation—I'm fucked.

As I pull over and squint against the spotlight shining directly into my side mirror, practically blinding me, I realize that I'm not out of London city limits yet. That means that London PD's finest is behind me. And the man I haven't been able to get out of my head the past several months is a London cop. *Fuck me.*

A man gets out of the cruiser and makes his way forward, but with that light behind him, I can't see shit. My pulse kicks up a few notches, and I tighten my grip on the steering wheel.

"Can you step out of the car, please, sir?"

Not him.

I release a heavy exhale and tell myself it's relief washing over me, not disappointment. "What happened to 'license and registration'?"

"Sir, I'm not going to ask you again. Step out of the car," he says, more forcefully this time.

A shadow passes over me from the passenger side. So, the pig has a partner. Something's off about this, but I don't have much of a choice other than to do what they say. They have the upper hand, what with the guns and the badges they're toting. I'm just a small-time criminal with no one to care if I disappear. Something I can't let happen before I make things right for Starkey.

"Sure thing, Officer."

Making sure they can see my hands at all times, I do as he says. As soon as I rise to my full six-foot-three height, the guy spins me around and pushes my chest against the car. I grind my teeth together, using every ounce of control I have to keep from turning and busting this motherfucker's nose open with my fist. Just like I did to the Neverland cop who tried to keep me from Starkey the night he was arrested.

Turning my head, I glare at him over my shoulder. "What the fuck is your problem, man?"

"Shut up and hold still," his partner says from the other side of my car, shining his flashlight in my face.

The guy behind me starts patting me down. I don't make a habit of carrying my gun on me, but—

"Got a four-inch switchblade," Handsy Cop says after retrieving it from my jeans' pocket and flicking it open before setting it on the trunk of the car. I'm about to really start bitching when he reaches into my inside jacket pocket and comes up with several one-ounce baggies with the picture of a fairy on them. "What have we got here?"

Goddamn it. This night just went all to hell. I can't believe I forgot to stash them in the secure container under my seat before driving away from the club. Just goes to show how fucked up my head's been lately. All because of *him*.

"My niece asked me to sell some of her body glitter," I say calmly. "I think it's important to support our young entrepreneurs. You want some?"

"Funny," Bossy Cop snarls. "Let's see how funny you are down at the station."

Handsy yanks my arms behind me and slaps the cuffs on my wrists tight enough that I wince. I've had plenty of jerk sessions that involved thinking about a cop and handcuffs, but not with *this* cop and I'm never the one wearing the cuffs. "James Hook, you're under arrest for possession with intent to sell. You have the right to…"

I tune out the rest of the Miranda rights as my head spins with what the hell is going on here. They never asked for my license, didn't follow proper protocol. I never gave them my name. This wasn't an ordinary bust. I was targeted. They probably would've hauled me in for possession of a deadly weapon or littering because I tossed my cigarette out the window had they not found the drugs. Because something tells me they were sent to bring me in no matter what. The question is, what the hell for?

An hour later, I'm still sitting in an interrogation room at the London Police Department, chained to the plain white table and waiting for…who the fuck knows. No one's giving me any goddamn answers, and it's not helping my mood.

"Hey!" I shout, staring at the one-way mirror. "The least you could do is give me my smokes while I rot in here for no fucking reason."

A minute later, the door to my left finally opens. A tall man with a muscular frame walks in wearing a pair of black cargo pants, a tight-fitting black polo, and a badge hanging on a metal chain around his neck. His head is bent as he looks at the files in his hand, but I don't need to see his face to know who it is. It's the bane of my existence and my biggest fantasy all rolled into one magnificent, irritating package.

John fucking Darling.

Chapter Two

HOOK

THE DOOR CLOSES behind him as John lifts his gaze to mine. If I wasn't sitting already, there's a good chance those honey-colored eyes would've knocked me on my ass for all the heat they're throwing my way. I'm tempted to glance over at the one-way mirror as though I could see who's witnessing this potentially damning interaction, depending on how good they are at reading body language. But I hold fast and concentrate on schooling my features. I'm an expert on showing people what I want them to see. This won't be any different.

He tosses a pack of Marlboros onto the table, and I curl my lip. "What the hell are those for?"

His brows draw together. "You said you wanted to smoke, so I got these from one of the officers."

"I want *my* smokes. The Djarum Black clove cigarillos that were confiscated with everything else when I was brought in."

"You used to smoke Marb Reds," he counters.

"Yeah, when I was a kid. I've learned to appreciate the

finer things in life since then. I'm sure a rich boy like you can appreciate that."

"I'm not even going to dignify that with an answer." He turns to the mirror and makes a round-'em-up signal with his finger. "Someone will be in shortly with your smokes."

"Gee, thanks. It almost makes up for forcing me to sit here for an hour to stare at my reflection. What's with the casual attire? Your polyester uniform at the cleaners?" I droll, leaning back against the uncomfortable metal chair.

"I'm on a Joint Task Force with the FBI. More comfortable uniforms are one of the perks."

I don't even bother hiding my shock this time. "No shit," I say. "You're a G-man now?"

"No, not technically. I'm still London PD, but I'm also deputized as a federal agent. Being a task force officer allows me to operate under the same parameters as the FBI and occasionally work with them on local area cases."

"Not sure if I should be impressed or even more disgusted, Darling."

His eyes narrow slightly as he sits across from me, but his back is to the mirror, so I'm the only one who sees it. "As I've told you before, you can call me John."

Yeah, he did tell me that before. A couple of months ago at the beach when I had him shoved up against a brick wall after he offered to help get Starkey out of prison. Help I promptly refused, because it'll be a cold day in hell when I trust a cop.

I pick out another detail from our past—one from what feels like a lifetime ago.

"Or how about I call you…" I pause to lean forward, then dip my voice in low. "*Johnathan.*"

His jaw flexes and his nostrils flare as he takes a steadying breath. He's good, I'll give him that. He didn't even flinch. But I can see it there in his eyes, the memory of the first night we met. I can't tell how he feels about me bringing it up—maybe he's embarrassed, maybe he's pissed—but he's definitely *something.*

And that makes the corner of my mouth twist up in the closest thing I get to smiling.

"I'm going to get right to the point, Hook," he says, flipping his file folder open and spreading out eight-by-ten glossies of me conducting business at several clubs in the London area. "We've had you under surveillance for the past couple of months, and we believe you're the one heading up the distribution of the new club drug of choice, Fairy Dust."

Any trace of humor falls from my face, and the familiar heat of betrayal burns in my gut. So much for any kind of history between us earning me a little leeway. I should've known better. That night on the beach he told me he planned on bringing Croc down. I told him to stay out of it, but I shouldn't have trusted him to listen the same way he did when he was just a scrawny little kid who worshipped the ground I walked on.

Should've fucking known better.

"Far as I know, the FBI—Task Force or otherwise—doesn't make a habit of paying special visits to guys hauled in on drug charges. So cut the bullshit and tell me what the hell this is really about, Darling."

He shoves to his feet and appears to think of how he wants to start as I try not to notice how his shirt pulls taut across his wide chest and broad shoulders. Or think about wrapping that chain around my fist and dragging him down to his knees— *Shit. Knock it off or you'll be the first guy to ever spring wood during an interrogation.*

I take a slow, deep breath and release it carefully so my

thready control over my starved libido isn't noticeable. Then I arch a brow in John's direction. "Well?"

He drags a hand over his groomed goatee, then leans forward, bracing his fists on the table. "We know your boss, Fred Croc, is behind this new drug. What we don't know is if this is the only activity he's involved in or if there's potentially something bigger. We also have reason to believe that this drug isn't stable. Several young women have ended up in the hospital and almost died as a result of using Fairy Dust."

I clench my teeth and try not to react. That's news to me, but then it's not like I keep up on current events. I hate selling drugs. Hate perpetuating the lifestyle that ultimately put me and my brother in that damn school. I'm only doing it for one very important reason—to get Starkey out of danger. But I still fucking hate it.

Telling myself these kids would be getting drugs from someone else, regardless, helps to ease my guilt. But I didn't know that anyone could OD on the Dust. If it's unstable, like he says, and it proves to be fatal for some of these kids, that makes me their Grim Reaper.

That'd be a whole new set of sins on my head. Ones I'm not sure I'd survive.

"I told you before, and I'll say it again," he continues. "We intend to bring Croc and his operations down. For good."

The image of Croc behind bars is like a shining light at the end of the long, dark tunnel that's been my life. But if there's one thing I've learned over the years, it's that something that sounds too good to be true, always is.

"If it's Croc you want, what does all this have to do with me, Darling?"

John nails me with the look of a cop getting his man, his eyes lighting up like fire shining through dark amber.

"From now on, my name is JD. I'm the newest member of your Pirate crew."

My heart stops. "What the fuck are you talking about?"

"I'm going undercover to take Croc down from the inside," he says, his lips curving up in a wolfish grin, "and you're my way in."

Chapter Three

JOHN

Then

Age 11

I CAN HARDLY BELIEVE where I am. Part of me wonders if I'm dreaming this whole thing up, but I don't think even *my* imagination is this good, which means it must be real.

Last week I caught my sister, Wendy, climbing onto her bedroom balcony in the middle of the night. She tried telling me some dumb story about her sleepwalking, but I'm super smart and I pay attention to details—like how her breathing changed and she wiped her sweaty palms on her pants—so I knew she was lying.

But in a million years, I never thought my goody-goody sister would be sneaking out to see a bunch of kids in Neverland of all places, the city we're not even allowed to get close to. Our parents would *flip* if they ever found out.

Like, grounded for life, do not pass GO, do not collect two hundred dollars kind of flip.

Except she says she's been doing this for over a year, so I guess it's safe to say odds are in our favor that we won't get caught. I hope so, anyway, because the idea of breaking the rules freaks me out. Not a lot—I'm not a wimp or anything—but just a little. I like rules and laws. We have them for a reason, and I believe in following them to the letter.

Normally.

I'm bending them for this, because it's just too cool to pass up. The eleven kids Wendy hangs out with are orphans who live at the School for Lost Boys of Neverland. Tinker Bell is a girl, though. I don't know what she's doing at a school for boys, and when I asked her, she just glared at me and went to bed. One of the boys my age, Silas, laughed and told me to be careful not to piss off the fairy, which I thought was weird, but I figured I should maybe not ask any more questions about her until Wendy and I are home.

We've been here—in the second-floor room where they all live—for about a half hour. So far I've learned that they used to have weird names until my sister gave some of them normal ones. Looking around the room, I try to remember who is who and commit them to memory so I don't forget. Silas, Nick, Thomas, the twins Tobias and Tyler, Carlos, Tinker Bell, Smee, Starkey (those last three names are their original weird ones and even weirder is that Smee talks like a leprechaun), and their leader, Peter Pan.

It's totally obvious that Wendy likes Peter as more than just friends. I don't know if they're boyfriend-girlfriend or anything, but they act like they want to be, which is gross to think about, so I'm not going to.

"Wait a minute," I say to Wendy. "You said eleven kids, but I only count ten."

Wendy glances at the door that leads to the first floor. "The last one is James Hook—but don't call him by his first name—and he's still downstairs with Croc, the man who runs the school. Sometimes Croc keeps him after supper for training on how to run his mechanic business. Since Hook is almost sixteen, he'll be out of the school in a couple years and can work full-time there."

"Oh, that's cool," I say, nodding.

Peter snorts. "Not if you know Croc, it's not."

I look over at Peter for an explanation, but Wendy shakes her head and Peter shrugs. Before I can tell her to stop treating me like a baby—she thinks because I'm two years younger that I shouldn't know stuff, which is dumb because Mom always tells people I'm an old soul, so that should count for something—Thomas asks to play a game of I Spy, and they all start talking at the same time.

We're in the middle of the first game when the door opens and an older boy enters, and everyone gets real quiet.

Hook.

My eyes widen as I take him in. Dressed all in black, he's tall and thin, but I can tell he's not weak. His arms look strong, like my sensei's, and he seems like the kind of kid who would start a fight for saying the wrong thing to him. Shaggy black hair hangs in front of his eyes so I can't see what color they are, but he doesn't look at any of us anyway. It's like we're not even here as he passes.

Smee and Starkey jump up and run over to a dresser where they grab what looks like a fresh black T-shirt and pair of sweats, then rush to meet him at the bathroom door. "Here you go, Captain," Smee says. "Anything else you need?"

"Anything else, Captain?" Starkey echoes hopefully.

James doesn't answer. Just grabs the clothes and disappears into the big bathroom, closing the door behind him. The boys come back to the circle, and a few seconds later I hear the sound of a shower running.

"Is he always like that?" I ask Smee when he sits next to me on the floor.

His forehead crinkles. "Like what?"

"I don't know," I say with a shrug, trying not to look as curious as I really am. "Rude, I guess."

"He's not rude. Least not to me and Starkey."

Starkey, who's only seven and has the coolest white hair with dark brown eyebrows, bounces on his knees and says, "Captain likes us because we do stuff for him. Everyone else likes Peter better, but we like Captain better." His cheeks get red like he's realized what he said out loud. "Sorry, Peter."

Peter smiles and gives him a wink. "Don't sweat it, kid. I know Hook's your guy."

Wendy adds, "I think it's great how you boys look after Hook. Everyone needs good friends like you."

They smile at my sister. She's learned how to say the right things from our mom who always knows how to make us feel better. It's nice that she's using the mom tricks to make the Lost Boys feel good, too. It's weird to think that none of them have any parents. I can't imagine not having a mom or dad. I bet it makes them really sad sometimes.

I peek over at the closed bathroom door, thinking about the boy on the other side. Is *he* sad? Or is it annoying having to live with so many little kids? I only have Wendy and our younger brother, Michael, and sometimes I think living with them is annoying. It must be a lot worse with ten others in the same room. Or maybe he hates having to learn stuff with that Croc guy.

I'm curious to find out more about him. I like solving puzzles, and sometimes people are the biggest puzzles of all. "Well, he didn't seem very friendly when you guys brought his stuff," I say to Smee. "He didn't even say thanks."

The redheaded boy waves a hand in the air. "He's just always tired after his training sessions with Croc. Adult stuff must be awfully hard to learn."

The rest of the kids agree, and then we're back to playing I Spy. I pretend to listen, but on the inside all I'm thinking about is the mystery boy in black. When he finally comes out of the bathroom, he heads straight for the farthest bed along one wall and sits on the edge with his back to the rest of us.

Before I realize what I'm doing, I'm up and walking until I'm standing right in front of him. His hands are folded together between his legs and his head is down, his wet hair hanging forward. I swallow hard, then open my mouth to introduce myself. But before I get anything out, I see a drop of blood fall from his right thumb. "You're bleeding."

He raises his head, and when I see his eyes, air gets stuck in my chest. They're the bluest color I've ever seen, and his black lashes are longer than even Wendy's. I think maybe he can see inside of me.

"Who the fuck are you?"

His mouth is twisted in a snarl like a beast in a fairytale who found me wandering in his castle. It freezes me in place, and I can't think. Coming over here was a bad idea. I'm about to run away when I hear the plop of more blood hitting the floor and I forget to be afraid as something squeezes in my chest.

"I'll be right back," I say and rush over to where Wendy's backpack is slumped under the window we snuck in through. She brought it to carry a bunch of snacks and juice boxes for everyone, but I know she also keeps a small first aid kit in the front pouch.

As soon as I get back, I kneel in front of him and get out the antibiotic ointment and a Band-Aid that's shaped like an H that goes on fingertips. I'm a Boy Scout, and I had to learn first aid skills for one of my badges. I'm so focused on wanting to help him that I almost forget to ask permission first, which is a rule when the person isn't unconscious.

Looking up at him, I ask, "Will you let me help you?"

He glares at me for a long time without saying a word. Almost like he's daring me to get scared again and go back by the others. But I don't budge. Finally, he moves his hand closer. That answer works for me.

I take a closer look at his thumb and realize the tip by his nail is really messed up. It looks like he dragged it over a cheese grater again and again. I raise my eyes to his. I want to ask him what happened, but then he arches an eyebrow at me. I can practically hear him challenging me in his head, daring me to run away and leave him alone.

Well, he doesn't know a thing about John Napoleon Darling. Pushing my glasses up on my nose, I get to work cleaning the blood as best I can, then adding antibiotic ointment so it doesn't get infected, and finally securing the bandage.

"That's waterproof, so you can probably leave it on for a day or two and let that skin heal up good before taking it off," I say as I close up the first aid kit.

"Again," he says, "who the fuck are you?"

My cheeks get warm. I completely forgot to introduce myself once I saw the blood. "I'm John Darling, Wendy's brother." I hold out my hand. "Nicc to meet you…um…" I start to say Hook, but something stops me. I remember what Smee and Starkey called him, a title only used by the two kids who followed him. "Can I call you…Captain?"

He looks at me like he's trying to figure something out, but then he rolls his eyes and sits back. "Whatever, kid."

"Yessss," I hiss in victory. "That's so cool because it's like a special name that only some people get to use, right? And now I'm one of them. It's like a club or something."

"What are you talk—"

"But now I should have a special name, too, like Smee and Starkey. I mean, those are super cool. Oh," I say, excited, "my middle name is Napoleon. That's pretty cool, right?"

Hook looks at me like he's bored. "I'm not calling you Napoleon."

"Okay, yeah, I guess it is kind of dumb. Especially since Napoleon was a general and then an emperor, which is a lot higher than a captain."

"Kid—"

My mind races as I try to come up with something, because I feel like he's about to send me away, and I don't want to leave without having a special name like the other boys. I don't know why, but I want Hook to have something to call me that no one else does. Like that's what I need to make sure I'm part of his group. Maybe I shouldn't think too hard about it. I should make it something simple, but different… Then it hits me.

"Captain," I say, squaring my shoulders, "I would like it very much if you called me Johnathan."

He raises that one eyebrow again, and I hold my breath as I wait for his answer. "Johnathan?"

"Yes, Captain."

"Your own name."

"It's my full name, Captain, but no one has ever used it. Not even my parents. That means it would be special only to you. So…will you?" My hands are getting sweaty around the first aid kit. I'm not sure why I'm so nervous about him not liking me. He's like the cool kid I want to sit with at lunch, only we're nowhere near my school cafeteria and Hook is like ten million times cooler than the most popular boy in my class.

He sighs and lays back on his bed. "Whatever."

Yessssss. This time I manage to keep my excitement on the inside, although I pop up to my feet with extra energy. "I'll let you get some sleep. I think we have to leave soon, anyway."

I get to the end of his bed when he says, "Hey."

I turn back to look at him. Man, his eyes are *really blue.* "Captain?"

"Thanks for patching me up…Johnathan."

My chest puffs out with pride. He said that whole sentence with a clenched jaw like it hurt worse than his thumb does, but I don't care. If I had to guess, Hook probably isn't the kind of person to throw around thank-yous or special names just because someone wants them. So I'm counting those six words as a win. And who knows, maybe over time, I can even get him to say my name without snarling.

Hoping I'll get the chance to help him again in the future, I give him a serious nod and say, "Always, Captain."

Chapter Four

JOHN

Now

"YOU'RE out of your goddamn mind."

Well, that's better than the outright *no fucking way* I was expecting. I knew James wasn't going to immediately go along with the plan. That's why I was the one chosen to speak to him. I told my Supervisory Special Agent I had a history with the leader of the Pirates and would be our best bet to get him to cooperate. I didn't honestly believe the bullshit I fed them, but I figured it was worth a shot.

Now I'm in this small interrogation room with him that feels even smaller with the enormous chip on his shoulder taking up so much space. And while he's doing his best to glare me into the ground, *I'm* trying not to notice how hot he is. Seriously, he's like the poster child for bad boys everywhere. Over-long black hair that's constantly falling in his face, a scruffy beard, and his perpetual *I don't give a fuck* attitude, combined with all-black attire that molds to his body in all the right places.

And then, of course, his tattoos… Christ, his black-and-gray sleeves are sexy. All pirate-themed and incredibly artistic, one arm has a half-skeletal Blackbeard steering a ship's wheel with a metal hook instead of a hand, and below that is a writhing octopus that wraps around his forearm with a ribbon banner that declares *Dead Men Tell No Tales*. The other arm has a huge skull in a pirate hat with pistols crossed behind it, a treasure map, and a large compass, all filled in with decaying roses.

I could probably spend hours studying all the intricate details of his tattoos and never get bored, but if I don't do my job and convince him to go along with this plan, there's a chance I won't even get to look at them from a distance because Hook won't let me anywhere near him again if I blow this.

"I disagree," I say, trying not to notice the way his eyes burn with blue fire and wondering if they'd look the same in a moment of passion. We have an audience behind that mirror, and I'd do well to remember that. "I could give you dozens of examples off the top of my head where an undercover agent successfully infiltrated a large criminal operation, gathered enough evidence to break the case wide open, and brought justice to those responsible."

James claps his hands together a few times in mock applause. "Nice try, Darling, but you're gonna have to do better than that. Maybe you should let one of the seasoned guys talk to me while you go work on your pitch."

Damn him. He keeps using my last name on purpose, trying to get under my skin. It's working. He hates his first name—I still have no idea why—and I've never been fond of my last name. It's the opposite of manly. Growing up, other kids teased me all the time, insinuating that I was as much of a sissy as my name implied. After I became a cop, I hated the smirks or outright laughs every time I introduced myself as Officer Darling, so I switched it out for Officer John. Unfortunately, my new bosses don't let me play fast and loose with my name, so back to Darling it is. But it doesn't matter as much, because as soon as people find out I'm working with the FBI, they forget about everything else. It's the power of the acronym.

But I hate it even more when James uses my last name. He does it to put distance between us, to reinforce all the ways we're different. Throwing the "special name" idea in my face from the first time we met was a defense mechanism. James, like anyone chained to a table in an interrogation room, is essentially a wild animal backed into a corner, so he's using everything he can think of to get the upper hand. He intended to throw me off my game.

He did.

I didn't think he remembered that night. He never once called me Johnathan after that, not in the three years we were around each other before he moved out of the school. If you want to get technical, he didn't call me anything since he made it a point not to speak to me, no matter how hard I tried to get his attention.

In the beginning, it was a case of hero worship, plain and simple, but by the time I was thirteen, hero worship had morphed into a serious crush. His aloofness and utter disregard for anyone around him drew me in, but the dark secrets lurking in his eyes—secrets I wanted to uncover and eradicate for him—are what held my attention long after he seemingly disappeared into thin air.

But he also made a mistake when he brought that little detail up from our past. Because now I know that I wasn't quite as inconsequential to him when we were younger as I once thought. And I already know that he's not immune to me now. I can still feel the way his erection pressed against my ass when he pinned me against that wall at the beach the night my sister got engaged to Peter.

I'd suspected James was gay—or at the very least, bi—but it wasn't until that moment I knew for sure. Even better, there's a part of him—a very *large* part from the way it felt—that's attracted to me, whether he wants to admit it or not. And I'm not above using that to my advantage if that's what it takes. But sexual chemistry isn't the only bargaining chip I have.

"Okay, I can do better than that," I say. "You're right. After all, you're a hardened criminal without a conscience or moral code, so why would you cooperate with us for the sole reason of helping out your fellow man?" That's all a bunch of shit he couldn't convince me of if he tried, but it's what he wants people to think, so I'll play into it. "What if I told you that we're also aware that most of the Neverland Police Department is in Croc's back pocket and bringing him down means we break the NPD corruption, which means anyone being unlawfully held will be set free."

I grab the eight-by-ten mug shot of a young man—twenty-two years old with pale skin, white hair, brown eyebrows, and silver-blue eyes—and drop it on the table in front of James. The boy doesn't look like his normal handsome self with the two black eyes, swollen cheek, and busted lip, but his unique coloring is enough to make out his identity.

James swallows and pulls the picture closer. "Starkey," he whispers, his voice thick with emotion. His hands curl into fists, and his eyes shoot up to nail me with misplaced accusations. "What the fuck happened to him? He was perfectly fine when they put him in the back of that cop car."

"I don't know for sure, but I'm guessing they roughed

him up at the station. They booked him for possession of ten grams of methamphetamine. That's a felony that carries a minimum of five years."

James bolts to his feet, the chair flying backward and slamming against the wall. "That's fucking *bullshit*! He didn't have any drugs on him. Croc didn't supply us with Dust until *after* Starkey's arrest, and that kid wouldn't know what to do with anything stronger than weed."

I hold my hands up in supplication. "I believe you, but it's not hard for them to pull shit out of the evidence room and claim they found it on him, especially since the people who would normally question things are likely in on the false arrest."

James brings his fists down on the table, the sound bouncing off the walls of the small room. He's in a volatile state right now, which works in my favor professionally, but on a personal level, I hate seeing him like this.

"Let me outta here, and I'll go kill that piece of shit myself. I should've done it a long time ago."

Fuck. I'm trying to get him out of this with minimal jail time, but threatening homicide isn't going to help me convince the higher-ups to give him a deal for his cooperation. Walking over to the corner, I turn off the audio for the room. My boss probably won't be happy about it, but I told him there was a chance I'd do it as a trust tactic. What I didn't tell him was that I one hundred percent planned on doing it at some point in the interview. Some things just don't need to be heard by outsiders.

"Audio is off, but they're still watching," I say, turning my back on our spectators and walking over to set his chair back to rights behind him. "Listen, Hook, I get it. You want to save your guy who's been thrown to the wolves in what I'm guessing is a ploy to control you. You're pissed as hell and ready to burn the world down, but I'm telling you that isn't the way to get what you want. The only thing it accomplishes is getting your ass put in prison right along with him."

"And what *is* the way to get what I want? Working with you and your cronies? I don't trust cops. Never have, never will."

"Then trust *me*." He's still standing, so I sit in my chair across from him. It's a calculated move, one that lets him feel as though he's in the power position. He might be handcuffed to the table, but there's enough chain that he's able to walk around to my side if he wants. "Just because I'm part of the establishment you hate doesn't change the fact that I genuinely want to help you and Starkey and, by extension, the people of London and Neverland, and however far Croc's reach goes."

He takes a step around to the side of the table. "Why?"

"Why what?"

"Why do you care about me and Starkey?"

"You think seeing that mug shot didn't upset me, too? He might be four years younger than me, but Starkey was one of my friends for almost half of my childhood. And you…"

James lifts his chin as though bracing for some kind of impact or preparing to be let down by what I say next. Jesus, has this guy ever had anyone stick their neck out for him, or has it been one disappointment after another for the last thirty years? Fuck the power position tactic. He needs to know he has an equal, someone who's just as strong and willing to stand by his side.

Pushing to my feet, I walk around to stand in front of him. He's about an inch taller than me, but I've got him by about twenty extra pounds thanks to my intense lifting program. I'm careful to keep some space between us despite everything in me wanting to fist his jacket and haul him against my chest. I don't waiver for a second as I hold his gaze and speak honestly.

"I've always cared about you, whether you wanted me to or not," I say, my voice pitched low. "I can't explain why, but I also don't think it's something that needs an explanation. It just *is*. You know why I wanted to become a cop?"

His Adam's apple bobs as he swallows, but he doesn't spit back a snide comment or cocky rebuff, so I keep going. My mom always said honesty was the best policy. I hope she was right.

"Because of you and the rest of the Lost Boys crew. I saw the bruises and black eyes after Croc got his hands on one or several of the kids. I heard Tink and some of the boys talk about dismantling shiny new cars when they should've been studying for school or playing like normal kids. And I know I probably didn't even see half of what went on there, but I saw enough to understand it was a shitty situation with no one to help you out of it.

"I wanted to help you, Hook. I wanted to help *all* of you. But I was just a kid myself, there was nothing I could do other than be a friend and help Wendy sneak in food and games. So I decided that when I grew up, I was going to make sure I was in a position where I could help people who couldn't help themselves. I was going to be a cop and put the bad guys away, *especially* that asshole Fred Croc.

"But as I was growing, so was he, and by the time I was in the police academy, he'd already branched out to bigger things than his small-time chop shop. So I set my sights even higher and joined the JTF. Now I'm in a position—we're *both* in a position—to finally take him down. You just have to fucking trust me. For once in your goddamn life, let someone help you."

For several minutes, James doesn't say a word, but I know he's thinking. He's smart, which means he's running through all the possible scenarios of how this can go right…and how it can go utterly fucking wrong. "He'll know you're a cop," he finally says. "There's no way you pass for a Pirate. Croc deals in information; he has people who can sniff out your deepest secrets. He'll find out who you are."

I shake my head. "Believe me, he won't. We have guys who can scrub out my entire existence as John Darling and give me a new identity, complete with a criminal background and time served. You'll bring me in as someone to replace Starkey since you're down a guy. I'll pass, I promise. But if for some reason I'm made, they'll get us out of there and bring him down with whatever evidence we've managed to get to that point. It shouldn't take us long."

"I don't care about getting me out. I want Starkey out of there."

Not for the first time I wonder if Starkey isn't more to James than just another crew member. I know he's closer to him and Smee because they've been with him since childhood, but even Peter told me that there's something different about Hook's relationship with Starkey. Peter had never seen him so crazy over one of his guys getting picked up by the cops before. Logic would point to them being lovers, but my gut is telling me that's not the case. Or maybe it's just my blind hope.

"Starkey's already been to court and sentenced," I say, "so there are only two ways he's getting out of prison. Either Croc pulls the strings to make the whole thing go away and the prison suddenly has an inmate mysteriously disappear, or we bring down his house of cards, clear Starkey's name, and put Croc on the other side of those bars where he belongs."

James releases a heavy sigh and pulls on his midnight-black hair with his free hand before releasing it. I feel like I'm losing him.

"Hook..." Willing him to see the determination and sincerity in my eyes, I urge, "Trust me."

He levels a look of trepidation at me that cuts through my chest. For someone as distrustful as him, this has to be one of the hardest things he'll ever do.

"Fine," he says, and relief washes over me. "But when you're a Pirate, you do as I goddamn say or your cover will be blown, and I won't be able to lift a finger to help you. You got me?"

"Yeah, man. I got you."

Little does he know that Pirate or not, I'd do as he says anyway. If he actually knew the power he holds over me, I'd be in trouble. For now, I'll take this small victory. He might not admit it—would probably claim he has no choice—but he's trusting me. I hope like hell this means he can hear me knocking on those concrete walls he's surrounded himself with his entire life. If not, I'll keep on knocking and pounding and chiseling away until I finally get through to him.

Because whether he believes it or not, James Hook is worth the fucking effort.

Chapter Five

HOOK

Then

Age 14

"HOW LONG DOES it take to wash your dirty fuckin' mitts up there? Get your asses down here pronto!"

A shiver races down my spine, chilling me to the bone, despite the scalding hot water running over my hands. Every night when me and the other kids get back from working in the shop all day, I hope to fucking God—if there even is such a thing—that Croc ends up drinking with his buddies after hours, then sleeps it off on the couch in his shop office. Sometimes I get my wish.

Tonight, I didn't.

As I mentally steel myself for the next few hours, the kid next to me says, "Dirty work makes dirty hands, am I right, boys?"

The kids—eight other boys and one girl who thinks

she's a fairy thanks to the idiot talking—chuckle and continue to get the grease off their hands as much and as fast as possible.

Fucking Peter Pan.

I can't stand the kid. There couldn't be two more opposite people on the planet than me and Pan. At twelve, he's the next oldest here, but for some reason all the kids look up to him as their leader. Except for Smee and Starkey, who consider me their captain. Not that it's a huge accomplishment when a nine- and six-year-old follow you around like puppies, but I'm not about to tell them to take a fucking hike, either.

Especially not Starkey. No one knows he's my brother, not even him, and I intend to keep it that way. I got my reasons. But that doesn't mean I don't look out for him, and it's easier to do that when he's more or less my constant shadow. If I'm not around, he's stuck at the hip to Smee, so at least I know he's always got someone watching over him.

Glancing up in the long mirror above the row of sinks, I catch Pan's smirk and it rubs me the wrong way. "Everything's a joke to you, Pan. When are you gonna grow up? You act like it's normal for kids to be working in a chop shop. This is called a school, but we spend more time busting our asses taking cars apart or putting them back together for a small-time crook than we ever have cracking open our textbooks."

He shrugs. "It might not be normal for other kids, but it's *our* normal. There's nothing we can do to change it, so we might as well make the best of things. Besides, growing up doesn't sound like all that much fun to me. At least here we have food and a place to sleep. Growing up means getting banished from Neverland, and who the hell knows what happens to the kids then."

My eyes snap up to glare at him in the mirror. Sometimes I'd really like to shake some sense into him. He's so fucking clueless about the world and how cruel it is. Even before Starkey and I ended up here, my life was shit. Day after day of dealing with a junkie mom who was either strung out on heroin or figuring out how to get her next fix. Then Starkey came along, and I became a substitute dad at the age of eight because our mother could barely take care of herself, much less a baby.

But I'd take those days in a heartbeat over the ones I have here.

"Doesn't matter to me," I say. "I don't care where I go, as long as it's far away from this place."

"Says the teacher's pet."

Narrowing my eyes in his direction, I grind out, "You got something to say, Pan?"

"Just that I don't know why you're bitchin' about being here when you're Croc's favorite. I mean, you're the one he's taking under his wing, right? Teaching you how to run the business? That's what you said he's doing when he calls you down at night. Or maybe he's not teaching you anything. Maybe it's something fun like watching TV together, and you're lying because he told you not to tell us what you're really doing."

Pan's words ping around in my brain. *Croc's favorite... taking you under his wing...calls you down at night...something fun...* Rage burns in my blood and I get sick to my stomach all at the same time. That's pretty much my default setting for the past couple months since Croc started "training" me to take over for him someday. He's training me all right, but it has nothing to do with the damn shop.

"You talk too much, Pan."

He smirks. "Yeah, I get that a lot. Doesn't mean what I'm saying isn't true, *James*."

That name triggers me, and all I see is red. "Call me that again, asswipe, and see if I don't plant my fist right in your face."

Fuck it, I'm ready to punch him now. I have more pent-up anger in me than I know what to do with. It'll feel good to let it loose on Peter. But just as I clench my fist, tiny Tinker Bell steps in front of him, all kinds of pissed. "Touch a single blond hair on his head, and I'll tell Croc you were the one who took his pack of cigarettes."

I feel the blood drain from my face. Croc is already a nightmare. If he thinks I did something worth punishment… I shudder. "What the fuck ever, I'm outta here. Smee, Starkey, let's go."

"Coming, Captain!" they say together, but I don't bother to wait for them as I start putting as much distance between me and Pan as possible. That kid is constantly dancing on my last nerve. The others don't know that I have shit so much worse than them, but they *do* know they don't have it great. Croc beats us when he gets pissed, takes away our meal privileges—as if it's not our right to eat every damn day—or locks us in dark closets for days at a time and calls it solitary confinement.

Yet with all that, Pan still manages to smile and laugh and play games like he doesn't have a care in the fucking world. Nothing that happens to us gets him down, and he always finds a way to twist the bad things into good things. To give the younger kids hope for a better future when none of us have a clue what waits for us when we get out of here.

He even figured out a way to make nights a little more bearable by telling us stories he's been getting when he sneaks out. They're like short vacations for our brains, letting us escape into worlds where magic exists and the good guys always win. It's nice for the kids to hear that kind of stuff. They've even started using their imaginations, something they never used to do. For their sake, I hope he keeps bringing them stories. But he still pisses me off on a daily fucking basis.

Supper goes as it always does, in complete silence with the exception of the clinking of silverware, ravenous chewing, and inane complaints hurled back and forth between Croc and his bitch of a wife, Delia.

I'm not hungry, but I force myself to choke down enough stew and bread not to draw attention to myself. Unfortunately, it doesn't work. I can feel Croc's beady black eyes on me like lasers burning holes into my flesh. The seconds are marked with the sound of his ancient pocket watch *tick, tick, ticking* like claps of thunder in my head. And every one of those seconds feels like an eternity, stretching thin from one heartbeat to the next and feeding my dread until it eventually consumes me and I'm no longer Captain Hook but a vessel for fear itself.

Croc's cell phone rings. He gets up to answer it, moving into the living room to talk. A speck of hope blooms in my chest. I just need to make it upstairs. Once I'm up there, I'm safe for the night.

The meal ends.

Tink is ordered to clean the kitchen, as usual.

The rest of us are dismissed.

I'm first in line, and I don't even wait to see who's behind me as I start climbing the creaking wooden stairs.

Halfway there.

My heart is thundering so loud. I swear it's echoing off the walls of this narrow passageway, muffled by the sound of our heavy footsteps.

Almost to the top.

I don't know if I'm paranoid as fuck or my time is

running out, but I think I hear the ticking of Croc's ancient pocket watch getting louder…

Three more steps.

…and louder…

Two more.

…*tick*…*tick*…

One—

"*James*."

We all freeze.

Every muscle in my body clamps around my bones so hard I'm surprised I don't collapse. Croc is the only one who uses my first name. It's why those five letters make my skin crawl. The moment it left his lips to hang over me in the sticky air of his office several months ago, it ceased to be my name, instead morphing into a twisted extension of *him*.

But I refuse to show weakness. I refuse to let on to the kids that anything is other than what they think it is. We might not live the charmed life, but if I can prevent them from seeing the monster lurking beneath the asshole's surface, I will. I'm already damaged goods; there's no saving me.

And that's where this will end.

With me.

I'll make damn sure of it.

I turn and step down to Pan's level. "You getting the end of the story tonight?" Last I remember, we were nearing the end of one called *Cinderella*.

"Thought you didn't care about the stories."

There's no fucking way I'd ever give him the satisfaction of knowing I even listen to the things. Looking over at him, I deadpan, "I don't."

"Yeah," he says after a few seconds, "I am."

I nod once and continue down the stairs, the boys all

shifting over to let me pass. With each step, the ticking gets louder and the world around me blurs more and more, until everything becomes fuzzy and unfocused, like crossing from the real world into a dream.

Except I'm very much awake, and this is no dream. It's a nightmare.

When I get to the bottom, Croc palms the back of my neck, making me want to puke up what little I managed to force down earlier. Taking a deep breath through my nose, I fight the reaction and win. But I can't help the dry mouth and cold sweat. There's never any controlling that. I've tried.

"Come on, boy," he says huskily. "I've got lots to teach you tonight."

I glance over my shoulder at Pan one last time, willing him to read my mind. *I'll keep him busy. Get the story. They need it.*

I stop in front of Croc's desk and flinch when I hear the lock click over behind me, then I slip into my routine of turning off the different parts of my brain. One by one, I imagine powering them down or yanking the plugs. Doesn't matter so long as all that's left is a subconscious ability to follow orders and the muscle memory to carry them out.

"Time for tonight's lesson, James."

James? Who's James? Not me. I'm no one. I'm nothing. You can't hurt nothing. You can't violate *nothing. I'm fine, I'm fine, I'm fine—*

"You waitin' for a formal invitation, boy?"

He moves in behind me.

It's okay. Behind is better. Better than in front.

By now, I've managed to deaden most of myself. But there's a tiny voice deep in the shadows still thrashing around, demanding attention. Demanding revenge, retribution. Demanding I do something—*anything*—other than what I'm told. I want to listen to that voice. I want to listen to it *so fucking bad*. But then images of the other kids flash in my mind, of what would happen if the monster is forced to find different prey. An image of Starkey. Sweet, innocent little shit that he is.

Like every other time, I slam the door on that voice.

I know it doesn't stop his screams. But it's better if I don't hear him. For everybody's sake.

Hot breath sticks to my neck as he says, "Take your pants down, James."

And as I do, I have one final thought: I hope the prince finds Cinderella tonight.

Chapter Six

HOOK

Now

AS THE CREW shuffles into the Crow's Nest—the name we gave our clubhouse meeting room—I study each member and make mental notes. I watch for any signs that one or more of them might not be happy, either with me or each other. I pay attention to body language and whether they're avoiding my gaze or giving each other meaningful looks.

Because even though they're loyal to me as their captain, I never assume that their loyalty is blind. All it would take is for one of them to think they could do better in my position, and I'd have mutiny on my hands. I don't think it would ever happen, but a complacent leader is easy to stick a knife into. Metaphorically or otherwise.

After I turned eighteen and had to leave the school, I told Croc I'd stay on as his employee for whatever he needed if he put me up somewhere and let me run my own crew. As much as I wanted to, I couldn't take off and start a new life. I still had Smee and Starkey to think about—okay, yeah, and maybe the others, too—and the only way to make sure Croc didn't fuck with them was to stick around.

So I made a deal with the Devil.

Keep your friends close and your enemies closer.

My last year at the school, I told him me and the kids would need a new place to live as they all started coming of age, so if he wanted us to stick around for the cheap labor, he'd better do something to fix it. In reality, I had no illusions of any of them following me except for Smee and Starkey—I don't even think I would've let the others if they tried—but Croc didn't need to know that at the time.

He bought an abandoned bar called the Jolly Roger on the outskirts of Neverland. The old highway sign is still out front, and the stupid name just kind of stuck, but we usually just refer to it as "the clubhouse" like any respectable gang does. What made the property perfect are the four rental cabins out back. They all have two bedrooms, a full bathroom, and small living room.

None of the buildings were in great shape when Croc got the place, but they were livable. He told me if I wanted nice, I'd have to fix it up myself, so I did. I watched videos, read manuals, and even asked questions at the Home Depot in London. It was all trial and error, but over a long period of time, I managed to get everything the way I wanted, including remodeling the second floor of the bar into a huge two-bedroom apartment for myself, which I call my loft.

Originally, I'd planned on Starkey taking the other bedroom, but it would've looked suspicious to single him out. I couldn't treat him different from the other Pirates.

Besides, he might still have a hero worship thing where I'm concerned, but him and Smee are more like brothers than we'll ever be. It only made sense to keep them together once Starkey moved in.

For four years I'd been working for Croc and living at the clubhouse while keeping a discreet eye on things back at the school. By then I was twenty-two, and Pan, Silas, Nick, and Carlos were all out, and they definitely weren't joining me at the Jolly Roger. Croc was pissed that my "plan wasn't panning out" like I'd promised. But I'd been prepared for that conversation and had already scouted out some morally bankrupt individuals to bring on instead. It wasn't hard to convince him that guys with reps for breaking the law would be infinitely better than inexperienced and soft-in-the-hearts Lost Boys.

I played to his ego, while also satisfying mine. I knew Croc was looking to expand his operations, which meant dirtier jobs for me. I wanted guys who I could pass as much of that shit onto as possible. Plus, there's always strength in numbers, and when the shit hits the fan, I need guys who will ultimately stand by my side.

As everyone takes their seats around the massive wooden table, I look around the room and do a mental roll call: Smee, Cecco, Cookson, Noodler, Skylights, Bill Jukes, and Robert Mullins. Starkey's empty spot at the other end is a sharp reminder of why I'm about to send my crew into a fucking upheaval that could very well cause one of those mutiny situations I was talking about.

But even if it doesn't—even if John manages to pull this operation off—the deal I made with the FBI is going to put everyone sitting at this table behind bars, including me. Smee and I will supposedly get somewhere around six months for helping with the investigation and as part of our cover. If we're the only ones without consequences, word would get around that we worked with the feds and everyone knows what happens to snitches. Fuck the stitches, because in our world, snitches get *dead*.

Guilt over what I'm doing has been gnawing away at me since I left the LPD that day. The others stand to do a minimum of several years depending on their records, outstanding warrants, and whether they make plea deals. When it comes down to it, it's not like we don't deserve to do the time. I just hate the fucking idea of selling out my guys. But I hate the idea of Starkey's life being in danger even more. So I'll go through with this charade and hold up my end of the bargain. Then Starkey will be free, and I'll send him to stay with the Lost Boys while I'm on the inside. After that…well, I haven't gotten that far, but there's a good chance Neverland won't be part of my long-term plans.

I glance at my watch's digital face (nothing around here is allowed to *tick*) and realize I only have about ten minutes before John arrives. I told him to walk in around a quarter after seven. That gives me enough time to get the guys settled and in meeting mode—where I'm doing the talking and they're doing the listening.

The only one who knows what's coming is Smee. I had to read him in on the mission because he knows John. As soon as I told Smee about our new objective, he was all in. He didn't even balk at working with the feds. He wants Starkey free just as much as I do, maybe even more. When I wanted to raze Croc's world, Smee was right there with me. It was the other Pirates who held us back until we calmed down enough to realize fighting him would get us nowhere. We had to play his game to win, which is still true today. But now I'm changing the rules.

I'm in the middle of handing out club assignments for

this weekend when I hear a knock on the door frame and catch John out of the corner of my eye. He's ten minutes late. I lean back and swivel my chair to the right, ready to fire off a reprimand, but the words get stuck in my throat. I've seen Cop John, Civilian John, and Task Force Officer John. But I don't think my imagination ever bothered to picture what he'd look like as Badass John.

Worn jeans that stretch around his muscular thighs are bunched above a pair of black motorcycle boots that match the leather Harley jacket over a faded Metallica T-shirt. His short, chestnut-brown hair isn't in its usual combed style but mussed like someone's been running their fingers through it. Gone is his goatee and clean-shaven jawline, replaced by a couple days' worth of sexy scruff. And if that isn't enough, the top of a tattoo is peeking out from his jacket collar on the side of his neck.

I'm simultaneously turned on and pissed off. There's looking the part, and then there's taking dumb risks. What happens when that temporary tattoo flakes off at the wrong time? Because I'd bet my left nut—hell, *both* my nuts—that it's a fake, and if any of these guys realize he's a fraud, there'll be hell to pay.

"It's about time," I droll. "What's the matter, McRae, get stuck in Neverland's nonexistent traffic?"

John smiles wide like he doesn't have a care in the world. Good. At least he's off to a decent start. I wouldn't bother bringing on anyone who'd be easily intimidated. "Nah," he says. "I only have my bike right now, so I had to borrow a truck to bring all my stuff. Took a little longer than I expected."

"Borrow?" I say, a single brow raised. "Or steal?"

He shrugs. "Six in one hand, half a dozen in the other."

"What is it?"

"1996 Silverado."

I scoff. "Junk. Croc can't use that for anything but scrap metal, and it's not worth the extra heat right now. Get your stuff into the loft, then get rid of it."

"You got it, boss."

"Captain," I bite out.

"Sorry, right. Captain. I'll take care of it right away." For the first time since arriving, John appears properly, if not mildly, contrite. Under different circumstances, I'd love for him to do something to earn my wrath and watch him beg for my apology, offer to make it right however I wanted. Fuck, the filthy things I would make him do…

My cock stirs to life in my jeans, shocking me back to the present. If I don't stop fantasizing about Darling, he won't be the one to blow our cover. *I will.*

Punctuating the matter with a nod, I spin back to the table to address my crew. When I sense John still standing there, I add, "Why are you still here?"

"Don't I get to sit in on the meeting? Meet the guys?"

"No, you fucking don't," I say, nailing him with a cutting glare. "You get to do what I told you to do and sit up in the loft and not touch anything until I get there. And if you manage to piss me off any further, introductions won't be necessary because your ass will be out before it was ever in. Are we clear?"

John glances at the rest of the guys, who are staring at us curiously, before clenching his jaw and replying stiffly. "Crystal, *Captain*," he bites out, then turns on his heel and disappears.

Thank fuck he put some heat behind his words. I need a delicate balance of obedience and an aversion to authority. Maybe I didn't give him enough credit, because so far his acting skills are on point. I shouldn't get too excited, though. Just because he passed the first five minutes doesn't mean jack shit. Jesus, worrying about this whole thing blowing up in our faces is gonna give me an ulcer.

"What's going on, Captain? Who the hell was that?"

I turn to Cecco, a handsome Italian guy with small hoop earrings. If I need someone to look the part of an upstanding citizen, he's the man for the job. He can pull off a suit like he was born into it, but underneath he's still just a thug who's done a lot of prison time with the shitty tats to match.

"His name's JD McRae. Heard about him through some of my contacts, and we're down a guy, so I'm bringing him on board. Probationary, obviously; he's not a Pirate yet. He has to earn that right like all of you did."

"Why's he staying with you in the loft? Why not take Starkey's room?" Bill Jukes asks in his impossibly deep voice. Dude is huge and black and the scariest motherfucker I have, but he has pipes like Barry White. If he sang while dismembering you, you'd thank him for it.

"Because while I think he'll be an asset to us, I don't fully trust him yet. Half his old crew in Atlanta went down for drug trafficking and the rest disbanded when no one stepped up to lead. When I offered to give him a trial run with the Pirates, he accepted."

Cookson narrows his eyes in a challenge. "Who was his old crew?"

"The Scavengers," I say and hold my breath as I study their reactions. This was a risk, naming a crew only a couple of states away. It's not likely that any of my guys will have old associates from that area, but it's not impossible either. The Scavengers were a well-known club, and news of the bust last year has made the rounds. We're counting on the fact that it had a couple hundred members to make it much harder for someone to get a straight answer just by flashing a picture or asking about a name.

The guys all seem to relax and even mildly approve. I release my breath. It goes a long way to claim that John was with a respected criminal club, but that doesn't mean any of them will trust him right off the bat. John's got his work cut out for him, so I hope he knows what he's doing.

"All right, you have your assignments for this weekend. Smee, since he's standing in for Starkey, I want JD with you. Anything suspicious gets reported to me immediately."

"Aye-aye, Captain," Smee says in his faint Irish lilt and signature smirk. "I'll keep a close eye on him."

Skylights laughs. "Don't try gettin' in his pants, Smee. You'll scare the new guy off."

"Are ye kiddin', lad?" Smee gestures to his well-built body, then circles a finger around his model-handsome face. "Who wouldn't want *this*? Even you straight boys think about me, you know you have. Don't lie now."

Everyone starts laughing and giving each other shit about who's fantasizing about Smee, which I guess concludes our meeting. But that means I have to face a frustratingly sexy John Darling, who's parked his fine ass in my loft, around my things, in my space, and I'm not ready for that. Not sober, anyway.

"Meeting adjourned, boys," I say, pushing to my feet. "Let's go drink till we can't see straight."

That gets their attention, and we all file out into the main part of the clubhouse. The old bar is still intact and displays a full range of alcohol on the mirrored shelves, with a fully stocked cooler of beer. We all get our own drinks—something that Starkey used to do as the lowest man in the Pirate hierarchy—texts go out inviting the regular party crowd, and then we proceed to get good and shit-faced.

Well, *they* do. I get a good buzz on, then drink just enough to keep it without going overboard. If I go upstairs completely smashed, I'm liable to do or say things I can't undo.

Like fuck my new roommate within an inch of his life.

Somewhere around three hours later, I leave the boys to their debauchery and head out. The whiskey's taken the edge off any nerves I had earlier. There's no reason any of this should bother me. We have a job to do. I've always managed to ignore John in the past; this'll be no different. I'll talk to him only when I have to, avoid looking at him, and beyond working together to bring Croc down, there's no reason for us to interact at all.

Yeah. This'll be easy. I don't know what the hell I was so anxious about.

I have two entrances to my place. One is a set of stairs behind the clubhouse that lead to my deck, and the other set is accessed through my office. After relocking the office door, I head up. When I reach the top landing, I hear what sounds like rhythmic pounding muffled by the door. Pissed he's not sitting in goddamn silence like I assumed, I enter the loft, slamming the door behind me.

The floor plan is an open concept with this entrance being off the kitchen, which is in the back-left corner of the building. On the other side of the breakfast bar is the huge living room set up to face the rear of the property with that entire wall boasting big picture windows that look onto the deck and the other door. On the front wall are the doors to both bedrooms and the full bathroom between them.

But none of those places are where my eyes are glued right now. No, I'm looking at the front-left corner of the loft, opposite the kitchen, where I created an open area for working out. It has a treadmill, a complex weight system, free weights, and a heavy bag hanging from the ceiling. A heavy bag that John—a *shirtless* John—is currently working over like it threatened his entire family.

"What the fuck do you think you're doing?"

Chapter Seven

HOOK

He stops, dropping his wrapped hands to his sides as he turns to face me, his chest heaving with labored breaths and sweat glistening on his skin. His *very tattooed* skin.

"Working out," he says between breaths. "I got bored."

"I mean, what are you doing covered in fucking stick-ons?" I don't think that's what I meant originally, but now it's all I can think about.

John looks down at his own body as though he forgot they were even there, which gives me time to take them all in, too. An American Traditional-style rose with crossed daggers behind it on the side of his neck, the words *No Shame, No Mercy* curve under his collarbone, a squawking raven is on his upper left arm, a skull and crossbones on his right pec, and a grim reaper with a scythe along his ribs on his left side.

My throat goes dry, but my mouth waters with the images my alcohol-weak brain flashes of me licking each and every fake tattoo plastered to his body. Of me cupping his cock through those thin track pants and squeezing until I feel him shudder beneath my touch. Of me shoving him full of my hard dick again and again until I explode and mark him as *mine.* No shame, no mercy? I'll show him exactly what that expression means.

"These are a lot better than the ones available to the public," he says. "They use these in movies and can last up to a week or more. I have five of each. I just remove the ones I have on every week to make sure they don't start rubbing off and reapply new ones. No sweat."

Is he fucking kidding? There's plenty of sweat. It's on every inch of his exposed skin, and it's driving me insane. "That's not the point," I bite out. "It's an unnecessary risk. You could've just as easily shown up as unmarred as a baby's bottom like you usually are."

I'm trying hard to make it sound like his tattoo-free body is a turnoff to me, when it's anything but. I'll admit Badass John has a lot of sex appeal, but there's something about his straight-laced appearance that makes me think of all the ways I can dirty him up. So maybe the fake tats are a good thing. Although the way I feel right now, they're not doing a very good job of turning me off.

Meeting my gaze, he cants his head to the side. "How many of your guys don't have tattoos?"

I clench my teeth. "None."

"Exactly."

He grabs a hand towel and his water bottle from the floor. Wiping his face, he closes the distance, coming to stand a mere two feet in front of me. Close enough that I can smell him, the musky scent of his sweat combined with hints of his aftershave. Goddamn him.

Smiling, he adds, "Gotta look like a Pirate if I wanna be a Pirate."

In a heartbeat, I'm in his face, my finger in his chest. "Let's get one thing straight, Darling. You are not now, nor will you *ever* be a *Pirate*. You're not cut out for this life, and I have serious doubts you can even pull this off. If you're made and it puts Starkey's life in jeopardy, I'm telling you right now, I'll work you over harder than you did that bag over there."

Damn it. In retrospect, "work you over" might not have been the best choice of words as unmistakable heat flashes in his honey-gold eyes. It's all I can do not to pin him against the nearest wall and kiss him until we've both forgotten why it's a bad fucking idea.

"Ja—"

And there goes my buzz. He didn't even get the whole thing out before realizing his mistake. If looks were swords, he'd be run through and bleeding out at my feet right about now.

Fisting his hands on his hips, he blows out a breath and starts again.

"Hook, you need to trust me if this is going to work. I have no intention of putting Starkey at risk. If shit goes south, we have a guy on the inside who can pull him out and get him to a safe house."

"*What?* If we can get him out now, then *why aren't we doing that?*"

"Because if we do, Croc will know he's compromised. He'll take measures to move the product, his operations, tighten security—he might even shut down until things cool off—but in the end he'll go back to selling his drugs that make people sick or worse. Is that really what you want?"

Growling with pent-up frustration, I stalk into the living room, rip off my jacket and throw it at the couch like I'm trying to put a dent in it. "This is never gonna work," I mumble, raking a hand through my hair.

"Yes, it is."

A warm hand grabs my forearm, but I twist out of his touch before the heat can sink in.

He holds his hands up and takes a step back. "Look, I've got years of police experience, great instincts, and tons of training. They wouldn't have given me this job if they thought I was going to fuck it up. The more you fight me on what we need to do, the more we put the mission at risk."

When I don't say anything, he crosses his arms and levels his flinty agent glare on me.

"The faster you let me do my damn job, the faster you get me out of your life. Something you've made clear you wanted from the first day we met."

I chuckle with no trace of humor. "Oh, Darling, you have no fucking clue what the hell I want. But if you're ever curious, all you have to do is ask. Until then, remember this," I say, stepping into his personal space. "When it comes to the mission, you might be in charge, but in here…" I swipe my thumb across a drop of sweat trailing down the rose tattoo on his neck, then suck it off my thumb while holding his gaze. "In here, I call all the shots. How's *that* for clear? Crystal enough for you?"

He swallows hard, his Adam's apple tempting me to follow its bob with my tongue, but I hold firm. In here, I am king. In here, he will obey me. That is my non-negotiable demand, and the steel in my tone says as much.

"Yes, Captain," he says gruffly.

"Good."

Then I turn away from him and head to my room for a long cold shower before he can see what it does to me to hear him utter those two simple words.

Yes, Captain.

That man is everything I shouldn't want, which only makes me want him that much more. He's a walking, talking, sexy-as-fuck temptation dangling in front of me. And the thing about being the bad guy is that I've never bothered to exercise restraint when it comes to something I want. I've always just taken it, consequences be damned.

I'd better find religion, quick. Because if I don't, there'll be a hell of a lot of sinning going on in this loft.

Consequences be damned.

Chapter Eight

JOHN

For the first time in my adult life, I might be out of my depth.

Not on the job. I'm confident in my abilities for this assignment. I have a good team behind me, and the background they created for me is solid. Croc can look all the way back to my kindergarten records, and he'll find that John Dorian McRae was excellent at coloring in the lines but also had issues with authority.

No, it's not the case that's got me tossing and turning on these Egyptian cotton sheets (I guess he wasn't kidding about enjoying the finer things in life). It's the man on the other side of this wall. The man who sucked my sweat from the pad of his thumb and demanded I acknowledge his authority over me in this loft. And fuck if I didn't want to agree before he even got all the words out. I would've done it on my knees if he'd pointed at the floor.

And that's what has me so twisted up—this insane desire to please James, whatever it takes. I want to give him what he needs, to make him feel good, if only in the context of the bedroom. But while I've always been in relationships where we switched off physically as tops and bottoms, I've never had any kind of submissive tendencies. Quite the opposite, in fact. I'm very Type A. I like control and my routines, and the only time I ever take orders is from my superiors at work. Full stop.

But with James…fuck, I don't know what it is. Maybe there's a part of me that's still that little boy trying to impress the older kid and get him to like me or even notice me. Maybe it's because I know he hasn't had it easy in life and the idea of being an escape for him, however briefly, speaks to my protective side. Whatever the case, I can't let it affect this assignment. Too much is at stake. I need to keep things strictly professional.

Strictly.

Professional.

Growling at the ceiling, I kick off the sheet and get out of bed. All this thinking about James is making me thirsty, and since I'm not getting any damn sleep, I might as well get some water. I contemplate slipping on a pair of lounge pants over my boxer briefs, but that seems like a lot of work for a ten-second walk to the fridge, so I don't bother as I leave my room and head for the kitchen.

His place is nice, understated and simple. But it might as well be a hotel suite—tidy and functional, with all the furniture and appliances one needs but without any of the personal touches that make it a home. No pictures, knick-knacks, or anything that would give any clue as to who lives here. I have a small house in the middle-class area of London. It's nothing fancy, but it's homey. I worked hard to put my stamp on it and fill it with things that remind me of the people I love.

Opening the fridge, I grab a bottle of water and take note of the blender in the corner on my way out of the kitchen. Good, I'll need that for my morning meal. I twist off the cap, drain half the water, and recap it as I pad my way across the huge living room.

I catch movement out of the corner of my eye and instinctively reach for the gun that isn't there. The water bottle drops to the floor and rolls under the couch somewhere as I try to recover from the near heart attack.

"*Jesus Christ*, you scared the hell out of me," I say to a very calm James who's sprawled in the chair, bathed in the light of the full moon streaming in through the windows. He's wearing only a pair of black lounge pants, his legs stretched out in front of him, his incredible torso on full display.

Holy shit, this is the first time I've ever seen Hook shirtless, and my eyes drink in every detail like a greedy sponge. He has another tattoo—a large, three-masted ship flying a pirate flag that takes up most of his right side—his nipples are pierced with hoops, and his chest is lightly dusted with black hair that disappears at his sternum and picks back up under his navel. He has the frame of a swimmer, broad at the shoulders and tapered at the waist, with plenty of defined muscles in between.

I feel like someone dumped water on my mental circuit board. I can't think, can't speak. And it's not even the tattoo, the pierced nipples, the blocks of abs, or the dips of his V angling into his low waistband that has me completely tongue-tied. It's the fact that he's reading a worn copy of *The Count of Monte Cristo* and wearing black Clark Kent eyeglasses. He looks like a fuckable, badass professor relaxing at home. Good goddamn, this part of the assignment is going to be one giant exercise in sexual frustration.

"What the hell are you doing over there?"

A single eyebrow rises above the rim of his glasses. "If

you can't figure that out, you might not be as good of a cop as you think."

I roll my eyes. "I mean, what are you doing reading at nearly three in the morning? You have insomnia or something?"

"Or something."

His tone has a hint of bitterness, or maybe resentment. Combined with the elusive answer, the wheels in my cop brain start spinning. "Do—"

He lifts his book again and interrupts me with a forceful, "Go back to sleep, Darling."

I've accepted that he's going to keep using my last name as a way to get under my skin, so it no longer bothers me. But fuck if I'm telling *him* that. "I wasn't sleeping, either."

He lowers the book to his lap, and his eyes take a slow perusal of my body. Everywhere his gaze lands feels like an intimate touch, making me burn in its wake, and if I don't distract myself, I'll be pointing due north in seconds. There's a trick I've used in the past if I found my mind wandering down a path that might lead to an awkward reaction. If I catalog the details of the person's face and mentally file them away like I'll need them for a report later, it keeps my mind out of the gutter. *C'mon, cop brain, don't fail me now.*

Jesus. How can someone with such a ruthless reputation be so goddamn beautiful? His features are an odd mix of harsh and lush that complement each other. Cold eyes are framed with thick lashes, his often-snarling mouth is made with sexy, full lips, and his granite-edge jawline is softened by his trim beard that looks like strands of black silk. My fingers itch to stroke it as my lips lay claim to his, then trail lower to where the silky strands fade into the top of his throat, kissing their way down…

Fuck. So much for that trick. There's no hiding my reaction to him when the only armor I have is a pair of gray boxer briefs. His eyes drag back up my body to meet mine, his mouth twisting into a smug grin. "Insomnia?"

"Or something," I answer huskily.

"Need help with that? A good release might be just the thing you need to get some sleep."

My dick is shouting *YES* so loud I almost can't remember all the reasons that would be a colossally bad idea, but thankfully my logic does. Barely. Clearing my throat, I say, "As much as I would love to—and believe me, there's nothing I've thought of more in the past few months than that—I think it would be best that we don't cross that line while we're on this case."

"And what line is that?"

I frown. "Sex."

"Since I don't plan on touching you, I think it's safe to say I won't screw with your lines. Pun intended."

If he isn't touching me, does that mean I'm touching him? Will he demand a blow job? Would sucking him off even make me come? What am I talking about, of course it would. This is Hook we're talking about, the man I've wanted since before I even knew what those tingly feelings in my belly meant. Getting my lips around his huge cock would probably make me shoot on contact, I want him that badly. But that's still a form of sex.

"You have three seconds, Darling. Yes or no. Two… O—"

Before my brain even registers my mouth moving, I croak out, "*Yes.*"

Chapter Nine

JOHN

James pauses, like he's waiting for me to take it back. I don't.

"Fine," he says, "here's the one and only rule: you don't want to do something, you say no. Not 'stop' or 'red' or 'pineapple' or any of that other bullshit. You say *no.* Got it?"

I nod. "Yeah. Got it."

James doesn't react one way or the other. He simply removes his glasses, closes his book, and sets them both on the small table next to him before settling back into the chair, his elbow on the armrest and two fingers braced against his temple as he stares me down.

"Grab your cock."

I don't know what I expected him to say, but the blunt order takes me aback. "What?"

"Don't play coy with me, boy. Grab your fucking cock over your underwear."

I do, and the pressure from my hand forces a groan from my chest.

"The next time you balk at one of my commands, I'll assume it's a nonverbal no and we'll be done. We clear?"

"Yes."

"Yes, what?"

I haven't done anything other than grab myself because I have a feeling if he wanted me to do something else, he'd have told me. But now that I've started, my body is urging me to keep going, do more, chase down that mind-bending moment that leaves me in a state of tingling euphoria.

"*Darling*."

"Yes, Captain." My voice is thick with gravelly lust, and I don't fucking care. Let him see how much he affects me. Let him see how much I want him. This is my truth, and he deserves every bit of it.

"Show me," he says, almost as though he'd just heard my thoughts. "I want to see everything."

Eager to obey, I shove my right hand into my briefs and palm my heated flesh as my left thumb anchors the waistband under my sensitive balls. Arms at my sides, I stand with my heart racing and hard cock straining. I'm on lewd display, exposed for this man who makes no move to do the same for me. He's still very much covered in black pants, and with the shadows in the room, I can't tell if he's even the slightest bit hard.

He makes some kind of gruntish sound, like a "huh" without the actual word. "Looks like little John Darling is all grown up."

"You felt pretty grown up yourself the night you pushed me against that wall."

He narrows his eyes the slightest bit before recovering. He might not like being reminded of the effect I had on him that night, but it was a moment I'll never forget.

"Too bad you'll never know for sure." His gaze drops

to my throbbing erection. "I suggest you stop talking and do something with that."

I don't make him suggest it twice. I gather saliva in my mouth, then take it out with my fingers and slick it over my cock. I give myself a couple of long, slow strokes and hiss out a breath at the friction making every nerve dance. Up and down, I grip and twist, keeping a steady pace while I use my other hand to roll my balls and tug on my heavy sac.

"That all you got?"

Shit, he sounds bored. I don't want him bored. I want him *aching* like *I'm* fucking aching. "What do you want? Tell me and I'll do it."

James pulls his bare feet back and leans forward, bracing his elbows on his knees. "I want you to fuck yourself like it's my hand." The steel is back in his voice, every word a command that I want—no, *need*—to obey. "I want you to jack yourself like it's my fingers encircling that billy club you call a cock, my calluses dragging along the pulsing veins, my thumb roughly grazing over that fat head as precum leaks from its slit."

"*Christ,*" I bite out through clenched teeth.

His words alone are doing more for me than my own hand is. I might be staring at him staring back at me, but what I'm seeing is the image he painted with the added details my mind has filled in for me. *In bed, I'm on my back with him lying next to me on his side. We're kissing and he's jacking me off as I do the same to him. His cock is thick and hard, the top of my fist bumping over the sensitive ridge of his glans and sliding back down. I squeeze. He groans into my mouth…*

My strokes are getting faster, less coordinated, more erratic. Every erogenous zone in my body has relocated to my dick. The intensity is unreal. I don't know how much more I can take. I'm so close. Dropping my head back on my shoulders, I squeeze my eyes shut and mentally start listing the different MMA submissions. *Arm bar, triangle, rear naked choke—*

"Eyes on me, Darling."

Jesus. My lids fly open and my head snaps back to center, shocked to find him standing only a couple of feet in front of me. He's tall and ridged with muscles, and I want to tongue and suck on his nipple rings and *fuck fuck fuck.*

"Close them again and I'll bind your hands for a lesson in orgasm denial."

I groan. I've never had a lover control my orgasms. Yet the idea of James telling me when I can come—and when I can't—sends sparks of electricity sliding down my spine to swirl heavily in my balls.

"Yes, Captain," I rasp.

A new stream of pre-cum leaks from my tip and spills onto my fist as I pump myself harder and faster.

"Look at that." His voice is husky as he takes a step closer and studies what I'm doing. *For him*. "You're already making a mess. Imagine how you'd be if I actually touched you."

"Shit, yes. Please, please touch me."

"You haven't earned my touch, Darling. Besides," he says, "you say that now, but you'd regret it in the light of day."

"No, I wouldn't." That's a lie, or maybe a wish. But the moral and responsible part of me—the only part that's *not* drunk on the heat of this moment—knows he's right. And I fucking hate that part of me right now.

"You would," he insists. "And I refuse to play the bad boy to your good one. I won't give you a convenient excuse to explain away what you truly want. Now squeeze harder and yank faster. Because the next time you fucking beg me to take you, Darling, I might just give you what you want. But if I do, I won't be gentle with you. I will goddamn *ruin you.*"

I let out a string of curse words between my erratic breaths, and my strokes get shorter and faster until everything is concentrated at the top near the head of my dick as my orgasm bears down on me. I'm close, so fucking close. Flames are licking along the base of my spine, drawing my balls up tight.

Fiery blue eyes hold me captive. I'm unable to look away, unable to move forward. I'm in a holding pattern of torturous pleasure. I bite my lower lip so hard I taste the coppery tang of blood, praying for my release.

"Do you wish that was my hand on your cock?"

"Yes."

"Do you wish that was my cock in your hand?"

"So much."

"Would you want me to come on you? Mark you with long stripes of my hot cum all over your chest and stomach?"

"*Fuck yes.*"

"Then do it. Right now," he commands harshly. "Mark yourself for me."

I roar as my orgasm explodes through me, aiming it just in time as my cock pulses in my hand and shoots ropes of cum across the ridges of my abs and pecs. My chest heaves as I try to catch my breath and keep my legs from buckling with the aftershocks.

James leans in. Still careful not to touch me, he whispers in my ear. "Welcome to the dark side, Darling." Then he turns and ambles back to his chair, stretching out like a lazy cat as he replaces his sexy-as-fuck glasses and picks up his book. Without glancing up, he dismisses me with a casual, "Go clean up."

On autopilot, I tuck myself in and make my way to the bathroom, half-dazed and wondering if I'm not actually dreaming this whole thing. But no, I know that's not true. Because as imaginative as I am, I never could've conjured up something as hot as that in my dreams. That was all James.

I use a washcloth and reluctantly wipe all traces of "his mark" from my body. After tossing it in the hamper, I study myself in the mirror. I'm a twenty-six-year-old man, accomplished in my field, respected by my peers, and always professional. I'm a rule follower. A by-the-book kind of guy.

But I haven't *always* done the right thing.

When I was young, I risked punishment every time I snuck out with Wendy to spend time with Peter and the Lost Boys, all with the hope of seeing Hook. All with the hope that he would finally *see me.*

And now he has.

He sees me, and he wants me. But for how long? James isn't the type to do things on anyone else's terms. He does them on his. I can stick to my principles and not let anything happen between us while we're working this operation, but I think once this is all over and he's done his short stint in prison, James won't bother sticking around Neverland. He never said as much, but it's a gut feeling I have, and I've learned to trust my gut.

I won't give you a convenient excuse to explain away what you truly want.

"Screw it," I mutter, making my decision as I head for the door. I can compartmentalize the mission and keep it separate from what happens in this loft, same as he can. I'm not going to waste whatever he's willing to give me while I'm here because of a few professional guidelines.

Yanking the door open, I stride into the main living area, ready to admit what it is that I truly want…

But he's gone. The chair is abandoned, along with the book and his glasses, and his bedroom door is now closed.

"Shhhhhit," I say as I plow my hands through my hair. I'm still all messed up from what just happened. Must be the endorphins or the blood hasn't made its way back to my brain. Getting involved with James Hook would be the worst thing I could ever do as far as this case is concerned. And if I'm being completely honest, it's probably not a great idea for my heart, either. Because what used to be a boyhood crush could easily turn into so much more if I let it.

"Damn your hero complex all to hell," I mutter to myself on the way back to my room. "The Pirate doesn't want to be saved, and you don't belong on the dark side."

Chapter Ten

HOOK

I OUGHTTA HAVE my ass kicked.

I don't know what the hell I was thinking last night. Shit, I *hadn't* been thinking; that's the problem. The second he came out of his room in nothing but a pair of boxer briefs that clung to him like a second skin, I lost all brain function. It's a damn good thing I was mostly hidden in shadows, because if I thought the view of his muscular back and tight ass was great, the view as he walked toward me was a goddamn revelation.

What happened next was not part of the plan. The plan being *stay the fuck away from Darling*. But I've never been particularly good at taking orders, and that extends to my own, apparently. If I want to get childish about it, I could say he started it. Standing in my living room in nothing but thin cotton that didn't do shit to hide his cock that was getting bigger and harder the more he stared at me was like the adult version of saying *Tag, you're it.*

We're like two Adams in the Garden of Eden up here. Every time we're around each other, it's like the forbidden fruit—the fruit being me fucking his brains out—is hanging between us.

John's the good Adam, doing his best to resist temptation at every turn. But me? I'm the Bad Adam. Temptation is like my foreplay, it's what happens before the main event. And when something is forbidden, it might as well have a neon sign flashing *come and get me*.

So I did.

Not as much as I would've liked to, though. I should get a damn medal for the restraint I showed last night. But I meant what I said. I refuse to be put in a position where I'm even mildly coercing someone who isn't thinking clearly. Last night, I was dancing on the knife's edge of doing just that. If I'd caved and actually touched him, the few principles I hold myself to would've been trampled into the dirt in seconds.

It's not that I don't *want* to fuck John Darling. Being able to have John whenever I want, testing his boundaries in and out of bed has my dick hard just thinking about it—or it would if I hadn't just jacked off three fucking times in the shower to the memory of him marking himself for me—but it'll never happen because of his principles. I'm not doing anything unless he can admit in broad daylight that he wants the bad boy to fuck him six ways from Sunday. But he's too set in his ways as a moral, upstanding good guy to do that. Not while working a case, anyway. And once this is over, I'm gone.

So, like I said, never gonna happen.

I finish tying my boots and pull on my black T-shirt before grabbing my phone and keys off my nightstand and shoving them into my pockets. Then, raking a hand through my damp hair, I steel myself as I leave the safety of my bedroom.

John's already in the kitchen. He's wearing a shirt,

thank fuck, even if it is one of those muscle shirts body-builders wear when they work out. It's better than nothing. Maybe I should make shirts a loft rule. Or coveralls.

"Morning," he says, not glancing up at me.

There's a twinge of annoyance—I'll be damned if I'm calling it disappointment—that he can't even look me in the eye after last night. It only proves I was right not to let things go any further than they did. Technically, Darling just had a jerk-off session in my living room.

While I watched.

And directed.

Fuck.

"Why the hell are you shoving a salad into my blender?" I ask, making a beeline for the coffeepot.

The corner of his mouth tips up slightly as he dumps in a scoop of beige powder. "It's my kale smoothie. I have one every morning after my workout."

"Because you hate your taste buds?"

He chuckles softly behind me, and now *my* mouth is tipping up in the corner. Which I quickly correct. I don't do lighthearted amusement, and we're not some happy couple sharing candid quips in the kitchen after a night in each other's arms.

"It's not as bad as it sounds," he says. Then he turns the blender on.

I lean back against the counter with my cup of coffee —I drink it black because I'm nothing if not on brand— while he purees the hell out of whatever disgusting things he has in there. When it's done, he pours the bright green liquid into a tall glass and drinks half of it down in one go.

"Gross. Is that what passes for food in your life?"

"I don't think of it as food; it's fuel. I make sure I get all the nutrients I need, and I don't put unnecessary crap into my body." I don't bother to hide my disgust. "It's healthy. Just try some."

At least he got over the not-looking-at-me thing, but I'll happily go back to that if it means not drinking that shit. "Pass."

He shrugs, then downs the rest of it before placing his glass in the dishwasher. "I'm grabbing a shower; then we should talk strategy. We need to get intel on what Croc is doing and where he's doing it."

"Yeah, fine."

Instead of watching John walk across the loft, I force myself to grab the ingredients to make my own breakfast that doesn't involve liquefied rabbit food. Thirty minutes later, I'm sitting at my small kitchen table, eating my eggs Benedict drowning in homemade hollandaise sauce with a side of bacon and hash browns.

"Damn, it smells like a diner in here."

I glance up and immediately regret not keeping my eyes on my food. A freshly showered John dressed in criminal-casual attire of ripped jeans and a white T-shirt that stretches across his broad chest is making my mouth water more than my breakfast. "That's the smell of *real* food, not that shit you choked down."

He sits in the other chair and gapes at my half-eaten plate. "You made all of that?"

"Yep."

"From scratch," he says doubtfully.

I stop in the middle of cutting my next bite and glare over at him. "I like to cook. You got a fucking problem with that?"

"No, of course not. I'm just surprised is all," he says, rubbing the back of his neck.

"Stop that."

"Stop what?"

"Rubbing your neck. For one thing, it's a nervous tell of yours. And for another, it'll fuck up your stick-on tattoo."

"I didn't realize I was doing it," he says, his expression thoughtful like he's trying to remember every time he might have done it. "I'll be more conscious of it, though, thanks."

I shrug and dig back into my food, glad I managed to derail the chit chat portion of the morning.

"Anyway—"

Or not.

"—I was saying that I didn't peg the badass Captain of the Pirates to be a culinary wizard, but it's impressive. I only know the basics of how to cook what I need—steamed veggies, brown rice, baked chicken and fish, that kind of thing."

"Yeah, well, if you'd suffered through Delia's cooking all those years, you'd have learned to make yourself good food, too."

Shit. Why am I telling him these things? I'm like a loose cannon around this guy. I need to rein it the hell in. He's silent for a bit, and it makes me wonder what he's thinking, but I don't look up as I continue eating. If I'm lucky, he'll just let it go.

"What was life really like at the—"

"No." I stop him before he goes any further, but the look in his eyes effectively ruins my appetite, so I shove my plate back.

I silently curse his stupid empathy. It's not like I meant to bring up my tragic childhood, for fuck's sake. Besides, our shitty dinners were the least of my problems at that school. But John didn't take note of my flip tone, he only heard a sad tale of a boy with improper meals, because John has a knight-in-shining-armor complex. He said as much in the interrogation room that day. His entire mission in life is to save people from the bad guys of the world.

That's great, good for him and the people he helps. But he needs to keep that shit aimed at someone else. There's no saving someone like me.

"What's the plan for today?" I say, leaning back and folding my arms over my chest.

He sits up straighter, and his cop face makes an appearance. Just like that, he's all business. "What would you normally do?"

"Go get this weekend's supply of Dust at the shop. Then tonight we hit the clubs and sell it."

"Do you see Croc when you get the new supply?"

"Not if I can help it."

He nods and scratches his stubbled jaw as he thinks. "Would you say he does more of his business at the shop or the shipyard warehouse you told me about?"

"Shop. He only goes to the warehouse for periodic checks on the production, as far as I know."

"Okay, then we need to get a bug into his office at the shop since that's probably where he makes his phone calls. Maybe if you distract him outside, I can sneak in quick."

"Not a chance," I say, shaking my head. "As soon as the door to his office closes, it automatically locks with an alarm that requires a code to get back in. And he doesn't bring anyone into his office, either. He's a cagey bastard, doesn't trust anyone."

John blows out a breath and scratches at the scruff on his jawline. "We could try sticking it on him personally, but it's too risky. He could find it, and even if he didn't, as soon as he changes clothes, it's useless. Maybe we can put it on something that he carries into his office himself. I'll talk to the team and see if they can put something together in the next few hours."

My phone vibrates with a text message. *Fuck.* "We don't have time," I say, getting up to go grab my jacket. "Croc knows about you. He wants to meet."

Behind me, his chair legs vibrate on the tile as he pushes back from the table and follows me, his booted steps eager. "Perfect, when we're in his office—"

I snag my jacket and spin around. "I already told you, he won't bring us in there. He'll interrogate you right in the middle of the shop where everyone can watch him act like a tough guy."

"Okay, fine. Then we'll stick with the idea of bringing something new into the office with the bug in it. We might not get it in today, but it shouldn't be too much longer."

I punch my arms into my sleeves like I'm gearing up for a fight, but the only war I'm in is with myself. Since Croc won't bring anything foreign into his office, I'm our only chance of getting anything in there. The thought of being alone with him in a confined space makes my skin crawl, but I'll do whatever I have to do. For Starkey's sake.

"I can get in."

John stops and looks at me. "You can?"

"That's what I said, didn't I?"

"Perfect. All you need to do is stick it right under the edge of his desk, and we'll be golden. Hold on a sec, I'll get it."

He heads straight for his room and comes back with a small, round device that looks like a watch battery. I hold out my hand, expecting him to drop it in, but he doesn't. He places it in the center of my palm, his fingertips grazing my lifeline, giving me goose bumps all the way up my arm. I'm sure the thing costs more than what my miserable life is worth, but the way he's looking at me with those golden-brown eyes, it's almost like he's being careful with *me*, not the expensive piece of equipment he's entrusting me with.

"When we get there, keep it in your hand. It'll look natural since your hands are usually balled into fists anyway," he says with a teasing smirk.

I give him a wolfish grin. "Never know when I'll need to punch a smart-ass cop."

He bites the inside of his cheek to keep from smiling, but it doesn't work all that great. "Assaulting a police officer is a Class C felony. I'd have to put you in cuffs for my own safety until backup arrived."

I step into his personal space, nice and close. "If you want to get kinky with handcuffs, Darling, I'm totally down. Just know that you'll always be the one wearing them, bound and completely at my mercy. That's the only way I play."

He swallows hard but holds his ground, which —*goddamn it*—might actually be hotter than when he submits. Pulling his shoulders back, he holds my gaze. "Wearing the bracelets is pretty fun when you're not on your way to jail. Maybe you should try it sometime."

"Not in this lifetime, kid."

He raises a single brow. "Trust issues?"

You have no fucking idea.

I turn and head for the door. "Let's go. He doesn't like to be kept waiting."

Chapter Eleven

JOHN

"A FEW SECONDS near his desk, that's all you need." I try to make it sound instructional and not reassuring. James doesn't like to be considered weak, so I'm pretending not to notice how on edge he's been ever since he told me he could get Croc to take him into his office.

Not that I'd ever think he was weak for not wanting to be alone with a man who used to beat him as a kid. How he's managed to be around him all these years without wanting to give him a taste of his own medicine is a mystery to me. In fact, *why* he stuck around is an even bigger mystery. I don't know for sure, but I have to wonder if Croc hasn't been holding something over James all these years. Even if he wanted to wait until Smee and Starkey were safe, I can't think of why he'd stay after that.

I'm hoping that one of these days he'll talk to me about it, but I'm not holding my breath. I accused him of having trust issues, which is like saying "cops wear blue." It's merely stating the obvious. But I think it's way deeper than that. I think his trust issues have trust issues, to the point I have to wonder if he's been able to depend on anyone his entire life.

James pulls into a spot at the Wrench and Go, Croc's front for what's essentially the chop shop where Hook and the rest of the kids from the school were forced to work growing up. He cuts the engine on his Challenger and nails me with a serious look. "Let me do the talking. Answer his direct questions, nothing more. Got it?"

"Don't worry about me; I can handle myself."

"You'd better hope so."

I follow him into one of the open garage bays with my bad-guy-don't-give-a-shit-about-anything attitude in full effect. This is nothing like LB Automotive, which is owned and run by Peter, Tink, and the rest of the Lost Boys on the other side of Neverland. Their shop is clean and organized. The Wrench and Go would be more aptly named the Wrench and Stench. Every surface looks like it was dipped in motor oil, including the mechanics, and the random piles of tires and other car parts don't instill a sense that they'll be very careful with your vehicle. Any car that pulls out of here likely drives away with a few less original parts than they drove in with.

We stop at the service desk where a balding man in his late forties sits with his feet up on the lower counter, watching *Jerry Springer* on a small television. His mechanic coveralls look like they haven't been washed in months—or ever—and they're only zipped partway up his stomach, revealing a sweat-stained wifebeater underneath. The name patch on his chest says *Tito*.

"Well, well, if it isn't the Captain himself." Tito's mouth widens in a mirthless grin, his lower lip distended with so much chewing tobacco it looks like he tucked half a finger in there. "Your lackeys finally get sick of doing your dirty work and bail on you?"

James leans an elbow on the high counter. "Now, Tito, you know better than that. Lackeys never leave on their own. After all, you've been doing Croc's dirty work since I was just a kid."

Tito's amusement morphs into a disgusted sneer as he drops his feet and stands, leaning forward as he spews his hate. "You're no different than the rest of us, you little shit. You'd better show me some fucking respect or I'll—"

Up till now, I've been hanging back, letting James do his thing. But all it took for my blood to boil and fists to curl was hearing this slobbish waste of space even *start* to threaten James. It takes me two large steps to reach James's side and nail that fat fuck with a glare that promises pain. "You'll *what*?"

Tito takes notice of me for the first time. I enjoy the way he pales and his mouth drops open before he recovers his fake tough-guy act. "Who the fuck are you?"

James smirks. "That's JD, my newest lackey. He's very loyal with twice as much muscle as you have fat, and that's saying a lot. I wouldn't piss him off if I were you."

I crack my knuckles for effect and smile with satisfaction when Tito slowly sits back in his chair.

"That's a good boy," James says to him. "Now do your job and tell Croc we're here."

Tito picks up the phone to presumably do just that, but James doesn't bother to wait. As he leads me farther into the shop, I scan my surroundings with outward mild interest. Tactically, I'm taking in every detail: searching for exits, weapons, and surveillance cameras. Other than the one stationary camera up front that's pointed at the cash register and service desk, I don't notice anything out of the ordinary.

Not surprising since this isn't where the majority of the

criminal activity happens, just where it's planned. Hopefully we can get the intel we need, things like whether he has other players in the operation, if he's the one making it or having it smuggled in from somewhere else, and if he's dabbling in anything other than the drug trafficking.

All the way in the back, a man emerges from an office. The heavy metal door swings shut behind him, and the keypad next to it blinks red with a long beep that signals it's now locked. It doesn't look incredibly high-tech, but it's good enough to keep the average person out. Plus, there's another stationary camera aimed at the door, so you'd have to disable that before attempting to get past the alarm system. All things that would add a lot more risk to the operation than if James can just get the bug placed in the office without suspicion.

Croc saunters up to us with confidence and authority. I've studied his file. I know everything about him that the bureau knows and I've seen pictures, but I've never seen him in person. Not even when we were kids. He looks a lot older than his fifty-five years thanks to his wrinkled, leathery face and gray-streaked brown hair perpetually in desperate need of a wash and cut. At six-feet tall and pushing three hundred pounds, most people are probably intimidated by his size if not his menacing black eyes. He might be tough, but even the toughest predators have soft underbellies. That's usually a metaphor, but in Croc's case, it's also literal, courtesy of his love for beer and shitty food. I'm not impressed.

"What took you so long? You two sucking each other off instead of following my orders?"

From the corner of my eye, I can see my partner's shoulders tense, but his face doesn't give anything away. "Tito wanted to run his mouth instead of doing his job."

Croc grunts and turns his attention on me, giving me a once-over like he would with a potential car purchase. "Guessing this is your new crew member. The one I never gave you permission to recruit."

"I'm down a guy thanks to you," James says. "You want the product moved, I need people to move it."

"New guy have a name?"

"JD." I'm careful to stay just this side of respectful without offering more than I need to. A guy like JD wouldn't give out information about himself he didn't have to.

He narrows his beady eyes at me. "Your *full* name. I run checks on anyone who does business for me. That a problem for you?"

I shrug. "Only problem I'll have is if I don't get a cut of what I'm selling. I don't hustle for free."

"No one does," Croc says with a toothy grin. "Name."

"John Dorian McRae."

James cuts in. "He was in the Scavengers down in Atlanta."

That piques Croc's interest. "What'd you do for them?"

"I collected debts owed to the club. If people had problems paying up, I convinced them it was in their best interest to try harder."

Another grunt and another once-over, this time slightly more appreciative because now he's probably imagining me torturing some poor schmuck for him. Something I'd never be able to do in real life, but as JD, I give him a smug grin because I know how valuable a guy like "me" is to a guy like him. Every criminal boss needs reliable muscle. The more sadistic, the better.

"Enforcer, huh? I think your talents might be wasted pedaling Dust," Croc says, rubbing his chin. "I have other things you could do that would better suit you."

"Hey." James takes a step forward. "He's *my* find, *my* guy."

"Do I need to remind you that all your guys—including *you*—are mine? I can damn well do whatever I want with him."

"We had a deal, so I don't give a shit what you do with him as long as it's *after* he helps me," James says with a snarl. "You need to keep your eye on the bigger picture here. Only an idiot wouldn't give me the support I need to complete the job he gave me."

Croc glares and speaks in a low voice. "You forget who you're talkin' to, *Captain*."

Hook appears to almost shudder, like Croc's sarcastic use of his title is in place for something else that only they know about. But it doesn't stop James from taking another step forward into Croc's space. "Then maybe you should remind me," he taunts, his eyes stony and jaw set.

An evil grin slides onto Croc's face. "In my office. *Now*."

As they walk away, I'm torn between a mental fist pump and pulling a fire alarm to abort the mission. This feels off to me. Croc's expression didn't change, but something had flashed in his eyes, like anticipation or excitement, and I don't like it. I should've pressed James to tell me how he intended on getting an invitation into the office where no one is supposedly allowed. I don't know why I thought it wouldn't be a big deal. Like James would just say, *Hey, I need to talk to you in private*, and that would be it.

But James intentionally pissed Croc off to get some kind of punishment or consequence for his insubordination. I assume the very least he'll get is a major tongue-lashing. What I'm worried about is the other end of that scale—the very worst. How badly did Croc beat James as a kid? Does he still do it? Is that how Croc keeps him in line?

I have a really hard time picturing James taking a beat-down now that he's an adult, but I don't know the extent of the hold this asshole has over him, and it's eating at me more and more every second.

Chapter Twelve

JOHN

CROC PUNCHES a code into the keypad, it blinks green as the lock disengages, then he pushes the door open and holds it for James to walk through before it slams shut behind them.

My relief that I can see them through the large window is short-lived as the blinds are snapped closed. *Fuck.* The bug will transmit the audio back to our local headquarters where only a select few have clearance to the information recorded. My name is on that short list, but I won't get the transcripts from it for a while. Which means I have no way of knowing what they're saying unless James gets chatty, and I have about as much chance of that happening as I do an Acme anvil spontaneously falling on my head.

Anxiety rides me hard and I want to pace the floor, but that would raise suspicion. While it appears as though everyone's busy doing shit, I have no doubt I'm being watched. Grabbing a nearby metal folding chair, I park my ass on it backwards, forearms resting on the back. Then I get out my butterfly knife and start running through some simple tricks. Nothing flashy, but enough to keep my nervous energy busy while showing anyone who cares to pay attention that I've got some obvious knife skills, which should at least make them wary of what else I might have up my sleeve. With my extensive martial arts background, I have a lot more weapons training than what flipping around this Balisong implies, but they don't need to know that.

Jesus, what the hell is going on in that office? I check my watch and blow out a breath like I'm bored as fuck when I'm anything but. It's been five minutes already. Not long in the grand scheme of a day but an eternity when I think about all the shit that might be going on behind that door.

I have to stop thinking worst-case scenarios. James isn't a teenager powerless against his guardian anymore. He's a strong man who chooses to work for the snake who bit him repeatedly when he was a kid. I have to believe he wouldn't put himself in that position if Croc was still a viable threat to him.

In my peripheral, Tito pushes himself up and waddles his way over to two of the other grease monkeys standing about twenty feet away from me. I'm sure they're supposed to be working on the cars lifted in their bays, but they don't appear to be in any hurry to do their jobs. The entire time we've been here, they've been leaning against the back wall, smoking and drinking cans of beer. Tito starts speaking to them in hushed tones as they sneak glances at me.

I mentally roll my eyes. Look out for these guys; they're regular spies. "Keep looking at me like that, Tito, and I'm gonna think you have a crush on me," I say with a smirk and a wink.

I've never seen a man turn beet red so quickly. What

tiny bit of logic he has—the part that should remind him that I'm twice his size and currently holding a large blade —snaps, and he charges in my direction. "I'll show you a crush, you fucking fa—"

I pop to my feet, prepared to introduce this homophobic bastard to my fist, when the office door bursts open, interrupting Tito's tirade. James storms out like a tornado with a mind for destroying everything in his path. His stride doesn't break as he cocks his arm back and lays Tito out with a single right cross to the jaw.

The other guys react like they're ringside spectators at a WWE match, obviously not giving a shit that their coworker is lying prone and spitting out blood and a couple of his teeth.

James crouches next to him. "Stay down, Tito. Slugs belong in the dirt." He pats Tito's already swollen face hard enough to make the guy groan and flinch away, then gets up and walks out of the shop.

Staying in character, I smile and flip Tito off as I follow after my captain. *Oh Captain, my Captain.* My teenage self is ready to stand on a desk and spout poetry after that virile display of power, but I shove all that down when I get to the car. As soon as I climb inside, I turn all my attention to the man sitting next to me, doing his best to pretend I'm not here as he pulls out of the lot and takes off down the road like a bat out of hell.

"What happened in there?" I ask.

"I placed the bug under the edge of his desk; what do you think?"

"I didn't doubt you would. I meant what happened between you and Croc?"

His jaw clenches so hard that the muscle jumps beneath the dark hair, and his hand tightens on the steering wheel until the leather groans in protest. "Nothing happened."

"Really," I deadpan. "You just stared at each other for ten minutes, and then you decided to leave in a murderous rage for no damn reason?"

"We talked business, Darling," he bites back, shifting into a higher gear. "What else would we talk about? He's my fucking boss."

Which brings up another line of questions. "Why is that, by the way?"

"Why is what?"

"Why is he your boss? Why do you work for the asshole who abused you and the other kids? A criminal with no moral compass who doesn't care who he hurts or kills to gain power."

His laugh makes the hairs on the back of my neck stand on end. "I think you forget you're talking to a criminal with no moral compass."

I scoff. "Don't give me that shit. You might be a Pirate, but you live by a code. It's a limited one, but it's still a fucking code." He answers me with silence, so I fill it. "You didn't answer my question."

"Which one?"

"Either of them. Hell, *any* of them."

"Then that's your answer, isn't it?"

He's trying to appear apathetic, but his body is strung tighter than a drum. Something had to have gone down in that office. My gut's telling me shit is not right, and everything in me needs to know what it is so I can help him. "Come on, Hook. You're not sticking around for the fun of it. Does it have something to do with him training you to take the shop over? Is he holding that over your head?"

He yanks the wheel, taking a left turn so fast I can't

believe all four tires stick to the road, and I barely stop myself from slamming into the window.

"One more word out of your mouth, Darling, and I'll find a better fucking use for it," he growls. "Call Smee. Tell him to pick up the Dust and meet us at the Jolly Roger. We have work to do."

Chapter Thirteen

JOHN

CRASH!

The distant sound of glass exploding rips me out of my fitful sleep. In one fluid motion, I grab my Glock from under my pillow and pop to my feet, wearing only the boxer briefs I wore to bed. Bracing my gun with both hands, I make my way out of the bedroom. Once I clear the main living space, I do the same with the bathroom and Hook's bedroom—which is empty.

Where the hell is he?

The thought of him taking off without me knowing where grates on my nerves. I tell myself it's only because his actions might affect the case and I can't risk any surprises, but I know it's so much more than that.

From the moment I successfully inserted myself into his life—regardless of the reasons why—I resent anything that takes me out of his presence. I can't protect him if I'm not watching his six, and I can't assure myself he's not doing something destructive if I can't see it for myself. All of which is fucking ridiculous, because James Hook isn't some naive kid who needs my help. He's older than me, has more experience in surviving life than I'll ever have, and is the captain of a motley crew of criminals.

He's a Pirate with a heart as black as the ocean on a moonless night; he doesn't need anyone for anything, much less me. And yet...

And yet I can't kill this compulsion I have to care for this man who doesn't want to be cared for.

I check my watch. It's a little after four a.m., which means I've been asleep for less than an hour. We didn't get back from the club until almost two; then James went straight to his room and kicked the door shut behind him. He hadn't said two words to me all night. Hell, he'd barely spoken to anyone, instead choosing to communicate through glares and silent commands his crew members must have been familiar enough with to understand.

Another crash sets my heart pumping with adrenaline and focuses my senses. The sound came from the ground floor of the clubhouse. I decide to spare the extra fifteen seconds it takes to yank on my jeans; then I use the stairs off the kitchen that lead to the office. If someone's broken in, I have a better chance at sneaking up on them coming from the back.

Once I'm downstairs, I stick close to the shadows along the hallway leading to the main room. I keep my steps silent and try to listen for any signs of movement up ahead but hear nothing. When I get to the end of the hall, I place my back against the wall and grip my sidearm with both hands, keeping it pointed at the ground and my finger off the trigger. Taking a deep breath, I round the corner as I lift my arms and do a quick scan for potential threats.

But all I find is Hook, slouched in a wide armchair wedged into the far corner. The room is dark with the sole exception of the wall sconces on either side of the bar that give off barely enough light to see what woke me up—the shattered whiskey glass and broken Jack Daniels bottle littering the floor over by the bar. Looks like he did some cathartic vandalism before grabbing a fresh bottle and settling into the chair.

I stand still, unwilling to give up the rare chance to study an unguarded Captain Hook. He's still in his all-black club attire: fitted V-neck, jeans that hug his ass and thighs, and his ever-present motorcycle boots. His head is resting on the low chair back, legs spread apart, body relaxed with the bottle clutched in his left hand. I'd think he was sleeping except for the fact that his right hand is moving in some kind of repetitive motion.

I squint, trying to sharpen my focus in the dim light to see what he's doing from this far away. As my eyes adjust, I finally see his hand splayed against the exposed brick wall, his thumb bent and moving up and down on the gray mortar between the bricks. Mortar that's stained unnaturally dark.

With his blood.

A memory sparks to life of a brooding boy with a bleeding thumb after he'd taken a shower—a shower with walls made of tile and grout. *Oh Jesus.* The acid in my stomach churns. How many times has he shredded his thumb like this? Does he do other forms of self-mutilation? I have plenty of questions I don't have answers for, but I don't have to wonder what triggers this. All those years ago at the school, he'd been downstairs with Croc in his office.

Just like he'd been with Croc earlier today.

I still don't know what happened between them. Not today and obviously not back then. But I'm not looking at everything with the eyes of a sheltered kid anymore. I've done a lot of growing up over the years, and I've encountered a lot of things that made me sick in my time as a cop.

When your job is to protect the innocent, you're forced to face the evils that threaten them.

With the wide-open eyes of a more worldly man, I'm starting to suspect things that I can't bring myself to think about. If I do, I'll find Croc and spill a thousand times more blood than what's dripping from James's thumb.

For long moments, I stand in place, unsure what to do. Undoubtedly, he wants to be left alone, to suffer his darkness in solitude. But everything in me wants to go to him, to comfort him. Something I know he'll reject, maybe even despise me for. The possibility of provoking him into wedging more space between us almost has me retreating.

In the end, I can't do it. James can reject me all he wants, but I can be just as stubborn as he is, and I'm not leaving until I've helped ease his pain, even if only for tonight.

Chapter Fourteen

HOOK

MUSCLES GRIP MY BONES TIGHTER, even as something inside of me releases on a sigh.

He's here.

I didn't hear John come in, and it wasn't because I was too deep in my own head to pay attention. I'm always on high alert. No one's ever gotten the drop on me, and they never will. But with years of martial arts and law enforcement training, he can move ghostly silent when he wants to. Doesn't matter, though. Even with my eyes closed as they are, I knew the second he entered the room.

Because whenever he's near, I can *sense* him.

I feel him moving toward me now. The closer he gets, the more my skin tingles, his presence charging the air with electricity like an approaching storm. I don't move, but I crack my eyes open just enough to see him. My heart thuds harder in my chest with every slow step he takes, closing the gap and eliminating the space I need to keep a level head around this man who makes me question my fucking sanity.

Unable to look away, my gaze roams over his bare

upper body, taking in the way his tattooed muscles ripple with every movement. His jeans are unbuttoned and hardly zipped, as though he'd hastily done only what he needed to keep them from falling off his trim hips. He steps around the shattered glass—courtesy of my recent outburst—and places his gun on the bar as he passes.

I'm assuming he heard the crash and came down to investigate. I picture a half-naked John skulking in the shadows, his big hands locked around his gun, arms straining with tension and ready to take out the nearest threat. *Fucking hell.* My cock starts to wake up, growing harder by the second, and I almost groan in relief. The redirection of blood flow from my pulsating thumb and the brief distraction from the toxic shit in my head is like getting my first taste of air in hours.

Finally, he reaches me. As he stands between my spread legs, I focus on keeping my breaths even, determined not to show him how much his nearness affects me. I am a rock. An island. I don't need him. I don't need anyone.

Then why do you want to chain him to your bed so he can never leave?

Other than opening my eyes all the way, I don't move, curious as to what he'll do next. After a few seconds, he grabs the bottle of Jack from me and takes a healthy swig before setting it out of reach on the floor. I arch a brow, then retaliate by grabbing a smoke from my pack on the side table to my left. I place it between my lips and light it with my Zippo. The cloves crackle as I take a long drag, the tobacco burning down and the red-hot cherry making the space between us glow.

Exhaling a long stream of spice-scented smoke, I fall back on our regular script. "Go back upstairs, Darling."

It's lacking my usual bite of command, but I don't have the energy—or maybe the desire—to correct it. He can stand there all fucking night for all I care. Closing my eyes again, I take another drag…and almost choke on it when I feel the cushion dip under John's weight.

My eyes snap open to find his hands braced on the chair back as he straddles me, his knees hugging my hips. This is the part where I demand to know what the hell he's doing. Except my brain short-circuits when he lowers himself onto my lap, his firm ass settling onto my thighs and—*fuck me*—his hard, denim-clad cock pressing against mine.

I watch him as he moves his hands to my shoulders, then slowly trails down my arms. His expression is one of determination, a single-minded goal swimming in that honey gaze. To seduce? No. To distract, I realize, as his left hand curls around my bloodied thumb, pulling it away from the punishing mortar, subtly protecting me from myself. Taking care of me like he did that first night we met.

I resent and appreciate the action, just as I resent and appreciate this man and everything he does—everything he makes me *feel.*

I should pull my hand away from his, but I don't. A voice in the back of my mind is warning me to be wary and stay on guard. That I should be pushing him away, both physically and mentally. But as he plucks the black cigarette from my fingers, takes a drag, and releases the smoke in a stream above my head, I can't seem to remember why.

"Look at you," I muse. "The good boy doing bad things. Since when do you smoke?"

He shrugs one powerful shoulder. "I've been known to do things out of character from time to time."

"For undercover work."

"Usually," he says, regarding the cigarette pinched

between his thumb and forefinger, "but now I'm starting to see the appeal in doing things simply for the sake of being bad."

John's lips wrap around the tip of the filter again, and the way his cheeks hollow as he draws the smoke into his lungs gives me ideas of him sucking my dick. Just as he's about to exhale, I grab his jaw with my left hand and drag his face close.

"Open," I command.

Amber eyes stay locked on mine as he obeys. Inhaling, I drag the white plume of smoke from his mouth into mine, careful not to give in to the temptation to close that last inch between us. As much as I hunger to take what I want—what we *both* want—I can't bring myself to surrender to this need. If I do, I'm not sure I'll be strong enough to come back from it. Somewhere a world might exist where a man like John Darling can be with a man like me...but this isn't fucking it.

I release him as I exhale and take my cigarette back. John's bad-boy act is hot, but for some messed-up reason, I prefer the original version. He's only been living the life of a Pirate for a couple days, and the small changes he's made to fit in—temporary as they may be—grate on me. Although, the view of his tatted and ridiculously ripped body is going a long way in making me forget everything but the fantasies now running through my mind.

"I hate that you do this," he says, lightly squeezing the base of my shredded thumb as he presses my hand on his warm chest, holding it to him as though he expects me to pull it away. I should. I will. Any second.

John rakes his teeth over his lower lip, his tell for when he's unsure about something. It makes him look more like that boy I used to ignore than the man I can't seem to.

"What happened today in that office?"

Whoosh. His question is like a punch to the solar plexus. So much for forgetting. The conversation in that office has been on a constant loop, one I've been trying like hell to sever. Almost succeeded, too. Now my breaths pick up and my pulse spikes with Croc's words slicing through my mind yet again.

"So, you don't want the new guy to work under me. What's the matter, James? Afraid JD will want what you didn't?"

"Considering you don't have a pussy between your legs, I highly fucking doubt it," I bite out with my fists clenched. "I need the extra manpower. I can't be a good little lapdog and do what you want if you don't give me what I need to do it."

Croc laughs. "That man's not interested in pussy, not with the way he looks at you. Not saying I blame him. Always been something about you. Even for a non-faggot like me, ain't that right?"

I'd heard this shit so many times it doesn't even faze me anymore. There are two kinds of closets that gays shut themselves into. The kind where you accept who you are but don't want the world to know, and the kind where you refuse to accept who you are to the point your closet is more like a deep, underwater cave. I'm in the former. Croc needs an oxygen tank for his.

For years, I've wondered if Croc targeted me because he could sense I was different from the other kids, even way back then. Or maybe there was something I did or said that tipped him off. Either way, I have to assume my preference for men is what got his attention, which is why I can't forgive that part of me. I accept it, but I also hate it. It's a weakness, one that can be exploited to ruin my reputation. Just as I threatened to ruin Croc's once upon a time.

"I don't give a shit how he looks at me, as long as he does his job." Swallowing back the bile in my throat, I force myself to add, "After that, you can do whatever the hell you want with him."

His lips twist into a lascivious grin that awakens the nightmares from my childhood. "Oh, don't you worry about that, James. I'll do plenty *with him."*

I'm vibrating with the need to kill him. To wrap my hands around his throat, crush his windpipe, and watch with satisfaction as that evil gleam slowly dies in his black fucking eyes. Instead, I dart my tongue out to lick my lips. Croc's gaze instantly locks on to the move like I knew it would. Predictable, sick fuck. *Then I use the distraction to stick John's bug under the lip of the desk.*

He sneers. "I bet he'll even take my cock without choking and crying like a little bitch. But then," he says, stepping in so close I want to vomit, "nothing got me off faster than seeing those tears streaming down your face."

Shoving him away, I bolt for the door, his maniacal laughter following me as I flee from yet another of Croc's offices.

"Hook!"

I snap back to the present and realize that wasn't the first time John had called my name. My hand he's still holding to his chest is now clutched into a fist, my blood marking his skin in a streak. I twist out of his hold and try to sit up, intending on unseating him, but he grabs the back of the chair and holds fast.

Faced with the choice of wrestling him for my freedom or feigning apathy over my imprisonment, I sag back to my original position. "What the hell do you want?"

"I want you to talk to me. You were thinking about earlier, weren't you? Something happened. What was it?"

Stalling, I take one last drag on the cigarette, squinting to keep the smoke out of my eyes. I pull on it long and hard, relishing the burn spreading deep in my lungs, then crush it out in the ashtray as I exhale off to the side. "Nothing worth talking about."

"But—"

Glaring at him, I grate out, "Fucking *drop it,* John."

His eyes widen, no doubt just as surprised as I am that I called him by his first name. Desperate measures and all that shit. He's too perceptive not to have at least some idea of what my problem is with Croc. He knows I wouldn't still be screwed up from typical beatings when I was younger. And I can't open this wound with him. I fucking *can't.*

"I don't need a goddamn head shrink, all right? Stop trying to fix me."

John shakes his head slightly, like he can't understand me. *Welcome to the club, kid.* "I'd have to consider you broken for that. But I don't think there's a damn thing wrong with you. Never have."

I study him, searching for the same pity in his gaze I'd gotten from Peter after he accidentally walked in on one of my "lessons." The pity had been a thousand times worse than the humiliation. Seeing that on John right now will send me over the edge.

But it's not there. Instead, I find reverence and…desire.

"Tell me what you need," he says softly.

His hands move to my stomach, and my abs jump at his touch. Even with my shirt as a barrier, his warmth seeps into me, spreading unsolicited comfort. My apathetic act is slipping with every shallow rise and fall of my chest, but I forge ahead like I'm not dying to feel him skin to skin.

"I don't need anything," I say, my voice thick and raspy.

John leans in, his lips grazing my ear, barely a whisper of flesh on flesh. I nearly groan from the carnal promise. "Let me take care of you," he whispers. "I wanna make you feel good. *Please.*"

Goddamn him. I've tried resisting this man at every turn, tried sparing us whatever fallout is bound to follow if I don't. There's no world in which getting involved with me ends well for him. You can't play with fire and expect to get away unscathed. It's not a question of whether he'll get burned, but just how badly.

Digging deep, I search for the strength to deny him—

and find none. He's got the advantage. My head's been fucked up all day, my usual barriers feel paper-thin, and I'm probably half in the bag. So, when John's big hands cradle my face as he leans in to kiss me for the first time…I don't stop him.

Gods help us.

Chapter Fifteen

HOOK

I DON'T SO MUCH AS TAKE a breath as John closes the distance, his muscular body rounding over mine. He pauses, his golden eyes holding me hostage, even as he gives me one last chance to stop him. I should, I *fucking know* I should.

I don't.

Full lips press to mine, and tingling heat shoots down my spine to swirl in my stomach and straight to my aching cock. I open to him and somehow hold back a groan at the first sweep of his tongue. He tastes like my whiskey and cloves, like virility and vulnerability; a heady combination that echoes a single word in the back of my mind.

Mine.

John fucking Darling. He's everything I was afraid of and more. Tonight, he's just the temptation I'm succumbing to, but he has the potential to be my Achilles' heel, the chink in my armor. And that weakness scares the ever-loving hell out of me.

"Let it go," he whispers against my mouth. "Everything eating you up inside. Give it all to me."

The last tether to my control snaps. I fist his hair in my hands, slant my lips over his, and delve into his wet warmth. He moans, and I eat at him like a starving beast, shoving back the regret I won't rectify. It's done. John Darling has sealed his fate—whatever that may be.

Fuck, he tastes so goddamn good, but I need more. My hips rock, my aching cock needing the pressure, the friction, but he denies me by breaking our kiss to sit back. The dominant reflex to drag him back to me dies as soon as his hands drop to my waist. John tugs my shirt out from my pants, inching it up as he watches for my reaction, as though wondering if I'll allow it. I answer by rising enough for him to pull it completely off before I settle back again.

Black pupils swallow his amber irises as his gaze follows the path of his hands on my shoulders, down my pecs, and over the ridges of my abs. The drag of his calluses on my sensitized skin leaves sparks in their wake. When his fingers tease along the barrier of my jeans, I suck in a breath. Clinking metal echoes in the silence as he undoes my belt buckle, then works the button and zipper open.

My dick jumps with anticipation, but I don't take charge and rush the process like usual. I've never let a lover have free rein with me—I know what I like and what I want, and I don't see the point in tap-dancing around that—but Darling's not making this just about pleasure. The look on his face and the softness in his eyes gives him away. No one's ever wanted to take care of me before. No one except this sexy-as-hell man who walks on the right side of the law and shouldn't have a damn thing to do with me.

And that's my undoing in this moment. I have no idea what to do with that or how to accept it other than to sit here and let him do what he wants. For now.

Bracing one hand on the chair back, he leans forward and lifts just enough to slip his other one into my pants, squeezing me through my boxer briefs. "*Jesus fuck*," I hiss, letting my head drop back.

"You have no idea how long I've wanted to touch you like this," he rasps.

"Get your fill now," I choke out. "Could be your last."

That's a lie. Unless he changes his mind, I have every intention of corrupting him as often as possible now that I've opened the floodgates. But my warning does its job and spurs him on. His mouth finds my neck, his stubble scratching me as he kisses, licks, and bites a path down to my chest. He latches on to my left nipple, sucking and tonguing my hoop piercing. Frissons of electricity light me up with every tug, streaking down to swirl in my heavy balls. Then he kisses his way over to my right nipple and does it all again.

I lift my head so I can watch him worship my body, see my skin glowing red with irritation from the scrape of his rough beard and the suction of his mouth. I've never been turned on by sexual marks before, but now I find myself wanting them from John. Something to remind me of all this when his hands and mouth aren't on me tomorrow.

As much as I wanted to let him run the show, my control is slipping. Or rather, it's *returning*. With the way he's palming my cock and rubbing me from tip to root, all the things I've fantasized about are rushing to the surface. Lust is overriding the darkness, urging me to act.

Fuck it. He claims to want this—to want *me*. If that's the case, then I'm ready to show Darling how to obey his captain. With one caveat.

"Fair warning: I don't do blow jobs and I don't bottom. If that's gonna be a problem for you, we should stop this right now." At the last second, I add, "It's nothing personal; they're just not things I'm willing to do. Ever."

I try not to think about why I want him to know my

hang-ups aren't about him. Whenever I hooked up with men in the past, I gave them the same warning so they don't expect shit out of me that's non-negotiable. But I've never given any kind of explanation to spare their feelings. Jesus, I'm going soft. Metaphorically speaking, since I'm currently hard enough to pound nails. Forget a cold shower. If he does want to stop, I'm going to need a damn ice bath to get this thing to go down.

A slow, sexy smile curves his lips. "Then I guess it's a good thing I'm willing to do both. And by 'willing', I mean I'm willing to beg for the pleasure of doing both if I have to."

Fuck. Me. The thought of Darling begging me to fuck him is enough to send me over the edge. Plowing my hands into his hair, I yank his head back to meet my gaze and growl, "On your knees, *Johnathan*."

His eyes snap open in surprise, but he doesn't move to follow my order. His inquisitive nature wants to ask why, after all these years, I'm finally using his full name—the name no one else uses for him, making it mine alone. *Mine.* It feels fitting in this moment, though fuck if I want to think about why. If I start examining shit, I'll call this whole thing off and send him away. I can only be pushed so far before I have to push back.

John must realize this because he bites his lip, then answers with an eager, "Yes, Captain."

As he slides off my lap, he trails wet, openmouthed kisses along my abs. He dips his tongue into my navel before following the dark line of hair that disappears into my boxer briefs. Without missing a beat, he tugs them and my jeans down to mid-thigh. I grunt in glorious agony when my cock springs free to bob against my stomach.

John gazes at my thick length hungrily, his tongue darting out to slick his lips as one of his hands encircles the base. Pre-cum leaks from my tip. Peering up at me from beneath his lashes, he dips his head and laps it up with the flat of his tongue. I suck a breath in through my teeth, his first contact like the lick of a flame. *Not enough. Want more, so much more.*

"God, you taste good. Like saltwater and sin."

My voice is gravelly with need when I answer. "Then stop fucking around and swallow my cock already."

He gives me a mischievous smirk. "Aye-aye, Cap'n."

Just as I'm about to berate him for being a smart-ass, he makes good on the promise and swallows. Me. Whole. *Fuuuuuuuuuck!* I'm so deep inside his mouth, his nose is mashed into my lower stomach, and the head of my dick is lodged in the tight space of his throat. I've never been sucked down so completely. It's fucking heaven. Warm, wet heaven.

He withdraws slowly, maintaining tight suction, his tongue dragging along the vein pulsing on the underside of my cock. The frenzy of sensations is making me go insane, my grip on the armrests bone-crushing as I fight for control.

As much as I want to think of this as just another sexual escapade, I know this is different, if only for the fact that John's on his knees because of his hero complex and inexplicable desire to take care of me—whether I want him to or not. Which I *don't*. Except…it stirs something in me I'm not familiar with; something that makes me want to do right by him, too. Or at least, not be careless with him.

Which is why I'm keeping my hands to myself. We haven't talked limits or boundaries, what *gets* him off versus what *turns* him off. If I let go and dominate him the way I've imagined, I could end up taking things too far or taking them in a direction he's not comfortable with, so I need to keep my alpha instincts in check. But *goddamn it*, he's not making this easy.

He sinks down on me again with a hum of pleasure that sends vibrations zinging straight to my balls. "Look at you," I rasp. "Taking my cock like a fucking pro."

That thought has me wondering just how much experience Darling's had that he's this good, which makes me think of him with other men, which makes me instantly murderous, and I have to mentally shake those phantom images before I say something I regret. Like make him swear he won't so much as *look* at another man ever again.

He pops off my dick to swirl his tongue around the head, then he dips the tip into my leaking slit. My hips jerk, and a tortured grunt slips out before I can stop it.

"You're holding back." His tone is a mix of accusation and disappointment, even as one hand jacks me off with the other rolling my balls. "You don't have to hold back with me."

Curling my body up, I loom over him and grab his chin, my thumb and fingers gripping his jaw tightly. "Be careful what you wish for, Johnathan. There's rough, and then there's *me*. You slip the leash off my beast and I'll use your mouth like my own personal fuck hole until I'm good and spent."

"Yes, *that*," he says, honey eyes glazing over. "I want the *real* you, not some watered-down version of you. Let yourself go. Please, Captain."

Jesus Christ. The more I learn about this man, the more perfect for me he seems, which I remind myself is stupid. There's no such thing. He has to have a flaw somewhere, something that'll put a dent in his shiny packaging, and the day I find it, this godforsaken hunger for him will finally go away.

But today is not that day.

Muttering a curse, I surrender to this clawing, aching need and crush my lips to his, demanding his submission in return. I've never kissed someone so savagely, never craved a kiss this desperately. I'm beginning to suspect John Darling of dark magic and lust potions. Our tongues twine and fight against each other in a war for dominance. He shudders on a moan, and I swallow it down like he's about to swallow my cock.

Shoving to my feet, I fist a hand in his hair and grasp my aching shaft in the other, aiming it at his face. "You need me to stop, you pinch my thigh. *Hard*. Got it?"

The idea of being too lost in how he feels to notice if it's too much for him scares the shit out of me. Almost enough that I consider putting a stop to this right here and now. But John's choosing this, and I'm going to trust him to give me signals. Because I'm a selfish bastard who wants this more than I should.

"You won't hurt me," he says with confidence, briefly shedding his submissive role. "I won't let you. I promise."

Giving a quick nod, I take a deep breath and succumb to the overwhelming lust crashing over me. "Open," I command gruffly for the second time tonight. As soon as he obeys, I plunge inside to the hilt, sliding into the back of his throat once more. When he swallows around my engorged head, my eyes nearly roll into the back of my skull.

"*Jesus fuck*."

I pull almost completely out, then hold him in place as I work my hips at a punishing pace. The sight of his lips wrapped around my cock and the way his watering eyes stare up at me in dazed pleasure nearly makes me embarrass myself, but I clench my teeth and manage to hold out, needing this to last.

When his hands rise, I brace myself to feel the pinch

on my thigh, but it never comes. Instead, he fondles my balls and reaches around to dig his fingers into my ass cheek, spurring me on. "You want more? I'll give you more. When I'm done, you won't be able to suck another man's cock without wishing it was mine. *Only mine.*"

I ride him harder, if that's even possible. My breaths are ragged, my skin slicked with sweat, and the gorgeous John Darling has strings of saliva dripping from his chin as I fuck his mouth like I own it. I've never seen anything so goddamn hot in my life. Wait. "Take out that bat you call a cock and jerk yourself off. But you'd better be quick about it, because if I come first, *you* won't be coming at all."

John moans, approval written all over his face. In seconds, his jeans are shoved over his hips, and he starts jacking his magnificent dick like it's offended him. There. *This* is the hottest thing I've ever seen, and now there's no more holding back. My climax bears down on me like a runaway train, and I'm giving it the green light.

"You've got ten seconds, tops. Better hurry, big guy."

And goddamn is he *big*. My gaze is transfixed to his fist sliding along his thick shaft, fast and rough, the flushed crown glistening with pre-cum. I'm ready to burst at the seams, and watching him is only building that pressure more and more with every passing second. Pulling him off me, I tilt his head back with a yank on his hair.

"Stick out your tongue," I grate. He does, and I start jerking myself furiously over the open invitation. "One of these days, I'm going to bend you over the nearest surface and bury my cock so deep in your ass you'll still feel me days later."

That does it. John groans as long ropes of cum paint the peaks and valleys of his chest and abs. *So fucking hot, this man.* And then I'm just as gone. A string of curses leaves my lips as I come on John's tongue, marking him with every hot lash I give him. *Mine.*

When I'm completely spent, my hand relaxes in his hair and shifts lower to cradle the back of his head. I feel a tug behind my ribs as I watch him lap at the remaining drops of cream on my cock like a contented cat until he's swallowed every last bit.

Bending down, I whisper in his ear, "Good boy, Johnathan." I feel him exhale on a shudder, a sigh of satisfaction from hearing he did a job well done. From knowing that he pleased me. *Killing me. Absolutely killing me.*

After pulling my pants up and tucking myself back in, I hand him my shirt to clean himself up, then I settle back into the chair. I don't know what I expected him to do after that, but I sure as hell didn't think he'd remain kneeling between my legs and rest his head on my lower stomach.

I tense up at the unexpected intimacy and almost brush him off. But then my hand finds his head and I start to relax as something in me shifts. I feel lost and found all at once. Lost in an unfamiliar territory that I have no idea how to navigate, but somehow, he found me—the first person to successfully scale my walls to get a glimpse at what's behind the iron curtain.

Releasing a slow breath, I rest my head back and melt into the chair. "Thank you," I say on a barely audible whisper.

His response is just as soft but filled with conviction. "Always, Captain."

Something in my chest clenches. It's an echo from our past. The first night we met, when he insisted on taking care of me then, too. John Darling is an anomaly. No one's ever gotten me to give in to them before, yet he's managed it, time and time again. Even crazier is that every time he does, I find myself grateful.

I never realized how taxing it is to be the untouchable Captain Hook. Not until John forced his way through to the man underneath. A man whose name was stripped from him half a lifetime ago when he was just a kid.

I might not be able to resurrect that long-dead part of me, but as I stare up at the ceiling, sifting John's silky hair between my fingers and feeling his warm breaths on my stomach, I wonder if it's not possible to lay down the weight of who I've become. At least for a time. At least when I'm with him.

Chapter Sixteen

JOHN

THIS MORNING, I got a coded text on my burner phone letting me know I have something at our drop location. Before I went undercover, my team and I decided on a place where I could pretend to go on a run and pick up small items without risking an in-person meeting.

As I jog through the seedy streets of Neverland, past businesses sporting bars on their windows and very few vertical surfaces not covered in graffiti, all I see are the beautiful things. The sound of a little girl's giggles drifting down from an apartment window above me. A dog happily chasing the birds that his owner is attempting to feed with scraps of bread. The way the vandalism looks like vibrant artwork in an outdoor gallery illuminated by the sun's rays.

I can't help it. I've been wearing these rose-colored glasses the past seven days. And since I can't go around smiling like an idiot as JD, Pirate Prospect and Heartless Badass, once I'm in the safety of the loft it's almost impossible to keep the stupid grin off my face. James does his best to ignore it or he rolls his eyes, but I've caught the corner of his mouth quirking up the tiniest bit when he thought I wasn't looking. And that feels better than if I'd won millions in the North Carolina lottery.

I'm probably shooting myself in the foot by crossing the line with him. I know there are a hundred-to-one odds of this ending any way other than me going down in flames. The thing is, I can't bring myself to care. Being with him is like…I don't even know. I'm not eloquent enough to put it into words. I just know that, for me, it feels *inevitable*. Like a part of me has been holding out hope that something could still happen between us. And the second our lips met, I sighed with relief, like a decades-long wait had blessedly come to an end.

That night a week ago was the best sexual experience of my life, and it was nothing more than mutual foreplay. He'd finally let me in, and it was more amazing than anything I'd ever imagined. Watching him lose himself in my touch, my kisses, *my mouth*. Fuck, it was so damn hot. And kneeling at his feet—letting him command and control me—has been the most eye-opening thing of all.

I've never been submissive with anyone else, not like that. And I've argued with myself that it's only because I waited so damn long to be like this with him that I'm willing to play whatever role he needs. But then he said something to me that night that changed everything.

Good boy, Johnathan.

That was it. Three little words whispered at my ear that melted into my soul. Words that unlocked a part of me no one else knew existed, not even me. But James knew. He's probably known since the first day we met and I knelt in front of him to bandage his thumb. And now that he's brought this side of me to light, I can't keep pretending my submissive tendencies with him are driven by anything as simple as altruism. It's so much more complex than that. My need to serve him, to please him, to care for him…it's overwhelming at times, but in the best of ways.

Good boy, Johnathan.

God, that still slays me when I think about it. A rush of pride and utter contentment had swelled and crested inside of me until I was sure I'd burst. He'd praised me *and* used my full name without a hint of derision. He'd said it, and it had meant something. Still, I'd braced myself to be brushed off and dismissed once the moment was over.

Never in a million years had I expected him to let me rest on him as he feathered his hand through my hair while we both recovered. It was in those quiet minutes that I did the most reckless thing I've ever done: *I fell hard* for Captain James Hook.

Which brings me back to reminding myself—*often*—that I'm happy to accept however much he's willing to give me. And when this case is closed and he never wants to see me again, I'll embrace that bullshit adage about it being better to have loved and lost, I'll ignore the Pirate-shaped hole in my heart, and I'll move on with my life.

Until then, I'm living on cloud nine, otherwise known as the loft, where we shed our undercover personas and get kinky. Not that there's been much time for the fun stuff. We had a dirty shower where he jerked my cock and finger fucked my ass, milking my prostate until I came so hard my legs buckled. And one morning, he commanded me to suck him off while he drank his coffee and read his book—an act that was made ten times hotter by his black-rimmed glasses and blasé attitude. But that didn't last long. I sucked him so good that he lost his fucking mind and threw me onto the floor. Before I even registered my new position, he had my hands pinned above my head. Then he spit on my bare chest and rutted against my saliva-slick skin until I was the proud new owner of a pearl necklace.

Add that to the ever-growing list of things I never thought I'd find sexy but now fantasize about on the regular. All in all, it's been a great week. But still no sex. I've debated asking him for it, but my gut tells me to wait him out. I just hope he doesn't wait too long, because we're on borrowed time as it is.

As for the case, we've been keeping busy with the Fairy Dust distribution, trying to actively slow it down to keep it from spreading as much as possible while still making it look like we're trying to expand. Smee and I have been "selling" Dust (we don't actually sell it, instead telling anyone who asks that we're waiting on a new shipment) at the regular clubs, and Hook goes out with the other guys to new spots in Neverland, London, and the surrounding cities to scout for new locations to add to the distribution list. They take a small amount with them, as a kind of trial run process; to see whether the clubbers are receptive to buying the Dust. At least, that's the story Hook is giving his men.

I made James promise he wouldn't let the rest of the crew in on the "thwarting Croc's operation" plan—loyal to their captain or not, it doesn't mean Croc can't get information out of them if he starts to suspect anything—so as far as the Pirates know, they're really looking for new places to sling their toxic shit to unsuspecting clubbers.

It must be fooling Croc into thinking we're expanding his operation because he's rewarding James with a visit to see Starkey today for the first time since he went in. Before I left him earlier, I could tell he was excited but nervous. Not that he'd ever admit to feeling anything other than indifference, but I've gotten pretty good at reading the many brooding faces of Captain Hook over the past few weeks.

Turning a corner, I head to the back of a bar that was

shut down and seized by the IRS last year—*pay your taxes, kids*—and remove a broken brick in the alcove of the rear entrance. Tucked inside the hole is a brown paper bag that I retrieve before setting the brick back in place and dumping the contents into my hand: a flash drive and a drop phone.

Slipping the flash drive in my shoe, I use the cell to call my handler.

"Pablos's Pizza, how big do you want your pie?"

I laugh and lean back on the metal door, still relatively cool in the shadows. "That the best you got, Henderson? I'm pretty sure anything called Pablo's Pizza would be a dead giveaway for a fake place."

"If someone other than you found that package and knew the phone number to get me, we'd have bigger problems than an unconvincing pizza joint."

"True story. What's on the stick?"

"Updated dossiers on all of Croc's known associates with some new ones added. It also has all the recordings from Croc's office so far that gave us any information to add to the case."

I freeze. "Is the first day on here? From when Hook planted the bug in Croc's office?"

"Yeah, it's on there," Matt says, his tone wary. "It's the only clip that doesn't have anything about the case, but it reveals some stuff about Hook you might want to know."

He has no idea. I've wanted to know what Croc said to James that day since he came barreling out of the office like a runaway train. "Yeah, okay. I'll check it out," I say nonchalantly.

"How's it going over there? Hook giving you any trouble?"

Only if you consider constantly fighting off hard-ons around the man "trouble." I clear my throat to cover up the chuckle trying to escape. "No, not at all. I mean, he's a surly bastard, but he's cooperating. He wants to take Croc down just as much as we do."

"Yeah, I can see why," he mutters into the phone.

I'm torn between hanging up to go in search of a laptop in the area and demanding he tell me what's on the tape when my cell phone for JD pings with a text message. "Shit," I mutter. "Noodler is looking for me to do a liquor run with him to replenish our stock. Because that's just what those guys need is more booze."

"Make sure you go through the stuff on that flash drive when you get a chance, and call me if you need anything."

"Thanks." After hanging up, I dismantle the drop phone and toss the pieces in a nearby Dumpster. If I'm caught with a burner, my cover is as good as blown, which is why my other one never leaves my room in the loft.

Jogging back to Neverland, I keep my head on a swivel even though I know there's no one following me. No one questions my extreme workout regimen; they all just dismiss me as a CrossFit jockey that keeps up with my training to back up my former identity as an enforcer.

I want to text James and see what his status is, but he wasn't leaving until around now and I don't want to bother him when he's with Starkey. I know he's been out of his mind with worry for that kid. He says it's because he's young and not a hardened criminal like the rest of his crew, but I can't help but feel like there's more to it than that. Then again, though he refuses to admit it out loud, James feels a bond with Starkey and Smee for obvious reasons. So, it's very possible it's his sense of responsibility for the kid that has him worked up over Starkey's incarceration.

But I still think it's more.

Maybe there's something on the flash drive about it.

When I get back to the clubhouse, Noodler is out front tuning up his bike. Watching him work a wrench—or anything, really—is kind of trippy. The man had sketches of the bottoms of his hands and fingers tattooed onto the tops. It looks like his hands are literally on backwards. When I asked him why he did that, he gave me a grin that hinted he wasn't dealing with a full deck and said, "Why not?"

As I bring my jog to a stop in front of him, I place my hands on my hips and try to slow my breathing. "Hey, man. Let me grab a quick shower and we can head out. Cool?"

"Cool with me," he says, wiping the grease from all four of his palms on a rag. I start to pass him when he cackles and adds, "Hey, JD. If you see Smee inside, you better make a run for it. He has a thing for sweaty dudes."

I want to laugh, but that's the John Darling reaction. JD McRae is slightly disturbed at the thought of being chased down by a sweat-hungry redhead, which I convey with a proper snarled expression. "Thanks for the warning. Now I definitely want that shower." This only sends Noodler into a bigger fit of cackles as I hurry into the clubhouse.

Seconds later I'm bounding up the office stairs and entering the loft. I head straight for Hook's room and grab his laptop. With Noodler expecting me, I don't have enough time to look through everything, but I do have enough time to listen to a specific audio clip that should only last a couple of minutes.

I insert the flash drive into the USB port and click on the file folder for the audio surveillance. There it is. The very top one with the file name as the date James planted the bug in Croc's office. I move my finger on the mouse pad and hover the arrow over the file…but I don't click.

"Shit," I mutter, scrubbing a hand down my face. I can't do it. It's none of my business what was said in that office. Henderson was clear that there isn't anything helpful for the case on that recording. If there was, then I'd have a reason to listen. But there's not, so I don't. Listening to something that James has already refused to tell me would be a huge violation of his privacy.

And, more importantly, his trust. I'm not willing to risk what little of it I've gained just to slake this gnawing curiosity. I have my suspicions about some things, and I'd love to have them dispelled, but I'll have to wait until Hook tells me himself.

Deciding to get rid of temptation altogether, I delete the file from the flash drive and delete it from the Recycle Bin on the computer. I put it back where I found it, then hide the stick next to the burner phone in my room before heading to the shower. The faster I get this liquor run over with, the faster I can be back for when James returns.

I just hope everything goes okay at his visit with Starkey. The guy could really use a fucking break for once.

Chapter Seventeen

HOOK

I CAN'T BELIEVE I'm finally seeing Starkey.

It's been six months since the crooked NPD arrested him for no damn reason while we were at one of Peter's house parties. Six months since he begged me to believe he didn't do anything wrong as they shoved him in the back of a cop car. Six months since I was helpless to stop them from driving away with my baby brother.

Six months that I've lived with the suffocating guilt of knowing he's in here because of me. The only thing that's eased that guilt even the slightest is the reassurance John's given me that we can take Croc down by cooperating with the feds. Then me and the boys will be free of him for good, and I'll finally have my vengeance.

John's not with me right now—he said he needed to pick up some stuff from his handler about the latest case developments or whatever. It's strange not sensing him at my back. Somehow in only a week, I've grown accustomed to him being around. Hell, that's downplaying it. As much as I hate to admit it, even to myself, I've come to depend on him and his calm strength. He has a way of muting that deep-seated rage. It's not gone—I don't think it'll ever be gone—but it's quieter with him. And the few times we've fooled around, it's blessedly silent.

I don't think I realized how much of an effect he had on me until I left the loft alone today. I feel more exposed and raw, like I'm entering a knife fight, naked. But maybe that's because I don't know what I'm walking into. It's actually a good thing John's not with me. Starkey would recognize him and blow his cover, not to mention I don't need an audience for this. I have no idea how this is going to play out, but none of the scenarios end with me leaving with my brother, so it's gonna be shitty no matter what.

The heavy door to the visiting room buzzes as the guard pushes it open and waves me in. "Number five," he says, indicating which of the six viewing booths I should go to.

I'm the only one in here. I'd think I was lucky if I didn't know Croc better than that. As always, he's the puppet master pulling all the strings, and he has a reason for everything he does.

Including letting me come here today.

I'm not stupid enough to think he's doing this for my benefit or as some kind of reward. He has an ulterior motive; I'd bet my life on it. I'm just not willing to bet Starkey's, and I need to see with my own eyes that he's okay, regardless of whatever Croc has planned.

The door slams shut behind me, the *bang* echoing ominously in the bare room. It's so quiet that every little sound is magnified. The thudding of my rubber soles as I cross the room, the high-pitched scrape of the metal chair legs against the floor. My breaths. My heartbeats. All of it is so fucking loud, and if Starkey doesn't get here soon, I might jump out of my own goddamn skin.

The door on the other side of the partitioned room

opens, and I get my first glimpse of my brother in half a year.

Jesus fucking Christ.

I don't know what I expected, but it wasn't this. Even with a daily weight-lifting routine, he's always been on the thinner side, like me, but his standard-issue gray jumpsuit is literally hanging on his gaunt frame. His shoulders are slumped, and his white hair is long enough that with his head bent forward like that, it hides his face. He shuffles slowly, the metal of his cuffs clanging, drawing my attention to where his hands and feet are chained together like he's some kind of animal. Like he's not the sweetest fucking kid on the planet.

I clench my fists on the counter and tamp down the burning anger. I have to keep my shit together. The last thing Starkey needs is to see me all worked up.

He drops into the chair across from me as though relieved, like he couldn't have summoned the strength to go any farther. Finally, he rakes the hair back from his face with his bound hands, and I get my first *true* look at my little brother.

For several seconds, I can't breathe. It feels like I've been sucker punched and had the wind knocked out of me. Like an invisible wraith reached into my body and violently ripped the air from my lungs. All I can do is stare in horror at my brother who looks like he just boxed twelve rounds with his hands tied behind his back. Somebody's used him as their personal punching bag. From the severity of his current swelling and the different healing stages of various wounds, it's obvious the abuse is a recurring thing that's happened as recently as right before he was brought to me.

So, this is what you wanted me to see, you sadistic fuck. I'm gonna kill you. Slowly and painfully. If it's the last thing I do.

Despite the swelling on his cheek distorting the left side of his face, the partially healed split lower lip that has to hurt even with the slightest of movements, and the angry red scar that stretches from an inch above his right eye to two inches below it, the fool kid still lights up when he sees me and does his best to smile.

I curse a blue streak but realize he can't hear me when he picks up the receiver of the phone on his side of the glass and indicates I should do the same. As soon as I have it up to my ear, he says, "Captain, you're here."

His relief is palpable, like I just offered him a running garden hose after months of crawling through the desert. But I'm not his savior. I'm his damnation. He's a starved and beaten junkyard dog who still wags his tail at the sight of his master. I've never hated myself more than I do in this moment.

"Starkey," I rasp. "Jesus fuck, what'd they do to you, kid?"

His dark brown eyebrows furrow in confusion until he tests his lower lip with his tongue, and it's like it all comes back to him. "Oh yeah." He shrugs. "This wasn't so bad. Just a couple pops to the face. I'll take that over the steel-toed kicks to my ribs and kidneys any day."

Godfuckingdamnit! Inhale…exhale…

"And this?" I ask, drawing a line on my own face to match the scar on his while trying to ignore the sound of blood rushing in my ears enough to hear his answer. "How the hell did you get that?"

The dim light that had sparked in his silver-blue eyes when he saw me dies out, and his gaze slides to a spot on the beige partition separating his booth from the next one over. "It's no big deal."

"Starkey," I bark and instantly regret it when his entire

body flinches. I lower my voice but keep it firm. "Tell me how. That's an order."

"Happened shortly after I got here," he says flatly. "Few of the inmates cornered me. Said if I was a Pirate, I should have an eye patch. They came at me with a shiv. I saw it at the last second and pulled back fast enough to keep my eye. Still got fifty-six stitches, though."

It takes every shred of my control not to start throwing chairs and demanding the names of the bastards I need to kill to make this right. Freaking out isn't going to help him. He needs me to reassure him that I got this, and that I'm getting him the fuck out of here.

But on the inside, I'm shaking with the compulsion to commit unspeakable violence. Last time I sought vengeance, I went to prison for arson. That was nothing —*nothing*—compared to the fiery malevolence coursing through every inch of my body right now.

Of all of us, Starkey's the last person who deserves to be locked up. Every one of the Pirates are stone-cold criminals. Even Smee has a dangerous streak in him. He hides it well, but push that Irishman's buttons and you won't want to be on the other side of his knife. He might not kill you, but once he's done, you'll wish he had.

Starkey's not like the rest of us, though. I should've sent him to Peter when I took him out of that school. I should've sent both him and Smee to the Lost Boys. I was going to. And then I didn't. I hadn't always liked it, but the ten other kids I grew up with were as close to any kind of family as I'd ever had. Peter got seven of them. It was sheer pride and selfishness that wouldn't let me give him the last two. They could've had a better life, and I prevented it. In that respect, I'm not any better than Croc.

"Captain," he says, his eyes welling up with unshed tears and his voice thick with emotion.

"Yeah, kid."

"They told people I'm in here for..." He swallows hard and whispers into the phone. "For raping kids. Underage boys. But I swear to God, Captain, I never did anything like that. I would *never do that.*"

My eyes close as I blow out a heavy sigh. I have to pull the phone away from my ear for a second because Starkey's pleas for me to believe him are blades plunging into my chest. I bow my head and rap the heavy receiver against my skull several times, the sharp spears of pain only a fraction of what I deserve.

I did a measly two years of hard time, but you only have to be inside *two days* to know which crimes the inmates consider heinous enough to break their loose moral codes. One of those unforgivable crimes is anything sexual with a kid. You go to prison for that and you might as well have a target carved into your back. And prison justice is of the biblical sort. Very eye for an eye, what you've done, they'll do unto you, and all that shit.

If that's what Starkey's been going through, then everything I've done in my life up to this point has been all for nothing. The one fucking thing I tried to do as his big brother was spare him that kind of suffering...and I failed.

Starkey bangs his phone against the plexiglass to get my attention. I force my eyes open and lift them to meet his gaze. He's shaking his head, and when I press the phone to my ear again, his pleas continue to slice me open.

"Stop," I snap, unable to hear it another second. "I *know* you didn't do it. You didn't do *anything*. You're in here because of me, Starkey."

"What?" A hank of his hair falls in front of his eyes, but he doesn't move to fix it. That would require taking the phone away from his ear, and I have his rapt attention now.

"It's Croc's power play to get me to do what he wants. It's taking me longer than I thought, but I'm gonna get you out of here, I swear it."

He frowns. "I don't understand. How—"

Before he finishes his question, the door behind him opens and a guard walks in. Starkey starts to argue that he needs more time, but the guard doesn't make a move to haul him away. Instead he hands him a folded piece of paper, then disappears the same way he came.

The hairs stand up on the back of my neck as he opens the note. "What is that? What's it say?"

My questions fall on deaf ears because the phone is still in his right hand with the note in his left. Confusion is etched on his battered face, and when he finally looks up at me, it's like he's seeing me for the first time.

"Damn it, Starkey, *what's it say*?"

He turns the note around and presses it to the glass. Bold capital letters are scrawled across the paper: **HE'S YOUR BROTHER**

Oh. Fuck.

Chapter Eighteen

HOOK

"Is...is it true?"

I'm still trying to process the rabbit Croc just pulled out of his hat, so when I don't say anything, Starkey raises his voice in desperation. "Captain! Is it true? Are you my brother?"

My secret is finally out after all this time. Relief and terror collide inside of me, fighting each other for dominance. Swallowing around the fist in my throat, I nod. "Yeah," I finally manage, the word shredding my vocal cords on its way out. "I'm your brother."

A multitude of emotions cross his face—elation, more confusion, back to elation, then doubt. "What's my real name?" he asks carefully, like he's testing me. Not that it's a very good test since he doesn't know the answer.

I scrub a hand down my face. There's no point in holding anything back anymore. Croc dealt me the hand. I have no choice but to play it.

"Your full name is Marcus Allen Hook. We have different fathers, neither of which were ever in the picture. Our mother, Marion Hook, was a heroin addict who OD'd when you were almost two, which is how we ended up at the school."

He blinks back the moisture and sniffs hard. "Then what's Starkey from? Is it really because of my hair?"

"Yeah, kind of. We called you Markey. One day someone commented on your blond hair. Mom said, 'That's not blond; it's stark white.' Then she started calling you Starkey Markey, but she always dropped the second part whenever she was high, which was more often than not before you were even a year old. By the time we got to the school, you refused to answer to anything but Starkey."

He chuckles a bit, like everyone does when they hear a cute story about themselves from when they were little. It gives me hope that this might all be okay, that maybe I'd been worried about him finding out for nothing, so I continue.

"Mrs. Anderson, the nice old lady who ran the place, said it was okay to indulge you with whatever name you wanted for a while. You were young; she said she'd switch it back to Markey gradually over time once you were settled. But three weeks after we got there, she and her husband were killed in an accident, and the school went to Croc and Delia. Since they didn't care to read any of our files and all the kids knew you as Starkey, that's what stuck."

He frowns. "I don't understand. *You* knew my real name," he says, and I can practically see the wheels spinning in his head. "But you never corrected anyone. And you never told anyone I was your brother, not even me. I've been following you around my whole life, but you treated me no different than everyone else. Why?"

"I did it to protect you. Croc's a manipulative bastard who's always had it in for me. Who knows what kind of bullshit he would've tried with you?"

Starkey seems to think about that for a second, then shakes his head. "That doesn't exactly wash, though, does it? That only explains why you didn't let Croc know. Maybe even why you didn't tell the others. But why not me? Why not tell me when I was old enough to understand and keep a secret?" He swallows hard, and the tears finally spill over to stream down his cheeks, one swollen and one scarred. "You should've told me."

Frustration at this shit situation—that I can't get him out of here now, that Croc is fucking with us, that I can't strangle that asshole with my bare fucking hands—builds in my chest and expands until my rib cage feels ready to tear through my skin. "I couldn't take the chance you'd let it slip. I told you, it was for your own protection."

"Bullshit. Me and Smee have been loyal to you from day one, but we barely rank above the rest of the crew. Even without the shared blood, our shared past should make us more like brothers. Like me and Smee are to each other. Like Peter is with the Lost Boys. But fuck anyone who could ever give a shit about you, right?" He scoffs and swipes at his eyes. "You wanna know what I think? The secret wasn't about protecting me. It was about protecting *yourself*."

I pound the counter with my fist. "You have no idea what kind of sadistic fuck Croc is. He would've used our relationship against us."

"Oh, you mean like he is *now*? Guess this means the cat's out of the bag, huh? That's fucking great," he says, his words stained with sarcasm. "Glad I went twenty-two years without a brother so that the very reason I couldn't have one ended up making my worst nightmares come true anyway."

"Starkey—"

Starkey pops up to his feet, sending the chair toppling

over behind him. "Do you have any idea what they're doing to me in here? *Do you?*"

I stand and brace my fist against the glass. "I'm gonna get you out of here, I fucking swear it. I just need a little more time."

He shakes his head, causing some of his hair to fall forward, but not enough that I can't see the fresh tears gathering in his silver eyes before he blinks them back. "Don't do me any more favors…*Captain*."

And with that, he hangs the phone up, turns, and shuffles away.

He bangs on the door to be let out as I bang on the glass to get his attention. I yell his name and pound with my fists and the flat of my hands, even the end of the receiver, not giving a shit if I bust the phone or scratch the plexi. I need him to turn around, to come back, to listen to me, anything, *anything* but walk away from me.

But it's no use.

The door is pushed open by the guard, and Starkey walks through it without a second glance in my direction. Then the door slams shut…and he's gone.

He hates me he hates me he hates me.

I fucked up. I fucked up bad, and I can't fix it, even if I could get Starkey out of here right now. He's a mere shell of the easygoing, eager-to-please, quick-to-laugh kid he was six months ago. Once the innocence is stripped away, there's no getting it back. I know that better than anyone.

I feel sick and helpless and murderous. Like I could puke until I'm empty or scream until my throat bleeds or kill someone until *they* bleed.

That's when my cell phone rings. Thinking it's Smee or maybe even John, I pull it out from my back pocket. But the contact picture staring back at me isn't a playful

Irishman or the tatted version of a certain LEO. It's an image of a crocodile I'd grabbed from Google.

Taking a deep breath in through my nose, I remind myself that I can't promise to end his life. Whether I like it or not, he holds all the cards right now, or so he thinks. I can't show him my hand; it's too early for that. His goal with this was to break me down and keep me in line, so I have to give him what he wants. For now.

"Was that fun for you, old man?"

"Come on, now, you don't think I enjoy hurting you, do you, James?"

"That's exactly what I think," I say, my tone defeated for his sake. "How long have you known?"

"Shortly before I had him arrested." I can hear his smile and blatant pride through the phone. "I'm not stupid. I know my ambitions aren't yours. You play your part, but you lack the sense of urgency I need from a captain. So I finally looked in your file and found something to motivate you. Imagine my surprise when I discovered the white-haired kid is actually your baby brother. Incarcerating him was a no-brainer."

"And today," I say, referring to this whole fucking charade he put me and Starkey through, "this was just for kicks? To remind me who pulls my strings?"

"No, this is because you've been slacking," he growls, his harsh ire slicing through my eardrum. "This was to show you that your poor brother's life hasn't been a picnic in there, but it'll get a hell of a lot worse if you don't redouble your efforts to move this product. A *lot* worse."

Fucking hell. Starkey won't survive *worse*.

My body vibrates, fighting to keep the bear trap of control snapped shut on my basest instincts. Without it, I'd be tracking him down with a single-minded purpose: to once and for all, *end* Fred Croc. I doubt John has enough sway with the FBI to get me off Murder One, and rotting in prison for the rest of my miserable life means I leave Starkey on his own. On the other hand, he'll always have Smee. Forfeiting my freedom to spare the world from a sadistic tyrant is quicker than waiting for this undercover bullshit to work. If it even works at all.

"Even loyal dogs can turn on their owners if provoked, Croc."

"I wouldn't recommend it," he sneers. "I've made sure that if anything happens to me, your brother's as good as dead. You hear me, Hook?"

Grinding my teeth into dust, I grate out, "Yeah. I hear you."

"Good. Do *not* fail me—or your brother—more than you already have." Maniacal laughter echoes through my head before I manage to end the call.

My cell drops from my hand to the counter where I brace myself as air saws in and out of my lungs, the thread of my control fraying with every exhale…and then it snaps. Hatred—for Croc, for myself, for a system that failed us as kids and set all this in motion—rips through me from the bottom of my black soul until I let out a deafening roar and tear the visitor's phone off the partition wall to whip it across the room.

Reining myself back in, I plow my hands through my hair, fisting it at the scalp and pulling until the pain makes my eyes water. I can't lose my shit, not now. My need for vengeance is what kept my baby brother in harm's way. I was so goddamn naive to think I could get the upper hand on the monster who's controlled my every move from the time I was nine.

I was so fucking stupid, and now Starkey's paying the price. And if I don't get him out of here soon, he might end up paying it with his life.

Chapter Nineteen

HOOK

THEN

Age 9

"JAMES, WOULD YOU LIKE A DOUGHNUT?"

My eyes whip up from the plate in the middle of the table to the old lady sitting across from me. Her name is Mrs. Anderson. She has silver hair and rosy cheeks, and she hasn't stopped smiling since my caseworker, Miss Janell, dropped us off. It's kinda weirding me out. The only time Mama smiled was after using her "happy kit" or if she wanted me to do something for her. Since I don't think Miss Janell would bring me to someone else like Mama, I'm guessing she wants something.

"They're jelly-filled," she says, pushing the plate closer to me before checking on my brother who's playing with some blocks on the floor.

My mouth is watering. I really, really want one. But

what's it gonna cost me? I shift in my seat and fist my hands in my lap under the table. As much as I want it, I hate what comes with getting special treats.

Remember when I bought you that ice cream cone, James? Be a good boy and feed your brother, then give him a bath, or I won't get you any more ice cream.

Here's a candy bar. Share it with your brother tonight. I'll be back tomorrow.

James, bring me my happy kit… Don't tell me what I need, you ungrateful little shit! You don't need to play with friends, that's what I gave you a brother for, so bring me my kit and fucking play with him!

That was the last thing Mama ever said to me. After I took the kit to her and Officer Ricky—he came over after work all the time—they stuck the needle in their arms, then stumbled down the hall to her room.

My mom had lots of guys she did that with. Sometimes they passed out right away. Sometimes they made noises I didn't want to hear, so I'd take the baby out of the apartment and sit in the stairwell until they stopped.

But that last time, there weren't any noises. I was in the kitchen feeding my brother our last can of SpaghettiOs when I heard Officer Ricky freaking out in Mama's bedroom. I ran in and found him shaking her and yelling at her to wake up but she didn't move. When he put his fingers on her neck and then backed up real fast, I knew. My mom was gone.

I thought he would call for help—we didn't have a phone but he was a cop, so I know he did—but he didn't. He grabbed his shirt and gun belt and told me that if I ever told anyone he was there, he'd make sure I never saw my brother again. Then he left.

On her better days, Mama liked to talk about life lessons. I didn't always listen, but as the door shut behind Officer Ricky, I remembered one of her favorites. *Just because someone says something doesn't mean it's the truth, James. It's their actions—what they* do—*that speaks the truth.* That day I learned to never trust a police officer. And if I couldn't trust the "good guys," there probably wasn't anyone I *could* trust. Even if I'd asked a neighbor for help, they'd just call the cops and then what? Would Officer Ricky really take my brother away? I couldn't risk it.

So I stayed in the apartment and did what I always did: I took care of my brother. I didn't cry over Mama. Kids and babies can cry but I had to be Starkey's parent, and parents shouldn't cry.

After a couple days I opened the window in her bedroom, then closed the door and put a towel under it because she started to stink bad. We ran out of food and diapers after five days, and when I tried to steal some from the corner store, I got caught. Cops showed up, but I didn't tell them who I was or where I lived. That's when they called Miss Janell. She said she wasn't part of the police, so I told her about Mama so I could get back to Starkey. But I kept my mouth shut about Officer Ricky.

Now me and my brother are here, at some Lost Boys school or something. I don't know if it's a good thing or not, but I'm guessing it could be worse. At least we're still together.

"Usually we don't give out big snacks right before lunch, but something tells me a doughnut won't ruin your appetite," Mrs. Anderson says.

She's still smiling. It doesn't look like the weird kind of smiles Mama had, though. Maybe she's not all bad. "What do I have to do?"

Her mouth curves down for the first time. "What do you mean?"

"If I have a doughnut. What do if I have to do for it?"

"Oh, sweetheart," she says, her hands pressing over her

cross necklace, "you don't have to do anything. We don't use food as punishments or rewards here. You'll get three meals plus snacks or special treats every day. All you're expected to do is your schoolwork, which you'll get help with, and then you get to play with the other boys. Sometimes we'll take trips to the park and go for walks. And Mr. Anderson loves baseball, so he likes taking everyone to the occasional game.

"You *will* have simple chores, however, like keeping your areas picked up and organized, setting the table for meals, small things like that. But we always help you, and it's only to teach you responsibility for when you grow up, not because we want you to do the work for us."

I chew on my lip as I think about what she said. She doesn't look like she's lying. And I saw some boys playing outside with a ball when I got here, and they seemed like they were having fun. Maybe this place isn't going to be that bad. If it is what she says, it'll be like heaven.

"Please, James," she says, her eyes shimmering like she's going to cry for some reason. "Have as many jelly doughnuts as you want. I won't even care if it spoils your lunch this one time, okay?"

Unable to resist any longer, I snatch one from the plate and take the biggest bite I can. Powdered sugar gets everywhere—smeared on my face, spots on the table, and streaks down my shirt—but I don't care. I'm going to eat as much as I can before she changes her mind.

When I'm halfway through my first one, my brother falls onto the blocks and starts to cry, holding his arms up for me. I drop my doughnut to the table and growl in frustration. "Why can't you leave me alone for just five minutes?!"

Before I get a chance to move, Mrs. Anderson is there, picking him up and bouncing him on her hip as she shushes him and dries his tears. "James, honey, it's okay. Go ahead and eat; I've got him."

I look at my doughnut, then over at my brother. I want to keep eating, but I'll have a better chance if I put him down for his nap first. The only time I don't have to worry about him bothering me is when he's sleeping. Sighing, I stand and hold my arms out for him. "It's time for his nap; that's why he's cranky. If you show me where he's going to be sleeping, I'll go put him down."

"Actually, I was thinking Mr. Anderson could get some time with him while we talk. He absolutely loves babies. Then after you're done stuffing yourself with doughnuts, I'll take you to see where his crib is so you can make sure he's okay. Would that be all right with you?"

I lower my arms slowly. Part of me feels like I should say no and do what I've always done. But there's another part of me, one that's never been there before because I was never given the choice, and it wants to let Starkey be someone else's problem for a change. Guilt for even thinking that makes me cringe. But Mama's been dead for a week. I was taking care of him that whole time, and even before that because she wasn't much help. And I'm just so, so tired.

"Yeah, okay," I croak out.

She calls for her husband as I sit in the chair again. Mr. Anderson's hair is white, but he smiles as much as his wife. When he takes Starkey, he acts like he was given the best gift ever.

"Well, hello there, little guy. Gosh, aren't you adorable. Look, we have matching hair!" he says, laughing. Starkey giggles back at him, which makes me feel a little better about letting him go with a stranger. "Let's get you into a clean diaper and all snuggled up in your new crib." Then to me, he says, "You like those doughnuts? They're my favorites."

"Yeah, they're good."

He nods. And smiles more. So much smiling here. "They have at least fifty different kinds; you won't believe your eyes. Next time I'll take you into town with me and let you pick the flavors for you and the rest of the boys. Sound like a plan?"

My shoulders lower and something in my chest feels lighter. I'm starting to believe that these people really do love kids and want to help. I know there are people like that; I'd just never met any before. Until now, I guess. And if that's the case, maybe I can stop being Starkey's fill-in parent. I could just be…*a kid.*

"Sure," I finally say. He winks at me, then takes Starkey out of the room, talking to him the whole way.

I get back to scarfing down the doughnuts and reassure myself that it's not a big deal that my brother is out of my sight for the first time since he was born over a year and a half ago. I'll see him soon. After a few minutes, Mrs. Anderson starts talking again.

"James, you're obviously a very good big brother to Marcus." *Marcus, ha!* I huff a quick laugh through my nose as I'm taking a bite, scattering powdered sugar everywhere. It's weird to hear someone call him by his real name. Thanks to Mama's dumb nickname, he doesn't answer to anything but Starkey anymore. I've even gotten so used to it that it just feels like his name.

Mrs. Anderson doesn't even blink at the mess I made. "Even though my husband and I are here to take care of both of you, the same as we do for all the boys here, you can still take care of your brother as much as you want."

I freeze, then swallow the chunk in my mouth as my free hand curls into a fist again. "But I'm *sick* of always having to take care of him. It's *all I ever do*." The more I think about it, the madder I get. I'm finally in a place where I might not have to worry about whether he's getting enough to eat or if his diaper needs to be changed or how long it's been since he's had a bath. "I don't *want* to take care of him anymore. I don't even want anyone to know he's my brother!"

I expect her to get mad at me for saying something so horrible—I'm halfway mad at *myself* for saying it, except I can't stop this anger bubbling inside me—but she stays calm and speaks gently, like I did whenever I put Starkey down to sleep. "Okay, James, that's of course entirely up to you. May I ask why?"

"Because," I say through clenched teeth, "if the other kids know, then he'll still be my responsibility. I don't want it. If they don't have to take care of him, then I don't want to either. He has you now, anyway, right? So he doesn't need me anymore."

"Ah, I understand." She's still smiling at me, but it looks kinda sad. "That had to have been very difficult. You've been forced to act like an adult, and that wasn't fair to you. You're right, he has us now. We'll take good care of him, and we won't tell anyone he's your brother until you're ready. I bet after a while you won't mind them knowing. You just need a chance to get used to things and find your place here."

Maybe she's right. I think of Starkey's pudgy cheeks, his white hair that sticks up in the middle like a Mohawk, and his big blue eyes that always get soft when he sees me. Then I remember all the things I had to do for him when Mama couldn't even get out of bed. I even made a wish that there was someone else who could worry about the baby so I didn't have—

Oh no. My stomach squeezes, and I have to take a deep

breath so I don't puke everywhere. She'd done that needle stuff for years and always woke up eventually. But that day I'd made the wish—I wished *really hard*—and then she died.

"Do you want another jelly doughnut, sweetheart?"

I shake my head. I probably shouldn't talk in case I say something bad again. Mama always said I was no good. It doesn't matter what I do or don't want; I shouldn't be around Starkey. I'm not good for him.

I'm not good for anyone.

Chapter Twenty

JOHN

I ALMOST DON'T HEAR the knocks over the sound of my gloved fists hitting the heavy bag in the loft. When I pause my workout to see if I was imagining things, I hear, "Hey, boyo! Open the feckin' door already!"

Hoping he's heard from James, I tug the gloves off and drop them on my way to the door that leads to the deck. I open it and automatically scan behind him to check for anyone who might be watching, but don't see anything. My eyes return to Smee, and I realize he's in the middle of giving me a slow once-over, his gaze heated as it slides back up my bare torso.

"Feck me, Johnny-boy, you filled out nicely, didn't ye?"

Teeth clenched, I fist the front of his wifebeater and yank him inside before slamming the door shut. "Are you fucking stupid? What if someone heard you?"

"Relax," he says, moving farther into the room. "Your undercover name is John, too, or did ye forget? Besides, it'd be more suspicious if I *didn't* say somethin' when greeted by a half-naked fine thing glistenin' with sweat."

I roll my eyes and head over to where I left my water

bottle in the kitchen. "Then I guess I should thank you for playing the part of the thirsty pirate." I take a long drink, then almost bump into him when I turn around.

"Oh, it's not a part I'm playing at, boyo." A smirk plays on his mouth as he steps in close, his chest only a couple inches from mine. "In fact, I'm giving you an open invitation to frisk me. You know, whenever you might be feelin' *frisky*."

Unlike Starkey's leaner frame, Smee is built like a brick shit house. He looks like one of those bare-knuckled brawlers who fight for giggles and cash in dive bar basements. His size alone would make anyone wary about getting on his bad side, but he uses his playboy charm and roguish attractiveness to disarm people. If I was into fun-loving redheads with green eyes and easy smiles, I'd be all over Smee. But I've had a thing for broody, tortured bad boys since I was a tween, so Smee's SOL.

"Sorry, man, but you're not really my type." I give him a mock apologetic smile, because I'm not really sorry. "No offense."

I'm not even convinced Smee knows I'm gay. I think he's just helpless not to hit on anyone within spitting distance, regardless of their gender or sexual orientation.

He gives a careless shrug. "Can't blame me for tryin'." Then, just like that, Smee's humor is replaced by placid concern. "You hear from the boss? Thought he'd be back by now with news about Starkey."

Lines of worry crease around his eyes. I know he's hurting for his friend, and I wish I could give him better news. Blowing out a breath, I busy myself with unraveling the ten feet of cotton wraps from each of my hands. "No. I've been texting and calling, but he's not picking up."

"Don't you have a man on the inside? He can tell you if Hook's still there."

"That's not how undercover works. You can't just pick up a phone and call them for updates. If that was an option, I would've done it by now, believe me."

The door bursts open. Hook charges inside, a raging cyclone that seems to lose its steam as soon as he's secured inside the loft. Raven-black hair sticks out in ten different directions like he's been yanking on it, and his knuckles are bloody on both hands. Either he punished something unyielding, or someone was missing a mouthful of teeth.

"Captain, what happened?" Smee asks anxiously. "How's our boy?"

"He's beat to shit, is what he is," he grates out as he drops onto the couch, now completely deflated.

Smee's entire demeanor changes so suddenly a chill runs down my spine. Gone is the playboy, revealing the true man lurking underneath: a man who will kill you as soon as look at you if he finds you deserving, and he'll enjoy every fucking second of it. His voice is low and even. Deadly. "Who's doin' the beatin'? Who's hurtin' him?"

"Everyone. The guards are fucking him up, and the inmates are—" He breaks off like his throat is thick with emotion. Raising his head, he glances up at us. "They're just plain fucking him. They spread it around that he's in there for molesting kids."

"I'll fuckin' kill him," Smee whispers, then heads for the door. Before I can spring into action to stop him, Hook sparks to life.

"Stand down, Smee. You won't even sneeze in Croc's direction, do you hear me?"

Spinning on his heel, he stalks back to stand in front of his leader and roars, "*Why the bloody hell not?* I've never understood your loyalty to that fucker, but it didn't matter to me because my loyalty is to *you*. But how can you turn your back on one of our own for *him*?"

"Hey, no one is turning their backs on anyone. Let's stay calm and talk about this rationally," I say, but I might as well not even be in the room.

"Are ye scared, is that it, Hook?" Smee lowered his voice, but it's even more menacing with less volume. It's also the first time I've ever heard Smee address James by name and not his title. "Because I'm not. I'll rip his spinal cord out through his belly and not think twice about it. And if you won't do what it takes to fuckin' protect Starkey, then I will."

Lightning fast, Hook springs to his feet and grabs the huge knife holstered on Smee's hip in the process. In the span of a heartbeat, Smee's head is yanked back, his own knife poised millimeters away from his exposed throat in Hook's shaking hand. Smee and I both freeze in place, neither of us breathing for fear we'll do or say something that might make that hand slip.

"I don't give a *shit* about Croc," he growls. "I want him dead more than I want my next breath. But what I want more than that is my little brother's safety. From the day he was born, it's all I've ever fucking wanted."

Holy shit, did he say *brother*? Smee's eyes widen, mirroring the shock that's likely written all over my face. Apparently, I'm not the only one who was in the dark about this, but Hook continues like he didn't just drop a goddamn bomb in the middle of the loft.

"If we go after Croc right now, Starkey dies." Hook swallows hard and tightens his grip on the hilt of the knife. "I failed him once already. I *will not* let it happen again. Which means no one makes a move on Croc until I fucking say so. Are we clear?"

"Aye, Captain," Smee rasps. "Clear."

Hook releases the Irishman, flips the knife to catch it by the blade, then hands it back, before resuming his position on the couch. Smee returns the knife to its sheath on his hip, glancing at me with questions in his green eyes. *Did you know?* he seems to be asking. I give a subtle shake of my head.

Dots start to connect all over the place in my mind. Things that didn't quite add up before now make perfect sense. Starkey isn't just another random Lost Boy turned Pirate. He's Hook's baby brother. That's why he's been so turned inside out about Starkey's arrest.

Smee starts to pace the room while James hangs his head and flexes his hands dangling between his knees, testing the wounds on his knuckles. I'm beginning to realize he uses pain as a distraction or some kind of penance, and it drives me crazy. I want to wrap the man in cotton and prevent him from getting anything so much as a scratch ever again. Since that's impossible, I'll settle for the next best thing. I wet the kitchen towel with cold water, then cross the room and kneel in front of him.

"Always on your knees for me, Darling," he murmurs softly, not lifting his gaze from the floor. "It's becoming a habit of yours."

He's so in his own head right now, he doesn't realize Smee has stopped in his tracks behind the couch. The expression on his face tells me he's seeing us with new eyes, and his mind is a little blown from yet another revelation about the man he thought he knew inside and out.

Smee opens his mouth, but I shut him down with a look that promises pain if he so much as breathes in Hook's direction about this. Holding the Irishman's gaze, I answer James honestly.

"It's where I belong."

Smee gives me the barest of nods—a sign of his approval, I suppose, not that either of us need it—then gets back to pacing. James doesn't acknowledge my response, but I didn't expect him to. Hell, he may not have even heard me over the noise buzzing between his ears. Doesn't matter. In time he'll realize I'm right. For now, I'll take whatever allowances he'll give me.

I gather one of his hands in mine and begin to clean the blood with gentle swipes. I consider it a win that he doesn't pull away or tell me to fuck off.

"Captain," Smee says, his voice thick with emotion. "We have to get him out of there. I can't stand knowing...*fuck!*"

James finally raises his head, his eyes hardening at the reminder of what his brother is going through. "I know, Smee. We will. But to do that we need to play by Croc's rules. He doesn't know it's intentional, but he knows our sales have been shit lately. Today's visit with Starkey was a warning. We need to step up our distribution of Dust, there's no way around it."

I mentally cringe at the idea of selling more of that dangerous drug. I know it's part of the game we're playing, but I want to keep it to a minimum as much as I can. "Or," I say, an idea coming to me, "we can make him *think* he's expanding across state lines and hitting a much bigger market with more profit and better growth potential."

They both look at me. "What're ye thinkin', Johnny-boy? You got a plan?"

"Yeah, I do. In the meantime, we keep doing what we've been doing to keep up appearances—scouting for new locations and testing new markets with small doses. I'll get the ball rolling on the rest. It shouldn't take long."

Smee's gaze cuts to James because even though I'm in charge of this operation, he'll always defer to his captain. I'm good with that. After a few seconds, James nods. "Do it. But don't share anything about Starkey with the others.

It's nobody's fucking business. I won't have anyone looking at him different when he gets out, you hear me?"

"Aye, Captain." Smee glances at me. "I'm good at keepin' secrets."

I dip my head in silent appreciation, then wait for him to leave before turning my attention back to the man who needs me for so much more than just tending to his busted knuckles.

Chapter Twenty-One

HOOK

MY WORLD HAS BEEN FILLED with noise as far back as I can remember. The obnoxious laughter or exaggerated shouting from my mother and random "friends" as they drank and got high. Incessant chattering of Peter, Tink, and the Lost Boys at the school. The high-pitched whines of power tools and hydraulic lifts at the shop with the clattering of car parts dropping to the cement floor.

Even at night, when I'm finally surrounded by silence, the memories of a man grunting in my ear reverberate in my mind like the echoes of a banging gong. The only thing I've found that muffles them is losing myself in a book, which probably makes me the most well-read criminal in all of Neverland. But nothing has ever silenced the noise completely.

Not until John Darling.

The second he took my hands in his, everything faded to the background. All I see is him in front of me, all I hear are his steady breaths, all I feel is his strong yet gentle touch. It's both the most calming and unnerving thing I've ever experienced.

It's where I belong.

I've never wanted and dreaded something so much in all my life. It doesn't matter what I want, though. Keeping John isn't an option. He'll get hurt. It's only a matter of time. Our arrangement—or whatever this new reality we're indulging in is called—is only until we take Croc down and get Starkey back. Then the people I care about will finally be safe, and after I do my time, I'll disappear to a place where no one knows me. Where I'm not defined by my past, my sins, or my tarnished soul.

"There," John says, dropping his hands. "The blood's at least cleaned up. I don't suppose you'll let me apply ointment and wrap them up."

I arch a single brow that says, *What do you think?* earning me a half grin of that sensuous mouth that fills my head with more salacious thoughts than I can keep track of.

"Then I guess I'll have to be satisfied with doing this..."

Before I can even think to pull away, he proceeds to kiss all eight of my busted fucking knuckles, his soft lips pressing gently to each wound as though sealing them with his own magic brand of protection. The affection that's so innate in this man seeps into the cracks of my battered heart, slipping into my bloodstream like a dose of morphine, lulling me into a state of serenity—

Goddamn it!

I don't have a right to feel at peace. All-consuming anger, hatred for my enemy, plans for vengeance—those are the only things I should have room for in my life. They've sustained me for over two decades, nourishing me more than the food I ingest and fueling my every move.

Grabbing a handful of his sweat-dampened hair, I yank his head back and glare down at him. "Why do you do these things? Why do you insist on making more of this than what it really is?"

Honey-gold eyes, so guileless and trusting, stare back at me. "Because I care about you. I always have."

"You shouldn't," I grate. "People who care about me get hurt. Or dead."

"Is that why you push people away? Because you care about them?"

I scoff. "Don't project your sense of nobility on me, Darling. Know why I called my crew the Pirates? Because they have the ultimate freedom. Pirates aren't tied down by anything. Not by people, not by land, not even by their own ships. Their code is loose and given to mutiny, cutting down any man who tries to control them beyond what they allow. A pirate might live and work with his shipmates, but ultimately, he doesn't need anyone but himself. So to answer your question, I push people away because I *don't* care."

His eyes bounce back and forth between mine for a few seconds while he thinks. But if I thought my impassioned speech would have any sort of impact on young John, I was wrong. "Sorry," he says with a shrug, "not buying it."

I narrow my eyes into glaring slits. "I don't give a shit because I'm not selling you anything."

"As much as you pretend otherwise, I know you cared about Peter, Tink, and the rest of the Lost Boys. Wendy told me how you used to protect the younger kids by stepping in front of them or drawing Croc's wrath so he'd turn it on you instead."

He has no fucking idea the things I did to draw Croc's attention from the others. If he did, he'd see me for what I really am. Damaged goods. A broken, pathetic shell incapable of human connection and unworthy of his naive adoration. But the thought of losing it—however undeserved—makes my insides shake. Smee and Starkey have always had a case of hero worship when it came to me, but we were raised together as brothers against a common enemy. John's loyalty wasn't forged from a sense of family. It was something else entirely—not that I pretend to understand what that something is—and it makes it feel more significant. More *necessary*.

But old habits die hard, and the one that's always reinforced my rep as a loner instantly coughs out a protest despite the fact that it's bleeding out under John's supportive assault. "Just because I don't think little kids deserve to be beaten by a lowlife sack of shit doesn't mean I care. It just means I wasn't a complete asshole."

He crosses his arms over his bare chest, not willing to let this go. His tone is firm, but his gaze is soft with compassion. "Even if I believed that—which I don't—what about Starkey?"

I grind my molars together, wary of the path this conversation is on. "What *about* Starkey?"

"Do you care about him?"

Hundreds of thorny memories of feigning indifference for the little boy with stark white hair pierce my lungs, making it impossible to draw in enough air, and I explode. "Of course I care for him, *he's my fucking brother*."

My chest expands and contracts with rapid breaths as it fights against the steel band of helplessness threatening to crush my rib cage. Unable to sit here any longer, I shove off the couch and stride over to where the blaze-orange rays of the setting sun penetrate the loft with false promises of a better tomorrow. I rest my forehead on the warm glass of the large window, using it as a preventative measure. I wouldn't think twice about punching through drywall, but even I'm not dumb enough to put my already busted fists through double-paned glass.

I hear John crossing the room, and I mutter a curse. The guy's a goddamn Labrador retriever, doggedly following my every move. It's annoying as all hell. That's what the zing tripping down my spine is as I feel him getting closer—not awareness, not contentedness, not *rightness*—annoyance.

He stops with barely more than an inch separating us. His breath fans across my neck, the heat from his body radiating through the thin cotton of my shirt. The fact that I'm letting him have my back doesn't escape my notice. I don't let people get behind me. *Ever.* It's a position of vulnerability, of weakness; a position I've refused to put myself in with anyone for more than a decade.

But I'm not prepared to turn around, either. To face the only man with the power to see through my walls to the black void where my soul should be. My darkness is my cross to bear, no one else's. Especially not someone like John who's only ever lived in the light.

His hands squeeze my shoulders, then travel down my arms hanging at my sides. But instead of closing his hands over the tops like I expect, he slips them underneath mine, the backs of his hands resting against my palms. He doesn't force anything further, doesn't take more than I'm willing to give. He simply offers himself to me…and waits.

I want to tell him he'll be waiting a long time because I don't need his comfort or his support or the feel of his strength in my shaky grip. But I don't tell him that. I don't tell him anything because I'm too weak to fight this truce between us right now. I'm too weak to fight *him*.

Expelling a slow breath through my nose, I allow myself to thread my fingers through his, curling them tightly, like he's the only thing keeping me from dropping into a chasm of despair. John leans forward and erases that last yawning inch between us. The second his chest presses into my shoulder blades, the tension leeches from my muscles until I'm practically sagging against him. And suddenly I'm so damn grateful he's here. Not just for this moment, but for a whole myriad of reasons I can't bring myself to unpack just yet. Or maybe ever.

He nuzzles his nose against my neck and presses chaste kisses in a line up to my ear, disarming me a little more with each new touch. "Talk to me," he urges quietly. "What happened when you saw him today?"

"He was...*fuck*." I pause to choke back the guilt threatening to cut off my airway. "He was in real bad shape. Jesus, his face looked like they'd been using it as a speed bag. But you know what he did when he saw me?"

"What?"

"He fucking smiled. Just like he did when he was a baby and I walked into the room. He'd grin and look up at me like I hung the goddamn moon." I chuffed out a short laugh, devoid of any humor. "I used to deserve that look. It was us against the world. Now he hates me. I don't blame him, though; he should. I turned my back on him before he was even two years old."

"I don't understand," John says. I can feel his furrowed brow where it's resting against the side of my head. "How did you turn your back on him as a baby if you were placed at the school together?"

"Doesn't matter," I rasp. Images assault me of the haunted look in Starkey's eyes when he realized I'm the reason for his daily beatings and rapes. "I fucked up. Can't fix it."

John pulls his hands out and turns me around to face him. I manage to keep my head lifted with the last shred of my pride still intact. But its hold is tenuous at best, and it feels like at any moment it'll snap, leaving me to crumple to the ground in a boneless heap.

Framing my face with his palms, he gazes deep into my eyes for what feels like an eternity, silently demanding my secrets. As though he asked for them out loud, I admit hoarsely, "If I tell you, you won't like what you hear. You won't stay."

Without breaking eye contact, John presses his full lips to mine. It isn't sexual. It's a statement. One he follows up with a deep, "Try me."

It's in that moment that I decide I will. I'll lay my sins down at this perfect man's feet and bare my secrets for him to judge, one by one. Will he be disgusted? Horrified? Or worse, will he pity me? All of those reactions and more are possible. But I can't stand the thought of holding up these walls anymore. There's been no one in my life I could let my guard down with. I can't imagine the relief of having even a single person I could be myself around.

I have my doubts that I'll ever know what that's like. But if there's even the slightest chance that person could be John—even for a short time while we work this case—then I'm ready to take that risk. And if it does what I fear it will and destroys things between us…then it's only speeding up the inevitable, and I can stop fantasizing about a world where John and I are anything other than a spider and a fly with a temporary truce.

Chapter Twenty-Two

JOHN

I HOLD MY BREATH, hoping James will open up to me. Hoping beyond reason that he'll trust me and let me in. His Adam's apple travels the length of his throat several times as he works to hold back the anguish I can see gathering in his blue eyes before he blinks it away. And just when I'm afraid he's about to reinforce his walls and brush me off…he doesn't.

"Our mom died after shooting up too much heroin with one of her regular fuck buddies she got high with—one of Neverland's finest, a boy in blue," he starts bitterly. "Her death was a problem for him. His solution was to threaten me into silence and to leave us in the apartment with a rotting body."

It takes me a few seconds for what he's saying to sink in. "The guy abandoned two little kids with their dead mother. A fucking *cop* did that?"

His gaze hardened. "You calling me a liar, Darling?"

"No! Jesus, it's just… Shit, that's the exact opposite of what we do. We're supposed to *protect* people against scumbags like that, not *be* the scumbags."

"In my experience, cops are nothing more than bad guys posing as good guys. We're all the same, we all have our own agendas. But at least bad guys are up front about who we are and what we want. Cops use their uniforms and badges to disguise the criminals lying underneath."

I huff out a harsh breath as I plow my hands through my hair, then drop them at my sides, defeated. "No wonder you have issues with law enforcement. And now with the whole of NPD in Croc's pocket, it's not doing anything to help your distrust. I get it, I do. But, Hook, we're not all corrupt assholes. Some of us genuinely want to make a difference."

"While I reserve the right to assume that anyone carrying a badge is in fact a corrupt asshole," he says with solemn conviction, "I'll admit I no longer believe you're one of them."

I keep my features schooled, but on the inside, I'm celebrating like the Panthers just won the Super Bowl. I'm not sure there's higher praise to be had from *the* Captain Hook, self-proclaimed outlaw and hater of LEOs the world over. Clearing my throat, I move to stand next to him with my back against the sun-warmed glass, so I won't be tempted to pepper his gorgeous face with kisses of gratitude.

Baby steps, John. Don't scare him off.

Keeping my focus in front of us, I guide his story back to where he left off. "How old were you when your mom died?"

"Nine. Starkey was twenty months. I thought I could take care of us the same as always—it's not like our mom had been much help in the day to day, anyway—but I was only a kid. I didn't take into account how I'd get food or diapers or anything else once it ran out. I tried stealing from the corner store, but I wasn't very stealthy."

"And that's how you both ended up at the School for

Lost Boys." He makes an affirmative sound but doesn't elaborate. "Then I don't understand how you think you abandoned Starkey. As far as I remember, he was stuck to you more than your own shadow. Well, you or Smee. They were attached at the hip, too. I'm actually surprised he kept the fact that you're brothers from Smee all these years."

"Starkey didn't know," he says, his voice gravelly. "That's how I abandoned him. When we got to the school, I didn't want anyone to know he was my brother. I didn't want to have to take care of him anymore. I wanted him to be someone else's problem for once. And he was too young to remember, so after a while, he didn't know any better.

"I don't think I ever intended to keep it from him indefinitely. I just wanted a fucking break, just for a little while."

"Yeah, I get that. Little brothers can be super annoying." Michael is only three years younger than me, but I remember sometimes it felt like a lot more. There were plenty of days I wished he'd go away and leave me alone. And I'd never been in the position of being his sole competent caretaker before the age of ten. So I sure as hell can't begrudge a nine-year-old James for wanting to distance himself from his baby brother for a while. "What made you decide to keep the secret?"

"Croc." He speaks the name with all the vitriol it deserves, his drop in tone causing goose bumps to pop up on the back of my neck. "It didn't take me long to realize he was a manipulator. Any connection to the others would give him leverage. He'd use them to control me. And if he knew Starkey was my brother, it'd be the worst for him."

"Wow," I say, unable to articulate the whirlwind of realizations in my mind.

I've always suspected Hook wasn't as heartless as he wanted everyone to believe. That deep down he cared about the kids he grew up with, however reluctantly. Now he's confirmed it. People with drug addictions are great at manipulation; it's how they hustle their loved ones or even strangers to help them get their next fix. They take what you care about—whether it's other people or as simple as a favorite treat—and use it against you.

Hook's rough start in this world meant he knew how to recognize that trait and how to battle against it. And he used that knowledge to do what he could to protect the others by showing indifference and holding everyone at arm's length. What a heavy burden to carry for such a young soul.

Thinking back on what he said, my mind snags on a certain detail. "You said that Starkey *didn't* know he was your brother. When did you finally tell him?"

"I didn't." As if the strength he's been using to keep himself upright is sapped out of him, James slides down until he's sitting on the floor, his forearms resting on bent knees. I follow him down. "One of the prison guards handed Starkey a note while I was talking to him. He freaked out."

"Fucking Croc," I growl. "He set you up."

He shrugs. "Doesn't matter. He wouldn't have had a card to play if I'd done the right thing and come clean to the kid years ago."

"Why didn't you?"

"When he was young, I was afraid he'd let it slip. He was always shit for keeping secrets," James muses with a slight smirk. One that only lasts for a second before the amusement drops from his face. "But once he was older and out of the school, I should've told him the truth. Or at the very least, I should've made him and Smee go with Peter and the others. But I didn't. Because even though he had no idea we were brothers, having Starkey underfoot as a Pirate was better than losing him completely. Guess it was inevitable, though. He doesn't want anything to do with me now."

James lets his head drop back and thump on the wall, his eyes staring at where the orange rays are creeping onto the ceiling as the sun gets closer to the horizon. From my spot next to him, I can see the water shimmering in his eyes and his throat work to keep everything from spilling out. He's hurting, and I don't know how much he'll allow me to comfort him. If I move too fast or offer too much, I run the risk of him shutting down and shutting me out. Which is why I do what I can with my words and refrain from wrapping him in my arms like I'm dying to do.

"He's in shock. After he's had some time to wrap his head around it, he'll be okay."

"You don't get it," he says, his voice thick with emotion. "All I've ever wanted, from the time he was born, was to fucking *protect him.* At the school, I…I did th-things —" James chokes back what sounds like the beginning of a sob and turns it into a frustrated growl as he bangs his head on the wall once, twice, before trying again. "I did what I had to do to ensure he was safe, to ensure he'd never have to fucking go through any of that, *ever.* I was older and stronger. I could handle it. But Starkey and the others, they were too soft, too innocent. And they needed Peter, so it…" He swallows thickly, and a fat tear escapes the corner of his eye to stream down his temple. "It had to be me."

Oh, Jesus Christ, he's killing me. Again, my suspicions about what happened between James and Croc all those years ago slither to the surface. Stuff I can't bring myself to put into words in my own mind any more than he can bring himself to say them out loud. Knowing it is enough to make my stomach turn and my heart fucking break.

Then there's the rage. I want to turn this world upside down until I have Croc's life in my hands for the sole purpose of snuffing it out in the name of that broken boy who grew into this perfect but broken man.

I wish I could call him by his name, but for reasons I still don't understand, it's the one thing guaranteed to send him running, so I settle for the next best thing. "Captain…"

"Don't you fucking pity me, Darling," he bites out, closing his eyes and curling his hands into fists. "Don't you fucking dare."

"I don't pity you," I say honestly. "I am in *awe* of you." His eyes snap open, and he turns to look at me, questions knitting his brows together. Ones that I answer with an open heart. "I know you won't believe me when I say this, but you are the bravest and most selfless man I have ever known. The first night I met you, I knew there was something special about you. I didn't know what it was, but I didn't need to. No matter what people said about you—no matter what you said about yourself—I was confident about who you truly were. Hearing these things only proves I was right, and still am. You are exactly the man I thought you were. And that man is *amazing*."

When he answers, the quiet resignation in his voice is a hundred times worse than when he's sparking with violent fury. "That's where you're wrong. This man failed his brother. Every time he's beaten or…"

James squeezes his eyes shut, pushing more tears past his thick lashes to streak into his trim beard. I can't hold myself apart from him any longer. Reaching up, I cup his cheeks and use my thumbs to brush the moisture away, only to watch it get replaced with fresh streams. Leaning in, I rest my forehead on his and will all of my strength to transfer to him through every contact point we have, through our mingled breaths. Anything to help ease his pain.

He releases a shuddering exhale, then sniffs. "You should've seen him, John," he whispers as he looks into my eyes with a helplessness I can't bear. "Starkey's a mere shell of the kid he once was. His light…it's gone. He'll never again grin up at me when I enter a room. I did that, that's on me, and I just—"

Then the dam breaks, and so does the man I love.

I don't mutter words of solace in his ear. I don't quietly shush him like a mother soothing her baby. I just gather him to me and hold him and let him be broken, because he fucking deserves it. He's never had the luxury before. Always having to be strong and do what's best for the ones he cared about.

Everyone pegged him as a broody asshole, an outsider with no desire to be part of their makeshift family. Hell, I witnessed him still resisting any kind of connection as recently as a few months ago, the night my sister got engaged to Peter. For more than two decades, he's pushed people away to *protect* them. For years, he endured unspeakable horrors so that no one else had to. And he did it all while affecting a cool and collected demeanor, never so much as cracking under the immense pressure.

Eventually, he starts to calm down. His breaths stop hitching in his chest, and the tears have slowed to a couple drops every other minute as opposed to a steady flow. He presses a kiss to the side of my neck where his face has been tucked, then lowers himself until he's lying on the floor with his head in my lap. He sighs. Not one of relief, but like the weight of the world is settled firmly back on his shoulders.

Taking advantage of the rare opportunity to shower him with affection, I rest one hand on his arm and draw lazy circles on his skin with my thumb as my other hand sifts through his thick hair, over and over. I don't know what's going through his mind, but when I feel him suddenly tense, I have a good guess.

"John—"

"Stop," I tell him. "I won't breathe a word of this to anyone. I would never betray you like that. I know it's going to take a long time for you to fully trust me, but just try, okay?"

Instantly, he relaxes in my lap, and I continue to stroke and soothe him, the feel of him under my hands soothing me in return. Never did I think I'd get the chance to be with him like this, intimate in a way that has nothing to do with our sexual chemistry. And since I'm a realist, I know there's a good chance it'll never happen again, so I'm cherishing every second he allows me in past those walls, because eventually, he'll put them back up. He has to. It's how he survives.

"Johnathan," he whispers between the deep and even breaths of someone drifting on the fringes of exhaustion and sleep.

"Yeah," I say softly, unsure if he's actually awake.

"I trust you."

Those three simple words are my undoing, and now it's my turn to blink back the emotions welling in my eyes. I am so far gone for this man. The man who thinks he's the villain but is actually the hero. A beautiful, broken, battered hero. Even if no one else learns the truth, *I'll* know it. And I'll be here to worship him, on my knees and at his feet, offering my body, my heart, and my soul.

He is my Captain. And for as long as he'll have me, I am *his*.

Chapter Twenty-Three

HOOK

USUALLY FEELING the vibrations of my GSXR-1000's engine beneath me is enough to put me in a zen mood within minutes. But tonight, not even the twenty minutes it took us to ride out to the Lost Boys Lair in Buttfuck Nowhere was long enough to stop my nerves from fraying at the edges.

John went over the plan no less than half a dozen times and reassured me at least twice that many times that it'll work. And every time he did, I acted like he was being ridiculous. There was a lot of bored yeah-I-know looks, followed by glaring shut-the-fuck-up-already looks.

Annoyingly, he's more tuned into my moods than even I am. Because, despite my usual in-control-of-all-that-I-survey attitude, as soon as my crew and I left the Jolly Roger (John borrowed Starkey's white and blue Yamaha, and the man is sexier on it than he has a damn right to be), everything that could go wrong with this plan ripped through me. Every what-if slammed to the front of my brain so hard they would've burst through my skull to land on the pavement if my blacked-out helmet hadn't kept them locked inside where they continue to torment me.

Tonight, we're attempting to pull off a ruse, inside of a ruse, inside another ruse. The plan is a Russian fucking doll come to life.

One: The Pirates are pretending to attend one of Peter Pan's famous Friday Festivity parties like we've been known to do on occasion, covering up for the fact that we're actually here to meet with a prominent Atlanta drug kingpin to strike a deal for expanding the distribution of Fairy Dust into his territory.

Two: John, Smee, and I are pretending that the deal with the drug kingpin isn't a complete sham that was set up by the feds who struck some kind of deal with the guy so that he'd do a decent job acting like this fake deal is legit so that Croc thinks I'm falling in line with his demands without actually spreading his Dust shit around even more than I already have.

And three: John and I are pretending that we're merely associates and that I haven't been shoving my dick in his mouth at every available opportunity, among a myriad of other filthy things.

Oh yeah, and *I'm* pretending that I didn't break down in his arms like a little bitch last week as I spilled all my secrets, most of which no one else in the world knows. Even if some of them weren't mentioned in specifics, there's no way he didn't get a damn good idea about the stuff I'd intended to take to my grave. I don't necessarily regret it—somehow John knows when to push and when to back off—but I'm not entirely comfortable with it, either.

Guess that makes *four* ruses nestled inside of each other. Told you. Russian fucking doll. And it's going to take all my self-control and discipline to pull this off without any or every part of it blowing up in my face. A fact I'm trying to ignore as my crew and I wait for our guests to arrive in the huge outbuilding Pan uses as a secondary shop.

The Lair is an old, three-story farmhouse set on a couple dozen acres with the outbuilding set way in the back where Pan rebuilds custom cars. He bought the property years ago and made it into a home for him, Tink, and the boys who followed him—Slightly, Nibs, Curly, Tootles, and the Twins.

Side note: back when we were still kids, Wendy bestowed those six—the only ones who wanted them—with real names. Since then they've gone by Silas, Nick, Carlos, Thomas, and Tobias and Tyler, respectively. But after years of using the stupid-ass names Croc called them out of laziness, I usually default to those. Plus, I know it pisses some of them off, which amuses me because I'm a dick like that.

As it is every Friday night, the Lost Boys Lair is teeming with Neverlanders partying like oversexed college kids on spring break with no fucks to give. These parties are one of the ways Pan practices his "work hard, play harder" mentality. He's closing in on thirty but still acts like he's fucking thirteen most of the time. The Pirates attend for a lack of anything better to do in this shit town, and it's a good way for them to blow off steam. Between the booze, the women, and the axe-throwing competitions, it takes the edge off after a long week of working the criminal circuit. It does for my crew, anyway. I stay on the fringes and observe. Captain Hook doesn't do *fun*.

"Cookson, what time is it?" I say from where I'm leaning against the hood of a half dismantled '71 Dodge Dart. He's the only one wearing a watch right now, and since we all left our phones in our bikes—common practice when doing illegal shit, so no one can record or take pictures—I have no idea how long we've been waiting in here.

"Half past ten, Captain."

I level a glare in John's direction. "Your man's late, JD."

The cover story is that Trey Tannen is an old contact of JD's from his days in the Scavengers, so JD's the one who set up this deal. Which is true on two counts since Trey did have contacts in the Scavengers before they disbanded, and he was brought into this through John's team pulling the right strings.

"He's an important guy, Captain," John says without a trace of concern in his tone. "Guys like him always show up fashionably late."

"I don't give a shit *who* he is. He's wasting my goddamn time," I snarl.

The rest of the men shift uncomfortably from the tension in the air and the adrenaline coursing through their veins with the big bad unknown looming ahead. This isn't going to be a walk in the park. Just because we're meeting on neutral ground with the intention of working out a peaceful and mutually beneficial agreement, doesn't mean shit can't go sideways. And, when you deal with arrogant, trigger-happy thugs, it usually does. Those are the things running through my crew's heads right now. As for me, I'm hoping like hell that this Tannen guy doesn't decide to break his promise to the feds and go rogue on me, either by going back on this "deal" or trying to get a better one by going to Croc directly. Then we'll all be fucked.

Before I have to bluff that we're calling the whole thing off—or worse, that maybe JD set us up—the metal garage bay door is lifted to reveal Pan and a group of six mean-looking motherfuckers. Tannen, a badass Black man wearing a charcoal suit I couldn't begin to guess the worth of, steps into the middle of the room.

Pan shoots me an uncharacteristic somber warning look before closing us all in with him on the other side. As much as I'd like to, I can't blame him for the wicked side-eye. He and Wendy might have moved to their own house on the beach, but this was still his family we were placing in the line of fire by conducting business here. He knew this was the best choice we had, though. The more public a meeting was, the better the chances at everyone keeping their cool, and though this country party seems like neutral territory, the Pirates know this is more our turf than Tannen's, which will make it look good to Croc once he hears about it. So here we are.

The opposing lackeys square up behind their boss, matching the guys flanking me on both sides. I don't move, cementing my position of authority as the one who called this meeting, but John crosses to shake the man's hand as is expected of him as the liaison between the two crews. "Tannen, good to see you. Thanks for coming up."

"Been a long time, McRae," Tannen says warily. "Thought you'd gone dark. Or dead."

"Nah." John's mouth curves into a sexy smirk and winks. "You know as well as anybody, it ain't that easy to kill me off." Lifting the hem of his shirt, he shows off what looks like an aged, white knife scar under the left side of his ribs. It's a damn good thing the only Pirate to see John shirtless other than me is Smee because *that* wasn't more than a few hours old. Not to mention completely fake like the art decorating his body.

Tannen regards the "scar" with a chuckle. "Yeah, I remember." Then, to the rest of his guys, he explains, "JD, here, intervened when some asshole tried smacking my sister around in a bar. Got stuck for his trouble, earning my respect and gratitude in the process."

The release of tension is palpable. Every guy in the place relaxes a fraction more, knowing the men have history and trust between them. Smart move on the G-men's part, and Tannen deserves an Oscar for his performance already. Maybe this is going to work, after all.

At last, it's my turn. John steps back in deference to me as I meet Tannen in the middle. "Name's Hook," I say, choosing not to extend my hand. Pleasantries aren't my style, and if this meeting was real, I'm not the one who has to make a good impression. I'm doing *him* a favor by offering him a piece of the action, not the other way around. "I'll make this short and sweet, so we can all get on with our night. We're moving something big, something new. And if you're interested, I think we can work out a mutually beneficial arrangement."

"I like a man who cuts to the chase, Hook," Tannen says with the smile of a snake charmer. "Lay it on me."

"I work for a man named Fred Croc; maybe you've heard of him."

Rubbing his jaw with the backs of his knuckles, he nods. "Yeah, I've heard of him. Small timer who's been breaking into the big leagues the past several years, same as I did when I was starting. I got respect for a man like that."

I know it's all part of the script, but even hearing someone say they could have respect for Croc makes my blood boil. Hiding my true reaction, I smirk. "Don't we all. And he's about to go from the big leagues to the World Series. He's got a new drug, Fairy Dust. It's like MDMA, only stronger, and looks like body glitter. Absorbs through the skin, hitting the bloodstream in seconds for an instant high the club kids and ravers go crazy for. Plus, a small baggie of glitter is less conspicuous than a bunch of pills.

We're killing it in the local scene, but we're looking to expand."

"Body glitter." Trey raises a dubious brow. "Is it any good?"

I give him one of my rare and completely forced *I'm a normal person* smiles. "The best."

"What're the terms?"

"We'll give you a thousand kilos to start at 30%."

Tannen doesn't even flinch. "No fucking way, man. Not worth my time. I want two at 45%."

"I bet you do, but that's not how this works, and you know it. We start small and see how well you move it. Everything goes smooth, we can renegotiate for a bigger shipment and a bigger piece of the pie."

Sliding his hands into his pants pockets, Tannen rocks back on his heels as he pretends to consider my offer. "You got any product I can test?"

I snap my fingers and John steps forward with a small baggie. Before he even gets it open, Trey stops him—as planned.

"Not here," he says firmly. "No offense, but I'm not a fucking guinea pig. I have some girls who can try it out for me back home. Great opportunity or not, I won't risk bringing the feds to my door with a rash of dead or hospitalized clubbers in my territory. Assuming the girls enjoy themselves on your glitter, we have a deal."

Trey's following the script, but the reminder of all the girls who *have* ended up in the hospital from the drug has me grinding my molars into dust. How many of those girls did I sell to personally, placing the small baggie of iridescent glitter in their hands, then sending them off to their coma-filled fates? It doesn't matter that I'm selling Croc's shit to get my brother out of danger. Even *I* know that sins aren't canceled out by good intentions, and one way or another, the Devil is always paid his due.

Sometimes, in the stillness of the night, I wonder if I would've done anything different had I known the Dust was unstable. Would I still risk the lives of countless others to spare the pain for one? In my darker moments, I don't like my answer.

Picking up on my silence, John steps in smoothly to cover me. "I'm sure you can understand why my Captain is hesitant to let you leave with this, Tannen. I vouched for you. If you go out and reverse engineer this shit, it compromises our whole operation, and it'll be my ass. Then you'll have to explain to your sister why the man who stepped in front of a blade for her is six feet under. You feel me?"

Trey places one large hand adorned with flashy rings over his heart. "JD, I would never betray an old friend like that. And I'm not in the habit of making enemies of potential business partners, especially one like Fred Croc. You have my word."

John looks to me, and I give him a slight nod. One that says "go ahead" and maybe also "thanks for saving my ass." But just as John is about to hand it over, something slams into the side of the metal frame of the outbuilding —*BOOM!*—and all hell breaks loose.

Chapter Twenty-Four

HOOK

BOTH CREWS PULL THEIR WEAPONS. One of Tannen's guys steps in front of him and aims his gun straight at my head just as John does the same, shielding me with his big body and drawing on the thug. The only idiot in the room without firepower is me. I have a Desert Eagle stashed in the loft, but I almost never carry it. The way I conduct myself, I never need to. Now that we're in something right out of a Quentin Tarantino film, I suddenly wish I was packing.

Sharp accusations fly like verbal bullets as the situation escalates, neither side willing to be the first to back down. The danger right now is very real. Trey and his men are every bit the hardened criminals I have at my back, and none of them will hesitate to start a firefight at point-blank range if they have to. The gun pointed at John makes my stomach twist and my heart slam against my rib cage like a deranged animal trying to escape. I want to shove him out of the way, but I fucking can't. I need to get him safe another way.

Blasting the room with a shrill whistle, I shout at the top of my lungs. "Everybody chill the fuck out!"

Tannen follows my lead by tossing a command over his shoulder for his men to hold, but not to lower their weapons. The tension in the air is bowstring tight and so thick I can taste it, like sweat and too much testosterone. Now that it's quiet, we can hear the muffled sounds of a couple of drunks laughing, followed by Peter threatening to kick their asses if they don't get the hell back to the house.

Smee speaks up. "There, see? Just some assholes fuckin' around where they shouldn't be. No one's comin' to ambush ye, Tannen. Now let's all put our shit down and play nice."

"Come on, Trey," John adds. "You know me. This is a clean meet-and-greet. Tell your men to stand down, and we'll do the same."

Tannen lifts a hand, giving his crew the signal, and within seconds, everyone in the shop has tucked their guns back into holsters or waistbands. Discreetly releasing the breath I'd been holding, I tap John on the shoulder. When he doesn't immediately move, I use a gruff, "JD." Finally, he steps back over to my side, but the way the muscle in his jaw is jumping, I know he's not happy about leaving me vulnerable again.

Ignoring the light feeling in my belly his protectiveness gives me, I hold out my hand for the baggie of Dust, then pass it over to Tannen, who gives me a satisfied nod.

"We'll consider this a done deal, then," he says. "Let me know when you're ready, and we'll set up the exchange."

"I'll inform Croc of the good news. If you and your guys want to hang around, there's plenty of fun to be had at the party."

"Thanks, but we'll pass. We got what we came for. I'll be in touch, Hook."

I nod. "Looking forward to it."

As soon as Tannen's crew is gone and I excuse mine to go celebrate with what's left of the night, I cross to the far side of the garage and collapse into a metal folding chair in front of the work bench. Scrubbing my hands down my face, I allow myself the briefest moment to lower my walls and simply concentrate on dragging air deep into my lungs. Jesus fuck, that was close. Those thugs could've opened fire, and my crew would be nothing more than stains on the concrete floor by now. *John* would be… *Fuck!*

At the sound of the side utility door opening, my spine straightens like a metal rod is shoved up my back, and the mask of apathy I've perfected from the time I was nine snaps into place.

"It's only me," John says, closing the door behind him.

I stand and wing a single brow toward my hairline. "That's gotta be the most inaccurate way to qualify yourself, Darling."

His lips tip up on one side as he strides over to me. "Oh yeah? Can I take that as a compliment?"

Yes. "No, but I'll tell you what you *can* take," I say, fisting the front of his shirt to drag him closer, needing to feel his body to reassure myself that he's fine, he's fine, he's fucking fine. "My di—"

The sound of the door opening again acts like a bolt of lightning striking the ground between us, and we jump apart just before Peter and Wendy slip into the shop.

"Oh my God, John!"

In a blur, Wendy races across the open space and launches herself into her brother's arms. Smee's job this week had been to get word to Peter about the situation, including the fact that the top-secret mission John went off the grid for was practically right in their backyard, working with yours truly. That alone was probably enough to send Wendy Darling into a tailspin.

"Hey, sis, take it easy or you'll rub off my cool new tats. I need them for my street cred, you know," he says, chuckling as he gently breaks her chokehold.

Pan sidles up next to her and laces his fingers with hers. "Pretty sure whatever street cred the tats give you is canceled out by hanging around Captain Cinnamon Roll there."

"Oh, good," I reply drolly. "You finally have the same death wish I've had for you since the day we met. Glad we're on the same page."

Wendy smacks her fiancé's chest playfully. "Peter, behave yourself and apologize to Hook."

"You're right, Wen, I should definitely apologize." Grinning at me, I know by the stupid-ass twinkle in his blue eyes I'm not going to like what comes out of his mouth next. "Hook, I'm sorry your big, bad rep is trashed by the fact that you're such a cinnamon roll."

A few weeks ago, I probably would've cursed a blue streak and lunged for Pan's throat, succumbing to the desire to physically wipe that smirk off his face. But whether I simply lack the energy from the adrenaline drop or I don't want to traumatize Wendy by knocking his teeth out, all I do is cross my arms over my chest and deliver my practiced bored stare.

"I really hate you, you know that?"

He winks. "Must be opposite day, then, because we all know you secretly love me."

I sigh. "Christ, you're exhausting."

Pan's always been sickeningly cheerful—even when we were kids under the rule of abusive guardians. I'd resented the hell out of him for that luxury. It was one I'd never been able to afford.

Then again, I'm not sure Pan wouldn't still have been his freakishly happy self even if Croc had targeted him instead of me. Peter's "perpetually positive" gene was lodged firmly in his DNA. Or maybe it was a rainbow shoved firmly up his ass. Either way, if his glass was only half full, he would find a smaller glass and crow about his good fortune. I won't deny that the kids needed that kind of attitude from their leader, but that didn't mean it wasn't annoying as all hell. And fair or not, I've always kind of hated him for it.

Then, the year before I moved out of the school, he saw something he shouldn't have, and I hated him even more. Pan doesn't seem to care, though. Over the last decade, he's persistently tried including me as part of his Lost Boys family. And I've just as persistently told him to fuck right off. It's the only way we know how to co-exist—as bitter enemies. At least from my vantage point. I'm pretty sure he thinks we're more like bickering siblings.

Wendy gives John a scrutinizing once-over and shakes her head. "You look so…well, like a Pirate. No offense, Hook." I shrug. "If Dad saw you like this, he'd shit a brick sideways."

John tweaks a chunk of her hair and winks. "Dad has seemed like he might be a little backed up. Maybe I'll show up like this for Christmas."

She laughs. "Well, that would definitely make for an interesting event."

"Speaking of events," Pan says, draping an arm around Wendy's shoulders, "we've been making wedding plans."

I make a disgusted face. "And that's my cue." But before I can walk away, Pan stops me.

"Not so fast, Hook. As my best man, we'll need to discuss bachelor party ideas and a speech that emphasizes how awesome I am. These are not duties to be taken lightly."

He's done it. Peter Pan has finally struck me dumb. Because I have no response to what he just said. None.

Wendy is biting her lip nervously, and from the corner of my eye, I can see John holding a hand over his mouth to keep from laughing out loud. Oh, that's what this is. A joke! Of course it is because everything out of this man's mouth is a joke.

I blow out a breath and narrow my eyes at him. "Real funny, Pan. You almost had me there."

"Except I'm not joking, man." He's still smiling, but the expression on his face has toned down to one of sincerity. I can handle a lot of things from Peter, but seriousness is not one of them.

"No," I say simply as I cross the room, refusing to ask what would fucking possess him to want me—his lifelong nemesis—for his best man instead of one of his own guys.

"Great, so you'll think about it, then," he calls after me.

I give him my customary middle finger over my shoulder and walk through the door. Once outside, I make a quick call to Croc to let him know how the deal went with Tannen. To say he was satisfied with the news of his drug expanding into the Atlanta area would be a gross understatement. He makes a sickening comment about being proud of me, but all I care about is the fact that he says Starkey will be out before I know it. Hearing that gives me the sliver of hope I need. Whether by Croc's hand or by John's, my brother will be set free soon. And that knowledge puts me in the first good mood I've had in the past six fucking months.

When John emerges from the shop, I pull him around

the corner into the shadows. I bite his earlobe, and his groan travels straight to my cock. "Go enjoy yourself while you can, Johnathan. Because when we get home, I'm going to fuck you until every vein on my dick is imprinted on the inside of your ass," I growl as I palm the crease of his ass and squeeze over the denim where I plan on splitting him in two.

"Oh fuck," he rasps. "Let's go back now, Captain. *Please.*"

"No. You need to hang out with the rest of the crew, or it'll look suspicious. But *do not* get drunk. You get yourself a beer, and you nurse the hell out of it. I won't have you riding after drinking, and *I* won't ride *you* if you're wasted either. We do everything on my terms, my schedule. Understand?"

He nods and swallows hard. "Yes, Captain."

"Good. You better be convincing. We can leave in an hour or three, it all depends on you. I've got plenty of patience, and I don't mind making you wait." I want to smash our mouths together and show him with my tongue exactly how I'll fuck him later, but it's way too risky. Plus, I like making him crazy with anticipation. "Now go."

Without a word, he strides in the direction of the house, masculine power coiled in the flexing of his muscles and disguised by the grace with which he moves. He's a man on a mission, and I can't wait for him to complete it, so we can get to *my* mission.

Finally, I'll have every part of John Darling—at least all the ones I can afford to take. And I will take them, ruthlessly and unapologetically, like the villainous Pirate I am.

Chapter Twenty-Five

JOHN

TONIGHT'S BEEN one hell of a ride, and I haven't even gotten to the good part yet. My adrenaline has spiked so many times already—this afternoon as we planned the meeting with Tannen, running over a hundred mph on a crotch rocket down the highway, the explosive standoff in the shop, and then the eternity James made me play Pirate while his laser gaze bored into me. I should be exhausted from the multiple blood pressure drops, but I've never felt more alive.

I'd also never felt more scared than when that pistol was pointed at James's head earlier. I've stared down the barrels of a lot of guns in my career, but I've never been so consumed with fear as I was in that moment. In the second it took for me to place myself in front of James, an image flashed in my mind of the trigger being pulled and a bullet ripping through his skull. I nearly lost my fucking shit.

My training is the only thing that kept me grounded in my role as JD instead of acting on instinct and neutralizing the immediate threat. Which technically would've been *against* my training, considering it wasn't the smart move with a dozen other guns drawn in a twenty-foot radius. But everything in me had screamed to take down the bastard who dared to threaten my man. I need this case closed like fucking yesterday, so he can get through his couple months of jailtime and begin his life where he's not in constant danger anymore. I don't even want to think about the possibility of losing him. Not now that he's finally mine.

He *is* mine, whether he's ready to admit it yet or not. And I'm about to be his in every way that matters.

After we got back to the Jolly Roger, Cecco insisted I continue the party downstairs with the rest of them. I'd already been on edge for the two hours James made us stay at the Lost Boys' place. All I wanted to do was rush upstairs and fall at my man's feet. But turning Cecco and the others down would've looked suspicious. James is right, I need to keep up appearances with them, and that means acting like one of the crew, not the Captain's special first mate. So I stayed while Hook sauntered up to the loft without a backward glance.

I had two more beers downstairs, but it couldn't be helped. I'm lucky they were so shit-faced they thought I'd had closer to a dozen. Everyone except Smee, who kept a close eye on me all night. After an hour in the clubhouse, I think he sensed I was about to jump out of my skin and gave me the out I needed to make an acceptable exit.

Now as I climb the stairs to the loft, a pack of pterodactyls takes flight in my belly, great giant things that beat their wings in excitement and scratch my insides with anticipation. They inject me with lust so powerful it slips into my blood stream and rushes to my extremities until I'm on fucking fire with it.

When I walk into the space I've started to think of as our home, I find James in the same spot I found him the night he ordered me to jerk off for him—in that chair with his legs spread wide, looking for all the world like a king lounging on his throne. He's gloriously shirtless with his tableau of tattoos on full display and the gold rings in his nipples winking at me in the lamplight. But what really slays me are his sexy-as-hell black-rimmed glasses and that worn copy of *The Count of Monte Cristo* in his big hands.

He knows I'm here, but he hasn't so much as glanced my way as I cross the open space, and he continues to ignore me when I stop in front of him.

We do everything on my terms, my schedule.

I barely suppress an agitated growl. My skin is too tight, and I've been hiding a massive hard-on with my untucked T-shirt since James hauled me around the side of Pan's shop hours ago. The alpha male in me aches to take what I want, to shove him against the wall and kiss him until his careful control bursts into flames and he finally gives in.

But this new side of me, the part of me that Hook owns, wants to wait for as long as it takes. I know he'll give me his attention when he's good and ready, and fuck if that doesn't get me even hotter. My reactions to him continue to surprise me, but I don't question them, not anymore. They feel utterly natural with this man, and I'm comfortable enough in my own skin to surrender to them.

To surrender to *him*.

"Captain," I plead, not caring how eager I sound. "I'm here."

"So you are." He casually turns the page and continues to read.

Goddamn it, I'm desperate to make something —*anything*—happen. Sinking to my knees in front of him, I pull up my T-shirt—

"Don't even think about it, Darling," he snaps out in a low voice that might as well be a shout. I let my shirt fall back into place and meet his flinty blue eyes. He places his book and reading glasses on the side table and sits up. His contracting abs draw my gaze, and I lick my lips as the desire to nuzzle into that line of dark hair that disappears into his waistband punches me in the gut. "What do you think you're doing?"

My eyes flick up to his face as he braces his forearms on his knees and waits for my answer. "I thought—"

"That's your problem right there, you were thinking. More importantly, you were topping from the bottom, and that's not how this works."

I knit my brows together. Though I've never been in a D/s relationship, I'm familiar enough with some of the terminology. "No, I—"

"Yes, you were," he says, injecting steel into his tone. "You tried to control the situation by getting me to do what *you* wanted, when you wanted it, and that's where you fucked up. I told you that we go by my schedule, which means we'll do things whenever the fuck it pleases me. That was a test. You failed." A devilish smirk curves his lips. "Now you get these."

James reaches into the cushion between his thigh and the arm of the chair and pulls out a set of metal handcuffs dangling from one finger. *My* metal handcuffs. It would be too much of a coincidence that he has a matte-black pair just like mine. "You got those from my room."

"Correction. It's *my* room that I'm letting you borrow. Therefore, whatever's in it belongs to me."

I arch a brow and deadpan, "That's not how the law works."

"It is now. Keep talking and I'll get a ball gag. For the record, that's in *Smee's* room. Irish bastard's kinky as hell."

I press my lips firmly together. I have a feeling James could get me to try anything once, but right now I just need him to *fuck me*, hard and without mercy. But the only way I get what I want is by following his rules, some of which I don't even know yet. That's fine; I'm a quick study.

Then it hits me. He knew I'd be crawling out of my skin with need by the time I got up here. He knew I'd be desperate to get him to act. Narrowing my eyes, I say, "You set me up."

James reaches down and squeezes my straining dick through my jeans. A whoosh of air leaves my lungs, but I manage to hold my position and not shamelessly rut into his grip. "You complaining, Darling?"

"No, Captain," I grate. "Never."

"Then stand up," he commands and rises with me, tucking the handcuffs into his back pocket. "Don't move."

I'm almost afraid to breathe for fear he'll stop whatever he plans on doing, but by now I know that a direct order requires a response. More than that, I want to give him the words he craves from me. "Yes, Captain."

My pulse races as he grips the neck of my T-shirt with both hands. I brace myself for the forceful yank, but it never comes. Holding my gaze, he begins to *slowly* rip the thin cotton, dragging out the anticipation, shredding my patience along with my shirt. The sound of the fabric rending in two mixes with the roar of blood in my ears and the huffs of my quickening breaths. For every inch of my chest and stomach he exposes, my core temp ticks up another degree. When he finally gets through the bottom hem, he pushes the torn shirt off my shoulders and lets it fall forgotten to the floor.

Walking around, he secures my wrists behind my back with my handcuffs. Instinctually, I test my limited mobility. The clinking of the metal chain between the bracelets drives home the fact that I'm completely at his mercy, and fuck that turns me on.

His right hand snakes around the front of my throat and claims me as he squeezes, the smooth metal of his thumb ring pressing against my racing pulse. "As of tonight, Darling," he rasps at my temple, "you're fucking *mine*."

I let out a long sigh. "Finally."

James bites the shell of my ear, then keeps his face next to mine to peer down my body as his hands begin to roam. Long, graceful fingers travel over the peaks and valleys of my pecs and abs. They alternate between soft, grazing touches and hard scrapes from blunt nails across my sensitized, tattoo-free skin that mark me with his ownership in reddened furrows.

One second he's lightly thumbing my nipples and the next he's gripping and twisting until he rips a groan from deep in my belly. My cock is so hard and my balls so tight I'm in physical pain. The need to beg is almost unbearable, but I bite it back. Barely.

As though sensing my struggle, James makes it impossible for me to say a word. He grabs my jaw and turns my face for his domineering kiss, thrusting his tongue against mine in a mouth fuck so filthy it needs its own NC-17 rating. His taste of clove cigarettes, bad decisions, and dirty sex is drugging, and I hope I never come down from this high.

He presses his hips forward, grinding his jeans-covered erection into my restrained hands. I eagerly rub the thick length of him, wishing the material would disappear, needing to feel him skin to skin. He must have the same need because suddenly he makes short work of undoing his belt and fly. A second later we groan in tandem when his perfect cock is freed into my palms and I lavish him with long, firm strokes.

Growling, he breaks our kiss to lick and bite his way

over my stubbled jaw and down my neck, lighting me on fire. "That's it, Darling. Get reacquainted with it. The veins, the ridges, the fat head. Because I'm about to destroy you with every fucking inch."

"Oh Christ," I choke out. I know every *millimeter* of his cock intimately. I've worshipped him with my mouth every chance I got. Giving James head has become a constant craving. "Turn me around so I can suck you off. Let me—"

"No."

I clench my jaw so I don't do something monumentally stupid like complain or call him a controlling bastard just to get a rise out of him. Another time it might be fun to push his buttons and see what kind of punishments I can earn, but I need him too damn badly right now. I've been waiting weeks for him to take things all the way with me; I'm not screwing it up now.

As he finally reaches down to undo my jeans, I hold my breath in anticipation. Pants and underwear are shoved down past my ass, and the air in my lungs wheezes out as my painfully hard erection is given relief for the first time in hours.

He spits into his palm, the filthy act triggering a wave of arousal in me like one of Pavlov's dogs. James has a thing for marking me. With his teeth. His nails. His saliva. His scent. His cum. I fucking love it. I want him to brand me as his, I want his essence flowing in my veins and coating my skin until there's no denying who I belong to.

With his spit-slickened palm he grabs my dick and gives it a single rough tug. My body bows on a gasp. "*Oh fuck.*" When he ventures lower to squeeze my balls, my head drops back on his shoulder and my legs give out. The thick arm banded around my stomach is all that stops me from collapsing to the floor before I regain my strength.

"Don't even think about coming this soon, Darling. Get

your shit under control and hold it. That orgasm is mine, it belongs to *me*, and I want to feel it when I'm lodged deep inside your ass. You hear me?"

I groan. "Yes, Captain." I have no confidence in my ability to follow that order. The way he's working me over, I'll be lucky to last another minute. But I'm sure as hell going to try because the thought of clenching around his thick shaft as I come is my new idea of heaven.

"Look at you." I follow his gaze to where his large hand is slipping up and down my shaft. Every time he slides past the ridge and twists on the head before sinking back to the root, lightning crackles in my balls. "How long has this huge cock been hard for me, Darling?"

"Years, Captain," I admit freely. "Fucking *years*."

James growls into my neck, continuing to stroke me off. "I like knowing that. That you've wanted me for so long. I know that makes me an evil bastard, but I don't care."

"You're only evil if you don't fuck me like we both want."

"You say that now. We'll see if you still feel that way after I ruin you."

His words are slightly pensive, and I wonder if he's referring to the mind-blowing sex we're about to have, or if he's making predictions about our future. About what happens when this case is over and we're no longer tied together by our common goals and forced proximity.

I want to tell him that I'm not going anywhere. That after everything is over, I have no intention of giving him up. I've run the gamut of lovers the past decade—everything from one-night stands to long-term boyfriends—and none of them can hold a candle to this complex, impossible-to-label thing I have with him.

I'd rather be ruined by James Hook than be safe with anyone else.

But he doesn't give me a chance to say any of that. Pressing down between my shoulder blades, he bends me forward until the side of my face is planted on the cushion of his chair. With my bound hands resting on my back and my ass in the air, I stare up the line of my body at him looming behind me.

He kicks my feet out as far as they'll go with my jeans still bunched above my knees. His hands begin to roam, creating random patterns over my back, cheeks, and thighs. I revel in the feel of his rough touches, the feel of a man in control. The way his calluses abrade my skin and lightly pull at my body hair, the intermittent possessive digging in of his fingers into my muscles, the teasing of his thumbs as they skirt around the one place I desperately want him to touch.

"Mmm, Darling." Keeping his gaze locked with mine, he sticks his forefinger in his mouth, then runs the wet digit down my seam and over my tight hole, forcing a groan from my chest. "You look good enough to eat. And I'm starved."

Then he crouches down, and the absence I feel at losing sight of him is replaced with a blast of lust when his tongue laps a long line between my cheeks. I suck in a sharp breath and barely have time to release it before he's rimming my puckered hole with his tongue. He adds more pressure, then more, until he breaches that tight ring and delves inside.

"*Jesus fuck*," I say hoarsely. "Christ, that feels so good."

The growl he makes as he feasts on my body hums through me like electric currents, and I moan in ecstasy. I wish I watch him eating at me, wish I could look him in the eyes as he fucks me with his mouth and nips my flesh with his teeth. But all I can do is feel and hear. Feel the hot swipe of his tongue up my hypersensitive taint, hear him spit, feel the lash of his saliva on my crease before feeling the blunt tip of his finger rubbing it in.

"Please, Captain," I say, pushing my ass back against the pressure.

The hard smack of his hand on my cheek sends fiery pleasure right to my cock, and I press my face into the cushion to muffle my moan. "Hold still."

He teases me some more, testing my resolve and waiting for me to screw up again. But as much as I loved the correction, I want penetration even more, so I don't move a muscle. Unless you count the trembling from needing to come more than I need my next breath.

"Good boy, Johnathan."

His praise soothes me, and I'm suddenly confident I can hold out forever as long as he repeats those three simple words. But then I hear what sounds like a snap top on a plastic bottle and impatience buzzes through me once again because I know what's coming. Sure enough, I hiss between my teeth as the cold lubricant hits its mark. My devil chuckles as he spreads it around, but then grows serious.

"Tell me you want this, Darling. Tell me you want my fingers fucking your ass, stretching you open and getting you ready for my cock."

I don't hesitate. "I want it. I want it so goddamn bad."

"Then open for your Captain," he says, his voice gravelly with lust. "Open and let me in."

Finally—*fucking finally*—James pushes a single lubricated finger inside my ass in one slow motion. My eyes nearly roll back in my head at the familiar burn, and the pleasure only increases with every thrust. My jeans are low enough that he's able to reach between my legs with his free hand, and while he fucks me with that unrelenting finger, he tugs on my sac and rolls my testicles in his palm.

"Ah *shit*, I'm gonna come if you keep doing that," I grunt.

"No, you won't. You won't come until I tell you to."

His confidence adds another layer of lust onto all the others, and I have to focus on taking deep breaths to hold off my climax. It works, too, until he drizzles more lube onto my asshole and adds a second finger. Then a third. He scissors them inside me as he moves in and out, working me open more and more. I do a lot of moaning and begging and praising and swearing, but none of it fazes him. He has a plan, and no matter what I say or do, he's going to do things at his pace, just like he said.

When I think I might die from it all, he pulls out, and stands up. In a voice tight with unleashed restraint, he says, "It's time."

Chapter Twenty-Six

HOOK

DARLING'S GONNA KILL ME, I swear to fucking Christ.

I take a deep breath in through my nose to compose myself before I plunge into him without a second thought. I refuse to let my lust-driven need to sate myself in his ass put him at risk or hurt him in any way. If anything, my adult sex life has been sporadic and atypical. Choosing to keep my preference for dick under wraps (the men who follow me would see it as a weakness, and I can't afford that in my position) meant a lot of unsatisfying hookups with women and only the occasional anonymous fuck with random guys in other counties I found on gay hookup apps.

While the encounters did more for me than my own hand would, none of them were even a fraction of what it feels like being with John. With or without the tattoos, the man is drop-dead sexy. His body is a temple built with brick upon brick of solid muscle. I want to worship every single one of them with my tongue, test their firmness with my teeth. His cock is a work of fucking art, long and thick and deliciously veined. I'm big, but he's downright huge with the slightest curve north when he's hard, like it's straining for what it wants. Like it's straining for *me*.

I retrieve the condom from my wallet and tear the foil packet with my teeth.

"Captain, if…" He pauses, then bites his lower lip.

"Out with it, Darling."

"If you've always been safe before," he says hesitantly, "I'd be okay skipping the condom."

Shiiiiit. The idea of sinking bare into this man has my cock twitching and cum leaking from the tip. But it also pisses me off that he'd be so careless with himself. Grabbing the chain of his cuffs and one of his shoulders, I haul him up straight, then grip his jaw to turn his head. Narrowing my eyes on him, I speak low and clear.

"I've always used protection, but that's beside the point. Men will tell you anything you want to hear to skip the rubber. How many times have you let someone fuck you without a condom?"

"Never, it's just…" he says, pausing to lick his lips. "I've wanted this for forever. I want to feel you so fucking bad."

Ah, hell. That instantly banks my anger, and I can't stop myself from crushing our mouths together in a fierce, all-consuming kiss. I love the way his stubble scrapes against my lips and rasps beneath my fingertips. He tastes of beer and mint gum and *him*, and the combination is enough to get me drunk without a single drop of alcohol.

Tearing myself away, I reach down to grab his swollen cock and heavy balls together in my large hand and then I squeeze. He gasps and holds his breath, no doubt trying not to shoot his load before he's given permission.

"I wasn't planning on telling you until I got the results, but I had tests run at the clinic a couple days ago. If they come back that I'm clean, there will be no stopping me from fucking you bare. Until then, we use a condom. And the next time you're so flip about your safety or well-being —and that goes for any situation, Darling, not just sex—I'll tie you to my bed and whip your ass with my belt until my arm gives out. Are we clear?"

His golden eyes melt as he nods. "Yes, Captain. Thanks for taking care of me."

The tenderness radiating from him winds through me like slithering vines seeking out the black thing behind my ribs. Before I can cut them down, they wrap themselves around the barely beating mass again and again, until its completely cocooned in every soft feeling I've ever avoided.

No one's gotten to me as much as this man has. And for the first time in my life, I wonder if it's possible for my heart to emerge from this as something different…something alive and strong with a reason to keep beating long past this mission.

"Back into position, Darling."

He releases a groaning breath when I let go of his junk and push his shoulders down until the side of his face rests on the chair cushion again. I sheath my cock in record time and work a generous amount of lube all over my shaft. He still has plenty for me to enter without a problem, but my Johnathan likes it when I'm filthy, so I bend down and spit directly on his crack.

"*Ah shit yes,*" he hisses.

When I use my thumb to rub the splotch of saliva around his puckered hole, he moans and arches his ass up, chasing my touch. *Naughty boy.* I grin like the devil I am and capitalize on his small infraction with a hard smack to one round globe. He shudders on a groan, and I watch with immense satisfaction as my red handprint appears like magic.

"Goddamn, I like seeing my marks on you," I growl.

"Me too— *Oh fuck.*"

Oh fuck is right because I just pressed the crown of my dick to his tight hole and the heat kissing my tip has me sucking in a sharp breath. He clenches his cuffed hands and tries to reposition them at the small of his back. With the angle of his body and the sheen of sweat coating his skin, gravity is causing them to slide toward his shoulder blades, which can't be comfortable. Like before, I grip the chain between the metal bracelets. But instead of pulling him to stand up, I rest my fist at the base of his spine, relieving him of that added strain.

Once I see the muscles in his arms and shoulders relax, my focus returns to the spot my whole world is narrowing down to. Christ, he feels like heaven already, and I'm not more than a finger-width inside. Keeping the pressure steady, I slowly push past the ring of muscle trying to keep me out with the fat head of my cock.

"Jesus, you're big," he grunts.

I nearly snort because I'm nothing compared to him. I can only assume there's a slew of men permanently split in two from taking his weapon of mass destruction in their asses. Then I slam the door on that thought because thinking of John with anyone else makes me itch to set shit on fire.

I know from our cursory discussion about his past relationships that John's had a healthy sex life since coming into his own in high school. A fact that would've fueled my jealous loathing of him before…well, *before*. Admittedly, there's still a part of me that's jealous of his trauma-free upbringing, but I'm also glad he's not new at this. Though he said he's always been a natural top, he's also been the occasional bottom, so I don't have to worry about handling him with kid gloves. And the fact that he's never had anyone as big as me goes a long way in soothing my ego.

"You can take me," I tell him. "You know what to do.

Exhale and push out." He does, and the head of my cock finally slips past the tight ring, giving me unfettered access to bury myself to the hilt in his ass. We groan in tandem as I bottom out, my heavy balls smashed against his taint. "Good boy," I grate, holding my position while he adjusts to the invasion. I take deep breaths through my nose and count to five. I can't wait any longer than that. "Tell me you're ready, goddamn it. Tell me to ruin you."

"I'm so fucking ready. Please, Captain, I need you. Fuck me, ruin me. Make us feel good, *please please ple—*"

I pull out and slam back home; then I repeat the motion over and over and over. His cries of pleasure and strings of curses urge me on like a crop slapped to the flank of a racehorse. Keeping hold of the handcuffs with one hand, I grip his hip with the other and pull him to meet my every thrust. The sounds of our slick flesh smacking together, our grunts and growls and filthy words, our heaving breaths and hissing gasps—all of it creates a soundtrack worthy of an award-winning porn flick, and I've never been so fucking turned on in all my life.

There's nothing hotter, nothing tighter, than Johnathan Darling, and he's all mine, mine, *mine*. I want to lose myself in his body, I want to make it my home. I want to cover myself in his scent after every shower so I always smell like *him*. I want to brand him into my skin so he's forever a part of me, even after I inevitably fuck things up and he walks out of my life.

But that reality check is a kick to the nuts I don't need right now, so I push it from my mind. What I need is more of him. Always more. More, more, more. Pulling him up, I slip one arm through his to wrap it around his barrel of a chest and my other hand drops down to his cock. I gather his pre-cum on three of my fingers, hold them up so he can see what I do to him, then growl my command in his ear.

"Open."

On a whimper, he obeys, and I shove them deep in his mouth. With great effort, I slow my fuck down to match the thrust of my hand, reveling in the way he moans as he sucks and tongues my fingers like they were my cock. Pulling them back out, I gather as much of his saliva as I can. Viscous strands of shining spit keep us tethered, bottom lip to fingertips, in a sloppy-sexy display. Then I lower my hand to slather it all on his dick and start jerking him off with hard and cruel strokes.

"Oh my God," he gasps, dropping his head back onto my shoulder. I take advantage and attack his neck with my mouth as my hips work up to their previous punishing pace. My hand switches to fast, concentrated pumps over the sensitive flare of his fat cockhead. I can feel him getting close with the way his ass strangles my dick as I piston inside his tight sheath like a battering ram hell-bent on destroying him for all other men.

"Oh my God, that's so good. *Fuck fuck fuck*, I'm gonna come. Captain, please let me come, fucking *please please please*," he begs, squeezing his eyes shut and fighting to hold it.

My natural inclination to deny him permission, to edge him over and over until he practically explodes, is absent tonight. I'll never last long enough to do him any justice. I'll have plenty of time to play with him, but right now is not that time.

"Do it," I growl against the edge of his jaw, biting it for good measure. "I want to feel this ass strangling my dick as you come all over my hand. Do it, Johnathan. Come for me. Come for your Captain."

My big, strong man arches his back, every muscle

strung taut as he shouts to the heavens. His cock throbs inside my grip, and thick white ropes of cum spurt from his tip, covering us in a warm, sticky mess. And just like I knew it would, his ass clenches and pulses around me like a beating heart, milking my own climax before I'm ready.

The fire swirling at the base of my spine and gathering in my balls suddenly rips through my cock. I curse and moan and curse some more as I fill the condom, wishing I was filling John up instead, branding him from the inside. *Soon*, I promise myself. *Very soon.*

I give us each a couple of minutes to revel in the afterglow or whatever ridiculous name people give this heady post-orgasm sensation, but we're not in a position where I can let us linger for long. I need to get him out of those cuffs before his arms get too sore.

Gritting my teeth, I pull back to let my softening cock slip out of the greatest fuck I've ever had. He hisses a protest at the separation, and I can't say that I blame him. I already miss his heat surrounding me, which is the complete opposite of my usual need to sever all physical contact once sex is over.

"Shhh, just relax," I say against his temple as I reach between us and gently massage the lube-slick area to ease it back to its normal state. My dick twitches when I imagine someday doing it to make sure my cum stays where it belongs, but lucky for John, I'm too wrung out to start anything again so soon. "You okay?"

Sighing, he says, "I've never been this okay in my entire life." Then he turns those gorgeous eyes on me and smiles. "Are *you* okay?"

"Smart-ass." I crush my mouth to his for a quick, bruising kiss. "Let me take care of the condom quick, and I'll let you out of those cuffs." I pad over to the bathroom where I tie the rubber off and toss it in the trash before washing my hands and taking a towel back with me.

I find John kneeling on the floor, slumped against my chair, like his legs couldn't hold him up anymore. His jeans are still pushed down to mid-thigh, leaving him completely exposed. Canting my head, I pause to admire the view.

"Hook," he barks. "Cuffs."

"Watch the attitude, Darling, or I'll forget where I put the key." That's a lie. I know his shoulders have to be in need of a good massage, and as a responsible Dom, I'll give him one. In my bed. That may or may not (it absolutely will) lead to a round two.

John just looks up at me and laughs.

"What's so funny?"

"I can get out of these without the key."

"You brought *trick* cuffs with you on an undercover op? What are you, twelve?"

He shakes his head. "Not trick cuffs, and I can still get out of them in under thirty seconds."

Narrowing my eyes, I cross my arms over my chest. "Prove it."

John stays where he is, sitting on his heels, and never once takes his gaze off mine. I can't see what he's doing behind his back, but his arms are definitely doing something. I almost get distracted with the way his muscles bunch and shift with his movements, but my curiosity is stronger. As I get to the number twenty-five in my head, John brings his arms around to the front, his open handcuffs dangling on one long finger.

"Holy fuck, that's hot."

He arches a playful eyebrow. "Escaping custody is sexy?"

"Have you met me?" I deadpan. When he laughs, I hold out my hand and help him up. As he puts himself back together—totally pointless since I plan on taking him apart in less than five minutes—I ask, "How'd you do it?"

Slipping one of his boots off, he holds it up. "Special aglets on my shoelaces." Then he shows me the tiny metal shiv that tucks into the tip of his lace.

"I'll be damned," I say, rubbing my beard. "Teach me."

"You want me—a task force officer with the FBI—to teach a known criminal how to escape from handcuffs? I'm not sure that would be wise on my part."

I cross my arms again and raise a single brow in challenge. "And I'm not sure it would be wise for me—a known criminal—to fuck a pretty-boy TFO anymore."

His eyes widen. "I'll order you the shoelaces tomorrow."

"Good idea. Now get your ass in my bed, and if you're not naked in the next thirty seconds, I'll edge you so long you won't remember which one of us has a rap sheet."

Smiling from ear to ear, he sasses back with an, "Aye-aye, Captain." Then he slips his other boot off, turns in the direction of my bedroom, and moves slower than a bride single-stepping down the aisle.

So Bratty Johnathan makes his debut appearance. Chuckling, I grab the loose end of my belt and yank it from the loops with a *thwick thwick thwick* that echoes in the silence of the loft. I hear him whisper a curse before double-timing it into my room, but he's too late. He chose the game. I'm more than happy to play it.

Ready or not, Darling, here I come.

Chapter Twenty-Seven

JOHN

I GLANCE up at my rearview mirror again and pull off the interstate. So far, so good. My destination is only thirty minutes away, but I've been driving around for two hours to make certain I don't have a tail. I was probably fine after the first hour, but there's no harm in being extra vigilant.

Shifting in my seat, I wince, but a grin quickly chases it away. For the last three weeks, we've been entrenched in all manner of Pirate business during the day. But at night—and sometimes in the mornings—James has been fucking me senseless. I've never been so sore or so happy in my whole damn life.

Every day his walls seem to get a little lower, his defenses a little thinner. He appears more relaxed when we're in the loft now, whereas before he was like a tense beast confined in a cage of his own making. I've even managed to drag the occasional bark of laughter from him. Each time, he looked just as surprised at his reaction as I was. And each time, he promptly affixed his signature scowl and pretended like it never happened, which then made *me* laugh.

He's sleeping more now, too. When I moved in with him, I noticed he rarely slept, preferring instead to read in the living room. But once we started having sex, he switched to reading in bed while I slept tucked into his side. After about a week and a half, I realized he was finally sleeping more hours in the night than he was reading. I was excited to think that maybe our great sex life and my company in bed was reversing his insomnia.

Then I learned that his problem isn't insomnia; it's nightmares.

James doesn't wake up from bad dreams like most people, though. He doesn't thrash or shout out or bolt upright in bed. He jerks himself awake—his eyes snap open, his breaths come fast and shallow, and his heart races like a jackrabbit—but he just lies there, sometimes for less than a minute, sometime more than five, as he tries to get everything to slow down.

The first time he had one with me, I woke up when his body jerked hard under me. That time, he got up right away, slipping out from beneath my arm. I didn't let him know I was awake, but I watched him grab his book and leave the room. I didn't fully understand what happened. Not until the next morning when I asked him about it, and he shrugged it off like it was no big deal. That's when I knew it was a *very* big deal.

He doesn't have them every night, but since that first one, every time I wake up and he's not next to me, I pad out to the living room. I don't say a word when I pull him out of his chair and lead him over to the couch. Once he's sitting, I stretch out and lay my head in his lap, offering him my silent support without forcing him to talk or change his coping mechanism. Then I drift back to sleep while he runs his fingers through my hair as he reads his book. It's not exactly the recommended therapy for dealing with nightmares like his and all the suppressed trauma that's causing them, but it seems to help him.

For now, I'm glad I can offer him some measure of comfort when he needs it most. I think it says a lot for how far we've come, and things are only going to get better with time.

Turning my focus back to the mission at hand, I check the mirror one last time. Satisfied I haven't been followed, I pull into an industrial park located north of Neverland. I park the car and walk over to where Matt Henderson is leaning against his black sedan. He's in his midforties, lanky with dirty-blond hair, a hawkish gaze, and an ever-present cigarette from his two-packs-a-day habit. He's been my SSA—Supervisory Special Agent—since I became a task force officer with the FBI. He's a bit of a hard ass, but he's a good man, and we get along well. I'm used to seeing him in a dark suit, but today, he's wearing casual clothes—jeans and a black lightweight hoodie—in case anyone does happen to see us together, it isn't obvious who he is.

"Matt," I say by way of greeting as we clap hands in a quick shake. "Good to see you."

"You too." He drops his cigarette butt to the ground and crushes it with the toe of his boot. "Sure you weren't followed?"

I quirk an unamused brow in his direction. "I'm not even dignifying that with an answer." His laughter has a slight wheezing quality to it thanks to the smoking. Then, unbelievably, he lights up a fresh one. "That shit's going to kill you, Henderson."

"Yeah, well, if I didn't smoke, I'd stroke out from the stress of this job and then I wouldn't be around to enjoy our clandestine meetings, so there's that."

"If meeting with me, clandestine or otherwise, is the best thing you have to look forward to, you might want to reevaluate some of your life choices." A sly grin curves my lips. "Not that I blame you, you're just a little old for me is all."

He slaps a hand over his heart. "Wow, that hurt a lot more than I thought it would. I can't believe you called me old."

Chuckling, I change the topic to business. It's nice to be out and not have to worry about being someone else for a while, but I shouldn't be gone longer than a few hours. "What's the status on Starkey? Have they backed off him now that Croc's happier?"

Henderson's eyes slide away from me as he takes a long drag on his cigarette. A chill crawls over me. "Matt, what is it? Did something happen to Starkey? For fuck's sake, tell me."

Matt comes off the car, his stance no longer lazy but agitated. "We don't know how he's doing. We don't have a contact in the prison anymore."

I narrow my gaze. "What do you mean? What happened to Fallon?"

Seth Fallon is another special agent. They sent him into the prison to work in the security office. He'd know about any scheduled visits via the required forms he was in charge of processing. He'd also have access to any security footage. Not that we'd be able to use any of it in court without cutting through a lot of fucking red tape, but he'd be able to see if any *un*authorized visits to Starkey happened. He didn't have the clearance to do much else than be our eyes and ears inside a prison run by a corrupt warden and guards.

Matt blows out a stream of white smoke and scratches his chest, the thing he does when he's anxious. "No one's heard from Fallon in over a week, John. He's MIA."

Oh fuck. Please fuck no. Seth is a great guy with an awful sense of humor and fantastic hair. He has a beautiful family. I've met his wife and three little girls. Girls who might grow up without their father thanks to Fred fucking Croc, the ringleader of this shitstorm circus.

"*Goddamn it!*"

Turning, I pound my fists on the hood of the car, then hang my head as I breathe slowly through my nose.

"I know," he says, his tone softer than normal. "Look, we've got guys searching for him. Let us worry about recovering Fallon." The word "recovering" makes my gut churn. That's not the kind of word you use for someone suspected of still being alive. "I mean it, kid. You can't afford to lose focus when you're in the belly of the beast. Can you still do the job, or do I need to pull you?"

I shake my head and push off the car, locking away the personal shit until I can unpack it at a much later date. After I put Croc behind bars for the rest of his life. "I'm good. What else you got?"

Matt reaches through the driver's side open window to grab a file. Handing it to me, he says gravely, "We got an anonymous tip yesterday. We need you to check it out: see if there's any truth to it."

I flip the file open and do a quick scan of the call transcript. By the time I get to the end, the air has been sucked out of my lungs. There's a reason the FBI is involved in this case, and it's not because of any new drug. If it was only about drugs, the DEA would still be handling it like they were in the beginning, long before I infiltrated the Pirates. No, the FBI got involved when we started suspecting there was more to Croc's operation than just drugs. Something that made the Fairy Dust look like child's play.

"Jesus," I grate out. "I was really hoping we were wrong."

"We still might be. We don't know if this is a good tip or a setup. Going in without concrete proof could fuck everything up and Croc would walk."

Henderson's right. I need to check this out, make sure the tip is solid before I do anything else. I can't even tell James. Not until I have concrete evidence and a plan to take Croc down. Because if what I suspect about Croc and Hook is true, then this is going to bring a lot of shit to a very ugly head. Before that happens, I want to make damn sure I can deliver the head of the monster from his nightmares on a silver fucking platter.

Taking a calming breath, I square my shoulders and meet my handler's steady gaze. "What do you need me to do?"

After thirty minutes of strategizing and hammering out a plan for some recon, I get ready to leave. I'm anxious to get back to Neverland so I can get started on this mission and report back to Henderson. "Thanks, Matt. I'll be in touch."

"Make sure that you are," he says, extending his hand. "Be careful out there, John. I want to nail this guy, but not at the expense of losing another one of our guys."

I swallow the painful reminder that we've already lost one and nod. A minute later, I'm back on the road and praying I'll find enough evidence to drive the final nail into Croc's coffin. But at the same time, I'm hoping like hell the anonymous tip is a bust, because that kind of nail is the one that will hurt the man I love the most.

Chapter Twenty-Eight

JOHN

I DROP the clip of my Glock 19 into my palm to check that it's loaded before pushing it back into place and tucking it into the waistband of my jeans at my lower back. Yesterday's meeting with Matt shot this operation into phase two, and today's meeting is about getting into Croc's good graces enough to lay eyes on what's really going on at that warehouse. And I have to do it without James.

Even if I thought it would be okay to tell him what I'm investigating, I still couldn't tell him what I'm doing. All of his I-don't-care-about-anyone bravado is a bunch of bullshit. All that guy *does* is care. And if he knew I planned on meeting with Croc alone at the place where all the heavy stuff happens, James would insist on going with me. But my way in is to pretend like I'm trying to split from Hook and the mundane work as a low-level drug pusher. My goal is to get the evidence we need on the first try to finally take Croc down and free James from his clutches once and for all. That means I have to get creative with the truth, for the good of the case.

Taking a deep breath, I walk out of my bedroom and

try to act as nonchalant as possible. I was less nervous integrating myself into a group of hardened criminals than I am lying to the man I love. Metallica's *S&M* album is blasting from the stereo, something I've learned he loves to listen to as he lifts weights. Because of course he prefers the versions of the heavy metal band's popular songs that are accompanied by the San Francisco Orchestra. As much as Hook plays up the role of uneducated gang boss in public, in private he's more cultured than I am. He has an entire wall of shelves in his room with enough books in different genres and subjects to start a small library program.

I head over to where he's hefting a lot of weight over his head on the incline bench press. His legs are splayed in a tempting invitation to kneel between them, and his mouthwatering torso is covered in a sheen of sweat as his muscles ripple with his movements.

"Hey, I'll be back later. Gotta step out for a while."

My heart skips a beat when he places the bar back on the rack and waits expectantly for me to kiss him goodbye. Which I do. I lean down, cup his bearded jaw in one hand and press my lips to his, reveling in his salty taste and the subtle way he leans into my kiss.

When it comes to sex, James is more than happy to initiate things and usually does. But he still isn't the first one to offer affection outside the bedroom. He's holding on to that last wall of his for dear life. I'll knock it down eventually. Until then, it makes my heart melt every time he accepts any tenderness from me.

Reluctantly, I pull away before all that adrenaline flowing through him switches focus from weightlifting to ass-fucking. It wouldn't be the first time one of our workouts turned into a sweaty sex fest. But I can't risk missing my appointment. Too much is at stake.

As I straighten, his sharp blue gaze follows me up. "Where you going?"

"Gotta meet Henderson." *Eventually.* "Should only be a couple of hours or so." Ignoring the stab in my heart from the lie, I smile and tack on, "Don't worry. I'll be back in plenty of time for us to watch a few episodes of *Diners, Drive-Ins and Dives*. I know you have a secret thing for Guy Fieri." I give him a wink and then cross the room to the back door.

But before I can make a clean getaway, I hear, "Johnathan."

His use of my full name flays me with another stab of guilt, because that's *his* version of affection, and it feels like I'm tarnishing it with my dishonesty. Fixing a relaxed expression on my face, I turn back. "Yeah?"

"Everything okay? You just met with Matt yesterday."

"Yep, it's all good. He just has some more things he wants to go over with me." The lie tastes bitter on my tongue, but I force a smile for his sake. "I'll be back soon."

I hold my breath as he studies me for several, eternal seconds. When he nods and resumes his presses, I exhale and leave the loft. Twenty minutes later I'm parking Starkey's bike in front of a warehouse in an abandoned shipyard on the far south end of the city. When I get to the front door of the warehouse on the property, two military looking motherfuckers with AK-47s stop me.

"Arms out," the taller guy says, training his weapon on me. The second guy pats me down, easily finding the gun at my back. But then, I wasn't trying to hide it.

Satisfied I'm unarmed, they lead me inside into a huge industrial, open space. With a discreet scan, I don't notice any cameras, but I wouldn't expect them in this part. That'd be like doing our job for us, recording all the illegal activity for us to use in court.

The left side of the room has rows of tables with girls in their underwear and bras divvying up the glittery Fairy Dust into one-ounce baggies while armed men keep an eye on them. The scene is one Matt warned me about—the girls are made to work in their underwear so they can't easily steal the drugs for themselves—but it still enrages me. At least the girls don't look abused or strung out. It's possible they're paid well enough to show up every day and keep their mouths shut, with a healthy dose of fear heaped on for what will happen if they don't.

The right side of the space is where the larger quantities—approximately one-pound packages, if I had to guess—are stacked and wrapped in cellophane on pallets. No wonder Croc is pushing Hook for a larger distribution. It'd take us years to sell this much at the local clubs and raves, even if we covered the entire eastern half of North Carolina. Croc needs big dogs like Tannen in major cities dealing this shit if he's going to move this amount of product.

Acting totally unfazed, I keep pace with the goons on either side of me as we approach another double-guarded entrance at the back of the warehouse space. My escorts lead me through the steel door into what appears to be the administrative area of the building—or at least it was when the shipyard was operational. For as loud as the area up front is, the back is almost eerily silent. There's no one roaming around or guarding any of the rooms we pass as we wander through the maze of hallways on our way to wherever Croc is.

"You guys on the boss's permanent payroll, or are you one of those ex-mil third-party mercenary type groups?"

Without turning his head, the guy who almost got a little too personal with my junk earlier says, "If you were supposed to know that, you would."

"Can't argue with that," I say with a low chuckle, playing into my character's give-no-fucks attitude.

We arrive at one of the farthest rooms at the end of a hall, and I can't help but notice there's no camera covering the door and no keypad for a coded entry. Either Croc got lazy when he set up an office at this location, or he foolishly thinks that all the guard dogs he has stationed at the different entrances is more than enough security. One of the guards knocks on the door, then lets us in.

The room is fairly large, maybe twenty-feet-square, but the only piece of furniture in the whole place is a large metal utility desk where Croc is sitting with a money-counting machine and stacks of bills covering the entire surface. If he was a cartoon character right now, he'd be Scrooge McDuck, gleefully swimming in a silo of his own money.

"JD, it's good to see you." The smarmy grin on his face tells me he's not lying. Whether it's sheer curiosity or he's legitimately glad I called, I'm not sure.

"Appreciate you seeing me on such short notice."

"Nonsense. I'm always happy to discuss business with my employees. That is what you want to discuss, isn't it? Business?"

"That's right. More specifically, my role in yours. But I'd rather not speak in front of Thing 1 and Thing 2," I say, tipping my head toward his guard dogs.

Croc laughs and slaps his hands on the only open space on his desk in front of him. "I like you, McRae."

When he nods at his goons to leave, I hold out my hand and add, "But I'd like my piece back first." The men stop, and the one holding my gun snorts. I arch a brow at Croc. "Come on. If I wanted you dead, I sure as fuck wouldn't do it in a place crawling with Rambo wannabes."

Croc flicks his hand, and the guy reluctantly returns

my 9 mil before leaving the office. As soon as I feel the metal tucked against the small of my back, I breathe a little easier. Not that I'd stand a chance against the firepower under Croc's command, but after carrying a sidearm for so many years, I feel like I'm missing a limb without it.

Steepling his hands over his protruding gut, my mark studies me carefully. "Now, why don't you have a seat and tell me what I can do for you."

The man's clever, choosing words to lower my defenses, as though I'm the one with the power and he's just here to help me. Like he gives two shits about me or what I want. He's only interested in what it is that *I* can do for *him*. Which is exactly how I'm playing this.

"It's what I can do for you. Running the Dust is a decent gig and all, but it's not really my thing. Hook and the other guys seem content with the party perks that come along with selling in the clubs. I'm just used to a more...*serious* job, if you know what I mean."

He makes a low sound of understanding. "Like the kind you used to do in the Scavengers?"

"That'd be great, for sure. I enjoyed being one of Dante's enforcers, and I was damn good at my job." Dante Ellis was the head of the Scavengers until the gang was brought down last year. Now he's serving eighty to life in a maximum-security prison, so I'm relatively safe throwing his name around. "But Dante had plans to expand into a new business—plans only a few of us knew about—and I thought maybe someone with good business sense, like yourself, would be interested to know what it was. Because the money potential is ten times what you're doing with the Fairy Dust."

"And what was Dante so interested in?" he asks, narrowing his eyes slightly.

I stare him dead in the eyes. "Girls."

His eyebrows wing up his forehead before he catches himself. His expression smooths out and melts into one of smug pride, even as he keeps his cards close to the vest. "What about girls, exactly?"

"You know," I say, letting a wicked grin curve my lips. "Acquiring the ones who won't be missed but still have teeth in their head and keeping them in a place where they can offer specific services to a certain clientele willing to pay top dollar for an hour or two of the girls' time."

Croc rises and walks around his desk to stand in front of me. Crossing his arms, he leans back on the edge. "What does Hook think about that?"

I snort. "I didn't say anything about this to Hook or any of his crew. No offense to your top guy or anything, but I don't think he's got the stomach to run much more than drugs." Putting my hands up, I add, "No disrespect—all the Pirates are good at moving Dust—but dealing in girls is a whole different animal. I was set to head up Dante's operation before he got pinched. Now I'd like to do the same for you and make us a shit ton of money."

"I like the way you think, JD. Come on, I have something to show you."

Chapter Twenty-Nine

JOHN

OUTWARDLY, I'm calm and unaffected as I follow Croc out of the office, through several hallways, and up a back set of stairs to a second level. But on the inside, I'm cautious, wary, and nervous. Hearing about possible scenarios in a briefing is nothing like staring at the reality. I haven't even seen anything yet, and I already feel the difference.

The second floor is only a third of the size as the rest of the building with a single hallway flanked by four doors on each side. But instead of the typical wooden office doors downstairs, these are thick metal ones with small windows. Croc leads me to the first door on the right and gestures for me to peer inside, so I do.

Shock, rage, guilt, more rage…all of it slams into me as I stare at a girl with matted blonde hair lying on a mattress that sits on the dirty floor wearing nothing but her bra and underwear. The rest of her body is covered in glitter. She's alive—thankfully her chest is rising with her breaths—but she's listless with dilated pupils and a blank stare.

I whistle like I'm impressed, like I'm not holding myself

back from putting my fist through his wretched fucking face. "Are all these rooms occupied?"

"Yep. I have a whole stable of girls. This is my first batch, but I plan to have a steady rotation. In a couple of weeks, I'm transporting them by ship to my contact in Brazil. Then I'll get a new batch of girls, make money on them for about a month while they're here, and get even more money once I sell them to my associate. Rinse and repeat," he ends with an evil chuckle.

I smile wide. "Damn, Croc. Here I thought I was bringing something valuable to the table and you're already way ahead of me. Don't I feel like an asshole."

He claps me on the shoulder and squeezes. His touch makes me sick, and it takes all my control not to shake free of his grip. "Nah. Just proves you're exactly the kind of guy I'm looking for to run this. You're right, Hook's too much of a pussy for this sort of thing."

Pretending I want to check out the rest of the merchandise, I walk down the hall so I don't lose my shit and choke him out just for insulting James. "Where do you get them? From the clubbers buying the Dust?"

"That was the original idea, but it's too risky. The boys took a couple of them before I changed protocol to girls who don't have anyone to report them missing. Hookers and runaways, mostly. The Fairy Dust is a good side hustle and a distraction for law enforcement to draw their focus from the real moneymaker."

"Fucking smart." I'm hating myself a little more with every compliment I give this demented asshole. Every room I pass has another girl in it, just like he said. That one is crying softly…the next one is pacing and talking to herself or to someone who can't hear her…the one after that is covered in bruises and rocking in the corner… Christ, I feel sick to my stomach. I want to knock Croc unconscious and find a way to get every single one of them out of here.

But I can't. No matter how badly I want to save them, I can't. Not yet. Not like this. But so help me God, I will. Soon. I need to go back to my team with what I've found so we can get all the proper clearance to plan a bust and arrest him for his myriad of crimes. Putting him behind bars for life is the only way I free James and Starkey for good and prevent Croc from selling girls into sexual slavery.

Too deep in my musings, I don't realize I've stopped at the last door until Croc speaks. "She's a sweet piece of ass, huh?"

Mentally chastising myself for getting distracted for even the briefest of moments in this man's presence, I play the part of leering asshole and look in on the girl. She is beautiful, or she would be if she didn't look so gaunt and sad sitting in the corner and staring at the wall. Her raven hair hangs limp around her shoulders, and her cheeks are sunken in, making the angles of her face and jaw appear sharper than they should be. Like the other girls, she's stripped down to her underwear and covered in glitter.

"Definitely the hottest out of the ones I've seen so far," I manage to say with lust lacing my words. As though she hears me, she turns her head and locks her pale green eyes onto me through the window. Unnerved, I tear my attention from her and set it on Croc. "What's with the glitter? You got them all on Dust or something?"

He shrugs. "It makes them more enthusiastic about their jobs, but we only give it to them during business hours. Daytime is when I run the drug side of things; then at night, I clear everyone downstairs out of the building and open the second-floor business. The men who know about my live merchandise enter through a separate entrance in the back of the building. Payment is handled downstairs, then they're allowed up to make their choice of companion. There's a guard who stays up here to let the clients in and out of the rooms and to make sure they don't get out of hand."

"Sounds like you've thought of everything. I'm impressed."

"You should be. Care to take her for a test drive?" he asks, nodding to the brunette.

My stomach turns at the idea of taking advantage of her even for the purpose of keeping up pretenses. But if he's going to leave me inside the room to do my thing with her, I can get photographic evidence before I hightail it out of here.

"How much?"

"Free of charge this time. Let's call it a sign-on bonus."

Giving him a wicked grin, I say, "That's awfully fucking generous of you, boss, thanks."

Using a set of keys he takes out from his pocket, Croc unlocks the door and walks over to her. Before I can see what he's doing, he's dipped her thumb into a baggie of Fairy Dust and smeared it on her arm.

"That'll perk her right up. She's all yours," he says, standing up and sweeping his arm in her direction like he's Vanna White showcasing my prize.

Shit. I hate that he drugged her again, but there's nothing I can do now except maybe stay with her until she comes down from it to make sure she doesn't have a bad reaction to this dose. I saunter past him, my gait easy and unhurried. I don't hear him leave or close the door, but I wouldn't care about that as a lawless, immoral man who's about to sink inside of a woman—willing or not—so I keep my focus on her.

Beauty, as I've come to think of her, tilts her head and

watches me with deadened eyes and a faraway stare. She's not scared or upset, not crying or pleading with me to stay away. No, she's resigned, and that's so much worse. She's given up. Given up hope that she'll be rescued, that she'll be back with her loved ones, that she'll ever have autonomy over her body and actions again. I want to destroy the man responsible for the defeat I see in her green gaze and for the destruction he's wreaked on so many innocent souls, including James and all the Lost Boys years ago.

Then it happens. The drug starts to take hold, and her demeanor changes drastically. Her green eyes are now glassy as she drags her hands over her body and into her hair like she can't get enough of touching and being touched. But even though she's in an altered state that makes her restless and aching with manufactured desire, she stares at me with wariness and fear for what comes next, and it kills me.

For the first time in my life, I'm not viewed as the savior. Usually I'm the one coming in to put the bad guy in his place and rescue the victim. I've had people look at me with relief, gratitude, and even begrudging acceptance. But I've never had anyone watch me like I'm a hungry wolf advancing on my prey. I hate that the man behind me has put me in this position, that he's made me a predator in the eyes of this woman. I hate everything about this moment.

I wrack my brain for a way out of this. The only plan I can think of is to make my intentions convincing enough that Croc leaves me to it. Bringing her up to her feet, I press her against the wall and bury my face in her neck. I hear the faintest whimper escape her lips, and hope surges through me. She's not completely gone. There's still a part of her left to save. And with time and care, maybe the rest of her can be brought back, too.

Being careful to be quiet enough so only she hears me, I speak directly in her ear. “Shhhh, it’s okay, sweetheart. I’m not going to hurt you, I promise.”

Taking a step back, I start to undo my belt, then look over and act as if I’m just now realizing Croc is still in the room. “You get off on watching or something?”

“Maybe,” he says with a devilish smirk. “Or maybe I just want to make sure you’re the real deal. No room for soft hearts or soft dicks on my crew, JD.”

“Ain’t nothin’ soft about me, Croc.”

All traces of amusement fall away as he glares at me in challenge. “Prove it.”

Chapter Thirty

HOOK

I KNEW John was lying before he ever stepped foot outside the loft; I just didn't know why. I still don't. I only know *where* he went. Instead of the meeting with his handler like he claimed, I knew that John went to the warehouse, courtesy of the GPS tracker on his "JD" phone. I can track every one of my Pirates. I don't have to do it often, but I've had to check up on all of them at one point or another.

Funny enough, I didn't think I'd ever need to use it with John.

It fucking stung when he lied to me, but I don't know why I was so damn surprised. I've never been able to trust anyone. It was only a matter of time before he let me down, too.

As soon as he left, I choked back the bile of his betrayal and decided to find out what the hell he was up to. I took a two-minute shower, threw some clothes on, and sped after him on my bike. Ten minutes into the ride, his location stopped moving. At Croc's warehouse.

I parked on the far side of the building where Croc wouldn't see my bike, then strolled in with a friendly nod at the guards like I do any other day I conduct business here. I have clearance to come and go as I please, and the armed goons are used to seeing me on a semi-regular basis now that we've been picking up larger quantities of Dust from the warehouse as opposed to the shop.

Since I didn't see John in the front anywhere, I figured he must be in Croc's office. Acting as though I had a routine meeting with the boss, I approached the two guys standing guard at the door that leads to the administrative area in the back. I turned on my fake charm, greeted them by name, and bumped their fists. I'd made it a point to befriend the men of the security group Croc hired from the very beginning. Guys who are *cool* with each other, don't *suspect* each other. I knew I'd need their blind trust eventually.

After a minute of bullshitting and laughing at a dirty joke, they let me pass without a second thought, assuming I had business with the boss. I made my way through the empty maze of halls until I reached the rooms in the far back of the building. I could hear John's voice coming from the other side of Croc's closed door, so I hid in one of the adjacent rooms and waited with the door cracked. It wasn't long before they exited, and I watched Croc lead John in the opposite direction.

That was several minutes ago, and they still haven't come back, so what the hell are they up to? The only things in that direction are a back exit and a staircase leading up to the second floor. They didn't leave because John's location is practically on top of me, which means they're upstairs. I don't know what's up there—I never knew Croc used that space for anything—but I'm done waiting. I have a bad fucking feeling in my gut, and I need to confront John about what the hell he's doing.

Making a decision, I dial the only person walking free I can depend on.

"Go for Smee," the cheeky bastard says with a grin you can hear through the phone.

"I need you to call Croc and tell him someone smashed up the shop. Tell him it looks like someone was trying to get in, possibly a rival club."

Smee's tone is dead serious now. "He'll come running to see the damage for sure. Are ye sayin' what I think ye're sayin', Captain?"

"Trash the place. Make it look good and stay away from the cameras. But make the call *now.*"

"Aye, Captain. Consider it done."

It's not even a minute later when Croc is stalking in my direction. He makes a quick stop in his office then rushes back down the hall, looking like he's ready to spit nails. As soon as I know I'm in the clear, I make my move and head for the staircase. When I reach the top of the landing, I hear John's voice coming from an open room at the end of the hall.

"Come on, sweetheart, lay down on the bed."

His deep voice is indulgent and cajoling, the way you'd coax a lover into your arms. Blood rushes in my ears as my boots thud on the concrete floor down the corridor. When I round the corner, I see red. John's back is to the far wall and there's a mostly naked woman is climbing him like a goddamn tree, her arms locked behind his broad shoulders and her legs wrapped around his waist where his dark jeans gape open from the weight of his undone belt.

"*What in the fucking hell is going on?*" I snarl.

John's head snaps up. For a split second, a mix of shock, guilt, and panic flashes across his face. But then he sags in relief, like he's happy to see me. When I've caught him with his pants down. Almost quite literally.

"Help get her off of me. She's like a damn spider monkey."

"You should've thought about that before offering your dick for her to—" The girl looks back over her shoulder at me, and the bitter retort dies on my lips. "Brandy?"

Her green eyes are glassy, her black hair limp and tangled, and her soft curves have been replaced by sharp angles. But it's her. The last girl I sold Fairy Dust to at the Quarry. She looks strung out, reminding me even more of my mother than before. I don't realize I've started walking toward them until she physically recoils with a whimper and redoubles her effort to merge her body with John's.

"Shhh, it's okay, come on," John coos softly, stroking her bare back and down her knotted hair. "He's not here to hurt you, either, I promise." When she calms down in his arms again, he locks eyes with me. "You know her?"

I shake my head but then stop myself and nod. "I sold her some Dust the night your guys picked me up. Why the fuck is she here, man?"

He doesn't say anything, not with his mouth. But there's a message in his eyes I'm not decoding. It's like I can see all the puzzle pieces of what he's trying to tell me, but they're upside down and I don't know which pieces go where in order to solve it.

Yes, you do. You just don't want to look at it.

Clenching my fists to stop their slight trembling, I ease my way to where John's still trying to comfort the girl.

"Brandy, do you remember me?" She picks up her head from his shoulder and stares at me as though I'm not here. To John, I ask sharply, "Is she rolling?"

"Croc swiped it on before he left me with her. I don't know how long he'll be gone. You need to get out of here."

"He'll be busy for a while," I say. Then I get an idea. Taking off my skull ring, I hold it up for her to see.

"Brandy, remember this? You said you loved it that night at the club." A hint of recognition lights in her gaze. She reaches for it, but I pull it back. "I'll give it to you if you get off of JD."

She doesn't move for several seconds, but then she finally lowers her legs and scrambles down to the thread-bare mattress. As John zips up his pants, he opens his mouth to say something, but I stop him. "Not now," I grate. "We gotta get her out of here."

I turn, ready to scoop her up and carry her out the back to my bike. I'll give her my shirt and—

John's hand grabs my bicep. "We can't. Not yet."

Shaking out of his grip, I get right in his face. "What do you mean, we *can't*? I'll tell you what we can't do; we can't fucking *leave* her here."

"I'm sorry, Hook, but we have to." He's keeping his voice soft, but his tone is anything but. This isn't Johnathan who kneels at my feet and calls me Captain. This is task force officer John Darling, a man running point in a federal investigation to take down a dangerous criminal. He might bend to my will inside the walls of my loft, but out here, he's in charge, and I have a feeling he'll knock me unconscious to drag me home and ask for forgiveness later if I don't go along with his plan.

"John…" I shake my head, unable to voice the chaos banging around in my mind right now.

"We're going to save her." He palms the back of my neck with one big hand and presses his forehead to mine. "I *promise* you, we will."

I'm still pissed at him for lying and meeting with Croc about fuck knows what and putting himself in danger, but I know his heart and John isn't making idol promises. He won't rest until we rescue her from this place. I nod stiffly, then break away from him to crouch down to where

Brandy is curled onto her side. Her body is restless from the Dust rolling through her system, and I wonder how much of the drug she's been given since I last saw her. Almost every inch of her exposed skin is streaked with glitter.

"Jesus," I rasp. "She's covered in the shit."

"They all are." John's words are spoken softly, carefully. In saying so little, he's told me so fucking much. He's flipped those puzzle pieces over, forcing me to look at the picture I didn't want to see.

Girls. Croc is dealing in *girls*. I didn't pay attention as I passed the rooms on this floor a few minutes ago, but I now know that every one of them has a different version of Brandy in it. Alone. Naked. Drugged. *Raped.*

Rage, indignation, and weaker things I don't want to feel prick the backs of my eyes and constrict around my neck like a giant python cutting off my air. I blink hard a few times and clear my throat as I look down at the skull ring in my hand. The badass piece of jewelry that for over a decade has been the symbol of my mission to end Croc and his entire operation.

Now it will be a symbol of my promise to Brandy.

Placing the ring in her palm, I curl her fingers around the warm metal and hold her gaze, willing her to see the conviction in my eyes. "I have to go right now, but I'll be back. I'm gonna get you out of here, Brandy, I fucking swear. You hold on to this for me until I do, okay?"

Tearful green eyes gaze up at me, and her chin quivers. "I'm scared," she whispers.

God-fucking-damnit. Apparently it's possible for my black heart to break after all. I swallow the lump in my throat and ignore the way my hand shakes as I brush the hair off her face and gently tuck it behind her ear. "I know you are." *Fuck, do I know.* "But every time you get scared or feel like there's no hope, I want you to squeeze this in your hand and remember that I'm coming back for you. Can you do that for me?"

She nods, and it'll have to be enough because I have to get out of here before I lose my goddamn mind. Pushing to my feet, I turn on my heel and hightail it out of that room. I keep my head down in the hallway, and I don't stop. Not when I hear John close Brandy's door, locking her back into her own personal hell. Not when his boots eat up the space behind me as he follows me down the back stairwell. Not even when he calls my name as I take off on my bike and try to outrun my demons.

Chapter Thirty-One

HOOK

Then

Age 17

OUT-OF-BODY EXPERIENCES. Some people don't believe in them. They don't believe the mind can leave the body behind and look on as though you're another person casually observing the scene, or place itself somewhere else entirely.

They're wrong. I do it all the time. Every time Croc's hands touch me, grip me, manipulate me. My body clicks over to autopilot, and my brain goes into triage mode.

Most of the time, it transports me to the beach at the height of a new moon, when the water is just as inky as the night sky. That's when I like it best; when the world is a black void of nothingness, a giant blank slate, and the only signs of life are the sound of the waves crashing in my ears, the salt spray coating my lips, and the ocean breeze ruffling my hair.

Other times, I force myself to watch from across the room. I tilt my head and focus on random details with a cool detachment. The greasy hair that flops against his forehead with every thrust. The dirt caked under his nails that leave marks on my skin whenever he flexes his meaty fingers. The way he grits his teeth with exertion behind the sadistic smile of a wolf toying with his meal. I watch, I memorize, and then I renew my vow that one day I will have my revenge.

And then there are the rare times. Times like now, when I actually fight back. When I *don't* hold still, and I *don't* make it easy, and I *don't* keep my goddamn mouth shut. I know the outcome will still be the same—not because I'm too weak to win, but because I have no other choice than to lose—but every once in a while, I need to fight and gain that single *shred* of my dignity back, before losing it again the next time I comply.

But today, I have another reason for fighting back, one much bigger than regaining my dignity. There can be no mental trips to the beach at night, no detached observation. Right now I have to be present and in the moment, no matter what happens.

I keep that thought in the front of my mind as I twist my body up from where it was shoved over a dirt-covered desk (there's always a fucking desk) a few seconds ago. I keep it in mind when he hammer-fists me in the face to knock me back down and the explosion on my cheekbone radiates through my head with such force it feels like the top of my scalp blows open.

When he braces a thick forearm across my shoulders and leans his weight into me, I clench my jaw and remember my vow for revenge. When he captures my flailing arms and pins them against my lower back so hard I feel the bones in my wrists bend, I tuck that vow into a deep, dark place no one will ever find it.

And when my body jerks in time with his thrusts, in time with the ticking of that fucking watch as though he's a fucking musician keeping time with a fucking metronome, I feed that vow every drop of my hate, every ounce of my pain, and every wince of my shame. Then I watch it grow and grow and grow, until it's every bit the vile monster he is.

I growl like a rabid animal caught in a trap as he laughs in my ear between his grunts. "You're full of piss and vinegar today, aren't ya, boy?"

The swelling in my cheek has reached my right eye already, so I can't see him hovering over me. Thank Christ for small favors. "Fuck. You. You. Piece. Of. Shit."

I thought he'd appreciate me spitting out my words in time with everything else. But the quick right hook to my teeth indicates otherwise. I almost laugh as the copper tang of blood fills my mouth and spills out the corner of my lips, but I'm still aware enough of what I'm doing to control my reactions. *Stick to the plan. Control the situation.*

"Hope you enjoyed the last four years of forcing your dick in me, old man," I manage to choke out, blood spattering the desk when I speak. "I'm almost outta here; then your fun will be over."

"Nah. Your ass isn't the only one in town, James. I'll just get some nice, fresh meat. You're getting too old for my tastes, anyway."

Over my dead fucking body, asshole.

Again, I want to lash out, to use the strength I've worked hard for, and overthrow him, to pummel his face until not even the demon who spawned him can recognize him. Even my mind fights against my hold. It wants to leave, to go somewhere else until it's safe to return.

But I can't do any of that. I have to stay the course; I have to ride this out. And that means doing just enough to keep Croc pissed and on his toes, so that's what I do.

Too busy doing a half-ass job of struggling, I don't notice the door behind us opening until the last voice I want to hear right now shouts, "Hook!"

Before I can tell Pan to get the fuck out of here, the *thunk* sound of something heavy hitting something solid rings out. A second later, Croc falls away from me and slumps onto the concrete floor, his pants and underwear still bunched around his thighs with his ugly dick dragging a line through the filth as it deflates like a grotesque retreating snake.

Pan stares down at the bastard, his eyes wide and filled with confusion. I use his distracted state to put myself—and my clothes—back in order. There's no fixing my busted face right now, so I just drag my sleeve across my mouth to sop up the excess blood. That's when I realize there's a fire extinguisher in Peter's hand, and it dawns on me what he did. I swing my gaze back to Croc, hoping for a miracle… Nope. Still breathing. I guess an accidental death was too much to ask of the universe.

"What the hell, Hook?" Pan says, finally darting his gaze back and forth between me and Croc. Jealousy stabs me in the gut at the glaring innocence he still has at almost sixteen. Even though I'm the one who afforded him that luxury, it doesn't make me resent him any less for it.

"Why—" he tries again and then stops.

I see the exact moment it clicks. The moment he realizes that what he does with Wendy can be done other ways, and that it doesn't have to be consensual. The moment he realizes that my "training" hasn't been about learning the business after all. He actually turns five shades of green as his brain clicks through all the revelations, which I'm willing to allow. But the second he drops the extinguisher and looks like he's going to be sick, I pounce.

Jacking him up by his shirt, I slam him against the wall. "Don't you fucking puke, Pan. You keep that shit locked down, you understand? Lock. It. Down."

"Yeah." He nods and swallows hard. "Okay, but—"

"But nothing. You forget what you saw and get the hell out of here. You breathe a word of this to anyone—*ever*—and I'll fucking kill you."

His blue eyes go soft as his brows knit together. "Dude, I would never do that. Like it or not, we're family. Why do you think I crushed Croc's skull? He was hurting you somehow—that much I knew—and I couldn't let him do that." He shakes his head and steels his jaw. "I never would've let him do that. I'm sorry, Hook. I didn't know."

"You weren't supposed to," I say as I release him and push away.

Pan shoves a hand through his hair and looks down at Croc again. "You've been protecting us from this—from him—the whole time, haven't you?"

Great. The last thing I need is for him to place me on a pedestal I don't want to be on. "I didn't do shit, Pan. Don't go thinking I'm one of the heroes in your stupid fairytales, because that's not what real life is. I don't know how his demented mind works, and I don't fucking care, all right?"

"Yeah, all right." He blows out a breath. "Shit, he's gonna kill us for this one."

"He's not gonna do a damn thing."

Pan shoots me an incredulous look. "You think the guy who beats us for fun is going to let me get away with denting his skull?"

"I got it under control. He won't lay a finger on either

of us. Just get the fuck out of here already and forget this ever happened." When he hesitates as though unsure about leaving me alone with the guy who was violating me five minutes ago, I point to the door. "*Go!*"

Finally, he listens. As soon as he closes the door behind him, I step over Croc and retrieve the small video recorder from the shelf across from the desk. I stop the recording, check to make sure it captured what I need, then take my first full breath since walking into this storeroom earlier. My insurance policy is intact.

As much as I hate it, when it comes to my revenge, I have to play the long game with Croc. If I take him down now, the school will go under, and the kids will be split up. I won't know where they are or what kind of homes they end up in. I won't know what happens to Starkey. I need to keep the kids together at the school until they're all out while keeping Croc in check at the same time.

Sometimes the devil you know is better than the one you don't. So now that I'm about to move out, I need a way of controlling the situation at the school—one that doesn't involve him fucking me—and I could only think of one way to do it. By blackmailing the bastard.

It's not the greatest leverage, but it's all I've got, and so far, everything's gone according to plan—not including Pan showing up. Earlier, I'd planted the video camera. Then, when I knew Croc's eyes were on me, I pretended not to see him as I shook out a cigarette from my soft pack and slipped into this storeroom in the back corner of the shop. I've been punished for taking a smoke break in here before, which is how I knew he'd be on the warpath as soon as he saw me.

After that, it was just a matter of putting on a good performance. Instead of mentally checking out and being physically complacent, I made sure he looked like the rapist he is. As a bonus, I got him on tape admitting this wasn't a one-off; that he'd been at this for four years already and planned to continue with younger kids.

Since I don't have any smelling salts on hand, I go with the slightly more barbaric tactic of kicking Croc in the ribs to wake him up. He comes to, wheezing and curling in on himself.

"Wakey, wakey, asshole. It's showtime." I light another cigarette as he attempts to drag air into his lungs.

"I'm gonna make you wish you were never born," he rasps.

Blowing out a stream of smoke, I grin and stare down at him with my one good eye. "Too late. My mom already beat you to it." I crouch down next to him, hold up the camera, and hit play. I block out the sounds coming from the tiny speaker, unwilling to relive even a second of it, and instead I watch with satisfaction as his eyes grow wider with every passing second.

"Here's how this is going to work," I tell him. "We're gonna become business associates, you and me. We can call it entering into a mutually beneficial arrangement."

He growls and makes a grab for the camera, but I yank it away in plenty of time. "Nice try, but that concussion you probably have is making you slow as shit, so you're better off just listening."

"What do you want, you little prick?"

Now that I have his undivided attention, I give him my conditions. I tell him I'll work for him at his shop and otherwise, doing whatever he wants. I promise not to release the video as long as he lets me run my own crew and he doesn't lay a hand on another kid for as long as he fucking lives. He grudgingly agrees, even as he glares at me like he hopes I drop dead, but neither of us have that much luck. At least this time I'm not the one left behind to lick my wounds. It's his turn for a fucking change.

Just as I turn to leave, something metallic catches my eye. It's on the ground under the edge of a shelving unit. Ignoring Croc's groans behind me, I pick it up and study it. It's a pewter ring in the shape of a wicked-looking skull. *Finders keepers.* Taking it with me, I slide it onto my right thumb and smirk. It fits me perfectly and looks just as badass as I feel walking out of the shop. Heading back to the school, power surges through me. I finally won. I bested Croc at his own game, and now I won't have to worry about him turning his sick shit on one of the other kids after I'm gone.

But the farther away I get from my place of victory, the sense of power starts to dissipate as the usual ones settle over me. Disgust, shame, humiliation. Their weight is suffocating. And now it's worse because there was a witness. Someone knows. *Fucking Pan.*

Back in our room, I don't acknowledge anyone on my way to the bathroom, not even Smee or Starkey. I lock the door behind me, then strip out of my clothes on the way to the shower area, not caring where they land or if they spontaneously catch on fire. Turning the temperature knob in the corner as hot as it will go, I sink to the floor and pull my knees to my chest. I release a shuddering exhale as the scalding water sluices over my body. I imagine it burning away any flesh tainted by Croc, giving way to new skin that will never know his touch.

I don't even realize I've moved my hand until I see the blood running down the tile as I scrape the edge of my thumb on the grout. I don't know why I do this. It's become a compulsion, something I can't stop myself from doing after one of my "sessions." Maybe it's the idea that I can focus the pain to one specific point, then watch it leak from my body in watery red rivulets until I go back to feeling numb. Maybe I like the idea of wearing a hole in this grout, making it bigger and more pronounced to match the hole eating away at what's left of me.

My gaze drops to the ring sitting at the base of my thumb. Sunken black eyes stare back at me over its triangular nasal cavity and toothy smile. Its expression is menacing, like it's promising pain to anyone who dares cross it. *Don't fuck with me. You'll regret it.*

That's exactly how I'm going to be from now on. I won't let this hole inside of me take everything. I'll make sure there's just enough to finish the job I started, to make good on my vow for revenge. It won't happen tomorrow, or next year, or even in the next several years, but it *will* fucking happen.

In the meantime, I'll do what Croc expects of me. I'll work for him; I'll break the law for him. I'll become everything he wants me to be—a criminal with no moral code, a man who forgets his past and doesn't plan his future. Then, when he least expects it, *I will turn on him.* I'll bite the hand that feeds me with the ferocity of every dark memory and every gash he ever sliced into my soul. Croc's fate is sealed. One way or another…

I. Will. End. Him.

Chapter Thirty-Two

HOOK

Now

FORTY-FIVE MINUTES LATER, I'm pulling off Highway 421 and winding my way past the Fort Fisher Monument to the frontage road for the small stretch of Kune Beach I've been to at least a hundred times before. I slow my speed as the sand covers more of the pavement the farther I go. When I run out of road, I abandon my bike and take long strides to reach where the foamy surf curls over packed earth.

Though I'm not surprised I ended up here, I didn't have a destination in mind when I sped out of the shipyard. All I knew was that I wasn't going back to the Jolly Roger. Even if I managed to avoid the guys in my crew, returning to the loft was out of the question. It didn't matter if John was physically there or not, he'd invaded every square inch of my home. The fridge is stocked with his boring health food, his workout equipment is stashed all over the weight room, his toiletries litter the bathroom, and the entire place smells like him.

Including my goddamn bed.

I told him it was easier just to let him sleep with me so all I had to do was roll over whenever I got the urge to fuck him, but we both knew it was more than that. I'd gone soft where he was concerned. Somewhere along the line I'd let myself start thinking of us as an actual *couple*. Just two normal guys sharing a home, meals, workouts, and a bed. No big deal, right?

Wrong. It's a huge fucking deal.

Because while John might be a normal guy, I'm the exact opposite. That scene back at the warehouse proved it. It was a dose of reality that ripped through my normal-guy-facade like a bullet at point-blank range. The moment I placed my ring in Brandy's hand and knew I had to walk away from her—away from *all* of them—I left that self-made delusion on the floor to bleed out. There's no point in keeping up with a lie like that. It can only last so long before it burns away to expose the truth.

Despite the long drive, my body is still vibrating with the rage and anguish of what happened at the warehouse. If I have any chance of getting my shit under control, it's on this desolate stretch of beach. During the day it's teeming with tourists and locals, but at night it's empty. Far enough removed from the rest of my life, it's the one place I feel any sort of peace.

But I don't think I'm going to find any solace tonight. Not here, not anywhere. I'm too fucking consumed by *everything*. Rage. Anguish. Regret. Shame. It's all swirling inside me like a hurricane of pain and it's picking up speed, gaining more power with every memory from those four years, every reminder of what I am.

Broken. Damaged. Tainted. Debased.

Reaching the edge of the water, I throw my head back and roar at the slivered moon. I roar at whatever is casually deciding the fates of women and children who aren't able to fight back. Who have done nothing to deserve such wretched, tragic chapters in their life stories and have no way of rewriting those tattered pages written with the stains on their souls.

The salty breeze whips my screams away before they get anywhere near the heavens. There's to be no cathartic railing at the gods. I'm denied even that small retaliation.

"James."

It comes from several feet behind me, and every muscle in my body clamps on my bones like one huge vise. The last time he called me by my name—the night on the beach after Pan proposed to Wendy—triggered nasty flashbacks. I threw him against a wall and almost choked him out until his scent snapped me out of it and I realized he wasn't Croc.

This time, I don't have to smell John to know he's not my nightmare. The deep baritone of his voice is imprinted in my brain. I know it as intimately as I know every inch of his body. But it doesn't matter. I still don't want to hear that name. It's wrapped up in too much hatred and resentment. I ceased being James the first time it was uttered from the shuddering lips of a monster taking his pleasure from my pain.

"I told you to never fucking call me that," I growl, staring out at the inky water.

I feel him step closer. "Why? Why do you hate your name so much?"

Clenching my fists, I spin around and glare at him. I hate how fucking beautiful he is right now. The wind moves through his hair like a lover's fingers, the barely-there moonlight highlights the hard set of his stubbled jaw, and his leather jacket pulls tight across strong shoulders. Ones that look solid enough to hold the weight of my world without strain.

It's so tempting. The thought of unburdening myself, of feeling this crushing pressure lift so I can finally breathe is almost more than I can bear. But nothing could be more selfish. Because unloading that weight means putting it on the man who, against all odds, I've come to care for, and that's not something I can ever take back. Once it's out there, it's out for good. And I can't—I *won't*—do that to him. Not to Johnathan.

Gathering all my strength, I do what I do best. Deflect. "Here's a better question. How the hell did you find me? No one knows I come here. It's the only place I've ever had to myself. It's like you take perverse pleasure in invading every aspect of my life."

He sighs, the frustration in my subject change evident. "I was worried about you, okay? And you're not the only one tracking people. I stuck one on your bike and car as soon as the operation started."

"That's bullshit, Darling. You had no right to do that without my permission. And speaking of bullshit," I snarl, "you *lied to me*. You looked me dead in the eyes and lied right to my fucking face."

At least he has the decency to flinch and drop his gaze. "I know, I'm sorry. It made me physically ill, if that's any consolation."

I cross my arms. "It's a bonus."

Looking back up at me, Johnathan squares his shoulders and morphs from my repentant lover into the FBI's authoritative Officer John. "I'm sorry I lied, but ultimately, I have a job to do. We were tipped off that Croc is running more than just drugs, but we needed proof. I was tasked with acquiring evidence. To do that, I needed Croc to think I was going behind your back to meet with him about doing more than just pedaling Fairy Dust."

"Then you should've told me what you were doing." I hadn't had a lot of time to think about John's dishonesty before. I'd been too worried about what he was doing that he needed to keep secrets from me. But now that I know he's not in danger and not in the arms of another man—the two things I'd feared the most—I feel the disappointment spreading through me like syrup, slow and thick, filling in the cracks he'd made in my walls. "I trusted you—something I don't do with *anyone*—because I thought you were different. I won't be making that mistake again."

"*Fuck that.*" In three giant strides, John is toe to toe with me and breathing fire. "You know damn well that you can trust me. That I would *never* do anything to hurt you. You think I didn't want to tell you what I was doing? The lie was like a goddamn thorn in my heart."

The frayed thread on my control snaps. "Then you shouldn't have done it!"

"I didn't have a choice! Can you honestly tell me that you would've been okay with me going to meet Croc by myself on his turf? Even with all my training, even though I can hold my own against men ten times worse than him, I knew you would've never allowed it."

We're mirror images of each other, standing at the edge of the surf. Fists bunched, jaws clenched, bodies coiled. The ocean breeze picks up, whipping into a frenzy around us like its feeding off our tension. "You're wrong. You're a big boy; you can do whatever the hell you want."

"Now who's lying?" he sneers.

I try for a casual shrug, but with my shoulders holding the full weight of my demons since speeding away from the warehouse, I don't think they move. "Think what you want, Darling. I don't give a shit."

Liar.

He lied first. I'm just following his lead.

Real mature.

Fuck off.

"Good," he says, "because I'm going back to Croc and telling him I'm prepared to do whatever he needs."

He turns and walks away from me, his boots eating up the distance with ease like he's not susceptible to the struggles of walking in sand like the rest of us mortals. My throat starts to close, threatening to cut off my air supply, and my heart beats so fast and hard I swear I'm going into cardiac arrest. The thought of him…and Croc…

Christ, not Johnathan. "NO!"

John stops in his tracks. His shoulders rise and fall for several seconds. I hold my breath, waiting to see if he'll ignore me and keep going. I almost fall to my knees with relief when he spins on his heel and stalks back to me.

"*Why not?* You want honesty? Then practice what you preach. Tell me why you don't want me anywhere near Croc. Tell me why you hate him so much. Tell me why you hate your name. Fuck, tell me *anything*."

"Why?" I shout back. "So you can look at me with disgust? Pity me? *Fix me?*"

"No, goddamn it, so I can *understand* you. I have given you everything I am and everything I have. Things I never even knew I had to give until I met you. But it all means nothing if you won't do the same for me. *Let. Me. In.*"

Each one of his words are like his hands shoving me in the chest, trying to provoke me, to push me until I fall off the edge of my resistance. But if I go over, I'll be dragging him into the darkness with me, and I don't know if I can handle that.

"You act like we can talk it all out then just ride off into the sunset, but that's not how this works for someone like me. The bad guy doesn't get a goddamn happily ever after!"

"Why do you insist that that's what you are? Who you work for and getting dealt a really shitty hand in life doesn't make you a villain. When will you realize that *you're the fucking hero of this story*?"

Damn it! How can be so blind to all my faults? Plowing my hands into my hair, I tug until the pain in my scalp makes spots dance behind my squeezed-shut eyes. I've always kept my secrets to protect myself and my reputation and, by extension, my brother. Now, for the first time in my life, I want to keep my secrets to protect someone else. To protect *him*. The last thing I fucking want is for any of this to taint John. He's too good, too pure. I need him to stay that way. I can't be the one responsible for ruining him. Not when it comes to this.

I feel his big hand splay over my chest where my heart is still pounding faster than the hooves of a doped-up race-horse. But his touch acts like a physical form of Xanax, slowly calming me to a manageable level. Releasing my hair, I cover his hand with both of mine and release a heavy breath.

But just when I think he's finally backed off, he says, "You *are* the hero, and you deserve a happily ever after. I want to be the one to give it to you, to share it with you. But if you can't let me in, then you're dooming us before we even have a fighting chance."

He's got it all wrong. Not using him as a shrink isn't what's dooming us. It's the shit in my past. There's no such thing as a normal relationship for me because my demons aren't going anywhere. They'll lurk in the shadows and wait for any opportunity to drive a wedge further between us.

I knew getting involved with John was a bad idea, and

yet I wasn't strong enough to stay away. The temptation of tasting the smallest bit of happiness, however fleeting, proved too great. I gave in, knowing our tragic end was inevitable, but I didn't think it would come so soon.

Turning away, I pace along the shoreline as I growl so loud and long that it ravages my vocal cords. *End this before it goes any further. Before he gets hurt. Just fucking do it.* Changing direction, I charge back over to him and stab my finger in his chest. "You already know what I'm gonna fucking say, don't you? *Don't you?*"

He shakes his head once. "I only have an idea, nothing concrete. And if you decide not to tell me, I promise I won't look into it, or even beat it out of Croc once we have him in custody."

He's giving me an out. Despite his white lie to me earlier, John's a man of his word. If I say no, we'll ride to the loft, fuck out our frustrations, and go back to the way we were before all this went down. But every night we spend wrapped in each other's arms will only make it hurt that much worse when all this is over, and we're working on borrowed time.

"Fine," I say, my tone heavy with resignation. "You want to know so bad, I'll tell you. But then that's the *end of everything* and we never talk about it again. Agreed?"

Tension leaks from his body, and those gorgeous eyes soften as he nods. "Agreed."

He thinks I'm giving him what he wants.

I'm not.

By the time he realizes what he just agreed to, it'll be too late.

It already is.

This is the end of everything.

Chapter Thirty-Three

HOOK

John doesn't move a muscle. I don't even think he's breathing with how still his chest is. Like he's afraid he'll spook me into silence if he so much as blinks. He won't. I wouldn't stop now even if he asked me to. This is a runaway train with no working brakes.

For the past sixteen years, what got me through each day was suppression on top of suppression. Push it all back and shove it down deep. I did everything I could to not think about the events that torment me, and I sure as fuck never spoke of it. Not a single word about it to anyone. Not once.

As I get ready to do just that, every instinct I have is telling me to shut the hell up. Because once Pandora's box is opened, there's no closing it again. But now that I'm so close to confessing, something else is overriding that instinct like a siren's call. For the first time in my life, I can let someone else shoulder this burden with me.

I know I shouldn't. It's a selfish fucking move to put this on him—despite what he thinks he wants—and a better man would keep this shit to himself. But I'm not a better man. Hell, I'm not even a *good* man. I'm a Pirate, an emotionally stunted criminal who has no business screwing a cop with a heart of gold and eyes the color of honey. And it's time Darling sees things as I do.

"Croc was an abusive asshole. The only one he didn't smack around was Tinker Bell because she was Delia's problem. Life at the school wasn't a walk in the park, but it was survivable. Bruises healed and bones mended. All we had to do was deal with it as best we could until we hit eighteen; then we'd be free.

"But when I turned fourteen, something changed. I noticed Croc's gaze lingering on me as I worked in the shop. At dinner, he paid more attention to what I was doing than anyone else. I figured he was watching for me to do the wrong thing. The sadistic bastard enjoyed meting out punishments with the sting of his backhand or the blow of his closed fist, and as the oldest, I could handle more severe beatings than the younger kids."

John mutters a curse and shifts his weight like he's itching for a fight. This isn't news to him, though. Back when he and Wendy hung out with us a couple nights a week, it was obvious when Croc lost his temper with one or several of us. The details were never discussed, but John and Wendy did their best to patch the kids up when they could. Everyone except Tink, who was never touched, and me.

I never let anyone near me when I was busted up, with the exception of *one time*. The time a scrawny boy with golden eyes who talked too much wrapped a Band-Aid on my thumb and asked me to call him Johnathan.

Christ, that feels like five lifetimes ago. And look at us now. We went from being worlds apart to being so entangled I don't know if I remember how to be without him.

Sensing my distraction, he asks, "How long did the staring and watching go on for?"

"Long enough that I didn't even notice it anymore. Then one night after dinner, he told me to come with him to his office. Said he wanted to start teaching me how to run the shop so I could take over someday."

A tremor rips through me as the memory grows ghostly callused fingers that grip the back of my neck and rub along my hairline. I start to feel tight and itchy like I did back then, making me want to crawl out of my skin or shed it like a snake. Anything to get rid of the sensation of his touch.

I fist my hands at my sides to control the trembling, but I can't stop my stomach from cramping. Bile creeps up my throat as though my body wants to burn away my ability to spill the ugly truth. I *hate* how weak this makes me. No matter how old I get, whenever I'm forced to remember things, I turn into that scared fucking kid all over again. *Not today, I'm not. Not in front of John.*

"Hey," he says gently, "you okay?"

"Fine," I bite out, harsher than I meant to.

Jesus, what am I doing? Am I really going to say all this out loud? To him*?*

That siren's call that was tempting me earlier is suddenly gone, and I notice too late that my proverbial ship's course is set for destruction against the jagged cliffs. Nothing has ever given me a sense of pride and purpose like being John's lover has, and I'm about to throw that away sooner than I have to.

I should've kicked my demons back into the shadows where they belong, like I always have, and we could've enjoyed our time together while the undercover assignment lasts. I'll still be leaving Neverland for parts unknown after

I do my time, as planned, but at least he'd have good memories to look back on.

"James..."

I wince from the triggering word, but I notice it stings less with John's voice. Especially when I can see it coming from the full lips I've spent countless hours memorizing with my own, and not the reptilian snarl of a grunting sadist. I wish I didn't despise my own name. It was the one thing my mother gave me that I thought couldn't be taken. Croc proved me wrong. It wasn't enough to steal the autonomy I had over my own body; he had to rip away part of my identity, too.

"You wanna know why I hate my first name so much? I'll tell you. And listen close, Darling, because here's the last piece of the puzzle that puts the whole picture together," I say hoarsely. All the hatred, anger, and resentment lying dormant inside of me rises up and swells until it's seeping from my pores right along with the sweat. "It's because the only time Croc used it was when he was *raping me* or when he wanted me to *think* about him raping me.

"It was his own private joke, his sick little pet name for the boy he fucked in his office on a regular fucking basis. And every time he said my name and saw the disgust in my eyes, or the tears on my cheeks, he laughed, because he got off on my goddamn pain. I lived that hell for almost four years, and each of those years felt twice as long as the one before it."

Swallowing hard and breathing through my nose, I manage to beat back the urge to vomit. A minor victory, considering the rest of me is turning into a shit show. Even with the cooler nighttime temp and gusts of wind, beads of sweat pop out on my forehead and trickle down my spine as my heart begins to race again. Scrubbing a hand over my beard, I take several cleansing breaths as I try to calm the hell down. But releasing my demons from their cages so they can taunt me out in the open is doing fuck all to help the situation. Turning away from John, I face the ocean and try to focus on the low whitecaps rolling into the shore.

It almost works, until I lick my dry lips and have to choke back a Pavlovian groan. The salty sea spray tastes like John's skin during sex or after a workout, and I can't help my body's newly innate need to seek out his comfort. But no matter how much I want to tackle him to the sand and lose myself in him, I can't. Even if this wasn't the wrong time for sex, that's not something I get to do with him anymore. So instead, I keep my eyes forward and press on.

"As hellish as those years were, though, I made sure to keep Croc's attention on me. I couldn't let him turn his sick shit on any of the other kids. I was older and stronger; it was my responsibility to protect them, so that's what I did. Even before I left the school, I had a plan in place that protected them after I moved out. That's why I lost it when I found out what's happening to Starkey. It's why I lost it after seeing Brandy, naked, high, and covered in Dust, because that's when I realized Croc's real game is sex trafficking. John—" My voice breaks off, and I have to clear my throat before finishing. "You know as well as I do, those girls are facing a fate worse than death if we don't get them the hell out of there."

"We're going to, man, I promise." He says it emphatically enough that I allow myself a sliver of hope that he's right. "I have the evidence we need for a bust. I just need a couple of days to send everything up the chain of command for approval."

I nod, taking him at his word instead of grilling him for more details. "You know what the worst part of all this is?

Starkey and those girls wouldn't be where they are now if I hadn't set fire to the school."

"There's no way that's possible."

I chuckle darkly and turn back to him. "Oh, but there is. When I went in for arson, Croc ransacked my place and found the blackmail video I had on him of one of our more violent sessions—that's what kept him away from the other kids until they all moved out. But along with the tape, he found Starkey's personnel folder that I'd stolen from his office file cabinet years before. I planned on showing it to Starkey someday to prove we were brothers, but I never got the chance before Croc decided to use him as leverage so that I'd sell his drugs—something I never would've agreed to normally.

"Selling the drugs resulted in some girls ending up in the hospital and others getting kidnapped for sexual slavery. And Starkey's being abused and raped in prison worse than I ever had it. All of them are suffering, whether directly or indirectly, because of something I did."

John closes his eyes and whispers a harsh curse. His nostrils flare as he draws in a breath, and I know he's grinding his teeth by the way his jaw muscles flex—something he does occasionally in his sleep and whenever he's trying not to lose his cool, which is rare.

I'm not surprised by his reaction, though. He may have suspected the truth before but suspecting and knowing are two very different things.

When we woke up in my bed this morning, he was tucked into my side with his big body draped half over mine, and I was still his Captain. He saw me as a fierce leader of my crew, an equal partner in the loft, and an alpha Dom worthy of his submission, if not his love. I couldn't bring myself to acknowledge his love, but that didn't stop him from letting it shine in those golden eyes every time he looked at me.

But now that's all changing.

Now John knows I was defiled hundreds of times over by a monster who stripped away bits of my humanity with every encounter until there was nothing left.

Now he knows why I'm a rage-filled, poor excuse for a human who lacks the fundamental ability to return the gift of his love.

Now he knows how fucked up I truly am…and always will be.

And as he stands there and processes everything, the perception he's had of me from the time he was young is warping and twisting into something very different. Something darker and truer to reality. At this very moment, John is realizing what I already know: that I don't deserve to be his Captain. I don't deserve to be his anything. He thrives in the light, and I can only cast him in shadow.

This is the end of everything.

John releases a long exhale and finally meets my gaze. "I know you think this is all your fault, but the only one who deserves the blame in any of this is that scum-sucking bastard who I'm trying not to hunt down for the satisfaction of putting a bullet between his eyes."

"Get in line." That was meant as a joke, but not surprisingly, it landed flat. Worry etches into his brow as he traps his bottom lip between his teeth and stares at me for several long seconds. He's thinking too hard, which means I'm probably not going to like what he says next.

"Goddamn, I'm so sor—"

"*Don't,*" I bark out with a shove to his chest. "Don't you dare say you're sorry, or you wish you would've known, or any of that other cursory bullshit people say when faced with someone else's tragedy. I told you I don't want your pity, and I sure as hell don't want your emotional charity."

Indignation sparks in his narrowed gaze. "That's not your only problem with me, though, is it?" he growls. "It's not just about what I say—because God forbid I fucking empathize with you—it's about what I *feel*. You don't want me to *feel* anything for you, either."

Unleashing all the pain of the past and the hurt of today, I shout back at him. "No, I *don't*! Because that's not what this is! I don't know how many times I have to tell you that." I wave a hand back and forth between us. "You and me? This thing we've been doing? It's just *fucking*. Although, don't get me wrong, Johnny-Boy, you're an excellent fuck, so don't sell yourself short the next time you go trolling for dick."

"You've gotta be joking. You think insulting me and telling me all the bullshit lies you tell yourself is going to make me walk away?" He plants his feet and laughs, folding his arms over his wide chest like he's ready to hold the beach down by himself if he has to. "You're gonna have to do better than that, asshole. And I say 'asshole' with love, just so we're clear."

"And just so *we're* clear, Darling," I say, stepping into him until our noses almost touch. "When I say anything—literally anything I've said to you—I've said it with *nothing*. My words are as hollow as my heart. If I'm motivated by any emotions at all, it's hatred and guilt. I have none of the latter when it comes to you, but keep fucking pushing and I'll have plenty of the former."

He sucks in a sharp breath and studies my face, searching for any hint that I'm lying through my teeth, but he won't find any. I meant every word, just not how he thinks I do. There's no doubt that by the time this is all over, when it comes to him, I'll have more hatred than I know what to do with…for *myself.* Every time I have to push him away or cut him down in order to spare him far worse things in the future, the hate will eat me alive. For the rest of my life, I will burn with self-loathing for my inability to be the Dom he needs and the man he deserves.

Finally, his expression falls, heavy with disappointment. He takes a large step back and tips his chin down once in the universal sign for surrendering one's position. Staring into the eyes that have become my touchstone—honey-colored windows to the only soul that can soothe my own—I know I've effectively slayed everything between us. Just like I intended.

As I leave him behind on the shoreline of my sanctuary, I try not to care.

As I race down the highway at top speed, I try not to mourn what was and what can never be.

And as I lie awake in my brother's bed, without the warmth and weight of John's body next to mine, I try not to notice the wet trails at my temples.

Chapter Thirty-Four

JOHN

WAITING. Sucks.

Several months ago, I was helping Wendy rearrange the furniture in the beach house she shares with Peter, who was delivering a custom car he'd built for a client in South Carolina. About two hours into his trip, he stopped to gas up and use the restroom. While standing at the pisser, the dumbass thought it'd be funny to send Wendy a dick pic for his check-in text and dropped his phone in the toilet, completely frying it. In true Pan fashion, he laughed, tossed it in the trash, and continued on his trip, figuring he'd worry about a new cell when he got home.

But his trip turned out to be a comedy of errors including a flat tire, pulling over to wait out a flash flood storm, and a *second* flat tire. Meanwhile, my sister was freaking out because she couldn't get ahold of him and the GPS wasn't finding his location. I watched her pace, get sick with worry, and almost call every hospital and police department along his route at least four times. No matter how often I reassured her he'd be fine, she couldn't bring herself to relax and have faith he'd turn up.

He finally strolled through the door shortly after ten o'clock that night. Wendy squeezed the hell out of him and peppered his face with relieved kisses, until she remembered how scared she'd been. Not surprisingly, the story of the attempted dick pic as the catalyst for her shit day didn't go over well. He was grouchy as hell for the next two weeks for reasons I don't want to think about when it comes to my sister.

At the time, I thought my sister was being dramatic. I mean, this was Peter Pan we were talking about. He's matured a lot since getting back together with Wendy, but the dude's still not known for his superior adulting skills or rational thought process.

But now… Shit, now I get it.

Because it's been almost twenty hours since James walked away from me on that beach, and I've been going out of my mind with worry for the last nineteen of them. He'd found and removed the tracker I had on his bike and ditched his phone on the side of Hwy 421. When he didn't come home last night, every possible bad scenario ran through my mind on a constant loop.

I sat in his chair to wait up for him, but I passed out somewhere around four o'clock this morning with his scent in my nose and his book in my hands. A few hours later I jerked awake and listened for any signs of life, but the loft was deadly silent. My heart sank and my stomach twisted itself into knots, despite telling myself—as I did Wendy—that he was probably fine. It was that "probably" I couldn't get past.

That's when I went into Boyfriend Stalker Mode. I checked his bed to see if he'd slept in it (he hadn't), checked the tracker on his car (it hasn't moved from the garage out back), asked Smee if he'd seen or heard from him (negative, nor was he the least bit concerned, which just pissed me off), and called his dead phone every half hour in case he went back for it and plugged it in (straight to voice mail every time).

And now I've spent the last seven hours pacing, yanking on my hair, rubbing my neck raw, and chewing my nails to the quick. If Wendy could see me now, I'd never live this down.

I freeze mid-stride at the thudding sound of boots climbing the staircase off the balcony. I'm across the room in half a second. Yanking the door open, I'm ready to throw myself at my man, but I'm drawn up short.

"Cecco," I say, hoping the weight of my disappointment isn't written all over my face. "What's up?"

Holding up a small plastic container, he grins. "I need to borrow some sugar."

"Sugar?" I arch a brow at the man known for torturing his enemies.

"Now, JD," he says, "I hope you're not implying that a man like me can't enjoy the domestic simplicities of something like baking. I'm sure you've benefitted from the Captain's magical culinary skills, am I right?"

My cheeks flush. I've benefitted from a lot more of his magical skills than the ones involving food. "Nah, man, nothing wrong with baking. Just caught me off guard is all." Trying to hide my reaction, I discreetly clear my throat and head for the kitchen. "Come on, I'll grab you some."

"Captain around?" he asks, following me into the loft.

I pretend like that observation doesn't shoot another stab of worry through my heart as I grab the sugar from a cabinet. "Nope," I say casually. "He comes and goes a lot, but it's not like he tells me shit about what he's doing. I'm just the temporary roommate he barely puts up with."

Cecco hands me the container, then folds his heavily

tattooed arms on the breakfast counter. "Don't worry, man. Once we get Starkey back, the boss will be back to his old self, you'll have earned your spot in the Pirates, and we'll get you your own cabin like the rest of us."

"Looking forward to it."

I walk around the counter and give him the container filled with sugar. He squints his eyes at my shoulder, an earnest expression on his face. I freeze as he reaches up and picks something off my shirt. But then he smiles and holds up a couple of my hairs. "Looks like you're starting to lose your hair, JD."

Relief washes through me and I chuckle. "Maybe Smee will stop hitting on me if I'm bald."

He laughs, too. "Doubt it. Catch ya later, man."

"Later."

We bump fists and then I attempt to look busy as Cecco makes his way back to the door with his sugar. As soon as he's gone, the emptiness of the loft and worry for James rushes back in. It's fucking stifling. "I gotta get out of here."

Five minutes later I'm changed into my running gear, and for a solid hour and a half, I punish my body, pushing its limits, using the burn in my muscles to distract me. By the time I make it back, it's dusk and my shaky legs barely hold out long enough to get me up the stairs. I let myself in and head toward my room with the goal of collapsing on the bed, sweat-drenched clothes be damned.

I almost don't hear it over the rush of blood pumping in my ears: the sound of running water coming from the bathroom. *He's home.* The immense gratitude that he's okay is quickly replaced by the urge to throttle him for making me worry. He's got a lot of nerve pushing me away and bailing on me like I'm just another person in his life who won't stick around, who won't fight for him. Who won't fight for *us*.

Stalking to the bathroom, I open the door to give him a piece of my mind. But my indignation dissolves along with the air in my chest the second I see him.

Oh, James…

Standing under the shower spray, his head hangs between his shoulders with hands braced on the tiled wall in front of him. He's the picture of desolation, weighed down by a thousand and one betrayals from people who were supposed to care for him, to stand up for him, to *love* him.

He doesn't know it yet, but I'm the man who's going to stop the cycle. Not only will I stop it, I'll set that bitch in reverse until he's literally surrounded by people who love him and he spends his days rolling his eyes in disgust and growling complaints at us. And we're going to *keep* on loving him until those eye rolls and complaints are few and far between, and more still, until eventually they turn into easy smiles and unguarded laughter. It might take years for that kind of a transformation, but I don't care. From this day on, it's my number one mission in life.

I enter the bathroom and quietly close the door behind me. As I shed my sweaty clothes and drop them on the floor, I notice his right thumb moving and my stomach clenches. But instead of grinding the tip against the grout, it's lying flat and rubbing back and forth in jerky motions—like he's trying not to hurt himself. Like maybe he doesn't want to let his past continue to rule his present.

And that possibility, however small, is what gives me hope.

I open the glass door to the large enclosure and step inside. "Get the fuck out," he says, his voice sandpaper rough.

"No." I wrap my arms around him and press my front to his back. He tenses up, and I brace myself for an attempt to throw me off. When it doesn't immediately happen, I press soft kisses to his wet shoulder and along the side of his neck. When I get to his ear, I say, "I love you, James."

Growling, he spins around and stiff-arms me in the sternum, forcing me back until the shower spray separates us. He glares at me, his outrage slicing through the curtain of water. "I told you never to call me that. I even told you *why* and you *still fucking do it*! If that's the kind of love you have to offer, Darling, I don't want it." Dropping his hand, he shakes his head. "I don't want anything you have to offer anymore. You can bunk in Smee's cabin until this is over. Leave me the hell alone."

"I have no intentions of leaving you alone," I bite out, stepping through the water and bracing my hands on either side of him. "I'm also not going anywhere—not out of this loft and not out of your life—so pardon my disobedience, *Captain*, but you can take that command and *shove it*. As for your name…"

I angle my body and crowd him into the corner, using my larger frame and added muscle to enforce my rare moment of dominance. I'll be damned if I let him use our natural roles to keep me at a distance. He has to learn that while I have no problems getting on my knees for him, I will stand and go toe to toe with him when I have to.

"I understand why you left it behind, but that fucker doesn't deserve to have any part of you, not even your name." Cupping his bearded jaw in my hands, I hold his gaze. "Let me help you take it back."

He swallows thickly. "I can't get it back."

"Yes, you can." I know James will eventually need counseling, but I've learned basic psychology as part of my training, and if I can help him with this one thing, I have to try. Maybe then he'll see that he's not a lost cause. "We'll work on it a little at a time, and only when we're being intimate and affectionate, so there's no chance of your mind confusing us with the past."

His lip curls up in a snarl. "So now you're a fucking shrink who knows how my brain works?"

God, even when he's pissed, he's so damn beautiful. Jet-black hair slashes across his face in tapered strips and drops of water cling to the tips of his spiked lashes. But it's his blue eyes swirling with banked fire that pull me in. They're warning me to stay away, but all I want is to be consumed by their flames.

"No, James," I whisper, hope surging through me when he just barely stiffens. "I'm the man who loves you and knows how your heart works."

Before he can argue, I press my lips to his in a long, sweet kiss. There's no heat behind it. It's a declaration, a promise. *I love you. I'm here for you. I'm not going anywhere.* He doesn't move, doesn't return my touch or even the kiss, but none of that matters because he also doesn't push me away. And that more than anything tells me we're going to be fine.

I start to pull back, but I don't get far before he grabs my face and growls, "Goddamn you," then slams his mouth on mine.

Holy fuck, this kiss. *This kiss* has so much heat that it sets me on fire. He's ruthless and demanding, his tongue dueling mine in an ageless battle of dominance and submission. But I'm not ready to give him that power yet. Not until I'm satisfied he understands I won't back down on this. If he wants to communicate through sex, then I'm not above making him so mindless that he agrees to let me stay.

Pressing him into the corner again, I slide my hands over his slick chest and abs until they reach his thickening cock. Ignoring mine for now, I grab his shaft in one hand and his heavy balls in the other. He breaks the kiss to suck in a sharp breath. Dropping his head back, he releases it on a low moan as I squeeze and stroke, but I want those blue eyes back on me where they belong.

"Look at me," I command gruffly.

His jaw clenches, and I realize too late that his dominant side might be more than just a kink. There was a time when he was given orders, and because he chose to follow them instead of fight, it made him—in his mind—complicit in his own abuse. Nothing could be further from the truth, but perception is reality, and James has a lot of healing to do before he'll believe that.

Taking a deep breath, I release him and force myself to reset. I didn't come in here for sex. I want to comfort him and fix this rift between us, and that's exactly what I'm going to do. Settling my hands at the base of his neck, I gently caress him with my thumbs. Then, softening my tone, I try again. "Captain, please. Will you look at me?"

After a few endless seconds, he does, and that tiny seed of hope plants itself in my heart. "Damn. Yeah, just like that," I say encouragingly. "When you look at me, it feels like you're staring into my soul. That's what I want you to see when I say your name. That it's *me* touching you, *me* loving you. That it's *me* when I say… You are so damn beautiful, James."

His nostrils flare and the cords in his neck stand out in sharp relief above my hands as he draws in measured breaths. Remembering the care he takes with my safety, I do the same for him. "I'm going to keep saying it. If it gets to be too much, tell me to stop, and I promise I will. Okay?"

I don't demand a verbal acknowledgement like he does with me; I don't need to. He has the out if he needs it. He can tell me to stop right now.

But he doesn't.

Leaning my forehead to his, I continue staring into those ocean-blue depths. "James," I rasp, speaking his name like it's my prayer and he's my religion. He remains a statue except for the rise and fall of his chest, so I go on. "I'm so gone for you, James, you know that? From the first time I saw you, you drew me in; I was the moth to your flame. I think part of my heart has always been yours, even way back then. Now?" I pull back to study his gorgeous face. "Fuck, James, now you have the whole damn thing."

"This changes nothing," he grates out. "Whatever we had is done. *I'm* done."

I shake my head. "That's only because you don't think I'll stick around now that I know everything, but you're wrong. I'm not going anywhere." He opens his mouth, but I cut him off, my temper rising enough to make my tone sharp. "And it's not because I pity you or any of that other bullshit. Do I hate what happened to you? You better fucking believe it. I've never known the taste of bloodlust until now, and the temptation to act as judge, jury, and executioner gets stronger every time I think about it. But that has nothing to do with why I'm here."

"Why *are* you here?"

I can't stop the sigh. "Did you not hear me all the times I told you I loved you?"

"Just because you say or believe something, doesn't mean it's true."

"This *is*—"

"No, it's not!" Pinning me with his flinty gaze, he points angrily behind me. "*That wasn't real life, John*," he says, his booming voice echoing off the tile. "We were living in a bubble, pretending to be two normal guys, but nothing about this is normal and *we don't work* outside this loft."

"What are you talking about? Why the hell not?"

"For such a smart guy, you're doing a shit job of thinking about this rationally, so let me break it down for you. I'm always going to be the fucked-up bad boy on the wrong side of the law, and once this case is over, you'll go back to being the golden boy of the Task Force who saves the world, one fucked-up bad guy at a time."

He shoves his hands through his wet hair as he visibly tries to calm down. When he speaks again, his tone is resolute. "Everyone knows oil and water don't mix, Darling. We had fun in a situation that allowed us to fuck freely and often, but that's all it was. There's no room for feelings in this arrangement, and you're way past that already, so I'm calling it. We're done. Now get the fuck out and let me shower in peace."

Chapter Thirty-Five

HOOK

I FORCE myself to take steady, even breaths so I don't hyperventilate at the idea of John walking out of my life. I thought I'd had enough time the past twenty-four hours to come to terms with it.

I was wrong.

I'm also a fucking hypocrite.

I might be incapable of the L-word, but there's no denying I caught serious feelings for John Darling. As I laid in Starkey's bed last night, my mood swung like a pendulum from anger, arcing through frustration and misery, all the way to regret, then back again. I've never been so fucked up over another person other than my brother. I need to end this before I don't even recognize myself anymore. Once he leaves, I'll drink myself into oblivion until I'm too numb to feel a goddamn thing, and then I'll move the fuck on.

Except he's *not* leaving. He's studying me with those eyes that are like old souls. They look past what I show the world and see all the things not fit for public consumption, things I keep hidden for a reason.

Fuck it. If he's too stubborn to leave, I'll do it. But as soon as I move to go around him, he blocks my path. "Not so fast. Since you're putting our 'arrangement' on trial, I have the right to a counterargument."

"Jesus, everything's a cop analogy with you. I didn't put it on trial, Darling. I executed it."

He arches a brow and brackets me in with his big arms.

"Fine, say your piece so we can be done with this already. I'm tired of this game."

"This is *no* game," he says, his tone solemn. "I told you before why I went into law enforcement. I hated that you and the others had no one to fight for you, no one to protect you. Helping to protect those who can't help themselves is my calling; it gives me purpose."

John pauses to gather my hands in his. He dips his head to press a kiss to the tip of my scarred right thumb—the one I almost ruined again today until I thought of how upset it makes John when I hurt myself—and I have to swallow around the lump in my throat before responding.

"Thanks for proving my point. You can go now." I try to pull my hands from his, but he's strong as a damn ox. With his muscle and skills, if he wanted to overpower me, I wouldn't stand a chance. It's a painful reminder of how special his gift of submission to me really was. A gift that's killing me to return like some ill-fitting shirt, because no one could be a more perfect fit for me than John. Too bad I'm nowhere close to being the same for him.

"You didn't let me finish," he says, steel in his voice. "I know that what I feel for you is love—*true* love, not some temporary thing born of circumstance—because I would give it all up for you. I would turn in my badge and gun tomorrow and never look back if that's what you needed. I can find other ways of helping people that don't put us at such odds. But what I can't find is another heart that beats in time with mine. You're it for me. I want to help you heal, and I want to spend the rest of my life loving you—even when you push me away."

If my throat gets any tighter, I won't be able to breathe. Swallowing hard, I force the brick back into my stomach where I hope it crushes those stupid fluttering things taunting me with a future I can't fucking have. His golden eyes are the pathway to my undoing, so I drop them. My gaze slides past his neck tattoo that's flaking off at the edges to settle on the curved one along his collarbone. *No Shame, No Mercy.* Such a harsh motto for such a gentle soul. Harsh for him. Perfect for me.

I should've known lying to him wouldn't work. He's like a human bullshit detector. Gathering what's left of my shaky resolve, I play my last card and give it to him straight.

"I'm not worth that kind of trouble, John. Not that I would ever let you throw away your career, but I'm not worth *any* kind of trouble. That's not self-deprecation, either; it's simple truth. You haven't even scratched the surface of the shit going on in my head. I'm no good for someone like you. You might not see it now, but it'll only be a matter of time. And every night, as you fall asleep in my arms, I'll wonder if tomorrow will be the day you finally walk out that door."

"Then every morning when we wake up, I'll prove you wrong, one day a time, until all you wonder about are mundane things like what we'll have for breakfast." Erasing the space between us, he presses his chest to mine and cups my jaw in his strong hands. "I'm not saying we won't have bad days—we'll have fights like every other couple on the planet—but when we're done being pissed off, we'll apologize and fuck each other senseless. And I'm not afraid of the shit inside your head, so you can push me away all you want because I'm not going anywhere. Not today, not next year, and not fifty years from now."

My body trembles from the strain of holding itself together against the crashing tide of emotions inside me. "Damn it, Johnathan, you can't save me." Vision blurring with unshed tears, I plead for him to understand. "I've lived in the dark too long. You can't drag me into your light just because you want me with you."

Conviction shining in his golden depths, he whispers, "If you can't come into the light, then I'll live with you inside the dark. You don't need to believe you can be saved, James. I'll believe it enough for the both of us. You only need to let me love you."

I close my eyes, letting the tears spill over and his words sink in. *Let me love you.* It sounds like such a simple request, but for me, it feels insurmountable. Accepting love from someone means trusting them enough to let them in—*truly in*—and the thought of being so vulnerable terrifies me.

Except I *do* trust John, and despite my efforts to keep my walls in place, sometime in the past several weeks, I lowered them enough for him to climb in. All I have to do now…is let him stay.

Opening my eyes, I meet his pensive gaze, and surrender. "Okay."

I catch a glimpse of the relief flooding his features before he pulls me in for a sinfully sweet kiss. His lips mold perfectly to mine, forcing drops of water to stream around our sealed mouths, and the light scrape of his stubble sends tingles of electricity flowing south. With his scent in my nose and his body pressed to mine, a wave of indescribable rightness washes over me.

I memorize every detail, permanently branding these seconds into my brain. No matter how this turns out in the future, I don't want to forget the moment I placed my battered, black heart into the hands of the only man with the power to destroy it. For the first time in my life, I'm… shit, I don't want to jinx myself, but…I'm actually *hopeful.* John did that. If I'm not meant to be happy and John's destined to be my downfall, then I'm going to enjoy every sweet minute of my descent.

Breaking our kiss, he turns the water off, leads me out of the shower, and grabs a bath towel. I go to do the same, but he guides my hand back to my side, silently instructing me not to move. Biting the inside of my lip, I force myself to hold still as he dries me with long, slow swipes over my arms, back, and chest.

It goes without saying that I'm not used to anyone trying to care for me or show me affection. But my badass cop boyfriend has a softer side to him, one that thrives on giving me things such as care and affection. And that means I need to get better at accepting them in our daily life as easily as I accept (by demand) his submission and servitude in our sex life.

Admittedly, letting John tend to me like this doesn't suck, as evidenced by my cock growing harder in front of his face while he runs the towel down my calves. He glances up my body with a secretive smile but rises without so much as a lick. I frown and contemplate forcing him to his knees to remedy that. But when he presses a quick kiss beneath my jaw, my usual Dom tendencies melt in the face of his tenderness. This is a new dynamic for me, something I'm wholly unprepared for, but one I want to experience with John. So I wait as he dries himself off with a few efficient swipes, then let him lead me again into my bedroom.

Retrieving the bottle of lube from the bedside table, he says, "Lay down on your back."

I freeze. I'm going to ruin things already, and I fucking

hate myself for it. "John, I can't…" I clear my throat and try again. "I know you used to top, but I can't bottom for you or even take you in my mouth," I say thickly. "I wish I could, but—"

"Hey, I don't care about any of that. You more than make up for any deficits in those areas. I don't feel like I'm missing out on anything, I promise." Running his hands down my arms, he threads our fingers together. "Do you trust me?"

I do. I already admitted it to myself back in the shower. Now it's time I admit it to him, too. "Yeah," I answer gruffly. "I trust you."

"Thank you. Now get on the bed." With an easy smile, he adds, "Please."

Filing his mild attitude away to punish him another time—not because he's earned it since we're not in our typical roles, but merely because we both enjoy his punishments—I situate myself on my back in the center of the mattress. Then I watch as John crawls over to me like a powerful cat to straddle my hips and sit on my upper thighs.

Trust or not, I can't help the tinge of anxiety coursing through me. Intimacy has never been a part of my sex life. John was the first person I'd ever allowed in my bed, but even then, our fucking was always about satisfying carnal, deviant desires. And, because I'm me and needed to keep my walls intact, we've never had sex face-to-face. But John's in full wrecking-ball mode and won't be satisfied until he's demolished every last brick between us.

Holding my gaze, he pours a stream of lube into his palm before tossing the bottle to the side and gripping my throbbing cock. I suck in a sharp breath as he strokes up my shaft and twists over the flared head. His thumb swipes across the top, taking the bead of pre-cum with it before sliding down to the root of me. I expect him to switch directions again, but he flattens his hand and rubs the lube into my balls as he tugs and rolls them until I'm so damn close to exploding.

Right before I get to the edge, he backs off, then slips his fingers between my thighs. I tense and grit my teeth, bracing for a touch that's sure to trigger all the bad shit in my head and—

"Shhhh, trust me," John says soothingly as he stares into my eyes. I lick my dry lips and give him a jerky nod. I'm rewarded a second later when he presses his slick fingertips against my taint—that sensitive place just under my balls that I've always restricted during sex so no one was tempted to explore even lower—and massages the nerve-rich area in circular motions.

"Oh fuck." Blazing pleasure ignites in my belly and draws my balls up tight. An anguished groan is pulled from my chest as I drop my head back to the pillow. Once again, he drags me right to the brink of orgasm, then stops, and I regret introducing him to this brand of torture all those times I edged him.

He starts from the beginning and does it all over again —up, twist, over, down, lower, rub, and repeat. His other hand gets into the action, sometimes working in tandem with the first, sometimes straying in the opposite direction. He makes two hands feel like a dozen, and my stomach muscles are in danger of cramping from the permanent state of contraction.

When I feel the sudden absence of his touch, I lift my head to find him drizzling lube on the length of his shaft. I'm mesmerized as his fist begins to move on his huge cock, making it slick and shiny in just a few quick strokes. Just as I'm about to take over for him, he leans forward, bracing his hands next to my head and starts grinding our cocks together between our bodies.

"*Uhn*," he says with a grunt, "fuck that feels good." Then sinks his teeth into his plump lower lip and gazes into my eyes.

The tenderness swimming in those golden ponds and the sparks igniting at the base of my spine from our carnal friction is a lethal, unfamiliar combination.

Mine, mine, fucking mine.

It's not the first time that word has rolled through my mind with John, but it's the first time the claim doesn't feel twisted up in barbed wires of complications. Cupping the back of his head, I pull him down. He opens for me, and I lick into his mouth, claiming him with every thrust of my tongue as he lays claim to me with every pump of his hips. The vibrations from his moans travel straight to my balls, and the heaven he's creating with our dicks grinding together is threatening my usual stamina.

"Oh fuck," I grate out through a clenched jaw and fist his hair. "Want inside that tight ass, baby. Want what's mine."

He smiles down at me, and I swear his eyes shine with moisture. "I like hearing you call me 'baby.'"

It fell so naturally from my lips that I didn't even notice I said it. This man is unlocking all sorts of things in me tonight, and with each one, the steel band in my chest loosens, allowing me to breathe that much easier. "That's good," I say, framing his face and rubbing my thumb over his cheek. "'Cause it seems to be one of my many new things with you."

John rests his forehead on mine. "I think I'm going to like these new things."

"I'm glad. But if you don't put us both out of our misery," I warn, rocking my hips up to bring his attention back where I want it, "I'm going to do my *old* thing and take over." I reach toward the nightstand, but he stops me.

"No more condoms."

"John—"

"I know you got the results back," he says. "I saw them. We're both clean, it's safe, and I don't want anything between us anymore. Not emotionally or physically."

He's right. There's no reason we need to still use condoms, so why am I hesitating? *Because it's a way of keeping at least one barrier in place, that's why.* Jesus, that's messed up. I'm so sick of my shit screwing things up with him. I don't know how I'm going to do it or how long it'll take, but one way or another, I'm going to slay these demons and become the man John believes I am.

"Okay," I say hoarsely. "No more condoms. Just us."

He exhales in relief and kisses me, the tip of his tongue barely grazing my lips before he speaks against my mouth. "Thank you."

Pretty sure that's my line, but he doesn't give me the chance to say so. John grabs the bottle off the bed and slicks me up with more lube. My dick gets impossibly harder knowing it's moments away from sliding into its favorite place. When John reaches behind him to rub lube between his firm cheeks, I resent the limited view from this angle. I fucking love to watch his ass suck my fingers deep inside as I stretch him to take my cock. Then again, getting to watch the expression on his face when he does take me might just top it.

He rises on his knees and starts to guide me into place, but I grab his wrist. "I don't want to hurt you. Let me get you ready first."

"James..." My pulse still spikes when he says my name, but it's quick to even out. There's too much tenderness in the way he says it to be mistaken for anyone else. He removes my hand from his wrist and settles it on his hip. "I couldn't be more ready for you or for this moment. I don't want to put it off for another second."

With that, he lines me up at his entrance and slowly lowers himself onto my cock. Without the latex, his hot hole sears me with intense pleasure I never knew existed.

"Jesus fuck," I growl as his ass devours my dick, inch by inch, until he's fully seated. His pupils are blown with lust, his cheeks are flushed, and his plush lips are parted with shallow breaths. He's fucking gorgeous, and he's all mine. "Move, Johnathan. *Move now.*"

Groaning, he does. With long, measured strokes, he rocks back and forth, grinding himself on my shaft. I feel everything—every nerve, every vein, the flared ridge of my cockhead—all of it being dragged through the tight fist of John's ass, again and again. My eyes are locked onto my lower stomach where his huge cock rubs along the trail of dark hair that stretches up to my navel. I'm about to reach for him, but he twines our fingers together instead and pushes my hands to the mattress on either side of my head.

My breathing picks up, and my heart starts to pound. My body's at war, wanting to revel in the mounting rapture of John riding me but expecting my past to pounce on any hint of being restrained.

John lowers his body to mine and stretches our arms higher, staring deep into my eyes. "Shhh, it's just us here," he whispers. "Don't let anyone else in. I'm not holding you down; I'm simply holding you."

John's presence proves stronger than my demons, and I feel the chains binding me to those memories finally break and fall away. I know they'll imprison me again in the morning, but for now, I'm free. Taking a deep breath, I release it slowly and let everything go that doesn't belong in this moment.

Rolling my hips up to meet his downward thrusts, I start fucking him slow and hard. His face relaxes as he reads the change in me, and his mouth curves up with that easy smile that kills me in the best of ways. "I love you so fucking much, James," he says reverently.

John's repetition of my name is gradually dulling its effect. Every time he says it, the spike of anxiety gets weaker and dissipates quicker. Maybe he's right. Maybe someday I'll be able to hear my name from someone other than him and not think twice about it. Maybe my name really can become as mundane for me as they are for everyone else. I was trained to react a certain way when I heard it, so with time, it's possible I can be *un*trained.

"Say it again."

His smile grows. "I love you."

"With my name," I say gruffly as I squeeze his hands. "Say it again with my name."

His hips never stop moving as every emotion in his heart flashes in his honey gaze. "I love you, James. I'm yours and you're mine. No matter what I call you, the name branded on my soul is, and always will be, *James*." He presses his mouth to mine, then chants it like a devout prayer. "James, James, James. I love you, I love you, I love you."

My chest swells with feelings I don't recognize and can't label. I never imagined I was capable of anything other than guilt, hate, and for a select few, loyalty. Now I'm flooded with so much more. I don't know how to say things like John does, but I want to show him as best I can.

Pulling my hands from his, I roll us to the side without losing our connection. My bottom arm cushions his head and wraps around his broad shoulders while my free hand grabs him behind the knee and hikes his leg high onto my hip. I fuck into his tight ass with deep, measured strokes, reveling in the way he moans softly and whimpers with each one.

"I need you to understand something," I say, injecting a bit of my Dom tone and holding us still to ensure his full attention. "I can't say those words back to you because it would cheapen them. I'm not capable of love like you are, but what I feel for you is everything *I am* capable of. I don't want you to doubt that because I refuse to say something that would amount to empty words from me."

"I never expected you to say it back. I don't need to hear the words when I can see your heart just by looking in your eyes."

Jesus, I don't deserve this man. But I'm not letting that stop me from keeping him. Not anymore. "Then as of now, I'm claiming you. I'll be your everything, just as you'll be mine. My sub, my lover, and my partner. I will fuck you and hold you. Command you and cherish you. Punish you and protect you."

Unable to hold off any longer, I start to move again. "I held the door open and told you to run. You refused. Now I'm slamming it shut and tossing the key." I place my mouth at his ear and drop my voice an octave. "For better or worse, Johnathan, *you're mine*."

"I'm yours," he sighs, then buries his face in my neck and groans an "oh fuck" against my skin when my thrusts get harder. I hook his top leg behind my back and slide my hand over his rippling muscles as we move together. I lose all sense of self as the lines where I end and he begins blur and meld. The moisture from our shower has been replaced by sweat as our pleasure mounts. Our lower bodies slam together and pull apart in a steady rhythm. We kiss and suck and bite until the need for air forces us apart.

I spit into my palm and reach between us to fist his

cock. He hisses from my tight grip and curses when I start jerking him with rough strokes.

"Come for me, baby." I piston my hips harder and faster, driving us to our end. "I want to see how you look when I make you soar."

"James, oh God, I'm close, I—"

His words cut off and his mouth drops open on a silent shout, his entire body contracting with the force of his climax. I watch with satisfaction as ropes of his white cum lash my stomach and chest with every rough upstroke I give him until he's completely spent. It's the first time I've ever allowed him to mark me, but it sure as fuck won't be the last.

"Your turn," he says, framing my face in his big paw. "Come inside me, James. I want to feel you. Claim me. Fill me up until I'm dripping with you."

"*Fuck.*" I don't know what's hotter—his filthy mouth, the feel of his channel still clenching on my bare cock in pulses as I pound into his tight ass, or my primal need to give him the very thing he's begging for and brand him as mine from the inside. It's a lethal combination that sends me hurtling over the edge. Holding him in a vise grip, I press our foreheads together and pump him full of my cum.

"Fuck yeah, baby, take it from me," I say on a groan that matches his as he squeezes around my dick. "Christ yeah, just like that. Shit, you feel so fucking good."

We gradually slow our movements until all our energy is gone and neither of us can move. We're sweaty and sticky and in desperate need of another shower, but it'll keep until the morning. I also make a mental note to help him scrub off his neck tattoo so he can replace it with a fresh one.

When my softening cock finally slips from him, I

muster the strength to press my fingers to his puckered hole; then I say, "Tighten up, Johnathan. There will be times when I want to see your ass dripping with my cum, but tonight, I want everything I gave you to stay right where I put it." When I feel the ring of muscle close beneath my fingertips, I whisper, "Good boy."

John's eyes shimmer with love. I can only hope that he sees something similar in mine. He bites his lip thoughtfully, then says, "This was the best night of my life."

"Mine, too," I say honestly. "Now go to sleep."

I press a kiss to his damp forehead and relax when he sags in my arms and tucks his head under my chin. Tomorrow will be a whole new world of learning how to navigate this new relationship, but tonight, we get to enjoy the bubble a little longer.

"Love you," he murmurs sleepily.

I think for a second how I can respond, then settle on my truth as it relates to his. "Own you."

Chapter Thirty-Six

JOHN

"OH MY GOD, do you *want* me to get fat?" I stop grating the block of parmesan cheese I was tasked with and stare in horror at the butter melting in the pan held by my boyfriend.

Boyfriend. Every time I look at James, that word swells like a balloon in my mind until it bursts and rains bits of joy all through my body like confetti. It's only been a few days since we officially became a secret-for-now couple, but aside from all my unsavory duties as a thug, these have been the best days of my life.

As is his standard response to me, James rolls his gorgeous blue eyes. "It's alfredo sauce. You can't make alfredo sauce without butter. And even if you could," he adds quickly, correctly predicting my argument, "I *wouldn't*, because it's fucking wrong."

I'm smiling on the inside—he's so damn cute when he defends the integrity of his cooking, especially in those faded jeans that hug his ass and his fitted white V-neck—but I make sure to frown as I point my hunk of cheese at his frying pan. "Fine, but does it need a whole *garden spade* full of butter?"

"What the fuck's a garden spade?"

"You know, the hand shovel for digging holes in gardens."

He hitches a dubious eyebrow. "No, I don't know. How do *you* know?"

I shrug. "I used to help my mom plant flowers around the house every spring, and now I do it to keep the tradition going for my dad."

"For such a hard-bodied guy, you're awfully soft on the inside, you know that?"

"Keep shoveling fat into our meals and I'll be soft on the outside, too."

Smirking, he adjusts the stove's temperature and moves the butter around with a wooden spatula. "I bet you look pretty hot in a wide-brimmed hat and gardening gloves."

The smart-ass is being sarcastic, but I don't take the bait. Instead, I lay out some of my own. "As a matter of fact, I do," I say, resuming my cheese grating. "You can help me next time. I'm sure I can find you an extra straw hat and set of gloves."

He snorts. "Somehow I don't think gardening is really my thing."

"Okay," I say nonchalantly. "Then you can just supervise and get me stuff. It's not always easy to find what I need when I'm crawling around in the dirt on my hands and knees."

He stops stirring, and I can feel his intense stare boring a hole into the side of my head. *Gotcha.* "Your hands and knees? In the dirt?"

God, whenever he drops his voice like that, my cock twitches like a trained animal. Pretending I'm unaffected, I continue moving the cheese up and down the metal grater like it's the most important job of my life. "Mm-hmm. I get really sweaty and filthy, and my knees and muscles ache when I'm down there for a long time. It's hard and sometimes painful, but in the end, it's totally worth it."

In the span of a few seconds, James moves the pan off the burner and turns me in a one-eighty where he pins me against the counter. Just like that, my predictable man is ensnared in my trap. I might be the one caged inside his arms, but he's the one who snatched up my bait and put me right where I want to be.

"We still talking about gardening, Johnathan?"

He presses his hips forward, grinding his sizable and getting-bigger-by-the-second bulge on my cock that's straining to get at his. But I don't break yet. I bite back the groans and pleas for him to eat *me* for dinner instead of the alfredo. It's too fun to toy with him when the opportunity presents itself, and I've learned the punishments for teasing him are highly enjoyable.

"Of course," I say guilelessly. "What else would I be talking about?"

This is the part where he takes control and makes me pay for being cheeky. I'm practically vibrating with anticipation and need. But he flips the script on me when he grins and says, "Just checking." Then he pushes away and returns to his task at the stove. "Can you grab the small carton of milk from the fridge?"

Still scrambled from the abrupt switch, I get it for him on autopilot, rerunning the previous minutes in my head to see where my flirting went so wrong. But when he pours the thick, white liquid into the melting butter, I snap out of it.

"That's not milk; it's *heavy whipping cream*," I complain. "Jesus, this is the third night in a row you've made something like this. Which means it'll be the third night I have to put in a second workout after dinner. Do you have any idea the kind of cardio it'll take to burn that off?"

Yes, I know. I sound like a complete CrossFit douche, but my sudden case of blue balls is making me pissy. My boyfriend, however, seems unfazed by my attitude. As he continues stirring the mixture, his face breaks into a huge smile… And just like that, my irritation evaporates. I never dared to hope that I would see a genuine smile from the perpetually grouchy Captain Hook, but since we had our breakthrough the other night, they've been making brief appearances, a little more each day. And I melt faster than ice cubes under a blowtorch, every damn time.

He turns his head and peers at me from behind a slash of black hair, momentarily sidetracking me with how sexy he is. But when he quips, "I have a fairly good idea, yeah," then winks at me—*fucking winks*—I realize I'm the one who's been played.

"Holy shit! You're doing this so you can watch me workout and objectify me? Is that all I am to you? A piece of meat? A pretty thing to look at? I have feelings, too, you know."

Before I end up collapsing in a fit of laughter, I turn away and stomp off in a fake huff. I don't make it very far. Strong arms band around me from behind and maneuver me against the nearest wall. His deep chuckle reverberates through my back and sinks into my soul. The sound of a happy Hook gives me life. It's everything. *He* is everything.

"Come on, baby, you can't blame me," he rumbles in my ear, then sears a line of kisses down my neck. "The way sweat drips down every groove and valley of your body as you work out? I'd have to be dead not to enjoy that sight."

I tip my head to the side and rock my ass back against his still-hard cock. He hisses in a breath before he catches himself, making me smirk. "Keep trying to fatten me up and *dead* can be arranged."

He laughs and turns me to face him. Cupping my jaw, he kisses me soundly on the lips, twice, three times. "It's not my fault you're so fucking hot, Darling. Your workouts are like watching live porn from my living room."

"Oh, yeah?" I meant to say something snarkier than that, but he's back to trailing openmouthed kisses across the base of my throat and his hands are pushing up my shirt.

"Yeah." He pinches my nipples, and I drop my head back on a moan. "I want these pierced. Silver bars that keep them hard and sensitive for me. How's that sound, Johnathan?"

"Really good, Captain," I reply, my hips lifting from the wall, seeking the pressure my cock needs. "Really fucking good."

He pins me harder—

Ear-piercing beeps alert us to the smoke swirling in the kitchen. "Shit!"

Springing into action, James takes the pan with the burned ingredients off the stove and drops it into the sink while I grab a kitchen towel and wave it in front of the alarm to get it to stop before our ears bleed. Once that's accomplished, we make our way around the loft and open all the windows to clear the air.

"See? If you were fatter, I wouldn't get distracted and burn dinner. You're a damn fire hazard."

I chuckle and shake my head, ready to relent and admit to my faults, when the cell phone on the breakfast bar chirps with an incoming text. We freeze and stare at it like it's a bomb about to detonate. It's my burner phone. The one I've kept by me at all times in the loft the last few days because I'm waiting on word from Matt about whether the Powers That Be feel we have enough evidence to make our move on Croc.

"Read it, John. Whatever it says, we'll deal with it."

When this all started, I had to work hard to convince James to help me build a case against Croc. Now he's reassuring me that, no matter what, we're in this together. What a huge difference in just a couple of months. If I'd had a hundred guesses, I wouldn't have predicted that this is where we'd end up. I only hope what's yet to come doesn't fuck it all up.

I grab the phone and read the coded message. Adrenaline enters my bloodstream and rushes through my veins, making my muscles feel bigger, my skin tighter, like I've been injected with Superman's alien DNA. It's the thrill of the hunt.

The corners of my lips pull back in a wolfish grin. "We hit the warehouse this week."

He sags back against the counter, disbelief written all over his handsome face. "There's enough evidence? We actually did it?"

"Yeah, babe. We did it."

"Christ," he says, dragging a palm down his face and over his short beard. "I don't think I ever thought this day would come. That means Starkey—"

He cuts himself off and swallows the lump of emotion I know is making his throat tight. There hasn't been a day he wasn't worried sick about his brother. Gripping the back of his neck in a supportive squeeze, I hold his gaze. "It means Starkey can come home."

James nods stiffly. Neither of us mention the complicated feelings Starkey has for the captain he was loyal to and the brother he blames for his pain. Nor do we mention the long road he'll have ahead of him on his way to healing and hopefully forgiving James for his decision to keep their connection a secret. There will be a time to deal with all of that, but that time isn't now.

"What happens next?" he asks.

I release him and blow out a breath as I mentally run through everything that has to be done. "We put a team together, analyze the op from every angle, then come up with a plan to get those girls out and take down Croc. It'll happen anytime between two to four days, depending on how the planning goes."

"Okay, let's go."

I grab his arm, stopping him short. "Not you. I meant *we* as in the FBI with a DEA assist because of the Dust. You're staying here and pretending like nothing's out of the ordinary."

James yanks out of my grip. "You gotta be fucking kidding me, John. After everything I've been through with that asshole, you can't leave me behind for this."

Just as he has his Dom voice, I have my cop voice. "I *can*, and I *will*. This is serious shit, James. You're not trained for this. Even if I wanted to let you come—which I don't—no one else would let you get within a mile of the place. Your role was to get me inside the organization, and you did that. None of this would've been possible without your cooperation and help. Remember that."

"Don't you dare fucking patronize me."

"I'm not—"

"This bust is just as much mine as it is yours. *I deserve to take him down, goddamn it.*"

Grabbing his shoulders, I give him a light shake. "You *will* take him down, I swear it. But not right now. Your time will be in court as a witness for the prosecution. That was the deal we made, remember? Amnesty for Starkey with minimum jail time for you and Smee on the condition you testify against him. Your *testimony* is how you take him down. *Not* by getting *shot at* in a bust you have no business being at."

Blue sparks stop shooting from his irises and the angry slashes of his eyebrows soften, then knit together to form a worry line above the bridge of his nose. "Shit, you're going to get shot at. Before, it was like this abstract thing I knew was part of your job, but now…" He pulls me in by my belt loops, presses our foreheads together, and exhales as his eyes squeeze shut. "Just…don't get fucking hurt."

I slide my hands around to his back. "I'm trained for this, James. I'll be fine. But I need you to promise me you won't go anywhere near the warehouse this week. If I'm worried about you, I won't be able to focus. Then my chances of getting hurt go up exponentially."

Sighing, he steps out of my arms. I miss him already. "Yeah, okay," he says with a clipped nod. "Just promise me you'll bring him in."

"I promise."

"Then so do I."

He pulls me to him and kisses me like I'm going off to war, and I guess I kind of am. I feel him pouring every emotion he can't verbalize into this kiss. He might not be able to love me in the traditional way, but like he said the other night, I know what he does feel for me is the strongest he's capable of. To me, that's what love is, but he has to come to that conclusion on his own.

When we break away, he's back to the stoic, unflappable man with a single goal of taking down his enemy. "Go on. End this."

It only takes me five minutes to gather the few things I need, but I use that time to shed my undercover skin and slip back into my task force officer persona. I pause at the door, wishing I didn't have to leave him but knowing we can't truly be together until this is all over. That's motivation enough to get me moving.

"Remember, no resisting arrest or escaping from your handcuffs," I say like a kid trying to stall bedtime with random obvious statements. James knows the plan is to arrest him and Smee with the entire crew after the big bust with Croc. If any of the Pirates found out that Smee and James were working with the feds, they'd have targets on their backs for the rest of their lives. Their sentences won't be long, maybe six months or so, but it'll be enough to make it look like they cut deals for less time, which is what they'll all try to do anyway.

"Take away all my fun, why don't you," he says with a wry grin that doesn't quite reach his eyes.

This isn't easy on either of us. Everything changes once I walk out this door. Our bubble will pop, and the real world will rush in. Just as we learned to navigate *this* way of life, we'll have to learn another while he's in jail, and then another once he's out, and I can't help but worry how all that will affect everything we've fought to gain.

It must be written on my face because James crosses to me and gives me one last kiss. "We'll be fine. Go."

Infused with new confidence that we *will* be fine, I say, "See you on the other side."

"See you then."

Then I leave the loft and my boyfriend behind to prepare for battle. It's time to go slay some fucking demons.

Chapter Thirty-Seven

HOOK

THE GREATEST TRICK the Devil ever pulled was convincing the world he didn't exist.

It's only a line from a movie, but nothing has resonated with me more than that sentence. In the movie, it's referring to the bad guy, Keyser Söze—the guy everyone has heard about but has never seen. Some people believe he exists; others don't. Turns out he was hiding in plain sight the whole time, one of those plot twists you don't see coming, and when it happens, you're left slack-jawed as you start to rewind the movie in your mind to search for all the hints you missed the first time.

For the last twelve years, I've been trying to pull off my own version of a Keyser Söze. Croc knows I exist, obviously, but what he doesn't know is that I'm not the obedient dog he thinks I am. I've been biding my time, waiting for the right opportunity that would ensure his downfall. And while I waited, I made sure he thought I was his reluctant minion. There would've been no point in pretending to be as eager to serve him as the other Pirates; he would've seen right through that bullshit, and I'm not that good of an actor. But an abused and broken kid with nowhere to go who sticks around because it's the only life he's ever known? That shit's believable. More than that, it plays to Croc's ego and blinds him to the truth.

Now, after more than a decade of hiding in plain sight, the plot twist is only days away, and I've been relegated to sitting on my goddamn hands in the wings. Not even the wings. I've been ordered to stay metaphorically locked in the dressing room where I won't be able to see the look on that asshole's face when he realizes the curtain's dropping on his precious empire.

It grates on me like sandpaper on an exposed nerve. But like a fucking sap, I promised John I wouldn't make him worry. I was about to tell him where he could shove his worry until he said it could place him in danger. That stopped me cold. The possibility of losing him was the bucket of ice water that broke my fever for retribution. My need to be a part of the bust that takes out Croc isn't as strong as my need for John to make it out of that warehouse unharmed.

Which is why I'm here—in the Crow's Nest at the clubhouse with Cecco, Cookson, Bill Jukes, and Robert Mullins, while the others are at the warehouse picking up more inventory of Dust—instead of with John and his team. It's also why I'm in the foulest mood of my life. And all things considered, that's fucking saying something.

"Captain, should we go over tonight's assignments while we wait for the others?" Bill Jukes asks.

"I'm thinking maybe we don't do Croc's dirty work tonight," I say, flipping the Zippo Starkey gave me around in my fingers. "Maybe we should just stay in and get loaded. That sounds like more fun to me."

The men trade uneasy glances and silent "not its" for

who gets to question their volatile leader. As usual, Cecco steps up to the plate.

"Everything all right, Captain?"

All right? Fuck no, I'm not all right. I am ten kinds of not all right, but I can't let anyone know that I'm ready to jump out of my skin. That I'm wishing it was a week from now so the bust would be over, Croc would be behind bars, Starkey would be free, and I'd be able to see that John was safe with my own eyes. Even if it was from behind the plexiglass of a prison visitor stall.

"Just tired today." I take out a clove cigarette from my pack and light it. Smoking usually helps to calm my nerves and has the bonus of giving me something to do. "Don't worry, we'll do our job. We always do."

Cecco's phone rings. "It's Skylights," he says. Nodding at him to take the call, I settle back and take a long drag on my cigarette. Cecco answers and there's silence in the room as he listens to whatever Skylights has to say. Then his eyes jump to me as he asks, "Are you sure? Okay, sit tight."

When he disconnects the call, I lean forward and blow out a stream of smoke. "What is it?"

"It's Starkey." My heart rockets into my throat as my stomach plummets. "Skylights said when they were loading the Dust up, they saw a couple of guys pull in with Starkey in the backseat and drive around to the back of the warehouse."

I shove to my feet, my insides trembling. I don't know what's got me juiced up more: wanting to knock Croc into the ground for daring to fuck with my little brother or just getting my arms around Starkey to make sure he's alive and free.

"He's *sure* it was Starkey?"

Cecco nods. "Starkey looked right at them as they passed. Skylights said he doesn't look good, Captain."

"Where are they now?"

"They left the shipyard after loading so they wouldn't cause suspicion if they stuck around."

"Text him to meet us at the gas station a mile north."

In minutes, the five of us are flying down the highway in Cookson's blacked out Escalade. I know I'm supposed to be staying clear of the warehouse, but John said the bust probably won't happen for a couple of days yet, and I can't sit around to see what Croc's plans are for Starkey. Croc doesn't do anything without a reason, which means he's going to use him to manipulate me some other way. Over my dead body.

Taking Starkey out of prison was the worst move Croc could make. Because now I don't give a fuck about playing nice. I know what's coming down the pipeline for that bastard. My only objective is to get Starkey the hell out of there. I'll be in and out long before John's team makes their move. Then, if we need to, we'll hole up in a hotel somewhere until the dust settles.

We arrive at the gas station, pull up next to the cherry red Mustang, and join our waiting crew members. Except I'm short a Pirate.

"Where the fuck is Smee?"

Alf Mason says, "He's watching the office to make sure Croc doesn't take Starkey somewhere else."

"Good, that was smart. All right, listen up." Confident the huge SUV is shielding us from any curious bystanders, I pull out my Desert Eagle that I grabbed before leaving from the small of my back. After checking the clip, I tuck it safely into my waistband again. "This ends now. I'm done letting Croc use one of our own against us for his personal gain. I'm going in there to get our brother back. I have no idea what that'll mean for our future employment status"—*it won't matter because we'll all be doing time soon, anyway*—"so if any of you aren't on board, now's the time to speak up."

Robert Mullins checks his gun. "With you, Captain."

When everyone else follows suit, I nod, glad to have my crew backing me up. "We have no idea what Croc's up to, so keep your heads on a swivel, but my guess is they took Starkey straight to his office, which is why they drove around to the back. We'll go through the front like everything's normal; if anyone asks, we didn't pick up enough product and want to talk to the boss about some new ideas.

"The goal is to get out of there without setting off any kind of alarms because we don't have the firepower to win against all those AKs. So as soon as we get into the office, we need immediate control of the situation. I don't care if we hog-tie and gag the bastard or knock him unconscious, but we can't give him the chance to call for backup."

Noodler smiles. "I like it. How do we get Starkey out of there without raising red flags?"

"You'll all leave through the front, nice and casual. I doubt anyone will notice I'm not with you, but if they do, just tell them I'm in a private meeting with Croc. Then I'll take Starkey to the back exit. There's usually only one guard posted outside; I'll find a way to get rid of him. Drive around, pick us up, and we're out of there before anyone's the wiser. Questions?"

"Nah, Captain, we got it," Cecco says, cracking his knuckles and shifting his weight, ready for action.

"Then let's go."

We pile into the truck with a couple of the guys having to sit in the back hatch area, but both vehicles will look more suspicious. Cookson turns into the shipyard and pauses to tell the mercs standing guard at the gate that the other guys didn't get enough Dust on the first run. They wave us on and Cookson takes us through the graveyard of shipping containers until we finally come to a stop on the side of the warehouse. We spill out of the truck and I lead my men down and around the corner toward the double metal doors of the warehouse's main entrance.

My ever-present sea of rage is boiling just beneath the surface, surging in waves that propel me forward in a rescue march for my brother. Part of me realizes that Croc is setting a trap by bringing him here, but thanks to poor timing on his end, my guys were able to give us a leg up on whatever it is.

The two guards wearing body armor and AK-47s slung around their shoulders nod at us as we enter. Ultimately, they don't care what we're doing here. We have the clearance to be here or we would've been stopped at the gate.

I keep my eyes forward as I stride through the cavernous front room of the warehouse, deliberately avoiding the illegal shit going on around me and trying damn hard not to think about the tragic shit going on above me. *Almost over.* Then John will make sure the girls are taken care of and we'll pay for our part in these sins. Prison sucks, but we've all done time; it won't kill us to do more, and it's only right that we do. None of us are innocent men. None except Starkey.

Starkey. Hang in there, kid. I'm coming.

As usual, I use the fake charm on the guards at the door leading to the administrative wing, and they let us pass without issue. I don't know where Smee's vantage point is, but I don't worry about it either. He'll join the fray as soon as he sees us.

My boots eat up the distance of the long hallway, fueled by vengeance like a demon of reckoning with the hounds of hell at my back. I'm prepared to put Croc down by any means necessary and take my brother far away from here. But when I finally burst through the door, I'm not prepared for what I see.

With the desk shoved off to the side, two people are now the focal point of the otherwise empty room—neither of which are Starkey. Croc stands arrogantly next to Smee, who's on his knees with a gun trained at his temple. Hands bound somehow behind him with his face swollen and bloody, he looks like a stiff wind could topple him over.

"Ah, you're finally here. Just in time for the lightning round of my Q&A," Croc announces like we showed up with wine and snacks for game night. He'll lose his bravado real quick once he has eight guns aimed at his fucking face.

"*You motherfucker.*" I reach behind me, but I'm pulled up short when strong hands grab my arms and I'm relieved of my weapon. "What the fuck is going on?" A bolt of shock rips through me, then fury when I realize Cecco and Cookson are holding me back, and by the looks on their faces, it's not for my own protection. Struggling futilely against their combined strength, I rail at them. "What the hell are you doing?"

The only answer I get is someone behind me binding my wrists tightly together in zip ties. My gut clenches at the all too familiar sadistic glint in Croc's black beady eyes. His smirk grows, making me feel like a wriggling worm at the end of a rusty hook. The rest of the men fan out to flank my enemy, and it hits me like a two-by-four across the face.

My Pirates aren't my crew anymore. If they ever really were.

I wait for the rage and indignation to consume me, but they don't so much as throw off a spark. There was a time when a betrayal of this magnitude would've messed with my head. My entire identity has been hinged on being

Captain of the Pirates. It was proof that I'd risen from the ashes of my shitty past and became something better. I'd gone from never having power to having all the power I wanted. Power meant everything to me.

But I don't give a shit about any of that anymore. It was a means to an end. *His* end. Once this is over, I won't need the power or the title. So fuck them. Fuck each and every one of them. At least I don't have to feel guilty about giving them more time behind bars. They can all rot in prison as far as I'm concerned. I only care about my brother.

"What's the plan here, Croc? I'm the one you get off on making suffer. Why fuck with Smee? And where the hell is Starkey?"

Croc laughs. "So many questions, James."

A million spiders crawl over my skin when I hear my name spoken with that gravelly voice and see it shaped with those sneering thin lips. As easily as swinging a sledgehammer through a window, Croc blows the center out of my progress, leaving only the fragile jagged pieces desperately clinging to a steadily weakening frame.

"You're getting into the Q&A spirit, though, that's good. But I'm the one who asks the questions in this game. I asked Smee quite a few things, haven't I, boy?" Croc directs a nudging kick to Smee's ribs, which are probably already broken with the way he doubles over and gasps for breath. "I never bothered trying to turn this one against you. As for the rest… Well, you know what they say. There's no honor among thieves, or in this case, killers. I enjoyed letting you think you were the leader of your little gang, but they've always answered to me. All except the two, anyway," he says, disgusted, as he looks down at the Irishman.

Squaring his shoulders as best he can, Smee raises his

head to meet my eyes with his swollen ones. "To…the end…Captain."

My throat closes around a hard lump of shame and regret. This man has been by my side since we were young boys, yet I've never told him—never even hinted—how much his allegiance and friendship means to me. I give him a nod, hoping he hears it now. *You're my family. Not by blood, but by choice. Thank you for your loyalty, brother.*

"What a waste." Croc lazily points his gun at Smee—

"*NO!*"

Chapter Thirty-Eight

HOOK

THE SHOT IS DEAFENING, like an invisible crack of lightning that rips through Smee's body with a violent jerk. Time slows to a crawl as he lowers his head to stare at the dime-sized hole in his T-shirt over his abdomen. Crimson pools at the site, then spills over like thick paint, gaining in volume and pressure as though someone's turned a faucet on a steady stream. He glances up at me and opens his mouth to speak, but all that comes out is a slight wheeze before he slumps to the cement floor, eerily motionless.

Time zips back to normal speed as an anguished cry is torn from my chest. I lunge for my friend, but I'm held firm and forced to watch as Skylights and Alf Mason drag him to the corner as though he's a bag of trash.

"Oh, Jesus. *Smee…*" My legs give out, but I'm held up by my arms and set back on my feet. "Where's my brother, you sick fuck? *Where's Starkey?*"

The bored expression on Croc's face drives home just how big of a sociopath he really is. "He never left prison. But I did call the warden to let him know I wouldn't be needing the kid anymore. I left the specifics up to him, but he'll be joining Smee in that big pirate ship in the sky. If he's not there already."

Red rage bathes my vision. "*I'll fucking kill you!*"

"No, you won't," he sneers, walking toward me. "You could've done it a hundred times over by now, but you haven't. You pretend to be so tough, but you don't have the stomach for killing. Face it, James, you're gutless." He stops just out of kicking range but close enough that the stench of his boozy sweat burns my nostrils. "That's why I picked you, you know. Because you were easily manipulated. Broken. Damaged. *Weak.*"

Each flaw he lists blows a hole through the new narrative John wrote for me—one I started believing—that I have worth just as I am. That being broken doesn't mean I'm not fixable. However, faced with my reality, it's clear to see the rest for what it is: an elaborate fairytale like the ones John's mom used to tell them as kids.

But before I can dismiss it completely, I remember pieces of the conversation I had with John after my visit with Starkey.

I am in awe *of you…you are the bravest and most selfless man I have ever known. The first night I met you, I knew there was something special about you…You are exactly the man I thought you were. And that man is* amazing.

If I didn't know better, I'd swear John is projecting his thoughts directly into my head. But whether it's mental telepathy or an intuitive subconscious, it stops me from taking Croc's bait and spiraling out of control.

Reality is, it doesn't matter what I believe about myself right now, and it sure as fuck doesn't matter what *Croc* thinks, now or then. I don't care if it takes me years. If I survive this, I'm going to burn every shred of his existence in my mind until there's nothing left. Not even a goddamn memory.

Squeezing my eyes shut, I visualize setting fire to Croc's seeds of doubt, the same way I set fire to his precious school.

"Look at me when I'm talking to you, boy!"

My head snaps to the right as an explosion in my face reverberates through my skull. My cheek throbs in time with my racing pulse, and I assume he opened a sizable gash below my left eye when a trail of sticky wetness tracks downward and into my beard.

Glaring at him through the longer hair hanging in my eyes, I growl, "Fuck. You."

The corners of his thin lips pull back, and he replies with a creepy chuckle. "Maybe later, but right now we're gonna have a little chat. If you tell me what I want to know, I'll let you live."

Live? I just watched my only friend die and my baby brother—who's been my sole reason for living since our mom brought him home from the hospital—will be right behind him, if he's not already. Sticking around now seems pretty fucking pointless.

"Tell me who JD really is."

Johnathan.

One second Croc takes away my reason for living, and in the next, he gives me another. Every smile, every kiss, every embrace, every *I love you*… They flash through my mind like a mental resuscitation, breathing life into my heart and sparking hope in the darkness. Losing Smee and Starkey has destroyed me. But if I have even the smallest chance at a life with John, then I'll find a way to put myself back together, piece by fragmented piece.

I need to get through this, and I need to get the hell out of here.

I made him a promise.

"I don't know what you're talking about, old man. As

far as I know, JD's exactly who he says he is." Croc narrows his eyes like he's trying to decide if he should punch me in the face or the gut next. "Look, I'm not the information expert here, *you* are. I assumed you had him checked out after I brought him in like you always do."

"I did," he says through gritted teeth. "He checked out."

"Then what the fuck do you want from me? I don't know dick about any of that shit." My top lip curls up in a snarl, allowing my sarcasm to slip free before I can stop it. "I'm just an obedient dog, happily taking orders from his fucking mas—"

Croc's gaze shifts to my right, and Cookson plows his fist so deep into my stomach I think he grazes my spine with his scarred knuckles. I double over with a grunting wheeze, but I'm jerked back to an upright position before I fully recover.

"I don't believe you, James."

Another glance, this time behind him at Noodler. The crazy fucker grins like Jack Nicholson in *The Shining* as he steps in front of me and slips brass knuckles onto all eight fingers—four real and four fake—of his right hand. I have less than two seconds to brace myself. He cocks his arm back, swings, and connects with my jaw.

"FUCK!" Like a nail bomb detonating, the excruciating pain shoots in all directions, tearing through bone and flesh alike. My mouth fills with the coppery tang of blood from my teeth shifting in my gums. Before my ears stop ringing, he drives another punch into my side hard enough to crack a few ribs. All the air is forced out of my lungs with a *whoosh*, spraying my DNA onto Noodler's face like a preschooler's splatter paint project.

Not even fazed, he winds up for a third blow, but Croc calls him off at the last second. Stepping back into line,

Noodler makes a big show of licking my blood from around his mouth. Jesus, how did I never notice just how unhinged that man is? I try to take a deep breath but stop short at the piercing stab in my side. *Mother fuck, that hurts.* Okay, shallow breaths. Shallow breaths are good, too.

"Let me tell you why we're all here, James. You see, Cecco's been suspicious of JD for a while now," Croc says, bringing my attention back to him. "The other day, he stopped by your loft and noticed the tattoo on JD's neck flaking off like one of those fake ones for kids."

Goddamn it, I told him this would happen. If I make it out of here, I'm belting his ass for such a stupid move; one stripe for every tat and two stripes for every time he had to replace them.

"Now, I know not all gang members have tattoos, but they sure as fuck don't wear *fake ones*," Croc stresses, his frustration mounting. "Then he calls yesterday and says he's running down to Atlanta to check on the deal. Except I have it on good authority that JD never showed up, even though Tannen told me he *did*. Why do you suppose Tannen lied, James?"

"I don't really give a shit," I say lazily, my energy crashing.

"I think you do. I also think you know a lot more than you're letting on. So, for the last fucking time…" Croc grabs me by the throat with one meaty hand and *squeezes*. "*Who. Is. He.*"

Shit. Breathing… Breathing had been nice. Even the recently painful, shallow kind. Turns out you're never fully grateful for an involuntary function until it's taken away. I need to think fast before I pass out and Croc decides I'm expendable while unconscious. Trying to suck oxygen through an airway the width of a cocktail straw, I come up with two ways to play this.

One: I can pretend to bargain information for my life

then admit I was forced to cooperate with the FBI. I can hope like hell that Croc buys into the shit Hollywood sells and make up a story about the FBI and DEA working against each other, so John was pulled in for a couple of days to debrief the people in charge. *Then* I have to hope that John gets here in the next day or so before Croc manages to move his entire operation.

Two: Try to convince him that I'm just as clueless about "JD" as he is, then bargain for my life by promising to track him down and deliver him to Croc on the condition that afterward I'm free to move to the other side of the country, never to be seen or heard from again.

They're both solid plans. They might even work if it was any of the other Pirates in my place. The problem is, there's too much history between me and Fred Croc, too many secrets with too much intimate knowledge of how the other works.

He knows I won't really try to help him.

And I know he won't really let me live.

Which means bargaining on either of our parts would be nothing but empty promises.

It's a stalemate.

Except not really, because I'm the only one bound, bloody, and unable to breathe.

I know what he's going to do. I can see it in his eyes and feel it in his grip. He's past caring what I do or don't know, what I can or can't tell him. From the time I was nine, Croc has taken pleasure in controlling every aspect of my life. Being the one to snuff it out will be his Big Finale, one he's probably fantasized about for years, just as I fantasized about my revenge.

There'll be no *Count of Monte Cristo* ending for me now, though. Maybe things would've been different if I hadn't agreed to work with the FBI. But I can't bring myself to regret the decision that brought John into my life, fleeting as it was. I think I always knew Croc would somehow get the upper hand eventually, so I'm grateful I had the time that I did with John before my fate…my fate interve…

I don't remember where I was going with that… Thick fog is pressing down on my brain… Thoughts are leaking out like water through my fingers, I can't hold on to them… Blackness creeps in at the edges of my vision. I try to sip air into my lungs…even a tiny bit…doesn't work. Finally, the lack of oxygen tugs on the last thread of my strength, unraveling the hold my muscles have on my bones…my knees buckle.

This time I'm released to fall to my knees, but Croc's merciless grip only gets tighter…

"Holy shit, boss, you hear that? What the fuck's going on?"

The panic in Alf Mason's voice injects me with one last dose of adrenaline to fight against the relentless darkness.

And that's when I hear it, too.

A distant cacophony of shouts, commands, and screams among the peppering of gunfire.

The vise grip on my neck pops off and I collapse. I manage to twist my body at the last second and land on my side, preventing me from face-planting without the use of my hands. My head begins to clear with the return of sweet oxygen rushing to my brain, my lungs, my muscles—fuck, I never want to be without air again.

Still mentally sluggish, I try to follow what's happening. The bust is happening now. Not in a couple days. *Now.* Shit, this is so not good. Croc is barking orders, telling a couple of the men to stand guard and sending others out to secure an exit. Doubt he'll find one. Pretty sure the place is surrounded by federal agents. Not telling *him* that, though. As he continues to swear up a storm and threaten the lives of anyone still in the room, I take a move out of my old playbook and let my mind start to drift…

The cold from the concrete floor starts to seep through my clothes and into my skin. I try to adjust my position but freeze when I see Smee's lifeless body facing the corner not even ten feet away. The nightmare of losing him and my brother rushes back to me like a tidal wave of devastation. Tears fill my eyes and fall in steady drops to the ground from my temple and the bridge of my nose.

There's nothing I can do for either of them now. There's not much I can do for anyone, considering my current situation. But in one final, desperate act, I do the only thing I can think of. Closing my eyes, I offer up my first-ever prayer to a higher power I don't entirely believe in.

Dear God or whoever the hell is up there listening… Don't let John know I'm fucking here. Please. I need him to focus and stay safe. I can't let him worry. Goddamn it…

I made him a promise…

Chapter Thirty-Nine

JOHN

LASER-FOCUSED WITH ADRENALINE PUMPING, I slip through the shadows between the shipping containers with a small team on our way to the rear of the warehouse. Our job is to secure the girls and the back entrance while other teams work to clear the warehouse from the front and side exits. The main objective is to arrest, but with the type of hired firepower present, it's not likely they'll go quietly. As long as our guys make it out safely and the bust ends with Croc in cuffs, I'll consider this whole operation a success.

My need to take that fucker down has eaten at me forever, years before I ever became a cop. This day has been so long in coming, it's almost surreal it's finally happening. It's a small miracle we managed to put our plan in motion less than thirty-six hours after getting the green light. I don't know that I could've lasted longer than that. Croc is evil personified, a sociopath and predator, and he's grown more volatile with the added pressure of the human trafficking deal coming up. He's unpredictable, and my biggest fear is him fucking with James when I'm not there to protect him.

Not that he needs me for that—he's proven he can protect himself and everyone else—but I can't be expected to think rationally when it comes to him. James has survived more shit than any one person should have to in five lifetimes. He deserves to be shielded from any more shit, so that's what I'm going to do. As soon as we get Croc into custody and behind bars, James will be able to breathe easier and sleep better. Then we'll focus on healing from the past and building our future.

Staying low, we quickly cross the last twenty feet to crouch behind a shipping container. Once all my guys are ready, I speak quietly into my comms unit. "Blue Team in position."

"Red Team in position."

"Green Team in position."

That's all of us. We're minutes away from getting the order to go in.

"All teams hold," the Team Leader says. "We've got a black Escalade arriving."

Cookson? Shit. Is he alone or did he come with any of the others? We know that four of the Pirates were here to pick up their weekly Dust inventory and left about a half hour ago, but James and the other four were back at the clubhouse from the last report we heard.

"Be advised, the vehicle is parking on the west side of the building. I have the driver and two rear passengers exiting—wait. There was two in the very back, so that's five but I can't see if there are others. Schmidt, you got eyes on them?"

An answer comes through from Schmidt, leader of the Green Team that's positioned to take the main entrance. "I see them. Three exited on the passenger side. They're all heading toward the front."

Eight in the truck? That's one short of the whole

group. Dare I hope… Touching the unit in my ear, I ask, "Schmidt, is Hook with them?"

There's a few seconds of silence, then, "Affirmative."

My heart stops. *Oh God, no. No no no.* Suddenly my body armor weighs five hundred pounds and I break out in a sweat all over my body. What the fuck would possess him to come here? I told him to stay away. He *promised* me he would.

Goddamn it, I want to call the whole thing off, tell everyone to fall back and regroup for another night. But I'm not in charge of this op and I sure as hell don't have the authority to call off one of the biggest busts in the region for both the DEA and the FBI simply because I'm terrified the man I love will get caught in the crossfire.

No, there's only one thing I can do, and that's find James as fast as I can. Once I get him somewhere safe—I don't care if it's a fucking barricaded closet—I can focus on doing my job and helping my teammates. The only thing that gives me any consolation is that he won't resist arrest. He knows it's coming; he just doesn't know it's coming *now*. Once he realizes what's happening, he'll surrender.

It'll be fine. He'll be fine.

I repeat that in my head, over and over, like a mantra I can make into reality if I believe it hard enough. I refuse to think about the dozens of ways this can go sideways and end with anything other than James getting out of this unscathed. If I let myself go down that path, I won't be able to focus.

The Team Leader's voice comes through the comms. "They're in the building. All teams stand by to go on my command…"

An eternity ticks by as we wait for the final order. I mentally say a quick apology to the guys next to me. I'm about to abandon them for my own mission. There's enough of them to deal with whatever's on the second floor, but I'll catch hell for going rogue later. I don't care. It wouldn't matter if it meant my job; there's nothing more important to me than getting James out of here.

"Go!"

We spring into action and charge the rear entrance. There's only one guard. We yell for him to surrender as we advance. He raises his weapon. Never gets off a single shot. We sidestep his prone body and breach the building. Distant shouts and gunshots echo through the halls from the other areas, but we stay focused and head for the back stairs that lead to the rooms where the girls are being kept. Except when we get to the stairwell, I peel off down the hall in the direction of Croc's office. My gut tells me that James wasn't here with his entire crew to pick up a few more kilos of Dust. Something happened, which means Croc is at the center of it, like always.

"Darling! What are you doing?"

I turn around to see Sanchez stopped at the bottom of the stairs. He's a fellow task force officer and a good friend. Last night, I confided in him about my relationship with James. It was a risk to admit that I let an op get personal, but I've been shut off from my family for months and I needed to confide in someone.

"I have to find him," I say, praying he'll understand.

Sanchez curses, then gives me a chin lift. "Go. I'll cover for you. Don't get fucking dead or I'll kill you again myself."

"Deal. Thanks, man."

I spin on my heel and take off, sticking close to the wall as I approach the turn in the hall that will give me a clear view of Croc's office door. Before I get that far, the sound of boots pounding and voices I recognize has me ducking into an alcove. I move just enough to see around the wall and watch as five Pirates run toward the open warehouse, none of them the one I'm looking for. I don't know which Pirate is missing, but if the whole group of eight were in Croc's office like I thought, that means James and two others must still be back there.

Once the five are well past my position, I move to the end of the hall then flatten myself against the wall to look around the corner. *Skylights and Noodler.* That leaves James still in the office, and I don't like what that implies at all. Wasting no time, I spin out into the hall and raise my Glock. "FBI, put your weapons down, you're under—"

I don't know if they recognize me without the fake tattoos or facial scruff, but it ceases to matter as soon as they raise their guns. *POP! POP!* I get off two clean shots that drop them both to the ground. I run over with my gun still drawn, remaining cautious until I kick their weapons away and check their pulses. Gone. *Fuck.* I don't care how bad the person is or that I'm forced to do it in self-defense, it's never my goal to take a life. I've only done it once, and it still weighs on me.

Standing, I kick in the office door…and rush straight into my nightmare.

In just a few seconds, I take note of the situation. Croc is standing in the middle of the room, shielding himself with my boyfriend's body while holding a gun to his temple. James is roughed up. His cheek and lower lip are cut open, swollen, and bleeding, there are red marks on the sides of his neck in the shape of fingers and a thumb, and his hands are bound behind his back. Smee is in the corner, lying deathly still in a pool of his own blood. *Fuck, Smee.* A punch of grief hits me, but I can't let myself feel it yet, so I mentally shut the door on that for later.

"Croc! Put your fucking gun down. You're under arrest."

"I don't think so, *JD*," he snarls. "You pulled one over on me, I'll give you that. But I have the upper hand now. Kick your gun over or I put a bullet in his head."

My heart slams against my ribs at the speed of a strobe light, but I keep my features schooled. He doesn't know what James means to me. He doesn't know I'd fucking die for him. I don't have a clear shot, and I have no intention on risking James, so I hold steady and prepare to bluff my way out of this.

But then James leans his head against the barrel of the gun. "Do it, Croc. Stop being a fucking pussy and finish the job you were doing before."

"Shut up, Hook," I bark, hoping the panic riding me isn't coming through in my voice. "You're in no position to give orders here."

James locks gazes with me, his electric-blue eyes swimming with unspoken emotions. "He drops me, you drop him. It's the only way this ends."

"No, it's fucking *not*."

His eyes plead with me as he whispers, "Johnathan..."

I grit my teeth. "*No*."

"What's going on here?" Croc's gaze lands on my hands. I adjust my grip, but I can't stop the slight tremor. Then he looks at James, right as a set of tears slip between his lower lashes. "Oh, this is just too fucking perfect."

Croc's chuckle grows into arrogant laughter that sends a chill through my blood. We just lost any chance at having the advantage. I release a slow breath, trying to clear my mind and come up with a new plan. The stricken look on James's face kills me. Forcing a lopsided grin, I say, "You were supposed to stay gone."

"I know," he says, his voice raspy. "I fucked up. I'm sorry."

Two more tears fall, and I wish more than anything I could wipe them from his cheeks. I wish I could kiss him and hold him and let him know it's going to be okay. All I need to do is keep Croc talking, give my guys time to make their way here and take this motherfucker out.

"It's okay, babe," I say. "Everything's going to be fine."

"As touching as this is, I'm in a bit of a hurry." Croc puts the gun under James's chin and presses so hard it cuts off his air. "Kick your gun over here, *Johnathan*, and do it fast. If I'm going down, I'm taking James with me, so your best bet is to let me walk out of here."

James tries to shake his head, but Croc just shoves his gun in deeper, making James wheeze. "*Okay, okay!*" I say, holding my hands up in supplication.

I slowly lower my gun to the ground and shove it across the floor to him. I expect him to pick it up, which might give me a chance to overpower him if I act fast, but he doesn't. He just kicks it off to the side where it slides somewhere underneath the desk. *Goddamn it.* I'd have to move the desk away from the wall to even get to it.

Worse still, if Croc's willing to leave a gun in the room, then he's not planning on leaving anyone in here. At least not alive.

"Now," he says, pulling his lips back to bare his teeth in a grin fit for the devil. "Let's bring your story to a close, James. It's been a long time coming."

Chapter Forty

HOOK

I THOUGHT I knew fear intimately.

At the age of nine I stared into my mother's lifeless gaze with a baby crying at my feet. Not long after that, I knew what it was like to look into the gleeful eyes of a demon right before he hit me so hard I fell unconscious—the first time of dozens. And for four years, the mere sound of a ticking watch struck me with terror so deep it burrowed into my very marrow and never left.

Yet none of that comes close to the fear gripping me in its talons right now.

Not because there's a gun jammed against my carotid. But because I'm afraid that soon it *won't* be. As long as it's on me, it's not on John. I need to keep it that way. At least until I can get these fucking zip ties off.

John had made good on his promise to get me my own pair of Get Out of Jail Free shoelaces. Before Croc dragged me off the floor to use me as a human shield, I managed to get one of the tiny metal shivs without him noticing. I never really thought I'd get the chance to use the laces for anything serious; it was more of an inside joke. But that joke is about to turn the tables. If I don't sever my hand first.

Fuuuuuuck. I grit my teeth as I try to work one of the plastic strips around my wrist. I need to move as little as possible so he doesn't catch on to what I'm doing, but they were put on tight as hell. The plastic is cutting into my skin, which hurts like a son of a bitch but has the bonus of making shit slide easier from the blood. I need to get the locking mechanism at a certain spot on my left wrist for the fingers of my right hand to be able to slip the shiv inside and release the teeth. All I need is *one* tie free to have use of both my hands.

"Come on, Croc. You've got me as your hostage. Let's go," I say, hoping to keep his focus on me and his need for escape.

John counters my suggestion. "You won't get anywhere, Croc. Your best bet is to surrender and try to cut a deal in exchange for information on your Brazil contact. No offense, but you're not the biggest fish in the pond. Give them someone bigger and you'll get leniency."

Is it wrong to notice how sexy John looks in the middle of our lives being on the line? Maybe I'm slightly out of it —okay, probably a lot out of it—but I can't help but admire how strong and badass he is. His fake tats are gone and his jaw is clean-shaven now, but the way his all-black tactical clothes and gear hug his large frame is fucking hot. If this wasn't a life or death situation, I'd definitely be turned on. Speaking of turning…the zip tie is almost there…

Croc snorts. "I think I'll take my chances. But first," he says, turning his head to speak against my ear. "Say goodbye to lover boy."

The world slows down and speeds up simultaneously.

The gun leaves my throat as Croc switches targets, and

the resigned expression in John's eyes guts me. I can't let him get hurt. I *won't.*

I finally get the metal strip shoved into the zip tie and yank my wrists apart, immediately reaching up to grab the gun out of Croc's hands by using the element of surprise and sheer force of will. I refuse to accept an outcome that doesn't end with me giving my tormentor some poetic fucking justice.

And now I can.

Roaring with every second of pain and fear he's caused me, I spin around and thrust the gun against the center of his forehead, pushing him backward until he slams against the wall. "Now what are you gonna do, motherfucker? Huh? Not so tough *now*, are you?"

Croc doesn't give me the reaction I want, the reaction *I deserve.* He should be pissing his pants right now, begging me to spare his life, apologizing for every vile thing he did to me. But not Croc, no. He's chortling like I just told him the joke of the century.

"*What the fuck are you laughing at?*"

"You, James," he says, his black eyes taunting me the same as they always have. "I told you, you don't have the *balls* to kill me."

"You're right, I didn't. But that was before you had my brother beaten, raped, and killed." My left hand, bloody from the cuts in my wrist, strikes like a viper's jaw clamping onto his throat. As I press the barrel of the gun harder against his head, my fingers dig into the fleshy meat of his neck. Slowly, I squeeze, more and more, until I feel his life pulsing beneath my fingertips and hear the thready wheeze of his emaciated breaths.

Getting right up in his face so I can enjoy every second of his reaction, I say, "For years you've tried to break me, and after all this time, you finally did it. So, congratulations, motherfucker, because the broken me not only has the balls to kill you…he's going to *revel in it.*"

Croc's eyes flare wide. *There it is. At last.* True fear swirls in my demon's eyes for the first time, and I feel that teenage boy inside of me sigh as we merge into one and drink in this long-awaited justice. I'm so high on the power I'm shaking. Every minute of my existence has been leading up to this, the moment I take back my life and *end his*.

"James…"

My entire body flinches, and my mind tries to reconcile the vile word with the pleasant tone. Croc's lips never moved—

"James, baby, come back to me…"

That voice…I hear it say other things that don't really sink in—something about backup and medical attention—but I like the way it sounds, so deep and soothing. I want to burrow into its warm notes, wrap myself up in its comforting tenor…

But I can't. Not yet. Croc is in front of me with my gun to his head and his life in my hands. My tormentor is finally at *my* mercy…and I have none left to give.

I tuck my pointer finger through the guard and touch it to the trigger.

Movement on my left makes me freeze. *Johnathan.* He's here. Still in danger. "Get out of here, John."

"No fucking way," he says, "I'm not going anywhere without you."

"Goddamn it, *just go*," I plead through a clenched jaw.

"No. Give me the gun, James; you don't want to do this."

The shaking in my hand is getting worse. I have to fight to hold it steady, but my body rebels. As though the cost of a steady hand is that I break apart somewhere else, my eyes flood with more fucking tears before they spill over and follow the same path as the others. I resent them and the weakness they represent, branding me as the coward I've always been to *him*, and I'm so fucking sick of being afraid of him, of what he's done and what he won't ever let me forget.

"Yes," I whisper, staring into the soulless windows of my nightmare. "I do."

"No, you don't," John insists. "I know you; *I love you.* He's not worth—"

"*He killed my fucking brother!*"

"No, he didn't!" John takes a step closer to me. "We got Starkey out earlier today; he's *not dead.*"

My head snaps to the side, searching his golden eyes for the truth to match his words. "You got him out? H-he's…alive?"

He nods. "Yeah, babe, he's fine. I promise you."

Oh, thank Christ. Powerful relief nearly sweeps my legs out from under me, but I manage to remain standing.

"I'll take you to him as soon as we get out of here. But you have to let me do my job and arrest Croc, okay?"

I look back to where I still have a death grip on the asshole's throat. He's past red and on his way to dark purple. I'm suddenly disgusted that I'm touching him. Like realizing the garter snake is actually a king cobra, I snatch my hand back and begin reversing my steps, grabbing John's arm to take him with me. I keep my eyes and the gun trained on Croc as I put as much space as I can between him and us. I don't want to be anywhere near him, I don't even want us sharing the same air.

"James," John says calmly. "It's time to give me the gun."

Croc is still standing, but he's slumped against the wall with one hand rubbing his throat as he works to drag in enough air to satisfy his oxygen-starved lungs. His hair is messy, his shirt is halfway pulled out of his pants, and although his face is returning to its usual sallow color, his skin is dotted with newly broken blood vessels beneath his eyes. He no longer looks like the monster from my childhood. He's just a pathetic old man who's nothing without his criminal empire to back him up. Karma will be his constant companion in prison, and that will have to be enough.

Turning to John, I offer him the gun. He accepts it gingerly with a nod, letting me know I'm doing the right thing and everything's going to be okay. And maybe for the first time, I truly believe him.

"Thank you," I say, my voice gruff with overwhelming emotions, "for…" Fuck, there are so many things, I don't even know how to finish that. But he doesn't need me to.

"*Always*, Captain." John gives me a quick, reassuring tilt of his mouth, then slips right back into cop mode. "Hear that?" he says, indicating the sounds of men shouting to each other somewhere in the building. He looks over to make sure Croc hasn't moved—he hasn't—then glances down at the confiscated 9-millimeter as he drops the clip into his palm. "That's our backup and the medics. And don't give them any shit about looking you over, either. We're not leaving…"

I don't hear anything else. Not John's lecture, not the echoing sound of the backup in the halls, not their shouts to each other, not even my own thoughts. Because Croc is whipping out another gun from behind his back. And taking aim at John.

There's no time to think. No time to warn John. No time to disarm Croc. No time to wish for things to be different. There's only one thing I *do* have time for.

I take a lunging step to my left.

Chapter Forty-One

JOHN

YOU CAN FIT a hundred regrets into the span of a single heartbeat.

I wish I would have…

…cuffed him.

…kept my eyes on him.

…tried to stop the bust.

…stayed with James yesterday.

…told someone about Croc when we were kids.

All those regrets and more raced through my mind in a mere fraction of a second. If I'd done any of those things, maybe I could've prevented this moment from happening.

But I didn't. So I didn't.

I should have assumed Croc's gun was loaded and left it at that, but checking the clip of a weapon—especially one that's not mine—is second nature. I pressed the button and the clip slid into my left hand, something I've done thousands of times before.

But never in the presence of an unrestrained prisoner.

The second I pull out the clip to satisfy myself that it

still has bullets, I see Croc in my periph making a move. Then everything happens at once.

He pulls out another gun and straightens his arm to take aim at my chest.

I slap the clip into place.

James jumps in front of me.

I fist his shirt with my left hand, ready to jerk him to the side.

I raise the 9 mil.

Gunfire cracks like a whip in the air just before I see the muzzle flash.

James's body jerks and slams against me as I feel a concentrated punch in my chest.

I squeeze the trigger.

Blood wells up and spills from a hole from the empty space where Croc's heart should be, then he collapses in a heap.

"*James.*"

He starts to slump against me, losing his battle with gravity. I drop the gun off to the side, wrap my arms around him, and ease him down to the floor. I try not to jostle him as I dip my head to look for an exit wound. I know he has one because the bullet hit me, too, but I need to see where so I can try to staunch the bleeding. I hope to God the fact that he's not coughing up blood means it missed his major organs. But bleeding out is a very real threat, and after that, infection.

Shit, this is bad. Really fucking bad.

Once I locate both wounds, I whip off my vest and yank off my polo and undershirt. Then I carefully lift his head into my lap and press the balled-up shirts to each of his bullet wounds.

His beautiful face, caked with blood and streaked with dried tears, is contorting with pain. My throat constricts and I have to swallow around the fist-sized lump of gravel just to speak. "Goddamn it, babe, what the fuck were you thinking?"

"Croc gets perverse satisfaction from…taking things away from me." James grunts with a wince when he tries to breathe faster than his injury allows. Whatever expression is on my face, he tries to erase it with the hint of his crooked smile. "Wasn't about…to let him…take you away, too."

Jesus Christ. The man who thinks he's incapable of love jumped in front of a bullet for me. I don't know whether to kiss him or strangle him. When I finally decide that strangling my fatally wounded boyfriend is counter-productive to my end goal of keeping him alive, I shake my head. "You crazy, reckless man. I was the one wearing the bulletproof vest."

His gaze falls to my chest like he's remembering seeing my body armor with the bright yellow FBI letters emblazoned on it for the first time. "Well, shit…" Looking back up at me, he licks his dry lips, then adds, "I'm having some regrets…about the last few minutes."

I can't help but laugh even as tears blur my vision before falling through the air to land on his shoulder. The blood is starting to seep through my fingers. Before shit went sideways, Sanchez told me over the comms that they got held up with some wounded on the way, but they'd be here ASAP. Except I need them in here *now*. I hear the voices of my team, so I shout over my shoulder for a medic and turn back just in time to see James's eyes start to roll up into his head.

Shaking him, I don't even bother to hide the panic. "*No no no*! Don't you fucking pass out on me, Hook, do you hear me? Wake the fuck up!"

He opens his eyes again and gives a decent glare for how weak he is. "That's Captain…to you…"

"Yes," I say, clearing my throat. "You're my Captain, and you always will be. I just need you to hold on a little longer, okay? Just a *little longer*."

Finally, Sanchez and another guy from our team rush into the room with a stretcher and immediately go into triage mode. Sanchez heads for Smee and the other to Croc who is immediately declared deceased. I don't even have time to offer a quick explanation before Sanchez mutters a shocked "holy shit," then announces that Smee is still alive—but barely—with a gunshot wound to the abdomen.

Thank you, God. "Get him out of here and med flighted, do whatever you can to save him," I say, then look down at the man in my lap. "Make that two med flights."

Sanchez radios for a couple of medics to bring another stretcher and all their gear, then explains, "Between the girls and a few of our guys getting shot, they're swamped," Sanchez says. "Fucking AK-47s, man. But they're on their way, so just sit tight, and I'll get the birds in the air."

I nod. "We'll be here."

As soon as they're gone, I turn my attention back to James. They need to hurry. There's so much blood, I don't know how much can possibly be left in his body.

He stares up at me, and I swear I can see everything in his heart shining in those limpid blue pools. "Johnathan…"

"Captain," I whisper back.

"I l-love you…"

My eyes blow wide. *Holy shit, he said it. He said he* loves *me.* I'm full to bursting with everything I feel for this man, and I can't wait to spend every day showing him just how much he means to me.

"I love you, too, James. So damn much."

"Sorry…" he says, his voice gravelly and his eyelids sliding closed. "Gone…"

"No, baby, you just closed your eyes. Open them back up for me." He's so weak. When he raises his arm, it's like he's fighting against an invisible weight pulling it down. Grabbing his hand, I bring it to my face, kiss the center of his palm, then hold it against my cheek. When he finally does look at me again, I release a sigh of relief and smile. "See? I'm right here. I'm not going anywhere."

"I know…" A set of tears escape from the corners of his eyes and slip into his hairline. "I…am…"

His arm goes slack in my hand and his lids slide close.

"*Jaaaaaaames!*"

That's when the paramedics run in along with Sanchez, who pulls me back so the other two can work on James.

I've never felt so helpless in my life. After everything he's been through, everything he's fought for, everyone he's saved with his sacrifices. Goddamn it, this is not the end he deserves.

Villains die at the end, not the heroes. It's exactly why Fred Croc has a bullet in his fucking chest, and if I could kill him all over again, I gladly would.

James might never have considered himself the hero, but I know better. He *is* the hero. He's *my* hero, and that means he *has to live*.

Except this isn't a fairytale. It's real life. And I know all too well that in the real world, heroes die all the time.

Chapter Forty-Two

HOOK

CHRIST, no one said death would be so fucking painful.

If this is what the afterlife feels like, send me back to my hell on earth, please and thanks. Or maybe I'm in the actual hell—definitely more likely to be the eternal destination for someone like me—in which case, the Prince of Sin needs to step up his torture game.

I open my senses a little at a time, trying to assess my surroundings. I can hear muffled sounds of people talking somewhere in the distance, but I can't make out anything they're—

There's a soft snick, and then I hear everything clearly along with a woman's voice softly saying, "I'm checking on 322… Okay, yeah, I'm coming…" The rest of what she says is closed off with another snick, which must be a door closing.

Not dead, then. Just extremely fucking broken. I rack my brain, trying to remember what happened, how I got here, but my memory is fuzzy. It's like I'm squinting at a whiteboard with the details laid out for me, but a gauzy curtain hangs in front of it, blurring all the words.

Abandoning thinking for now, I focus on my body. It feels weighed down, like it's encased in concrete, and my heavy eyelids are reluctant to open, so I don't bother forcing them. I don't have any desire to fully wake up when half-consciousness feels this shitty. But now I'm suddenly worried on just how broken I am. Am I paralyzed? Fuck, that would suck.

Needing to end the suspense, I start small and try to wiggle my toes. When they obey and rub against each other, I heave an imaginary sigh. Okay, not paralyzed, so things are looking up. Bolstered with that small victory, I attempt to curl the fingers of my left hand. The motion is a bit jerky, and I don't get far before I feel a tug on the top of my hand that makes me stop, but it's more progress. I switch to my right hand, except this time my fingers don't budge. They're met with some kind of resistance. Silky, soft resistance.

My brain's still not supplying me with any puzzle pieces, so I'm going to have to figure it out myself. Avoiding reality isn't going to work.

With some effort, I crack my eyes open and blink a few times as I adjust to the muted light shining from somewhere on the wall behind me. Bracing myself for a possible unpleasant visual or an increase of pain from the movement—or both—I carefully lower my chin to peer down my body, covered by a thin blanket. I'm aware of the air blowing into my nose by the cumbersome oxygen line that stretches across my cheeks and hooks behind my ears. Snaking out from the loose neck of my paper-thin hospital gown are several gray wires, which I assume are connected to electrodes stuck on my chest. An IV is dripping fluids into my left hand, which explains the earlier tugging sensation.

But my other arm…my other arm is exactly where I need it to be.

Johnathan.

I sink farther into the pillow and mattress on a relieved sigh, releasing all the tension and unease I didn't realize I was holding. Just the sight of him makes everything right in my world, regardless of how wrong something must have gone for me to end up here. The memory is finally tickling my brain, and I think I'll be able to remember it if I try, but I'm not ready to face any of that yet. All I want to do is enjoy the calm before the storm with the beautiful man at my side.

Sitting in a plastic chair and hunched over the edge of the bed has to be giving him kinks in his back, but he's fast asleep with his head resting next to my leg. He looks so young like this, wearing a navy-blue hoodie, facial scruff, and his hair mussed like he just crashed after a long night of studying for finals. But it's the way his thick eyebrows are pinched together with his mouth turned down in a frown that gets to me. I've spent an embarrassing amount of time studying John while he sleeps, and this is far from his usual carefree-in-dreamland expression.

I lick my chapped lips and try to swallow past the lump of guilt clogging my throat. I *hate* that I've put him through any kind of distress. I want to take care of him, not cause him pain, and the blatant evidence of my failings is grating. I wish I had the strength to gather him in my arms, but it looks like John found a way to draw comfort from me even when I couldn't consciously offer it.

Keeping my upper arm on the mattress, John lifted my forearm and rested it against his left cheek. Then he held it there with one big paw while he slept so that my hand is gently cupping the crown of his head. I flex my fingers again, this time lightly combing through his soft hair and drawing my own comfort from the familiar act.

When John's lashes flutter, I stop moving, but it's too late. His eyes open to half-mast, and he stares at me, blinking slowly. "James…"

Damn. My name whispered in his sleep-roughened voice is the fucking best. I'll have to come up with creative ways to make it the first thing he says every morning. "Hey, baby. Miss me?"

My voice is less "sexy rasp" and more "my vocal cords were run over by a train," but the fact that I managed any sound at all is a win. John doesn't seem to notice, though, as his eyes fly wide and he jerks his head up from the bed.

"*James!* Oh, thank God." Embracing my hand in his, he brings it up for a long, prayer-like press of his lips to the center of my palm just like he did when I was…

…suddenly the gauzy curtain is ripped away and the details of that night rush in like a direct upload to my brain, *Matrix*-style. My temples start to throb with the overload of information, but that's nothing compared to the searing pain on the right side of my body.

"How bad?" I ask, pointedly glancing down at my chest.

"An inch in another direction and we might not be talking right now," he says, his voice thick with emotion. "You lost a ton of blood at the scene and passed out, which nearly gave me a heart attack. The doctor said the bullet just barely missed your lung, so you were lucky, and you also have three broken ribs on your left side.

"You made it through surgery with flying colors and they kept telling me you'd be fine but—" His eyes well up, though he manages to blink back the tears. "I was so fucking scared I was gonna lose you."

"Hey, come on, no more of that." Brushing my thumb

across his cheek, I wish we were back in my bed where I could hold him and kiss his worries away. "I'm sorry I scared you. I'm not going anywhere, okay?"

He nods and blows out a breath, visibly relaxing by increments as he lets go of his fears, then redirects his anxiety into a different avenue. "Can I get you anything? Maybe some water? I should probably tell the nurses you're awa—"

Suddenly aware of how parched I am, I pounce on the first option before he gets carried away. "Water would be good. Nurses can wait."

John reaches over to the side table and fills a Styrofoam cup with water from the plastic pitcher. He sticks a straw in it, then holds it to my mouth. When I scowl at the implication that I can't even hold a damn cup myself, he gives me his cop don't-challenge-my-authority look.

Raising a single brow, I say, "You're going to be more of a pain in the ass than the actual nurses, aren't you?"

"Only if you plan on being a pain-in-the-ass patient."

I roll my eyes but give in and let him help me. As usual, being fussed over by John feels both foreign as a general concept and familiar because it's what he's always done. And while I pretend that indulging that part of him is something I grudgingly accept, we both know I secretly take comfort in his need to dote on me. Though he'll never get me to admit it out loud.

Taking long pulls on the straw, the ice-cold water slides down my irritated throat like liquid heaven. After I finish the whole cup, I rest my head on the pillow and take a minute to gather the courage to ask my next question. "Smee…is he…"

"No," he says with a crooked grin. "He had more damage than you, but the stubborn bastard made it. He woke up a few hours ago and started hitting on the nurses

—both male and female—and insisting they need to check his groin."

I start to laugh, then *immediately* regret it. Searing pain steals my breath, and the room spins for a second before settling back into place. John jumps to his feet and reaches over me. He curls my fingers around something, then helps me depress a button with my thumb. I hear a beep right before a sharp sting hits the back of my hand that has me hissing through my teeth.

"Shit, sorry, babe. They said you might feel some *slight discomfort* when the medicine goes in. Obviously, that was an understatement," he grumbles, glaring at the device like he's filing that information away to chew someone out for later.

Trying to keep the everything-hurts-and-I'm-dying tone out of my voice, I say, "It's fine. Just surprised me is all."

"It's your pain meds. You can press the button when you need a hit of the good stuff, but it'll only allow you a specific dose at certain intervals." Before he even finishes explaining, the medicine begins taking affect. "There," he says, a soft smile playing at the corners of his mouth as he smooths the hair back from my face. "Looks like it's working already."

I breathe easier with the partial relief. It's not a magic cure, but the pain went from a screaming Level Ten down to a solid Level Four, which is probably the best I'll get at this stage. "The bust," I say, wanting to talk to get my mind off these remaining four levels. "What happened?"

"The *CliffsNotes* version is we arrested a lot of bad guys, seized a lot of Dust, found intel on more of Croc's associates, and got all the girls out safely. They're in the process of detoxing and getting any other help they might need, and their families have been notified."

"Pirates?"

He takes a beat before answering. "None of them surrendered."

The air is heavy with the words he's *not* saying. If they didn't surrender, then they didn't survive. My reaction is the same as if John had cited the day's weather. After years of friendship and camaraderie, their deaths would've bothered me a hell of a lot if they hadn't betrayed me and left Smee for dead. But since they did, I don't feel a damn thing. Not about that.

However, other events of that night make my chest tight. I know what I *think* happened, but if I'm wrong, then this nightmare is far from over. Steeling myself for the possibility that I'm wrong, I state what I'm hoping is true. "You killed him."

I don't want to speak his name for fear it'll somehow invoke his presence, like the scary kids' game Bloody Mary. In fact, I don't ever want to think or speak that name again. John's gaze drops to my chest as though he can see past the hospital gown and bandages to the spot beneath where the bullet tore through my body. The muscles tick in his jaw, and I wonder if he's seeing the blood pooling around his fingers as we waited for help.

Finally, he looks me in the eyes and answers. "My only regret is that I can't do it again."

Warmth spreads though me. It might be the drugs working through my system, but I prefer to think it's my visceral reaction to hearing the moment I've dreamed of for so long is now a reality. The moment I know without a shadow of doubt that my enemy has been vanquished and my revenge complete.

It's surreal that it's finally here, that I'm finally free. So much of my life has been about fear—feeling it, avoiding it, conquering it. I have no idea what it's like to not carry that weight around. But I can't wait to find out.

"It's over," I say gruffly, referring to so much more than just the undercover operation.

John wraps his hands around mine and gives me a light squeeze. "It's over."

My blinks are getting longer as my eyes grow heavy. But before I succumb to another mini-coma, I have one last question. "Where's Starkey? He okay?"

"He's with Smee, hasn't left his side. He was treated for some minor injuries, but that was all. Physically, he's okay. It's the mental stuff that'll take longer to heal. But he will. He'll get through this, and we'll be there to help him in whatever ways we can."

Tears prick the backs of my eyes. "That day at the prison…I finally got my brother back, then lost him minutes later. He isn't going to want my help."

"He will; you just need to be patient and give him time. He'll come around."

I don't have the same strength of conviction as he does, but there's nothing I can do about it right now. It's not like I can march over there and demand to hash this out. I can't even lift my head off the pillow anymore. Fuck, I'm so tired.

I'm also so in love.

I kept insisting it wasn't possible for me to ever fall in love, but jumping in front of a bullet for a guy wearing a bulletproof vest is a pretty good indicator that I was full of shit. I wish the first time I said it hadn't been while I was bleeding out in his arms, but I didn't know if I'd get another chance, and I needed him to know. I also wish the *second* time I say it wouldn't be while I'm falling asleep in a hospital bed, but again, I need him to know. John's been an open book about his feelings for me from day one, and while it might take me some time to be as open as he is, I owe it to him to start trying.

Willing myself to stay awake a few minutes longer, I tug on his hand until he follows it up and leans in. He stares down at me with those honey-colored eyes that owned my black soul from the very first look, and everything inside me melts.

"I love you, Johnathan. I'm sorry it took me so long to say it. You're the kindest, strongest, and most patient man I've ever known. I'm yours for as long as you'll have me."

His face splits into a brilliant smile as he chuffs out a short laugh and cups my jaw in his warm palm. "Always, Captain," he whispers. "I'll have you for always."

"Okay, good."

Unable to fight it anymore, I let my eyelids slide shut just as John presses a kiss to my forehead. As I drift along in that hazy space between sleep and lucidity, I realize that maybe John's been right all along. I must not be the villain.

Because this is, without a doubt, my happily ever after. And I can't wait to start living it with the man I love.

Epilogue

HOOK

Six Months Later

"WHISKEY NEAT." Remembering where I am, I tack on an awkward, "Please. I'd like a whiskey neat, please."

As the tux-wearing bartender nods and gets to work pouring my coping-with-high-society drink into a crystal tumbler, a hard chest presses to my back. "Make that two, please." Warm breath tickles my ear when he turns his head to speak low enough that only I can hear. "Have I ever told you how fucking sexy you are when you use your manners?"

I almost bark out a laugh, but manage to hold it in. "Let's see, so far today, it's been the way my ass looks in my underwear, the murderous look on my face as I fought with my stupid cuff links, the way I strut like a peacock in a tux —which I *still* deny doing anything so ridiculous, much less doing it like some cocky, flightless bird—and how I feigned interest when your dad gave me a lengthy rundown of the four types of stocks needed for a diverse financial portfolio. Now it's using my manners?"

"Mm-hmm." He nips at the shell of my ear. "All of those things make me hot."

"I hate to tell you this, Darling," I say, turning to face him, "but you're embarrassingly easy to impress."

"Am I?" John flashes me his brilliant smile—the one I'll never get enough of in a hundred years. "Or am I just completely infatuated by everything my super-sexy and mega-amazing boyfriend does?"

This time I can't help the twist of my lips as I try to hide my amusement. "Hmm, I do like the sound of your reasoning better. I might even reward you for it later. *If* you take back the shit about me strutting."

John retrieves our drinks from the bartender and hands one to me. I hold his gaze over the rim of my glass as I take a sip of the smoothest whiskey I've ever had. Mr. Darling probably requested some brand I can't pronounce for his daughter's engagement party, here at London's posh Empire Hotel. Though I'm way out of my depth at fancy functions like this, I can definitely appreciate the fancy alcohol.

Too bad I'm only allowing myself one glass tonight. Just enough to take the edge off my nerves about what I have planned for later.

After taking his own sip, John sighs dramatically. "I wish I could, but then I'd be lying, and a good cop never lies. It's in the handbook and everything. Plus, the fact of the matter is, babe, you strut in a tux."

"I. Do not. Strut."

"Dude, you *totally* strut," Peter interjects, crashing through our little bubble like the Kool-Aid Man on speed. When I glare daggers at him, he holds his hands up and laughs. "Whoa there, Hook, no need to make me walk the plank. I meant it as a compliment. It's nice to see you not doing the hunched-shoulders, head-down skulking thing anymore."

Peter Pan is giving me compliments? Ugh, shoot me now. And what the hell am I supposed to say? *Thanks for noticing I'm not as tortured as I used to be.* Or, *Yeah, it's nice not waking up every day and hating my life now, thanks.*

Pan's not the first person to mention something like that. My therapist, Bob, says I should go with just the *Thanks* part. He also made it a point to say that it should be free of sarcasm, though I don't know where the fun is in that. I know they mean well (something Bob forced me to acknowledge when I got all pissy about it in one of our sessions), but it still feels weird to outwardly discuss my "progress."

It took me a month to get up the balls to start counseling. The first three sessions consisted of us staring at each other in silence for an hour because I couldn't bring myself to say anything. Once I finally did, it took another month before I stopped ending every session with, "Fuck this, I'm done," to which Bob always replied with a calm, "If that's what you feel is best." Reverse psychology, oldest trick in the book. It worked, too, because I kept showing up, and eventually, I stopped treating Bob like he was the enemy. It's still not easy, but quitting isn't an option. I want to be the man John deserves; the man he already believes me to be.

An image of Bob raising a bushy eyebrow has me mentally adding *Yeah, I know, I'm doing it for myself, too.* Putting myself first still doesn't come naturally to me, but I'm working on it. Bob's a bit of a dork, but he's no pushover, and he doesn't take any of my shit. My glare has no effect on him. It's annoying as hell. I like him.

But I'm still not thanking Pan for saying something

nice, because I know him, and he's bound to follow it up with an equally dumb—

"Besides," Pan says, running his hands down his lapels, "you might not be anywhere near *this* sexy in a tux, but you still smash the look. You have every right to strut."

"Ooh, gossip," Wendy says, sliding into her place against Pan's side. "Who struts?"

I groan.

Pan grins. "Hook does."

Wendy nods appreciatively. "Oh, absolutely, it's very cute. Almost like he's preening."

John points at his sister. "Like a peacock, right?"

"Yes! Exactly like a peacock."

"I used to like you," I deadpan at her. She laughs and abandons her fiancé long enough to kiss me on the cheek. Wendy's as affectionate as her brother. The second she sensed I lowered my walls enough to even partially let people in, she attacked me with the longest hug of my life. I didn't hate it.

"Told you," John says to me. "From surly pirate to strutting peacock. It's like a magic trick."

"Careful." He shuts up, but the smile he tries to hide behind his whiskey glass says plenty. Angling my body away from Peter and Wendy, I speak in a low voice. "Enjoying yourself, Johnathan?"

"Immensely."

"And are you done now?"

"I don't know…" His smile widens, and there's a devilish twinkle in his eye. "Are you done strutting?"

I chuckle, and he joins me, thinking he's in the clear. He's so not.

Keeping my focus on John, I step back into our circle and have a little of my own fun. "Hey, Pan, about how far would you say it is from here to the ballroom entrance over there. Thirty feet?"

John's eyes widen, and he almost chokes on his drink. He knows damn well I don't care about the distance to anywhere. It's our code; my way of telling John in mixed company that he's due for thirty smacks with a paddle. The number is obvious, but each unit of length is a different implement I use to redden his ass—inches, feet, yards, and miles all correspond with hand, paddle, crop, and belt. It's a pretty clever system, if I do say so myself.

"From here?" Peter squints for a few seconds over at the double doors then shrugs. "I'd say closer to forty feet."

Nailing my man with a wolfish grin, I say, "Forty, it is."

Wendy's brows knit together. "That was an odd quest —John, you look flushed. Are you feeling okay?"

"Totally fine," he says right before downing the last of his drink. "But I'm gonna need another whiskey."

"No, you aren't, let's go. We're supposed to be mingling."

I take his glass, set both of our empties on the bar, then tell Pan and Wendy we'll catch them later. Threading my fingers through John's, I pull him farther into the room full of elegantly dressed guests with my night's mission in the forefront of my mind.

"Not that I'm complaining," he says as he walks with me, "but since when do you want to socialize so badly?"

"Since I know we need to make the rounds with everyone for our appearance to be counted as sufficient, and the faster we do that, the faster we can make our exit."

"Considering my future brother-in-law did me no favors with his *gross* overestimation, I wouldn't mind waiting the few hours for the party to be over."

Laughing, I stop and grab John by the back of his neck, then I pull him close and kiss the sullen look off his face. "Don't pout, baby. I'm saving that punishment for another time. I have something else planned for tonight. Something you'll love, I promise."

"In that case," he says, smiling again, "let's hurry."

There has to be at least three hundred people here to celebrate Peter and Wendy's engagement a full year after Pan popped the question. I guess they were too busy moving in together and getting Wendy's event planning business and Pan's custom car restoration business off the ground to plan anything until now. The wedding isn't until next year, though, so I guess now is as good a time as any for it.

Mr. Darling insisted on the fancy party, so he could invite the who's who of London, which is why I know less than twenty people here, and they're all from Neverland. For the next half hour, I let John introduce me to family, friends, and co-workers, while I play the part of his well-adjusted boyfriend, even if I feel like jumping out of my skin from all the socializing and pleasantries.

As we walk away from two of Mr. Darling's longtime clients, I scrub a hand down my face and remind myself not to be an asshole. This is the kind of thing I'll have to learn to deal with if I want to be with John. No matter how much it sucks, it's a small price to pay. Though I'll probably exploit my ability to demand special compensation for the sacrifice.

"How many parties like this do you attend every year?"

"It depends on how many charity dinners my family is a part of and who's getting married or having milestone birthdays or—"

"Holy shit," I mutter before I can stop myself.

John laughs. "Don't worry, I'll only make you come to the super important ones with me. Hell, maybe I'll start staying home with you instead."

"Now *that* I can get down with."

Finally, we reach the part of the room where our friends—yeah, I said it, don't make a big deal out of it—are hanging out. It's not hard to guess whether they're with the bride or groom. Even dressed in formal attire, they're still the same rowdy hooligans who party at the Lair on Fridays and hang out at the Jolly Roger on Saturdays, which is a newly added tradition now that Smee and I reopened it as a fully functioning bar.

Since waking up in that hospital room six months ago, my life has done a complete one-eighty. Smee and I both recovered, obviously, but his process took a lot longer and involved a temporary colostomy bag that he had way too much fun grossing people out with for the three months he had it. In other words, he's the same playful bastard he's always been with a few new battle scars to show off, which he does all the time, because it's a shameless excuse to bare his abs.

Thanks to all the major players of Croc's operation being six feet under, and because we helped with the investigation that allowed the feds to seize millions in Fairy Dust and end a human trafficking ring, we were both shown leniency for our crimes. It also probably helped that a certain task force officer—who is still kicking bad-guy-ass and taking names on the Task Force—went to bat for us, even though I told him not to.

But even though the judge didn't sentence us with any prison time, he didn't pull any punches with the probation and community service. We each got three years and a thousand hours, respectively. The community service was divided between local charitable programs, everything from soup kitchens to highway cleanup to running bingo night at the senior citizens center. Some of it was tedious, but a lot of it was kind of rewarding. Not that I'd ever admit that to anyone. Well, I told John. And Bob. And maybe a few others when I was drunk one night. Shit, therapy's making me soft. *Damn it, Bob.*

"Hey, there they are. How's it going, guys?"

Thomas, the youngest Lost Boy until my brother arrived and beat him by one year, gives John a big hug then gives me an awkward clap on the shoulder. He's probably the most tenderhearted of the group; smart, affectionate, and always a nice word to say about everybody—even me when I was a closed-off asshole. I've been fully integrated into the Lost Boys group for a while now, but some of them still aren't sure how to take me, which I get. Sometimes I'm not sure how to take myself either.

"Do you want a hug, Thomas?" I ask in a grudging tone.

"Only if you want one. I mean, I don't want to make you uncomfor—"

I sigh like I'm giving in to a toddler's request. "Make it quick."

He lights up and gives me a two-second hug that doesn't even give me the chance to lift my arms, then steps back to reveal a black-haired beauty wearing a navy blue dress and a soft smile.

"Hi, James."

"Hi, sweetheart."

This time, I open my arms wide, and Brandy eagerly steps into them, accepting my tight embrace. After she went through an extensive drug rehab program, she showed up at my door to return my ring. Turns out her family is one of those extreme religious types who practice the opposite of what they preach. When they heard what happened to her, they wrote her off as a casualty of Satan or some shit. She had nowhere to go, so I told her to keep the ring—I didn't need it anymore, my mission was complete—and gave her one of the rentals behind the Jolly Roger to live in.

Now she works for me as a bartender, along with Starkey, and she manages the other rentals. The whole group loves her. Smee hits on her every chance he gets, the girls do whatever it is girls do together a few times a month, and she and Thomas became best friends. To me, she's like a sister. She still has a lot of trauma to deal with, but she's going to counseling, too, so she'll get there. Either way, I told her she'll always have a place here with us. We've always been a family of orphans thrown together by circumstance, so she fits right in.

When I release her, John instantly pulls her in for his own hug. "Hey there, Beauty. Keeping Thomas on his toes?"

She smiles, popping a dimple into the center of her chin. "Always. I'm making him dance with me later."

Thomas groans playfully as John winks. "Atta girl."

I scan our crowd but don't see the ones I'm looking for. "Brandy, have you seen Starkey and Smee?"

"They left after dinner," she says, worrying her bottom lip. "Starkey was getting agitated. Smee took him home, so he could smoke and go to bed."

She means smoke weed, which Starkey does when he needs to calm down. And that better be *all* he's doing. Smee and I are keeping a close eye on him. We're worried his self-medicating with pot could expand to something worse. He refuses to go to counseling or even entertain the idea of temporary meds, because that requires a psych appointment.

Our relationship is tenuous at best and total shit at worst. Some days, he talks to me; others, he doesn't. John is constantly reminding me that he needs time and that he hasn't taken off anywhere, so there's still hope he'll come around. If I didn't have John keeping me grounded, I would've had weekly nervous breakdowns over my brother and our broken bond. But he's right; I just need to give him more time, make sure he stays safe, and be here for him when he's ready.

"Okay, thanks for telling me." Tears well up in her green eyes. Brandy feels a sense of kinship with my brother because they suffered similar traumas at the hands of the same evil tyrant. I suppose it's the same reason I feel a connection with her. I know that hell. "Hey, none of that now, okay? Smee won't let anything happen to him, and I'll check on him first thing tomorrow. Starkey's going to be fine. The only thing you need to be doing is dancing and taking advantage of the open bar that my boyfriend's dad paid ridiculous amounts of money for. All right?"

Brandy nods and gives me another of her sweet, half-smiles just as Thomas wraps an arm around her shoulders, offering his silent support. "Speaking of the open bar," he says to the whole clan, "we were just about to grab some drinks. Does anyone want anything while we're up?"

A few people shout their orders, so Silas, the arrogant pretty boy of the bunch, agrees to go with them, so he can tell the bartender how to make a better Manhattan (because of course he knows how to do someone's job better than they do—insert eye roll here) and help carry the drinks back. John and I sit at the table with Tiger Lily, Tinker Bell, Nick, and Carlos. They all pause their conversations long enough to say hi, then pick up where they left off.

I've never been the talkative type, and I don't see that changing anytime soon, but I'm content to sit with John's hand in mine as he argues with the guys about professional football. Tink and Lily are pink-cheeked and giggly as fuck

—a lot different from their usual stoic badass chick personas —probably due to the collection of empty champagne flutes on the table. They're laughing and not-so-discreetly rating the men in the room. Since I'm more qualified to judge hot guys than talk NFL stats, I tune in to the girls' conversation.

Following Tink's line of sight after she announces her most recent contestant for a possible hookup, I say, "If you're gushing over that douche with the pompadour hairdo and mouthful of veneers, you need your eyes checked."

The tattooed and pierced bombshell with a platinum blond pixie-cut smooths her hands over her glittering pale green minidress like she's getting ready to make her move. At least she's not still hung up on Pan, but her taste in men is seriously lacking.

"Your opinion can't be trusted, Hooky-poo, because you only have eyes for a certain cop."

"I'm taken, not *blind*, little girl," I clap back, calling her something equally as rude as the name she called me.

Crossing her arms over her chest, she hitches a single pierced brow. "Aren't you, though? You have your head so far up John's ass, I'm surprised you can see anything."

Oh, it's on. The insult sparks something in me I've learned to recognize as joy. As stupid as it sounds, I've missed the days before I shut myself off from the others when we bickered like normal siblings.

Smirking, I say, "Awww, that's so cute, Tink. You're *jealous.*"

"Ha! What do I possibly have to be jealous about?"

I glance past her to where Michael, Wendy and John's baby brother, is pretending to care about a conversation with two older gentlemen, all while his eyes are glued to the token girl of the Lost Boy clan. "You see how good Pan and I have it, and now you want a Darling of your very own."

I give a chin lift in Michael's direction, and she looks over her shoulder to see his smoldering gaze deadlocked on her pretty face. Tink gasps and whips her head back to center, narrowing her heavily lined eyes at me.

"Never gonna happen. Not even if he makes a thousand wishes on a thousand stars. Feel free to tell him I said so." She pushes herself to a stand, and if she had long hair, she would've flipped it over her shoulder. "Now, if you'll excuse me, I need more champagne, and Pompadour needs my digits."

Tink storms off in a huff in the direction of the bar and her intended conquest. When Michael immediately excuses himself to follow, I give myself a mental fist bump.

John shoots me an accusing eyebrow. "What'd you do now, James?"

I chuckle and squeeze his hand. "You should be thanking me. I'm basically Cupid. Only way hotter."

"I concede on that last point, but I'm not sure about the first. You intentionally pissed Tink off before setting her up to be ambushed by Michael, which means he's about to get his ass chewed out."

"Okay, so I'm a *slightly sadistic*, hotter Cupid. Different methods, same results. You'll see."

John's about to argue when Lily suddenly bolts upright in her chair and stares at us with excited dark brown eyes. "I just thought of something. Do you guys role play sex stuff as cops and robbers, except it's not really role play because you're *actually* a cop and a robber?!"

Nick and Carlos mumble something about that being their cue and hurry off to be anywhere else. From the corner of my eye, I see John press a fist to his mouth and turn his head, but the way his shoulders are shaking gives him away. I pinch his thigh through his tuxedo pants, eliciting a satisfactory curse. Then, like I did with her friend a minute ago, I set a trap for the very drunk princess of the Piccaninny tribe. It's nothing less than the inebriated minxes deserve.

"And what makes you think we role play?"

She places her elbows on the table and rests her chin in her hands. "I don't know, but it would be so hot if you did. Don't you think? Ooh! Did I just give you a new idea?" Another dramatic *aha* gasp. "Do you *need* some ideas? Because I could help with that. I could be, like, your love guru or whatever. I would be good at that. Maybe I should start a business. Not that I'd give up racing, because I don't care how much those assholes want me out of the circuit, I'm going to be the first female ASCRA driver, guaranteed. But professional love guru would be a cool side gig, don't you think?"

Damn, when she's drunk, the girl talks as fast as she drives. I chin lift to the two men standing just out of earshot who haven't taken their eyes off her all night. When they start moving toward our table, John catches on to my plan and groans. I ignore him. This is the most fun I've had all night.

"That would be pretty cool," I say. "Out of curiosity, though, what makes you qualified for something like that?"

"Oh, I know things. *Lots* of things." Cupping a hand on the side of her mouth, she speaks in a stage whisper. "I have a PornTube account."

"You *what*?" Tobias and Tyler, demand in tandem. Lily jumps with a squeak and twists around to find identical Lost Boys scowling down at her.

"What kinds of things are you watching on there, Lil?"

Turning away from them, she answers with a firm, "It's none of your business, Ty."

I have no idea how she tells them apart. The rest of us usually guess, knowing there's a 50% chance that we'll get it wrong. Tiger Lily's the only one who never calls them by the wrong names.

Tobias (determined by process of elimination) leans down to brace a hand on the table next to her. "If there's stuff you're curious about, Tyler and I would be happy to fill you in."

Ty mimics his twin's stance on the other side. "*More* than happy."

Something glints in Lily's dark eyes. Maybe it's a trick of the light, or maybe—

"Uh oh," John says near my ear. "Did you see that?"

I turn my head just enough to respond without losing sight of the princess. "Yep."

"Should I call Chief over?"

John's not referring to one of his superiors at London PD. He's talking about Gray Wolf, a.k.a. Chief, and Tiger Lily's over-protective half-brother. "No need. Sit back and watch a master ball-buster at work, Darling."

A deceptively sweet grin spreads across her face as she rises with all the poise of a woman who's accustomed to being revered by her people. Both men straighten with her, their eyes as hungry as ever when it comes to her.

"Would you really?" Her tone is mocking as hell, but the way she's batting her long lashes at the boys must have all their blood draining away from their brains because neither seems to notice. She turns her head toward Tyler and strokes a nail down his chest. "You'd be happy to teach little old me about all the things that make my belly quiver?"

He groans, but she's already moving on to her next victim, resting her palm lightly on Tobias's abs like it's an unconscious gesture and not a deliberate move to lull him into a false sense of security. "Would you be willing to teach me *everything*?" Lowering her voice to a whisper, she croons, "Even the really *naughty* stuff?"

Tobias growls. "Fuck yeah, we will. We can start tonight, but then no more PornTube, baby."

Ty chimes in. "You won't need any more now that you've got us."

"Wonderful," she purrs. "There's just one more thing."

John and I both say, "Oh shit."

Lily's hands strike low and fast, grabbing the twins by their…well, their *twins*. They curse a blue streak as she squeezes their junk. John and I cross our legs and wince in sympathy.

"If either of you ever deign to tell me what I can and cannot do again *or* decide to mansplain to me about *anything*, especially sex, I'll make earrings out of your testicles. Understood?"

There's a lot of nodding and grunting. "Perfect." Lily releases her hold then finishes her glass of champagne as the guys do their best to appear like they didn't just have their nuts crushed for a full minute, which might as well be an eternity. "I think I'll go grab another drink. Oh, and boys," she says, stopping a few feet away. When she has their undivided attention, Lily smiles wide. "If *you* ever need some sex education, let me know. After all, I've been a member of Fetish Fantasies for six years and running."

Their mouths come unhinged as she saunters away, and John and I laugh so hard we have tears in our eyes. Watching the twins learn that the woman they'd kill to have between them is probably kinkier than they are was worth suffocating in this penguin suit all night.

Standing, I grab John's hand and pull him up with me. "Come on, let's leave the boys here to ice their balls and bruised egos."

They gingerly drop into chairs and flip me off at the same time, doing that weird twins-in-tandem thing they do. John apologizes for laughing at their expense and promises to send one of the others back with ice packs—ever the caretaker, my Johnathan—then I lead him away. I've had enough socializing to last me a lifetime today. It's time we make our escape. I have something special planned, and even though I'm crazy nervous, I'm determined to make this a night we'll never forget.

I spot Pan and Wendy talking with Mr. Darling near the exit. *Perfect.* As the host and guests of honor, they're the only three we have to say goodbye to. Being with John in "the real world" for the past six months means I've learned a thing or two about social etiquette. Sometimes I forget and sometimes I just don't care, but I'm always very aware of the impression I make on John's dad. Someday, I'll need to ask him a very important question, and I want his answer to be an immediate yes.

"Ah, there you are," Mr. Darling says as we come to a stop in front of them. "James, I was hoping I'd get the chance to talk to you about starting a retirement fund. It's never too late to plan for your future, you know."

"Jesus, Dad, do you ever *not* talk business? James doesn't want to discuss his future when he's at a party," John says with a wry grin. "Hell, he might not even want to discuss it at all."

"No, I do," I say quickly. "John and I are on our way out right now, but I can call your office next week and set up an appointment. If that's okay with you, sir."

His face lights up, and I'm struck by how passionate he is for finances. The only thing I'm that passionate about is fucking his son, but I doubt he wants to hear about that.

"Fantastic! And, please, I think it's time you started calling me George. I wanted to make sure you were sticking around before dispensing with the formalities," he says, winking at his son.

"*Dad*."

"You don't have to worry about that, George," I say, squeezing John's hand. "I'm not going anywhere."

"Excellent. Here's my card. Call me next week and we'll discuss your options."

"Thanks, I appreciate it." I shake George's hand, then hold it out to Peter. He looks down at it, confused. Then glances back up at me like he's waiting for the punch line. "Christ, just shake it, Pan."

A smile ten times too big for his face breaks out as he grabs and pumps my hand harder than necessary. I don't say anything, though, because he's probably been storing it up for years. When he finally releases me, I accept a hug and cheek kiss from Wendy then wait for John to say his goodbyes.

"Night, boys," George says absently as he answers his cell phone.

"Yeah, night, boys," Pan echoes, holding up his own phone. "Now hurry up and go so I can take video evidence of Hook strutting on his way out."

I jab a finger in Pan's direction. "Keep it up, smart-ass, and you'll have to find yourself a new best man."

Peter's blue eyes blow wide just before I turn and start to walk away with my laughing boyfriend in tow.

"Wen, did you hear that? You heard him say it, right? Did everyone hear Hook say he's my best man?" Then he shouts after me, "It's a done deal now, Hook! I have witnesses!"

When we exit the ballroom, John about loses it. "Oh my God, did you see the look on his face? That was so perfect, babe. You should've told me; I could've gotten it on camera. Hey, the elevator for the parking garage is that way."

I continue leading him in the opposite direction. "We're not going home tonight. I got us a room."

A few months ago, I moved in with John at his house in London and gave the loft to Smee and Starkey. I thought for sure he'd get sick of me, but I should've known better. John worked tirelessly for a whole weekend, integrating our things until it felt like a shared home, and I've been living in domesticated bliss ever since. The world is officially upside down, but I like it like this.

"A hotel room? At the *Empire*?" We stop at the elevator banks, and I push the button to call the next car. "But we don't have any fresh clothes or—"

Like I did before, I pull him in by the scruff of his neck and force him to focus on me. "I brought us an overnight bag and dropped it off in our room earlier. We have everything we need for the night, so stop worrying."

He sinks his teeth into that plump lower lip, making me groan. "Don't start anything you'd rather not make a scene with, Darling."

"Sorry, it's just…you planned a romantic getaway for us."

The doors open with a *ding*. I gesture for him to board the empty car first, then follow, grateful for the privacy. I swipe the special key card over the panel that unlocks the access to the second highest floor. It took me a while to save up for one of the fancy suites, but the look on John's face makes it all worth it.

"It's not exactly a getaway, it's only one night."

He steps in close and presses me against the wall. "Stop downplaying everything, James. This is crazy romantic, and I'm blown away, so just accept it and kiss me."

"*That* I can do."

I kiss him all the way up to our floor. I kiss him as we walk down the hall, taking quick glances at the doors until we find the right one. I kiss him as we fall into the room and fumble with the privacy door hanger before shutting ourselves in and throwing all the locks into place. I kiss him as we rip off our bow ties and unbutton each other's shirts…

"Don't you want to see the room?"

"Later. Much later," he pants then attacks me again.

I'm so swept up in the moment, I almost forget my plans. Just as his hands drop to my waistband, I somehow find the strength to break apart. "Wait, wait, wait."

He freezes. "What's wrong? Did I do someth—"

"Shhh, no, baby, it's nothing like that," I say softly, framing his face with my hands. "I want to tell you something."

"Okay. What is it?"

We're still in the entryway of the suite with his back pressed against the door. I briefly consider taking him into the room but decide against it. I want to get everything out here, so that when we finally do go into the room, there's nothing left to talk about.

I take a deep breath and release it slowly, trying to quiet these damn butterflies wreaking havoc in my stomach, but it doesn't work. I'll have to ride this out with them sitting shotgun.

"Johnathan, you know that I love you," I start, my voice thick with emotion. "Six months ago, I gave you my heart, my mind, and my soul. They were dented and broken, but you wanted them just the way they were, so they became yours. At the time, that was all I had to offer you. But now…now I want to give you my body, too."

It takes a few seconds to sink in. And then it hits him.

Golden eyes flare, and he shakes his head. "James, I told you that I don't need—"

"I know, and the fact that you've never so much as hinted differently means the world to me. But I'm not the same man I was when we got together. I'm not saying I'm 100%, so we should go slow like we've been, but I'm ready for it all now. I know I am. More than that, it's what I *want*."

He bites his lip, and I can see his mind racing, trying to weigh the pros against the cons for multiple outcomes, always protecting me, even when he doesn't need to.

I worked hard in therapy to mentally separate the shame of being violated from the idea of inviting a lover into my body on my terms. Logically, I knew there was a difference, but before, the thought of penetration under any circumstance shut my brain down instantly. After I made progress mentally, John and I began to slowly test the waters. We'd agree on what he would do, and he always stopped at the slightest hint my discomfort was headed into panic attack territory. Sometimes it took several sessions before we could move on, but eventually, I accepted his whole finger, and that was a huge turning point.

He didn't waste his first opportunity to show me just how good he could make me feel, and when he milked my fucking prostate, *I saw stars*. Not only was it the most amazing thing I'd ever felt, but it retrained my brain. It was like saying *Penetration = Mind-Blowing Orgasm* and after that, things got a lot easier. Now I'm able to take three of his fingers, and I've learned to crave the burn as he stretches me to accept him.

I never thought I could get this far. I didn't think it was possible for me to heal. Honestly, I don't know that I'd even have tried if it wasn't for John. I couldn't ask for a better partner or a better lover, not only for this but for everything. I really am the luckiest fucking man in the world, that out of everyone, he chose *me*, and one day, I'm going to marry him in front of our friends and family and whatever God might be watching. But tonight, I'm ready for a different kind of union.

Resting my forehead on his, I breathe him in, reveling in the heady scents of whiskey and cologne with a trace of the mint he ate after dinner. My hands drop to press against his chest—one over his heart and the other over the skull and swords tattoo on his right pec that matches mine in the same spot. He smells and feels like home, and love, and hope.

Like my everything.

"Please, Johnathan," I whisper. "Make love to me."

Big hands come up to frame my face as his thumbs rub along my cheekbones. His whiskey-colored eyes swim with emotion he doesn't bother to blink away. "I love you so fucking much, you know that, right?"

The corner of my mouth hitches up the slightest bit. "Yeah, baby, I know."

"And you can say stop at *any* time and that's where it ends, no regrets, no worries, just like always."

This man. Every day, he fucking kills me. "I know that, too. Now that we got all that out of the way, will you please fuck me already?"

There it is. That's what I've been missing.

His smile finally returned, and with it, so did my sun. There was a time when I said that I'd never be able to live in the light with him, but I had it all wrong.

Johnathan doesn't live *in* the light. He *is* the light.

Every time he smiles at me or turns those golden eyes my way, I feel his love shining on me, and it burns as bright and as hot as that giant fireball in the sky. Every day I take another step out of the darkness from my past and toward my future with the man I love.

As he takes me by the hand and leads me over to the bed, my heart races. I'm mostly excited, but I can't deny I'm also nervous. I know I still have a long way to go before I'm completely free, or as free as I can be. But it won't matter if it takes me five more months or five years. Because John Darling will be with me every step of way, chasing away the shadows, picking me up when I fall, and reminding me that I'm always worth fighting for.

We spend the rest of the night making love and making plans wrapped up in each other's arms. And right before we drift off to sleep, I press a kiss to his temple and whisper, "Thank you, Johnathan."

"For what?"

"For everything. For being my happily ever after."

"Always, Captain. *Always.*"

Acknowledgments

I have so many people to thank for helping me with this book and starting this series. Apologies in advance if my tired, deadline brain forgets anyone. It is definitely not intentional.

As always, thank you to my loving husband and children who show great understanding and patience when I lock myself away for days and weeks at a time to finish a book, which interrupts our normal life more than I'd like. I couldn't do my dream job without their support.

Thank you to my work wifeys and soul sisters, Cindi Madsen and Rebecca Yarros, for everything and anything: plotting, reading, sprinting, blurb-shaping, whip-cracking, encouraging, supporting, laughing, and a thousand other things I could never list even if I tried. My life is immeasurably better with them in it, and I seriously don't know what I'd do without our daily conversations and weekly video chats. As a tearful Jerry Maguire once said, they complete me. #UnholyTrinity

To my incredible agent, Nicole Resciniti of the Seymour Agency, for her never-ending advice and support, talking me down from proverbial ledges, and working hard to get me awesome opportunities that allow me to share my stories with wider audiences. She's truly the backbone of my career, and without her, I would be lost. I'm incredibly grateful to have her in my life, and someday I hope to return all the good she's done for me, ten-fold.

To Miranda Grissom, Super Assistant Extraordinaire, who has literally saved my sanity more times than I can count. I proposed to her on the second day we worked together and continue to propose regularly. I never want to be without her again. Like, EVER. So, she's stuck with me.

To Lana Kart who makes my amazing graphic teasers and always accommodates my last-minute rush jobs because she's totally amazeballs.

To Lorelei James who has become one of my greatest friends and a constant source for fun texts, adorable baby pics, and writerly encouragement. I'm so grateful we're friends, and I'll never stop fangirling over her.

To Erin McRae who always drops everything to read every single chapter as soon as I hit send, even in the middle of the night most times. She's the best cheerleader a girl could ever ask for, and she sets me straight whenever I start to doubt my writing.

To Rebecca Barney and Lea Schafer, two amazing ladies, friends, and editors, who helped me polish this labor of love until it shined as bright as John's light. (Except neither of them saw this section, so don't blame them for all my incorrect punctuation and typos. LOL)

To Jaycee DeLorenzo of Sweet 'N Spicy Designs who created the beautiful covers for Pan, Hook, and Tink, and is literally the easiest, most pleasant, drama-free designer I've ever had the pleasure of working with. If you need design work done, she's the woman to see.

To Danni Stone who created the most amazing digital

art featuring Hook and John. (See after this section.) She truly captured my favorite boys and I could stare at the drawing all day. I've already told her I'm hiring her to draw every couple/throuple in the Neverland series, and we're making them available to the public as well, so make sure you check out her Etsy store!

To Brenda Ambrosius, the most kickass attorney I could've ever asked for. She truly has a gift for crafting legal letters with all the professionalism they require plus a healthy dose of ghetto subtext. Because of everything she's done and continues to do for me, I'm naming a heroine after her (with a slight variation) in this series. Look for her to be introduced in Tink's book!

To Hannah Murray and her Mister for putting up with my incessant questions about bullet wounds and recovery details, which helped me immensely for the end of the book.

To Liz, my FBI consultant who tried valiantly to make everything in my book accurate, despite my every plot issue that made it virtually impossible to work. I apologize profusely for straight up murdering most (all?) of the protocols, and I thank her for what little bits of realism I managed to squeeze into the story.

To everyone in the Maxwell Mob: thank you for sticking with me all these years and getting excited about my new projects in my ever-shifting publishing schedule. Your constant support, enthusiasm, and posts about Jason Momoa are what keep me going. Every. Single. Day.

A very special thank you to all the bloggers who work tirelessly and *for free* to shout out about my books, make graphics, invite me for takeovers, offer advice, take time to read and review my ARCs, and are just in general super amazing women whose passion is to lift up other women. You are the foundation of this book community we all live in, and we couldn't reach nearly as many readers as we do without you. I'm forever grateful for your help and humbled by your generous spirits.

And finally, thank you to everyone who's read this book. I hope you enjoyed my contemporary twist for another set of characters from the original *Peter Pan*, and I especially hope you'll stick around for the remaining books I have planned in the Neverland Novels. This series is a passion project for me, one I'm incredibly proud of, and I promise to work hard to make it the best I can for you. If you enjoyed it—or even if you didn't—I would super-duper appreciate your honest review on Amazon, Goodreads, or Bookbub. Sharing is caring, and reviews are what makes an author's world go round. :)

If you'd like to keep up with what I'm working on and when my next releases come out, you can sign up for my newsletter. And if you love sneak peeks, sexy men, dirty jokes, and Jason Momoa memes, make sure you join me in my reader group on Facebook, the Maxwell Mob.

HOOK + JOHN

Art created by Danni Stone

Prints available in her Etsy store

https://www.etsy.com/shop/ArtByDanniStone

The Neverland Novels series holds a special place in my heart. I hope you fall in love with the characters as much as I have. The plan is for the series to be ten books. I want to give all of the characters their own special Happily Ever After.

Stay up to date on the latest Neverland News and more from Gina L. Maxwell by signing up for her Newsletter.
www.ginalmaxwell.com/newsletter

If you haven't experienced Peter and Wendy's epic reunion in the first Neverland Novel, PAN, here's a s
mall taste of their love story.

Chapter One

PETER

Then...

Age 12
Neverland, North Carolina

WHEN SOMEONE IS LOST, it's because there's a place where they normally belong—one where people miss them and never stop looking for them. But me and the other boys have never belonged anywhere but here. No one misses us, and there sure as hell isn't anyone out there looking for us. So I'm not sure why they call us lost.

We know we came from somewhere—we weren't born at the Neverland School for Lost Boys—the only question is where. Not that *I* care to know—if my mother didn't want me bad enough to make sure I stayed with her, why would I? —but the younger boys who wish we had a mother sometimes ask me. I'm old enough to know that storks don't deliver babies to random couples, and even if they did, a stork would never drop an innocent baby—or eleven—into the care of Fred Croc and his wife Delia. But I still don't have the answers they're looking for.

"How long does it take to wash your dirty fuckin' mitts up there?" Croc yells up the stairs. "Get your asses down here pronto!"

The boys and I exchange glances in the rust-framed mirror over the row of sinks in our community bathroom. I hate the fear I can see in their eyes, especially over something as stupid as taking too long to wash their grease-stained hands. Living here is a constant practice in "damned if we do, damned if we don't." We get punished if we take too long to wash up after working our shifts at the body shop, but if we come down for dinner with so much as a smudge, we get punished for that too. If we're lucky, it's being sent to bed without supper. If we're not, we end up with belt marks across our backs.

I wink at them, all younger than me by a couple of years, except for Hook, and speak so that my words don't travel down the stairs. "Dirty work makes dirty hands, am I right, boys?" It's a play on words because not only is our work literally dirty, it's also illegal.

They all snicker and get back to washing and rinsing, the worry erased from their faces for a while longer at least.

Hook rolls his eyes with a shake of his head. "Everything's a joke to you, Pan. When are you gonna grow up? You act like it's normal for kids to be working in a chop shop. This is called a school, but we spend more time busting our asses taking cars apart or putting them back together for a small-time crook than we ever have cracking open our textbooks."

I shrug. "It might not be normal for other kids, but

it's *our* normal. There's nothing we can do to change it, so we might as well make the best of things." I wipe my hands on a towel that was dingy white at best last week but is now a shade of soiled gray. Looking over at Hook's overgrown black hair as he bends over the sink that's much too short for him, I add, "Besides, growing up doesn't sound like all that much fun to me. At least here we have food and a place to sleep. Growing up means getting banished from Neverland, and who the hell knows what happens to the kids then."

His ice blue gaze snaps up to glare at me through the mirror. He doesn't like the reminder that we don't know what happened to the older kids who used to live here. Croc tells us that he sends them off to work at a different shop, but he isn't known for his honesty, so we don't really believe him. Hook is two years older than me, and currently, the oldest kid in the house. He'll be the next of us to go.

"Doesn't matter to me," Hook spits out. "I don't care where I go, as long as it's far away from this place."

I study him and try to figure out what his deal is. This certainly isn't paradise, but it's not the worst life I can imagine, either. And, far as I can tell, he has it the best out of all of us. "Says the teacher's pet."

His steely eyes narrow on me. "You got something to say, Pan?"

I square up with him, crossing my arms. "Just that I don't know why you're bitchin' about being here when you're Croc's favorite. I mean, you're the one he's taking under his wing, right? Teaching you how to run the business? That's what you said he's doing when he calls you down at night. Or maybe he's not teaching you anything. Maybe it's something fun like watching TV together, and you're lying because he told you not to tell us what you're really doing."

The other boys mumble their agreements behind me. We don't have a television upstairs. Hell, we don't have anything up here. No books, no toys. Nothing but the beds we sleep on, the dressers that hold what little clothes we have, our imaginations, and each other. Sometimes it's enough for the boys. Other times, it's not.

"You talk too much, Pan."

I smirk. "Yeah, I get that a lot. Doesn't mean what I'm saying isn't true, *James*."

"Call me that again, asswipe," he says huskily, "and see if I don't plant my fist right in your face."

Before I can tell him to go ahead and try, a tiny thing steps in front of me, fists on hips and eyes throwing green fire. "Touch a single blond hair on his head, and I'll tell Croc you were the one who took his pack of cigarettes."

Hook blanches like he's seen a ghost—even I mentally wince at the little sprite's threat—but he recovers quick enough. "What the fuck ever, I'm outta here. Smee, Starkey, let's go."

He doesn't bother to wait before turning on his heel and striding out of the bathroom, but he didn't have to. "Coming, Captain!" they say, and as always, Smee and Starkey follow after Hook like the loyal lapdogs they are, offering apologetic glances at me as they pass.

I give them a small nod. I don't have a problem with either boy. Something about them is drawn to Hook's darker… I don't know what you'd call it. Presence? Attitude? Pissiness? Either way, it's not something I understand, and the rest of the boys don't either. They consider *me* their captain, and rightly so, because I'm the best man for the job. I'm a good and fair leader—all the boys would say so—which is why I don't make them *call* me captain even though I am. Unlike Hook who won't answer to anything else. See? Better.

"Tinker Bell, you shouldn't have done that. You're only nine, and I can take care of myself."

Her usually adorable face screws into an epic scowl. "How about you just say 'thanks, Tink' instead of spouting off dumb facts."

"Thanks, Tink." I ruffle her white-blond hair the way I imagine an older brother might, earning me a grunt of exasperation as she storms out of the room and calls me a *silly ass*, her favorite nickname for me. The tinkling of the bell around her ankle fades as she heads downstairs for dinner, and I turn to the remaining six boys: Tootles, Nibs, Slightly, Curly, and the Twins. "Come on, boys, let's get something to eat."

We shuffle out of the bathroom together, and as we near the top of the stairs, I feel a tug on my shirt. "Peter, are you gonna sneak out again tonight?"

"Tootles, shhh," I whisper, stopping the group. "You want Croc to hear? If he finds out, it's the end of our stories."

Six pairs of eyes widen, and one of the Twins—I don't know which because none of us can tell them apart—says, "But we need to know what happens to Cinderella, Peter!"

They're all whisper-shouting now, some worrying about never knowing if the prince finds Cinderella and the others about what will happen if I'm ever caught sneaking out of the school.

"Lost Boys, listen up." Using their group name does the trick. They all straighten like little soldiers and await my next command. "No more talking. Tonight will be like any other night. Got it?" In not so many words, I reassured them that I plan to sneak out, that I won't get caught, and that I'll bring back another piece of the story they're dying to hear. That we're *all* dying to hear. Even Hook, though he'll never admit it.

The rest of the night is like any other.

We sit at the long wooden table off the kitchen and eat in silence, using our eyes to carry on entire conversations that Croc and Delia never hear. Afterward, we clear our places and head up the stairs, oldest to youngest, except for Tink who has to stay and clean the pots and kettles and whatever mess Delia made when she prepared our barely edible meal.

The loud ticking of Croc's ancient pocket watch echoes up the stairwell. "James," he barks, and we all freeze on the steps.

Hook's entire body tenses in front of me. Man, he really does hate his first name. I wonder if Croc knows that and uses it on purpose. But that doesn't make sense if Hook's his favorite. More likely he doesn't know, and Hook doesn't want to tell him because Croc's temper is known to flare up over the dumbest shit and he's trying to avoid a beating.

Turning around, Hook takes the couple steps down to my level. "You getting the end of the story tonight?"

"Thought you didn't care about the stories."

He looks over and meets my gaze. "I don't."

That's it, that's all he says. He doesn't offer anything else. Just stares at me intently, waiting for my answer.

"Yeah," I say finally. "I am."

Something flashes in his eyes that I can't read. Like a mix of sadness and relief, but neither of those things wash with the boy I know. He's always been a pissy, jealous bastard for as long as I can remember. But since he started hanging out with Croc a couple months ago, he's been an intolerable asshole. He nods once and continues down the stairs as the boys shift to the right to let him pass.

Croc palms the back of Hook's neck when he reaches the bottom. "Come on, boy. I've got lots to teach you tonight." Hook glances over his shoulder at me one last time before they disappear into Croc's office, his expression emotionless like he's made of stone. Something's definitely off with him, but I don't know what.

Slightly pushes past me, followed by the others, jarring me back to the present and my mission at hand: sneaking out undetected. We go through our nighttime routine and get into our beds. Finally, Tink's bell can be heard as Delia leads her up the stairs. While Tink changes in the bathroom, Delia does a bed check, speaking to us as little as possible. We can feel how much she hates us, and we're happy to ignore her just as much as she does. Only Tink has to deal with her much.

As soon as Delia leaves, slamming the door at the top of the stairs behind her, I spring out of bed and do my thing. I jimmy open the window with the loose frame, whisper to the boys that I'll be back soon, and climb up to the flat roof of the building. In minutes, I've made my way over to Barrie Street in the neighboring city of London.

A few weeks ago, I was looking for an adventure when I walked under the balcony of the brick house in the middle of this block and heard a woman talking to her kids. But she wasn't just talking. She'd called it a bedtime story, and it was all about a girl called Snow White and her dwarf friends who all had funny names, just like the Lost Boys. I hid in the bushes and listened to the story floating down to me through the open balcony doors. But she only told them *part* of the story before telling them it was time for bed, and she'd continue the next night. They complained just like I was doing, but inside my head so I didn't get caught, and I knew I'd have to come back to hear more.

I also knew I had to tell the boys what I'd heard. No one had ever told us stories. We'd never heard anything like that before, and just as I'd known they would, they totally loved it. So every night since, I've returned to the same house to get the next part of whatever story she was telling. I'm not sure what I'm going to do when the weather gets cold and the lady stops opening the balcony doors, but I'll worry about that then.

As I approach the house under the cover of night, I hear a different voice. A younger one, soft and sweet sounding. "Nana, the longer you squirm, the longer it's going to take to brush you, you know." Looking up through the rails of the balcony, I see a gigantic dog shifting its weight from side to side and making unhappy grunts. Well that certainly wasn't who I—

Then she rises from behind the shaggy beast, and I forget to breathe. The light pouring out from the room surrounds her like it's protecting her from things that might be hiding in the darkness. I can't see any details of her face, but she's already the prettiest girl I've ever seen.

"Okay, Nana, that's good for now, you big baby. Go on."

The dog performs an oafish hop of gratitude before bounding back into the house. The girl laughs with a shake of her head, then leans on the bannister and gazes up at the stars. She runs a hand down her long braid and lets out a sigh like she's wishing for something. Maybe she wants an adventure, too. I could give her one. I don't know what it would be, but I know that I would search the earth until I found the right one for her.

As for me, I think I just found mine. *She*'ll be my greatest adventure yet.

I want to talk to her, to ask her name, for her to ask mine—

"Wendy, dear, come inside now, please."

"Coming, Mom." And with that, she disappears from sight.

Wendy… My adventure's name is Wendy.

Chapter Two

PETER

Now...

USING the back of my arm to wipe the grease-tinged drops of sweat from my brow, I duck out from under the hood of the Chrysler 300 and turn to grab my— Where the hell is it? Damn it, I hate it when I can't find my shit. I start pulling open every drawer in my tool bench, one after the other. Knowing that what I'm looking for isn't in the bottom drawer full of miscellaneous crap I never need, I squat down and open it to rifle through the contents anyway.

I shove aside a roll of paper towels, a mug of pens, a few dirty rags that I should really take home and wash... and then I freeze. There, in the back corner, is a small black box. The kind that a woman in love would freak out over. Except, if a woman opened this particular box, she'd be sorely disappointed. Any woman except for the one I'd intended to give it to, anyway.

The dust covering it is evidence of how long it's gone

untouched—half a dozen years, maybe more—but I know every detail of what's inside without even having to open it.

I pick up the box and swipe my thumb over the top, displacing the dust as my brain displaces the mental lock on that part of my life. Memories of a distant place and time flood my mind like a dam breaking under the pressure. Cornflower blue eyes, long hair the color of maple syrup, and a musical laugh I'll never forget as long I live.

When I was a boy, I thought she was my forever adventure. But just as they have a beginning, adventures also have an ending, and she had other things to explore. She wanted me to go with her, but even then, I knew there was nothing for me outside of Neverland. So she left, I stayed behind, and I did my best to bury her memory and avoid the ache I feel in my chest every time I think of her.

Fuck. Without opening it, I toss the box back into the drawer and slam it shut. Growling, I turn my agitation to my original problem and call out through the garage. "Which one of you assholes didn't put my 7/16ths wrench back?"

A man with black hair, short on the sides and long enough to curl on top, sticks his head out from the customer service area next to my bay. "Sorry, boss."

I roll my eyes. Even as a grown-ass man, his childhood habit of taking the blame for stuff is ingrained in him as it ever was. "It wasn't you, Carlos. You've been manning the front desk all day."

A boyish smile breaks across his face, popping the dimples in his cheeks that make every female customer swoon. "Oh right. Never mind."

The heavy metal being pumped across the four garage bays from the huge speakers makes it hard for any of the others to hear me, so I make my way down the line.

"Nick, you take my wrench?"

The muscles in his arms bunch, and a sheen of sweat covers his dark brown skin as he drags a wheel from the Jeep on his hydraulic lift and drops it to the ground. "Nah, I've done nothing but new tires and rotations today. People out here acting like it's about to snow in the middle of July or something."

"They can act however they want as long as they're spending money here and not over at Croc's place."

"I hear that," he says, grabbing the wheel to haul it over to the tire changer. "Good luck finding your wrench, man."

I know the next two bays will come up short as well. Thomas is our resident technology geek. Anything that has wires, computer chips, and mother boards, he's our guy. In the shop, that usually means custom sound systems on a fun day or aftermarket alarms or remote starts on a boring one. Either way, I know Thomas won't have my wrench. He has the strictest moral code of anyone I've ever known. He'd never take anything that wasn't his without asking first.

Then there's Silas. He'd never take anything that wasn't his either, but for an entirely different reason. He's an arrogant jackass—and I say that with nothing but love for the guy—who believes he's just a hair better at everything than you are and all his things are of slightly better quality. For lack of a better term, Silas is a one-upper. It usually annoys the shit out of other people, but we accept it as one of the many individual idiosyncrasies that make up our group.

Silas and I are two of the three body work specialists in the shop, but it's rare we get the opportunity to flex our skills. Pulling dents out of doors is child's play when you can take a rusted POS and turn it into an award-winning, custom beauty. But if we don't do the mundane crap that pays the bills, we won't ever have the money to open up the custom rebuild business we've been wanting forever. Something we'll get around to doing someday, but not anytime soon.

"Si," I say with a nod as I pass.

He gives me a chin lift and his signature smirk before going back to sanding the bondo on a Chevy Malibu's quarter panel.

I can hear the arguing before I even get to the next bay, which is nothing new when it comes to the twins. I find them standing underneath a lifted Toyota, one working on the exhaust and the other replacing brakes, their blond hair sticking up in different directions from running their hands through it as they do when working.

I stop in front of them and cross my arms over my chest, raising an inquisitive brow. "What's the argument today, boys?"

"Hey, Peter," they say in unison.

The one fitting the new exhaust pipe pauses to say, "Numbnuts over there says that a Camaro SS would beat a Mustang GT in a quarter mile."

His brother points a wrench—not my *missing* wrench, I notice—in his direction. "If they're both stock? Absofuckinglutely. Now if you're talking aftermarket mods, that might be a different story."

"What do you think, Peter?" they ask.

The creepy twin thing is something they do often, but I guess when two people are inseparable, it's bound to happen. They do everything together—including women, which is about the only thing they don't argue about. And they can easily turn around a job that has multiple issues in half the time with their tag-team approach, so I've never made them split up. We don't have enough bays for all of us to work separately, anyway. Carlos and Thomas share a bay and switch off with front desk duties since they're the best at customer service.

"Well, in my humble opinion—" There's nothing humble about it because I know everything there is to know about cars. "If you're talking stock and you're driving a Mustang GT, you might get him off the line, but his SS would smoke your ass before you get halfway down the track. So…" I glance at the embroidered name patch on the coveralls of the twin on the left. I wish one of them would dye their hair a different color for chrissake. "*Tobias* is right this time. Sorry, Tyler."

"Aha! Told you, asshole!" Tobias continues to rub his victory in a grumbling Ty's face as I move onto the last bay in our shop.

A pair of shapely legs in jean cutoffs sticks out from underneath the front of a Dodge Challenger, one black combat boot tapping along to the heavy beat of the music.

"Tink, you wouldn't happen to know what happened to my 7/16ths, would you?"

She rolls out from under the car, a huge smile on her face and a familiar wrench in her hand. "You mean *this* 7/16ths?"

I arch a brow down at her. "That'd be the one, yeah."

She raises her free hand up to me, and I help pull her up to her feet. She's wearing a tank top with a chopped-off bottom, leaving her stomach bare except for the grease smudges. I gave up telling her to wear a pair of coveralls years ago. She claims she can't work in restrictive clothing, and honestly, it doesn't hurt business when guys bring their cars in for unnecessary oil changes or diagnostic checks just to get a chance to chat up Tink. It's not like her Daisy Dukes and crop tops are distracting any of us. Tink's always been a non-sexual entity in our group, though we stopped referring to her as one of the boys after she nailed Si in the balls for it when she was twelve.

"Sorry, Peter, I couldn't find mine," she says, looking up at me.

"You need glasses, Tink?"

She furrows her brow under the longer fall of her blond pixie cut. "No, why?"

"Because yours is right there on your workbench."

She follows to where I'm pointing. Her skin flushes as she bites on the inside of her cheek, making the thin gold nose-ring glint in the light. "Well, would you look at that," she says with an embarrassed chuckle. "I swear it wasn't there earlier. But now that I've got you here, Peter, I wanted to ask you—"

"Boss!"

I turn to see Carlos gesturing wildly at me like it's a life or death situation. Shit, I hope the computer isn't on the fritz again. We can't afford to replace it. "Sorry, Tink, hold that thought."

"That's okay, I'll walk and talk," she says, falling into line as I make my way back across the bays, the bell she keeps on a long chain around her neck tinkling with every step. "I was wondering if you wanted to go to the Pitt County car show next weekend and pick out a custom project we could work on together. You know, to sell afterward as another way of bringing in money."

"We don't have the time or space to devote to a project like that right now. We need all our bays operational for the daily stuff that's paying the bills."

"No, I know. But we could make space for it in the pole barn and then after work—"

"Tink, what have I always said about after work?"

She sighs. "When work is done the fun's begun."

"Exactly. We only work as much as we have to, and

after that, we work hard at having fun," I say, dropping my wrench off in my bay as we pass. "Which, correct me if I'm wrong, makes me the best boss on the planet."

"You're absolutely the best boss, Peter. You're the best at everything."

I smile down at her. "Won't get an argument from me on that one." We stop in front of Carlos, and I put a reassuring hand on her shoulder. "It's a good idea, Tink, just not for right now. Someday, we'll be able to do stuff like that without pulling overtime hours. Until then, let's keep doing what we're doing."

"*Boss.*"

Carlos is practically bouncing in place as I finally turn my attention to him. "What is it?"

"There's someone who wants to talk to you about a custom rebuild."

I arch a brow in Tink's direction, but she holds her hands up. "Don't look at me. I didn't talk to anyone but you about that."

"Tell him we don't do custom rebuilds right now, but we can refer him to someone who does. Hold on, I think I have a number for J.R. at the Toy Shop in London…" I fish my phone out of the pocket of my coveralls and pull up my contacts.

"It's a *her*, boss," Carlos corrects. "And trust me, you're gonna want to talk to her."

"Trust me," I say, scrolling through the names in my phone. *Did I save it under the J's or the T's?* "I'm really not."

I hear the door to the waiting area open just as Tink whispers, "Holy shit," making me look up from my phone…and my heart stops.

"Hello, Peter."

A woman with cornflower blue eyes and long hair the color of maple syrup steps into the shop. Her smile is shy, and her small hands twist together in front of her like she's unsure of her welcome. So much time has passed since I've seen her, and yet, she's just as beautiful as that night I saw her standing on her balcony, wearing only a nightgown and rays of moonlight.

"Can you believe it?" Carlos says excitedly. "Wendy's home!"

Glossary of Neverland Characters
(as they are when the book starts 16 years before the present timeline)

Lost Boys

Peter Pan: Leader of the small group of children at the School for Lost Boys of Neverland.

Slightly (aka Silas/Si): Self-appointed right-hand of Peter since he's the next oldest and a classic one-upper as he believes he's slightly better than everyone else.

Curly (aka Carlos): Sweet and flirtatious with dimples that would get him out of trouble in most cases; yet, he's blamed for things so often that he adopts the habit of accepting blame even when it isn't his to claim.

Nibs (aka Nick): Most reserved of the boys, quiet and loyal; probably Peter's *actual* right-hand.

The Twins (aka Tobias and Tyler/Ty): Identical, fun-loving twins, no one can tell apart, who finish each other's sentences and argue about everything except girls.

Tootles (aka Thomas): Youngest and sweetest of all the boys; very empathetic and helpful.

Tinker Bell (aka sprite/fairy/pixie): Only girl living at the school for boys; sassy and feisty and fiercely loyal to Peter.

Pirates (a sub-group of the Lost Boys)

James "Captain" Hook: Oldest of the boys at the school, inexplicably hates Peter.

Smee: Red-haired and loyal to Hook unless he isn't around, then joins in with the Lost Boys.

Starkey: White-haired and loyal to Hook unless he isn't around, then joins in with the Lost Boys.

Darlings

Wendy Darling: Young girl who lives in neighboring city

of London; enjoys telling stories, nursing wounds, and pretending to be a mother.

John Darling: Wendy's brother, two years her junior; smart, cunning, and a martial arts enthusiast.

Michael Darling: Wendy's brother, five years her junior; genius level IQ and hates being the baby of the group.

George Darling: Father to the Darling children and financial planner in London.

Piccaninnies

Tiger Lily (aka Lily/Lil/T.L. Picc): Princess of the Piccaninny tribe; getaway driver with an affinity for knives and emasculating men.

Gray Wolf (aka Chief): Tiger Lily's older half-brother; outcast, nomad, and mischief-maker.

Crocs

Fred Croc: Guardian of the Lost Boys, small-time criminal, owner of chop shop.

Delia Croc: Wife to Fred and hates kids.

About the Author

Gina L. Maxwell is a full-time writer, wife, and mother living in the upper Midwest, despite her scathing hatred of snow and cold weather. An avid romance novel addict, she began writing as an alternate way of enjoying the romance stories she loves to read. Her debut novel, *Seducing Cinderella*, hit both the *USA Today* and *New York Times* best-seller lists in less than four weeks, and she's been living her newfound dream ever since.

When she's not reading or writing steamy romance novels, she spends her time losing at Scrabble (and every other game) to her high school sweetheart, doing her best to hang out with their adult teenagers as they learn to spread their wings, and dreaming about her move to someplace perpetually warm once they do.

You can find more information about her and all her online homes at www.ginalmaxwell.com.

Other Books By Gina L. Maxwell

Neverland Novels

Pan

Fighting For Love Series

Seducing Cinderella

Rules of Entanglement

Fighting for Irish

Sweet Victory

Playboys In Love Series

Shameless

Ruthless

Merciless

Stand-Alones

Hot for the Fireman

Ask Me Again

Tempting her Best Friend

Connect with Gina: www.ginalmaxwell.com

Newsletter Sign-Up: www.ginalmaxwell.com/newsletter

Follow on BookBub: www.bookbub.com/authors/gina-l-maxwell

Reader Group on Facebook: www.facebook.com/groups/TheMaxwellMob